The Witch's Head by H. Rider Haggard

Sir Henry Rider Haggard, KBE was born on June 22nd, 1856 at Bradenham in Norfolk, England.

After his education he was pushed towards an Army career but failed the entrance exam. Next Haggard was positioned to work for the British Foreign Office but he seems not to have sat that exam. Using family connections, he was sent to Southern Africa by his father in search of a further opportunity of a career.

Haggard spent six years there before a return to England and marriage. He had begun to write and publish some non-fiction in Africa but it was only after studying Law in the hope it might prove to be the proper career his father wanted for him that Haggard began to write fiction, using his African experiences as the basis.

His first fiction was published in 1885 and the following year King Solomon's Mines was published. It was a phenomenal success. His career was set.

Haggard wrote well and wrote often. He managed to sympathise with the local populations even though they were exploited and manipulated by Europeans intent on amassing fortunes in money, people and resources. His writing career covered the great sprint to Empire of several European powers and both reflects and criticizes these events through his well-loved characters including Allan Quatermain and Ayesha.

In his later years Haggard pursued much in the way social reform as well as standing for Parliament and writing a great many letters to The Times.

Henry Rider Haggard died on May 14th, 1925 at the age of 68. His ashes were buried at Ditchingham Church.

Swell out, sad harmonies,
From the slow cadence of the gathering years;
For Life is bitter-sweet, yet bounds the flood
Of human fears
A death-crowned queen, from her hid throne she scatters
Smiles and tears

Until Time turn aside,
And we slip past him towards the wide increase
Of all things beautiful, then finding there
Our rest and peace;
The mournful strain is ended. Sorrow and song
Together cease.

A. M. Barber.

Index of Contents

BOOK I

CHAPTER I

ERNEST'S APPEARANCE

"Come here, boy, let me look at you."

Ernest advanced a step or two and looked his uncle in the face. He was a noble-looking lad of about thirteen, with large dark eyes, black hair that curled over his head, and the unmistakable air of breeding that marks Englishmen of good race.

His uncle let his wandering glance stray round him, but, wandering as it was, it seemed to take him in from top to toe. Presently he spoke again:

"I like you, boy."

Ernest said nothing.

"Let me see—your second name is Beyton. I am glad they called you Beyton; it was your grandmother's maiden name, and a good old name too. Ernest Beyton Kershaw. By the way, have you ever seen anything of your other uncle, Sir Hugh Kershaw?"

The boy's cheek flushed.

"No, I have not; and I never wish to," he answered.

"Why not?"

"Because when my mother wrote to him before she died"—here the lad's voice choked—"just after the bank broke and she lost all her money, he wrote back and said that because his brother—I mean my father—had made a low marriage, that was no reason why he should support his child and widow; but he sent her five pounds to go on with. She sent it back."

"That was like your mother, she always had a high spirit. He must be a cur, and he does not speak the truth. Your mother comes of a better stock than the Kershaws. The Carduses are one of the oldest families in the Eastern counties. Why, boy, our family lived down in the Fens by Lynn there for centuries, until your grandfather, poor weak man, got involved in his great lawsuit and ruined us all. There, there, it has gone into the law, but it is coming back, it is coming back fast. This Sir Hugh has only one son, by the way. Do you know that if anything happened to him you would be next in the entail? At any rate you would get the baronetcy."

"I don't want his baronetcy," said Ernest, sulkily; "I will have nothing of his."

"A title, boy, is an incorporeal hereditament, for which the holder is indebted to nobody. It does not descend to him, it vests in him. But tell me, how long was this before your mother died—that he sent the five pounds, I mean?"

"About three months."

Mr. Cardus hesitated a little before he spoke again, tapping his white fingers nervously on the table.

"I hope my sister was not in want, Ernest?" he said, jerkily.

"For a fortnight before she died we had scarcely enough to eat," was the blunt reply.

Mr. Cardus turned himself to the window, and for a minute the light of the dull December day shone and glistened upon his brow and head, which was perfectly bald. Then before he spoke he drew himself back into the shadow, perhaps to hide something like a tear that shone in his soft black eyes.

"And why did she not appeal to me? I could have helped her."

"She said that when you had quarrelled with her about her marrying my father, you told her never to write or speak to you again, and that she never would."

"Then why did you not do it, boy? You knew how things were."

"Because we had begged once, and I would not beg again."

"Ah," muttered Mr. Cardus, "the old spirit cropping up. Poor Rose, nearly starving, and dying too, and I with so much which I do not want. O, boy, boy, when you are a man never set up an idol, for it frightens good spirits away. Nothing else can live in its temple; it is a place where all things are forgotten—duty, and the claims of blood, and sometimes those of honour too. Look now, I have my idol, and it has made me forget my sister and your mother. Had she not written at last when she was dying, I should have forgotten you too."

The boy looked up puzzled.

"An idol!"

"Yes," went on his uncle in his dreamy way—"an idol. Many people have them; they keep them in the cupboard with their family skeleton; sometimes the two are identical. And they call them by many names, too; frequently it is a woman's name; sometimes that of a passion; sometimes that of a vice, but a virtue's—not often."

"And what is the name of yours, uncle?" asked the wondering boy.

"Mine? O, never mind!"

At this moment a swing-door in the side of the room was opened, and a tall, bony woman, with beady eyes, came through.

"Mr. de Talor to see you, sir, in the office."

Mr. Cardus whistled softly.

"Ah," he said, "tell him I am coming. By the way, Grice, this young gentleman has come to live here; his room is ready, is it not?"

"Yes, sir; Miss Dorothy has been seeing to it."

"Good; where is Miss Dorothy?"

"She has walked into Kesterwick, sir."

"O, and Master Jeremy?"

"He is about, sir; I saw him pass with a ferret a while back."

"Tell Sampson or the groom to find him and send him to Master Ernest here. That will do, thank you. Now, Ernest, I must go. I hope that you will be pretty happy here, my boy, when your trouble has worn off a bit. You will have Jeremy for a companion; he is a lout, and an unpleasant lout, it is true, but I suppose that he is better than nobody. And then there is Dorothy"—and his voice softened as he muttered her name—"but she is a girl."

"Who are Dorothy and Jeremy?" broke in his nephew; "are they your children?"

Mr. Cardus started perceptibly, and his thick white eyebrows contracted over his dark eyes till they almost met.

"Children!" he said, sharply; "I have no children. They are my wards. Their name is Jones;" and he left the room.

"Well, he is a rum sort," reflected Ernest to himself, "and I don't think I ever saw such a shiny head before. I wonder if he oils it? But, at any rate, he is kind to me. Perhaps it would have been better if mother had written to him before. She might have gone on living then."

Rubbing his hand across his face to clear away the water gathering in his eyes at the thought of his dead mother. Ernest made his way to the wide fireplace at the top end of the room, peeped into the ancient inglenooks on each side, and at the old Dutch tiles with which it was lined, and then, lifting his coat after a grown-up fashion, proceeded to warm himself and inspect his surroundings. It was a curious room in which he stood, and its leading feature was old oak-panelling. All down its considerable length the walls were oak-clad to the low ceiling, which was supported by enormous beams of the same material; the shutters of the narrow windows which looked out on the sea were oak, so were the doors and table, and even the mantelshelf. The general idea given by the display of so much timber was certainly one of stolidity, but it could scarcely be called cheerful—not even the numerous suits of armour and shining weapons which were placed about upon the walls could make it cheerful. It was a remarkable room, but its effect upon the observer was undoubtedly depressing.

Just as Ernest was beginning to realise this fact, things were made more lively by the sudden appearance through the swing-door of a large savage-looking bull-terrier, which began to steer for the fireplace, where evidently it was accustomed to lie. On seeing Ernest it stopped and sniffed.

"Hullo, good dog!" said Ernest.

The terrier growled and showed its teeth.

Ernest put out his leg towards it as a caution to keep it off. It acknowledged the compliment by sending its teeth through his trousers. Then the lad, growing wroth, and being not free from fear, seized the poker and hit the dog over the head so shrewdly that the blood streamed from the blow, and the brute, losing his grip, turned and fled howling.

While Ernest was yet warm with the glow of victory, the door once more swung open, violently this time, and through it there came a boy of about his own age, a dirty deep-chested boy, with uncut hair, and a slow heavy face in which were set great grey eyes, just now ablaze with indignation. On seeing Ernest he pulled up much as the dog had done, and regarded him angrily.

"Did you hit my dog?" he asked.

"I hit a dog," replied Ernest politely, "but—"

"I don't want your 'buts.' Can you fight?"

Ernest inquired whether this question was put with a view of gaining general information or for any particular purpose.

"Can you fight?" was the only rejoinder.

Slightly nettled, Ernest replied that under certain circumstances he could fight like a tom-cat.

"Then look out; I'm going to make your head as you have made my dog's."

Ernest, in the polite language of youth, opined that there would be hair and toe-nails flying first.

To this sally, Jeremy Jones, for it was he, replied only by springing at him, his hair streaming behind like a Red Indian's, and, smiting him severely in the left eye, caused him to measure his length upon the floor. Arising quickly, Ernest returned the compliment with interest; but this time they both went down together, pummelling each other heartily. With whom the victory would ultimately have remained could scarcely be doubtful, for Jeremy, who even at that age gave promise of enormous physical strength which afterwards made him such a noted character, must have crushed his antagonist in the end. But while his strength still endured Ernest was fighting with such ungovernable fury, and such a complete disregard of personal consequences, that he was for a while, at any rate, getting the best of it. And luckily for him, while matters were yet in the balanced scales of Fate, an interruption occurred. For at that moment there rose before the blurred sight of the struggling boys a vision of a small woman—at least she looked like a woman—with an indignant little face and an uplifted forefinger.

"O, you wicked boys! what will Reginald say, I should like to know? O, you bad Jeremy! I am ashamed to have such a brother. Get up!"

"My eye!" said Jeremy thickly, for his lip was cut, "it's Dolly!"

CHAPTER II

REGINALD CARDUS, ESQ., MISANTHROPE

When Mr. Cardus left the sitting-room where he had been talking to Ernest, he passed down a passage in the rambling old house which led him into a courtyard. On the farther side of the yard, which was walled in, stood a neat red-brick building one story high, consisting of two rooms and a passage. On to this building were attached a series of low green-houses, and against the wall at the farther end of these houses was a lean-to in which stood the boiler that supplied the pipes with hot water. The little red-brick building was Mr. Cardus's office, for he was a lawyer by profession; the long tail of glass behind it were his orchid-houses, for orchid-growing was his sole amusement. The tout ensemble, office and orchid-houses, seemed curiously out of place in the grey and ancient courtyard where they stood, looking as they did on to the old one-storied house, scarred by the passage of centuries of tempestuous weather. Some such idea seemed to strike Mr. Cardus as he closed the door behind him, preparatory to crossing the courtyard.

"Queer contrast," he muttered to himself; "very queer. Something like that between Reginald Cardus, Esquire, Misanthrope, of Dum's Ness, and Mr. Reginald Cardus, Solicitor, Chairman of the Stokesly Board of Guardians, Bailiff of Kesterwick, &c. And yet in both cases they are part of the same establishment. Case of old and new style!"

Mr. Cardus did not make his way straight to the office. He struck off to the right, and entered the long line of glasshouses, walking up from house to house, till he reached the compartment where the temperate sorts were placed to bloom, which was connected with his office by a glass door. Through this last he walked softly, with a cat-like step, till he reached the door, where he paused to observe a large coarse man, who was standing at the far end of the room, looking out intently on the courtyard.

"Ah, my friend," he said to himself, "so the shoe is beginning to pinch. Well, it is time." Then he pushed the door softly open, passed into the room with the same cat-like step, closed it, and, seating himself at his writing-table, took up a pen. Apparently the coarse-looking man at the window was too much absorbed in his own thoughts to hear him, for he still stood staring into space.

"Well, Mr. de Talor," said the lawyer presently, in his soft, jerky voice, "I am at your service."

The person addressed started violently, and turned sharply round. "Good 'eavens, Cardus, how did you get in?"

"Through the door, of course; do you suppose I came down the chimney?"

"It's very strange, Cardus, but I never 'eard you come. You've given me quite a start."

Mr. Cardus laughed, a hard little laugh. "You were too much occupied with your own thoughts, Mr. de Talor. I fear that they are not pleasant ones. Can I help you?"

"How do you know that my thoughts are not pleasant, Cardus? I never said so."

"If we lawyers waited for our clients to tell us all their thoughts, Mr. de Talor, it would often take us a long time to reach the truth. We have to read their faces, or even their backs sometimes. You have no idea of how much expression a back is capable, if you make such things your study; yours, for instance, looks very uncomfortable to-day: nothing gone wrong, I hope?"

"No, Cardus, no," answered Mr. de Talor, dropping the subject of backs, which was, he felt, beyond him; "that is, nothing much, merely a question of business, on which I have come to ask your advice as a shrewd man."

"My best advice is at your service, Mr. de Talor: what is it?"

"Well, Cardus, it's this." And Mr. de Talor seated his portly frame in an easy-chair, and turned his broad, vulgar face towards the lawyer. "It's about the railway-grease business—"

"Which you own up in Manchester?"

"Yes, that's it."

"Well, then, it ought to be a satisfactory subject to talk of. It pays hand over fist, does it not?"

"No, Cardus, that is just the point: it did pay, it don't now."

"How's that?"

"Well, you see, when my father took out the patent, and started the business, his 'ouse was the only 'ouse on the market, and he made a pot, and I don't mind telling you, I've made a pot too; but now, what do you think?—there's a beggarly firm called Rastrick & Codley that took out a new patent last year, and is underselling us with a better stuff at a cheaper price than we can turn ours out."

"Well!"

"Well, we've lowered our price to theirs, but we are doing business at a loss. We hoped to burst them, but they don't burst: there's somebody backing them, confound them, for Rastrick & Codley ain't worth a sixpence. Who it is the Lord only knows. I don't believe they know themselves."

"That is unfortunate, but what about it?"

"Just this, Cardus. I want to ask your advice about selling out. Our credit is good, and we could sell up for a large pile—not so large as we could have done, but still large—and I don't know whether to sell or hold."

Mr. Cardus looked thoughtful. "It is a difficult point, Mr. de Talor, but for myself I am always against caving in. The other firm may smash after all, and then you would be sorry. If you were to sell now you would probably make their fortunes, which I suppose you don't want to do."

"No, indeed."

"Then you are a very wealthy man; you are not dependent on this grease business. Even if things were to go wrong, you have all your landed property here at Ceswick's Ness to fall back on. I should hold, if I were you, even if it was at a loss for a time, and trust to the fortune of war."

Mr. de Talor gave a sigh of relief. "That's my view, too, Cardus. You are a shrewd man, and I am glad you jump with me. Damn Rastrick & Codley, say I!"

"O yes, damn them by all means," answered the lawyer, with a smile, as he rose to show his client to the door.

On the farther side of the passage was another door, with a glass top to it, which gave on to a room furnished after the ordinary fashion of a clerk's office. Opposite this door Mr. de Talor stopped to look at a man who was within, sitting at a table writing. The man was old, of large size, very powerfully built, and dressed with extreme neatness in hunting costume—boots, breeches, spurs and all. Over his large head grew tufts of coarse grey hair, which hung down in dishevelled locks about his face, giving him a wild appearance, that was added to by a curious distortion of the mouth. His left arm, too, hung almost helpless by his side.

Mr. Cardus laughed as he followed his visitor's gaze. "A curious sort of clerk, eh?" he said. "Mad, dumb, and half-paralysed—not many lawyers could show such another."

Mr. de Talor glanced at the object of their observation uneasily.

"If he's so mad, how can he do clerk's work?" he asked.

"O, he's only mad in a way; he copies beautifully."

"He has quite lost his memory, I suppose?" said de Talor, with another uneasy glance.

"Yes," answered Mr. Cardus, with a smile, "he has. Perhaps it is as well. He remembers nothing now but his delusions."

Mr. de Talor looked relieved. "He has been with you many years now, hasn't he, Cardus?"

"Yes, a great many."

"Why did you bring him 'ere at all?"

"Did I never tell you the story? Then if you care to step back into my office I will. It is not a long one. You remember when our friend"—he nodded towards the office—"kept the hounds, and they used to call him 'Hard-riding Atterleigh'?"

"Yes, I remember, and ruined himself over them, like a fool."

"And of course you remember Mary Atterleigh, his daughter, with whom we were all in love when we were young?"

Mr. de Talor's broad cheek took a deeper shade of crimson as he nodded assent.

"Then," went on Mr. Cardus, in a voice meant to be indifferent, but which now and again gave traces of emotion, "you will also remember that I was the fortunate man, and, with her father's consent, was engaged to be married to Mary Atterleigh so soon as I could show him that my income reached a certain sum." Here Mr. Cardus paused a moment, and then continued, "But I had to go to America about the great Norwich bank case, and it was a long job, and travelling was slow in those days. When I got back, Mary was—married to a man called Jones, a friend of yours, Mr. de Talor. He was staying at your house, Ceswick's Ness, when he met her. But perhaps you are better acquainted with that part of the tale than I am."

Mr. de Talor was looking very uneasy again now.

"No, I know nothing about it. Jones fell in love with her like the rest, and the next I heard of it was that they were to be married. It was rather rough on you, eh, Cardus? but, Lord, you shouldn't have been fool enough to trust her."

Mr. Cardus smiled, a bitter smile. "Yes, it was a little rough, but that has nothing to do with my story. The marriage did not turn out well; a curious fatality pursued all who had any hand in it. Mary had two children; and then did the best thing she could do—died of shame and sorrow. Jones, who was rich, went fraudulently bankrupt, and ended by committing suicide. 'Hard-riding Atterleigh' flourished for a while. Then lost his money on horses and a ship-building speculation, and got a paralytic stroke that took away all his speech and most of his reason. I brought him here to save him from the madhouse."

"That was kind of you, Cardus."

"Oh no, he is worth his keep, and besides, he is poor Mary's father. He is under the fixed impression that I am the devil; but that does not matter."

"You've got her children, too, eh?"

"Yes, I have adopted them. The girl reminds me of her mother, though she will never have her mother's looks. The boy is like old Atterleigh. I do not care about the boy. But, thank God, they are neither of them like their father."

"So you knew Jones?" said de Talor, sharply.

"Yes, I met him after his marriage. Oddly enough, I was with him a few minutes before he destroyed himself. There, Mr. de Talor, I will not detain you any longer. I thought that you could perhaps tell me something of the details of Mary's marriage. The story has a fascination for me, its results upon my own life have been so far-reaching. I am sure that I am not at the bottom of it yet. Mary wrote to me when she was dying, and hinted at something that I cannot understand. There was somebody behind who arranged the matter, who assisted Jones' suit. Well, well, I shall find it all out in time, and whoever it is will no doubt pay the price of his wickedness, like the others. Providence has strange ways, Mr. de Talor, but in the end it is a terrible avenger. What! are you going? Queer talk for a lawyer's office, isn't it?"

Here Mr. de Talor rose, looking pale, and, merely nodding to Mr. Cardus, left the room.

The lawyer watched him till the door had closed, when suddenly his whole face changed. The white eyebrows drew close together, the delicate features worked, and in the soft eyes there shone a look of hate. He clenched his fists, and shook them towards the door.

"You liar, you hound!" he said aloud. "God grant that I may live long enough to do to you as I have done to them! One a suicide, and one a paralytic madman; you—you shall be a beggar, if it takes me twenty years to make you so. Yes, that will hit you hardest. O Mary! Mary! dead and dishonoured through you, you scoundrel! O my darling, shall I ever find you again?"

And this strange man dropped his head upon the desk before him, and groaned.

CHAPTER III

OLD DUM'S NESS

When Mr. Cardus came half an hour or so later to take his place at the dinner table—for in those days they dined in the middle of the day at Dum's Ness—he was not in a good mood. The pool into which the records of an individual existence are ever gathering, which we call our past, will not often bear much stirring, even when its waters are not bitter. Certainly Mr. Cardus's would not. Yet that morning he had stirred it violently enough.

In the long, oak-panelled room, used indifferently as a sitting and dining room, Mr. Cardus found "Hard-riding Atterleigh" and his grand-daughter, little Dorothy Jones. The old man was already seated at table, and Dorothy was busying herself cutting bread, looking as composed and grown-up as though she had been four-and-twenty instead of fourteen. She was a strange child, with her assured air and woman's ways and dress, her curious thoughtful face, and her large blue eyes that shone steadily as the light of a lamp. But just now the little face was more anxious than usual.

"Reginald," she began, as soon as he was in the room (for by Mr. Cardus's wish she always called him by his Christian name), "I am sorry to tell you that there has been a sad disturbance."

"What is it?" he asked, with a frown; "Jeremy again?" Mr. Cardus could be very stern where Jeremy was concerned.

"Yes, I am afraid it is. The two boys—" but it was unnecessary for her to carry her explanations further, for at that moment the swing-door opened, and through it appeared the young gentlemen in question, driven in like sheep by the beady-eyed Grice. Ernest was leading, attempting the impossible feat of looking jaunty with a lump of raw beefsteak tied over one eye, and presenting a general appearance that suggested the idea of the colours of the rainbow in a state of decomposition.

Behind him shuffled Jeremy, his matted locks still wet from being pumped on. But his wounds were either unsuited to the dreadful remedy of raw beefsteak, or he had adopted in preference an heroic one of his own, of which grease plentifully sprinkled with flour formed the basis.

For a moment there was silence, then Mr. Cardus, with awful politeness, asked Jeremy what was the meaning of this sight.

"We've been fighting," answered the boy, sulkily. "He hit—"

"Thank you, Jeremy, I don't want the particulars, but I will take this opportunity to tell you before your sister and my nephew what I think of you. You are a boor and a lout, and, what is more, you are a coward."

At this unjust taunt the lad coloured to his eyes.

"Yes, you may colour, but let me tell you that it is cowardly to pick a quarrel with a boy the moment he sets foot inside my doors—"

"I say, uncle," broke in Ernest, who was unable to see anything cowardly about fighting, an amusement to which he was rather partial himself, and who thought that his late antagonist was getting more than his due, "I began it, you know."

It was not true, except in the sense that he had begun it by striking the dog: nor did this statement produce any great effect on Mr. Cardus, who was evidently seriously angry with Jeremy on more points than this. But at least it was one of those well-meant fibs at which the recording angel should not be offended.

"I do not care who began it," went on Mr. Cardus, angrily, "nor is it about this only that I am angry. You are a discredit to me, Jeremy, and a discredit to your sister. You are dirty, you are idle; your ways are not those of a gentleman. I sent you to school—you ran away. I give you good clothes—you will not wear them. I tell you, boy, that I will not stand it any longer. Now listen. I am going to make arrangements with Mr. Halford, the clergyman at Kesterwick, to undertake Ernest's education. You shall go with him; and if I see no improvement in your ways in the course of the next few months, I shall wash my hands of you. Do you understand me now?"

The boy Jeremy had, during this oration, been standing in the middle of the room, first on one leg, then on the other. At its conclusion he brought the leg that was at the moment in the air down to the ground, and stood firm.

"Well," went on Mr. Cardus, "what have you to say?"

"I have to say," blurted out Jeremy, "that I don't want your education. You care nothing about me," he went on, his grey eyes flashing and his heavy face lighting up; "nobody cares about me except my dog Nails. Yes, you make a dog of me myself; you throw things to me as I throw Nails a bone. I don't want your education, and I won't have it. I don't want the fine clothes you buy for me, and I won't wear them.

I don't want to be a burden on you either. Let me go away and be a fisher-lad and earn my bread. If it hadn't been for her," pointing to his sister, who was sitting aghast at his outburst, "and for Nails, I'd have gone long ago, I can tell you. At any rate, I should not be a dog then. I should be earning my living, and have no one to thank for it. Let me go, I say, where I shan't be mocked at if I do my fair day's work. I'm strong enough; let me go. There! I've spoken my mind now;" and the lad broke out into a storm of tears, and, turning, tramped out of the room.

As he went, all Mr. Cardus's wrath seemed to leave him.

"I did not think he had so much spirit in him," he said aloud. "Well, let us have our dinner."

At dinner the conversation flagged, the scene that preceded it having presumably left a painful impression; and Ernest, who was an observant youth, fell to watching little Dorothy doing the honours of the table; cutting up her crazed old grandfather's food for him, seeing that everybody had what he wanted, and generally making herself unobtrusively useful. In due course the meal came to an end, and Mr. Cardus and old Atterleigh went back to the office, leaving Dorothy alone with Ernest. Presently the former began to talk.

"I hope that your eye is not painful," she said. "Jeremy hits very hard."

"O no, it's all right. I'm used to it. When I was at school in London I often used to fight. I'm sorry for him, though—your brother, I mean."

"Jeremy! O yes, he is always in trouble, and now I suppose that it will be worse than ever. I do all I can to keep things smooth, but it is no good. If he won't go to Mr. Halford's, I am sure I don't know what will happen;" and the little lady sighed deeply.

"O, I daresay that he will go. Let's go and look for him, and try and persuade him."

"We might try," she said, doubtfully. "Stop a minute, and I will put on my hat, and then if you will take that nasty thing off your eye, we might walk on to Kesterwick. I want to take a book, out of which I have been teaching myself French, back to the cottage where old Miss Ceswick lives, you know."

"All right," said Ernest.

Presently Dorothy returned, and they went out by the back way to a little room near the coach-house, where Jeremy stuffed birds and kept his collection of eggs and butterflies; but he was not there. On inquiring of Sampson, the old Scotch gardener who looked after Mr. Cardus's orchid-houses, she discovered that Jeremy had gone out to shoot snipe, having borrowed Sampson's gun for that purpose.

"That is just like Jeremy," she sighed. "He is always going out shooting instead of attending to things."

"Can he hit birds flying, then?" asked Ernest.

"Hit them!" she answered, with a touch of pride; "I don't think he ever misses them. I wish he could do other things as well."

Jeremy at once went up at least fifty per cent. in Ernest's estimation.

On their way back to the house they peeped in through the office window, and Ernest saw "Hard-riding Atterleigh" at his work, copying deeds.

"He's your grandfather, isn't he?"

"Yes."

"Does he know you?"

"In a sort of way; but he is quite mad. He thinks that Reginald is the devil, whom he must serve for a certain number of years. He has got a stick with numbers of notches on it, and he cuts out a notch every month. It is all very sad. I think it is a very sad world;" and she sighed again.

"Why does he wear hunting-clothes?" asked Ernest.

"Because he always used to ride a good deal. He loves a horse now. Sometimes you will see him get up from his writing table, and the tears come into his eyes if anybody comes into the yard on horseback. Once he came out and tried to get on to a horse and ride off, but they stopped him."

"Why don't they let him ride?"

"O, he would soon kill himself. Old Jack Tares, who lives at Kesterwick, and gets his living by rats and ferrets, used to be whip to grandfather's hounds when he had them, and says that he always was a little mad about riding. One moonlight night he and grandfather went out to hunt a stag that had strayed here out of some park. They put the stag out of a little grove at a place called Claffton, five miles away, and he took them round by Starton and Ashleigh, and then came down the flats to the sea, about a mile and a half below here, just this side of the quicksand. The moon was so bright that it was almost like day, and for the last mile the stag was in view not more than a hundred yards in front of the hounds, and the pace was racing. When he came to the beach he went right through the waves out to the sea, and the hounds after him, and grandfather after them. They caught him a hundred yards out and killed him, and then grandfather turned his horse's head and swam with the hounds."

"My eye!" was Ernest's comment on this story. "And what did Jack Tares do?"

"O, he stopped on the beach and said his prayers; he thought that they would all be drowned."

Then they passed through the old house, which was built on a little ness or headland that jutted beyond the level of the shore-line, and across which the wind swept and raved all the winter long, driving the great waves in ceaseless thunder against the sandy cliffs. It was a desolate spot that the grey and massive house, of which the roof was secured by huge blocks of rock, looked out upon, nude of vegetation, save for rank, rush-like grass and plants of sea-holly. In front was the great ocean, rushing in continually upon the sandy bulwarks, and with but few ships to break its loneliness. To the left, far as the eye could reach, ran a line of cliff, till it was as full of gaps as an old crone's jaw. Behind this stretched mile upon mile of desolate-looking land, covered for the most part with ling and heath, and cut up with dikes, whence the water was pumped by means of windmills, that gave a Dutch appearance to the landscape.

"Look," said Dorothy, pointing to a small white house about a mile and a half away up the shore-line, "that is the lock-house, where the great sluice-gates are, and beyond that is the dreadful quick-sand in which a whole army was once swallowed up, like the Egyptians in the Red Sea."

"My word," said Ernest, much interested; "and, I say, did my uncle build this house?"

"You silly boy! why, it has been built for hundreds of years. Somebody of the name of Dum built it, and that is why it is called Dum's Ness; at least, I suppose so. There is an old chart that Reginald has, which was made in the time of Henry VII., and it is marked as Dum's Ness there, so Dum must have lived before then. Look," she went on, as, turning to the right, they rounded the old house and reached the road which ran along the top of the cliff, "there are the ruins of Titheburgh Abbey;" and she pointed to the remains of an enormous church with a still perfect tower, that stood within a few hundred yards of them, almost upon the edge of the cliff.

"Why don't they build it up again?" asked Ernest.

Dorothy shook her head. "Because in a few years the sea will swallow it. Nearly all the graveyard has gone already. It is the same with Kesterwick, where we are going. Kesterwick was a great town once. The kings of East Anglia made it their capital, and a bishop lived there. After that it was a great port, with thousands upon thousands of inhabitants. But the sea came on and on and choked up the harbour, and washed away the cliffs, and they could not keep it out, and now Kesterwick is nothing but a little village with one fine old church left. The real Kesterwick lies there, under the sea. If you walk along the beach after a great gale, you will find hundreds of bricks and tiles washed from the houses that are going to pieces down in the deep water. Just fancy, on one Sunday afternoon, in the reign of Queen Elizabeth, three of the parish churches were washed over the cliff into the sea!"

So she went on, telling the listening Ernest tale after tale of the old town, than which Babylon had not fallen more completely, till they came to a pretty little modern house bowered up in trees—that is, in summer, for there were no leaves upon them now—with which Ernest was destined to become very well acquainted in after years.

Dorothy left her companion at the gate while she went in to leave her book, remarking that she would be ashamed to introduce a boy with so black an eye. Presently she came back again, saying that Miss Ceswick was out.

"Who is Miss Ceswick?" asked Ernest, who at this period of his existence had a burning thirst for information of every sort.

"She is a very beautiful old lady," was Dorothy's answer. "Her family lived for many years at a place called Ceswick's Ness; but her brother lost all his money gambling, and the place was sold, and Mr. de Talor, that horrid fat man whom you saw drive away this morning, bought it."

"Does she live alone?"

"Yes; but she has some nice nieces, the daughter of her brother who is dead, and whose mother is very ill; and if she dies one of them is coming to live with her. She is just my age, so I hope she will come."

After this there was silence for a while.

"Ernest," said the little woman presently, "you look kind, so I will ask you. I want you to help me about Jeremy."

Ernest, feeling much puffed up at the compliment implied, expressed his willingness to do anything he could.

"You see, Ernest," she went on, fixing her sweet blue eyes on his face, "Jeremy is a great trouble to me. He will go his own way. And he does not like Reginald, and Reginald does not like him. If Reginald comes in at one door, Jeremy goes out at the other. Besides, he always flies in Reginald's face. And, you see, it is not right of Jeremy, because after all Reginald is very kind to us, and there is no reason he should be, except that I believe he was fond of our mother; and if it was not for Reginald, whom I love very much, though he is curious sometimes, I don't know what would become of grandfather or us. So, you see, I think that Jeremy ought to behave better to him, and I want to ask you to bear with his rough ways, and try to be friends with him, and get him to behave better. It is not much for him to do in return for all your uncle's kindness. You see, I can do a little something, because I look after the housekeeping; but he does nothing. First I want you to get him to make no more trouble about going to Mr. Halford's."

"All right, I'll try; but, I say, how do you learn? you seem to know an awful lot."

"O, I teach myself in the evenings. Reginald wanted to get me a governess, but I would not. How should I ever get Grice and the servants to obey me if they saw that I had to do what a strange woman told me? It would not do at all."

Just then they were passing the ruins of Titheburgh Abbey. It was almost dark, for the winter's evening was closing in rapidly, when suddenly Dorothy gave a little shriek, for from behind a ruined wall there rose up an armed mysterious figure with something white behind it. Next second she saw that it was Jeremy, who had returned from shooting, and was apparently waiting for them.

"O Jeremy, how you frightened me! What is it?"

"I want to speak to him," was the laconic reply.

Ernest stood still, wondering what was coming.

"Look here! You told a lie to try to save me from catching it this morning. You said that you began it. You didn't, I began it. I'd have told him too," and he jerked his thumb in the direction of Dum's Ness, "only my mouth was so full of words that I could not get it out. But I want to say I thank you, and here, take the dog. He's a nasty tempered devil, but he'll grow very fond of you if you are kind to him;" and seizing the astonished Nails by the collar, he thrust him towards Ernest.

For a moment there was a struggle in Ernest's mind, for he greatly longed to possess a bull-terrier dog; but his gentleman-like feeling prevailed. "I don't want the dog, and I didn't do anything in particular."

"Yes, you did, though," replied Jeremy, greatly relieved that Ernest did not accept his dog, which he loved, "or at least you did more than anybody ever did before; but I tell you what, I'll do as much for you one day. I'll do anything you like."

"Will you, though?" answered Ernest, who was a sharp youth, and opportunely remembered Dorothy's request.

"Yes, I will."

"Well, then, come to this fellow Halford with me; I don't want to go alone."

Jeremy slowly rubbed his face with the back of an exceedingly dirty hand. This was more than he had bargained for, but his word was his word.

"All right," he answered. "I'll come." Then whistling to his dog he vanished into the shadows. Thus began a friendship between these two that endured all their lives.

CHAPTER IV

BOYS TOGETHER

Jeremy kept his word. On the appointed day he appeared ready, as he expressed it, to "tackle that bloke Halford." What is more, he appeared with his hair cut, a decent suit of clothes on, and wonder of wonders, his hands properly washed, for all of which he was rewarded by finding that the "tackling" was not such a fearful business as he had anticipated. It was, moreover, of an intermittent nature, for the lads found plenty of time to indulge in every sort of manly exercise together. In winter they would roam all over the wide marsh-lands in search of snipe and wild ducks, which Ernest missed and Jeremy brought down with unerring aim, and in summer they would swim, or fish, and bird-nest to their hearts' content. In this way they contrived to combine the absorption of a little learning with that of a really extended knowledge of animal life and a large quantity of health and spirits.

They were happy years, those, for both the lads, and to Jeremy, when he compared them to his life as it had been before Ernest came, they seemed perfectly heavenly. For whether it was that he had improved in his manners since then, or that Ernest stood as a buffer between him and Mr. Cardus, it certainly happened that he came into collision with him far less often. Indeed, it seemed to Jeremy that the old gentleman (it was the fashion to call Mr. Cardus old, though he was in reality only middle-aged) was more tolerant of him than formerly, though he knew that he would never be a favourite.

As for Ernest, everybody loved the boy, and then, as afterwards, he was a great favourite with women, who would one and all do anything he asked. It was a wonder that he did not get spoiled by it all; but he did not. It was not possible to know Ernest Kershaw at any period of his life without taking a fancy to him, he was so eminently and unaffectedly a gentleman, and so completely free from any sort of swagger. Always ready to do a kindness and never forgetting one done, generous with his possessions to such an extent that he seemed to have a vague idea that they were the common property of his friends and himself, possessing that greatest of gifts, a sympathetic mind, and true as steel, no wonder that he was always popular both with men and women.

Ernest grew into a handsome lad, too, as soon as he began to get his height, with a shapely form, a beautiful pair of eyes, and an indescribable appearance of manliness and spirit. But the greatest charm of his face was always its quick intelligence and unvarying kindliness.

As for Jeremy, he did not change much; he simply expanded very largely. Year by year his form assumed more and more enormous proportions, and his strength grew more and more abnormal. As for his mind, it did not grow with the same rapidity, and was loth to admit a new idea; but once it was in, it never came out again.

He had a ruling passion, too, this dull giant, and that was his intense affection and admiration for Ernest. It was an affection that grew with his growth till it became a part of himself, increasing with the increasing years, till at last it was nearly pathetic in its entirety. It was but rarely that he parted from Ernest, except, indeed, on those occasions when Ernest chose to go abroad to pursue his study of foreign languages, of which he was rather fond. Then, and then only, Jeremy would strike. He disliked parting with Ernest much, but he objected—being intensely insular—to cohabit with foreigners yet more, so on these occasions, and these only, for a while they separated.

So the years wore on till, when they were eighteen, Mr. Cardus, after his sudden fashion, announced his intention of sending them both to Cambridge. Ernest always remembered it, for it was on that very day that he first made the acquaintance of Florence Ceswick. He had just issued from his uncle's presence, and was seeking Dolly, to communicate the intelligence to her, when he suddenly blundered in upon old Miss Ceswick, and with her a young lady. This young lady, to whom Miss Ceswick introduced him as her niece, at once attracted his attention. On being introduced the girl, who was about his own age, touched his outstretched palm with her slender fingers, throwing on him at the same moment so sharp a look from her brown eyes that he afterwards declared to Jeremy that it seemed to go right through him. She was a remarkable-looking girl. The hair, which curled profusely over a shapely head, was, like the eyes, brown; the complexion olive, the features were small, and the lips full, curving over a beautiful set of teeth. In person she was rather short, but squarely built, and at her early age her figure was perfectly formed. Indeed, she might to all appearances have been much older than she was. There was little of the typical girl about her. While he was still observing her, his uncle came into the room, and was duly introduced by the old lady to her niece, who had, she said, come to share her loneliness.

"How do you like Kesterwick, Miss Florence?" asked Mr. Cardus, with his usual courtly smile.

"It is much what I expected—a little duller, perhaps," she answered composedly.

"Ah, perhaps you have been accustomed to a gayer spot."

"Yes, till my mother died we lived at Brighton; there is plenty of life there. Not that we could mix in it, we were too poor; but at any rate we could watch it."

"Do you like life, Miss Florence?"

"Yes, we only live such a short time. I should like," she went on, throwing her head back, and half-closing her eyes, "to see as much as I can, and to exhaust every emotion."

"Perhaps, Miss Florence, you would find some of them rather unpleasant," answered Mr. Cardus, with a smile.

"Possibly, but it is better to travel through a bad country than to grow in a good one."

Mr. Cardus smiled again: the girl interested him rather.

"Do you know, Miss Ceswick," he said, changing the subject, and addressing the stately old lady, who was sitting smoothing her laces, and looking rather aghast at her niece's utterances, "that this young gentleman is going to college, and Jeremy, too?"

"Indeed," said Miss Ceswick; "I hope that you will do great things there, Ernest."

While Ernest was disclaiming any intentions of the sort, Miss Florence cut in again, raising her eyes from a deep contemplation of that young gentleman's long shanks, which were writhing under her keen glance, and twisting themselves serpent-wise round the legs of the chair.

"I did not know," she said, "that they took boys at college."

Then they took their leave, and Ernest stigmatised her to Dorothy as a "beast."

But she was at least attractive in her own peculiar fashion, and during the next year or two he became rather intimate with her.

So Ernest and Jeremy went up to Cambridge, but did not set the place on fire, nor were the voices of tutors loud in their praise. Jeremy, it is true, rowed one year in the 'Varsity Race, and performed prodigies of strength, and so covered himself with a sort of glory, which, personally, being of a modest mind, he did not particularly appreciate. Ernest did not even do that. But, by hook or by crook, at the termination of their collegiate career, they took some sort of degree, and then departed from the shores of the Cam, on which they had spent many a jovial day—Jeremy to return to Kesterwick, and Ernest to pay several visits to college friends in town and elsewhere.

Thus ended the first little round of their days.

CHAPTER V

EVA'S PROMISE

When, on leaving Cambridge, Jeremy got back to Dum's Ness, Mr. Cardus received him with his usual semi-contemptuous coldness, a mental attitude that often nearly drove the young fellow wild with mortification. Not that Mr. Cardus really felt any contempt for him now—he had lost all that years ago, when the boy had been so anxious to go and "earn his bread;" but he could never forgive him for being the son of his father, or conquer his inherent dislike to him. On the other hand, he certainly did not allow this to interfere with his treatment of the lad; if anything, indeed, it made him more careful. What he spent upon Ernest, the same sum he spent on Jeremy, pound for pound; but there was this difference about it—the money he spent on Ernest he gave from love, and that on Jeremy from a sense of duty.

Now, Jeremy knew all this well enough, and it made him very anxious to earn his own living, and become independent of Mr. Cardus. But it was one thing to be anxious to earn your own living, and quite another to do it, as many a poor wretch knows to his cost, and when Jeremy set his slow brain to consider how he should go about the task it quite failed to supply him with any feasible idea. Yet he did not want much; Jeremy was not of an ambitious temperament. If he could earn enough to keep a cottage over his head, and find himself in food and clothes, and powder and shot, he would be perfectly content. Indeed, there were to be only two sine qua nons in his ideal occupation: it must admit of a considerable amount of outdoor exercise, and be of such a nature as would permit him to see plenty of Ernest. Without more or less of Ernest's company, life would not, he considered, be worth living.

For a week or more after his arrival home these perplexing reflections simmered incessantly inside Jeremy's head, till at length, feeling that they were getting too much for him, he determined to consult his sister, which, as she had three times his brains, he would have done well to think of before.

Dolly fixed her steady blue eyes upon him and listened to his tale in silence.

"And so you see, Doll"—he always called her Doll—he ended up, "I'm in a regular fix. I don't know what I'm fit for, unless it's to row a boat, or let myself out to bad shots to kill their game for them. You see I must stick on to Ernest; I don't feel somehow as though I could get along without him; if it wasn't for that I'd emigrate. I should be just the chap to cut down big trees in Vancouver's Island or brand bullocks," he added meditatively.

"You are a great goose, Jeremy," was his sister's comment.

He looked up, not in any way disputing her statement, but merely for further information.

"You are a great goose, I say. What do you suppose that I have been doing all these three years and more that you have been rowing boats and wasting time up at college. I have been thinking, Jeremy."

"Yes, and so have I, but there is no good in thinking."

"No, not if you stop there; but I've been acting too. I've spoken to Reginald, and made a plan, and he has accepted my plan."

"You always were clever, Doll; you've got all the brains and I've got all the size;" and he surveyed as much as he could see of himself ruefully.

"You don't ask what I have arranged," she said, sharply, for in alluding to her want of stature Jeremy had touched a sore point.

"I am waiting for you to tell me."

"Well, you are to be articled to Reginald."

"O Lord!" groaned Jeremy, "I don't like that at all."

"Be quiet till I have told you. You are to be articled to Reginald, and he is to pay you an allowance of a hundred a year while you are articled, so that if you don't like it you needn't live here."

"But I don't like the business, Doll; I hate it; it is a beastly business; it's a devil's business."

"I should like to know what right you have to talk like that, Mr. Knowall! Let me tell you that many better men than you are content to earn their living by lawyer's work. I suppose that a man can be honest as a lawyer as well as in any other trade."

Jeremy shook his head doubtfully. "It's blood-sucking," he said energetically.

"Then you must suck blood," she answered, with decision. "Look here, Jeremy, don't be pig-headed and upset all my plans. If you fall out with Reginald over this, he won't do anything else for you. He doesn't like you, you know, and would be only too glad to pick a quarrel with you if he could do it with a clear conscience, and then where would you be, I should like to know?"

Jeremy was unable to form an opinion as to where he would be, so she went on:

"You must take it for the present, at any rate. Then there is another thing to think of. Ernest is to go to the bar, and unless you become a lawyer, if anything happened to Reginald, there will be nobody to give him a start, and I'm told that is everything at the bar."

This last Jeremy admitted to be a weighty argument.

"It is a precious queer sort of lawyer I shall make," he said, sadly, "about as good as grandfather yonder, I'm thinking. By the way, how has he been getting on?"

"O, just as usual—write, write, write all day. He thinks that he is working out his time. He has got a new stick now, on which he has nicked all the months and years that have to run before he has done—little nicks for the months and big nicks for the years. There are eight or ten big ones left now. Every month he cuts out a nick. It is very dreadful. You know he thinks that Reginald is the devil, and he hates him, too. The other day, when he had no writing to do in the office, I found him drawing pictures of him with horns and tail, such awful pictures, and I think Reginald always looks like that to him. Then sometimes he wants to go out riding, especially at night. Only last week they found him putting a bridle on to the grey mare—the one that Reginald sometimes rides, you know. When did you say that Ernest was coming back?" she said, after a pause.

"Why, Doll, I told you—next Monday week."

Her face fell a little. "O, I thought you said Saturday."

"Why do you want to know?"

"O, only about getting his room ready."

"Why, it is ready; I looked in yesterday."

"Nonsense! you know nothing about it," she answered, colouring. "Come, I wish you would go out; I want to count the linen, and you are in the way."

Thus adjured, Jeremy removed his large form from the table on which he had been sitting, and whistling to Nails, now a very ancient and preternaturally wise dog, set off for a walk. He had mooned along some little way, with his hands in his pockets and his eyes on the ground, reflecting on the unpleasant fate in store for him as an articled clerk, continually under the glance of Mr. Cardus's roving eyes, when suddenly he became aware that two ladies were standing on the edge of the cliff within a dozen yards of him. He would have turned and fled, for Jeremy had a marked dislike to ladies' society, and a strong opinion, which, however, he never expressed, that women were the root of all evil; but, thinking that he had been seen, he feared that retreat would appear rude. In one of the young ladies, for they were young, he recognised Miss Florence Ceswick, who to all appearance had not changed in the least since, some years ago, she came with her aunt to call on Dorothy. There were the same brown hair, curling as profusely as ever, the same keen brown eyes and ripe lips, the same small features and resolute expression of face. Her square figure had indeed developed a little. In her tight-fitting dress it looked almost handsome, and somehow its very squareness, that most women would have considered a defect, contributed to the air of power and unchanging purpose that would have made Florence Ceswick remarkable among a hundred handsomer women.

"How do you do?" said Florence, in her sharp manner. "You look as though you were walking in your sleep."

Before Jeremy could find a reply to this remark, the other young lady, who had been looking intently over the edge of the cliff, turned round and struck him dumb. In his limited experience he had never seen such a beautiful woman before.

She was a head and shoulders taller than her sister, so tall indeed that only her own natural grace could save her from looking awkward. Like her sister she was a brunette, only of a much more pronounced type. Her waving hair was black, and so were her beautiful eyes and the long lashes that curled over them. The complexion was a clear olive, the lips were like coral, and the teeth small and regular. Every advantage that Nature can lavish on a woman she had endowed her with in abundance, including radiant health and spirits. To these charms must be added that sweet and kindly look which sometimes finds a home on the faces of good women, a soft voice, a quick intelligence, and an utter absence of conceit or self-consciousness, and the reader will get some idea of what Eva Ceswick was like in the first flush of her beauty.

"Let me introduce my sister Eva, Mr. Jones."

But Mr. Jones was for the moment paralysed; he could not even take off his hat.

"Well," said Florence, presently, "she is not Medusa; there is no need for you to turn into stone."

This woke him up—indeed, occasionally, Florence had an ugly trick of waking people up, and he took off his hat, which was as usual a dirty one, and muttered something inaudible. As for Eva, she blushed, and with ready wit said that Mr. Jones was no doubt astonished at the filthy state of her dress (as a matter of fact, Jeremy could not have sworn that she had one on at all, much less to its condition). "The fact is," she went on, "I have been lying flat on the grass and looking over the edge of the cliff."

"What at?"

"Why, the bones."

The spot on which they were standing was part of the ancient graveyard of Titheburgh Abbey, and as the sea encroached year by year, multitudes of the bones of the long-dead inhabitants of Kesterwick were washed out of their quiet graves and strewed upon the beach and unequal surfaces of the cliff.

"Look," she said, kneeling down, an example that he followed. About six feet below them, which was the depth at which the corpses had been originally laid, could be seen fragments of lead and rotting wood projecting from the surface of the cliff, and, what was a more ghastly sight, eight inches or more of the leg-bones of a man, off which the feet had been washed away. On a ledge in the sandy cliff, about twenty-five feet from the top and sixty or so from the bottom, there lay quite a collection of human remains of all sorts and sizes, conspicuous among them being the bones which had composed the feet that belonged to the projecting shanks.

"Isn't it dreadful?" said Eva, gazing down with a species of fascination: "just fancy coming to that! Look at that little baby's skull just by the big one. Perhaps that is the mother's. And what is that buried in the sand?"

As much of the object to which she pointed as was visible looked like an old cannon-ball, but Jeremy soon came to a different conclusion.

"It is a bit of lead coffin," he said.

"Oh, I should like to get down there and find out what is in it. Can't you get down?"

Jeremy shook his head. "I've done it as a boy," he said, "when I was very light; but it is no good my trying now; the sand would give with me, and I should go to the bottom."

He was willing to do most things to oblige this lovely creature, but Jeremy was above all things practical, and did not see the use of breaking his neck for nothing.

"Well," she said, "you certainly are rather heavy."

"Fifteen stone," he said, mournfully.

"But I am not ten; I think I could get down."

"You'd better not try without a rope."

Just then their conversation was interrupted by Florence's clear voice:

"When you two people have quite finished staring at those disgusting bones, perhaps, Eva, you will come to lunch. If you only knew how silly you look, sprawling there like two Turks going to be bastinadoed, perhaps you would get up."

This was too much for Eva; she got up at once, and Jeremy followed suit.

"Why could you not let us examine our bones in peace, Florence?" said her sister, jokingly.

"Because you are really too idiotic. You see, Mr. Jones, anything that is old and fusty, and has to do with old fogies who are dead and gone centuries ago, has the greatest charms for my sister. She would like to go home and make stories about those bones: whose they were, and what they did, and all the rest of it. She calls it imagination; I call it fudge."

Eva flushed up, but said nothing; evidently she was not accustomed to answer her elder sister, and presently they parted to go their separate ways.

"What a great oaf that Jeremy is!" said Florence to her sister on their homeward way.

"I did not think him an oaf at all," she replied, warmly; "I thought him very nice."

Florence shrugged her square shoulders. "Well, of course, if you like a giant with as much brain as an owl, there is nothing more to be said. You should see Ernest; he is nice, if you like."

"You seem very fond of Ernest."

"Yes, I am," was the reply; "and I hope that when he comes you won't poach on my manor."

"You need not be afraid," answered Eva, smiling; "I promise to leave your Ernest alone."

"Then that is a bargain," said Florence, sharply. "Mind that you keep to your word."

CHAPTER VI

JEREMY FALLS IN LOVE

Jeremy, for the first time for some years, had no appetite for his dinner that day, a phenomenon that filled Dorothy with alarm.

"My dear Jeremy," she said afterwards, "what can be the matter with you? you had only one helping of beef and no pudding!"

"Nothing at all," he replied sulkily; and the subject dropped.

"Doll," said Jeremy presently, "do you know Miss Eva Ceswick?"

"Yes, I have seen her twice."

"What do you think of her, Doll?"

"What do you think of her?" replied that cautious young person.

"I think she is beautiful as—as an angel."

"Quite poetical, I declare! What next! Have you seen her?"

"Of course, else how should I know she was beautiful?"

"Ah, no wonder you had only once of beef!"

Jeremy coloured.

"I am going to call there this afternoon: would you like to come?" went on his sister.

"Yes, I'll come."

"Better and better: it will be the first call I ever remember your having paid."

"You don't think she will mind, Doll?"

"Why should she mind? Most people don't mind being called on, even if they have a pretty face."

"Pretty face! She is pretty all over."

"Well, then, a pretty all over. I start at three; don't be late."

Thereupon Jeremy went off to beautify himself for the occasion, and his sister gazed at his departing form with the puzzled expression that had distinguished her as a child.

"He's going to fall in love with her," she said to herself, "and no wonder; any man would; she is 'pretty all over,' as he said, and what more does a man look at? I wish that she would fall in love with him before Ernest comes home;" and she sighed.

At a quarter to three Jeremy reappeared, looking particularly huge in a black coat and his Sunday trousers. When they reached the cottage where Miss Ceswick lived with her nieces, they were destined to meet with a disappointment, for neither of the young ladies was at home. Miss Ceswick, however, was there, and received them very cordially.

"I suppose that you have come to see my newly imported niece," she said; "in fact, I am sure that you have, Mr. Jeremy, because you never came to call upon me in your life. Ah, it is wonderful how young men will change their habits to please a pair of bright eyes!"

Jeremy blushed painfully at this sally, but Dorothy came to his rescue.

"Has Miss Eva come to live with you for good?" she asked.

"Yes, I think so. You see, my dear, between you and me, her aunt in London, with whom she was living, has got a family of daughters, who have recently come out. Eva has been kept back as long as possible, but now that she is twenty it was impossible to keep her back any more. But then, on the other hand, it was felt—at least I think that it was felt—that to continue to bring Eva out with her cousins would be quite to ruin their chance of settling in life, because when she was in the room, no man could be got to look at them. So, you see, Eva has been sent down here as a penalty for being so handsome."

"Most of us would be glad to undergo heavier penalties than that if we could only be guilty of the crime," said Dorothy, a little sadly.

"Ah, my dear, I daresay you think so," answered the old lady. "Every young woman longs to be beautiful and get the admiration of men, but are they any the happier for it? I doubt it. Very often that admiration brings endless troubles in its train, and perhaps in the end wrecks the happiness of the woman herself and of others who are mixed up with her. I was once a beautiful woman, my dear—I am old enough to say it now—and I can tell you that I believe that Providence cannot do a more unkind thing to a woman than to give her striking beauty, unless it gives with it great strength of mind. A weak-minded beauty is the most unfortunate of her sex. Her very attractions, which are sure to draw the secret enmity of other women on to her, are a source of difficulty to herself, because they bring her lovers with whom she cannot deal. Sometimes the end of such a woman is sad enough. I have seen it happen several times, my dear."

Often in after-life, and in circumstances that had not then arisen, did Dorothy think of old Miss Ceswick's words, and acknowledge their truth; but at this time they did not convince her.

"I would give anything to be like your niece," she said bluntly, "and so would any other girl. Ask Florence, for instance."

"Ah, my dear, you think so now. Wait till another twenty years have passed over your heads, and then if you are both alive see which of you is the happier. As for Florence, of course she would wish to be like Eva; of course it is painful for her to have to go about with a girl beside whom she looks like a little dowdy. I daresay that she would have been as glad if Eva stopped in London as her cousins were that she left it. Dear, dear! I hope they won't quarrel. Florence's temper is dreadful when she quarrels."

This was a remark that Dorothy could not gainsay. She knew very well what Florence's temper was like.

"But, Mr. Jeremy," went on the old lady, "all this must be stupid talk for you to listen to: tell me, have you been rowing any more races lately?"

"No," said Jeremy; "I strained a muscle in my arm in the 'Varsity Race, and it is not quite well yet."

"And where is my dear Ernest?" Like most women, of whatever age they might be, Miss Ceswick adored Ernest.

"He is coming back on Monday week."

"O, then he will be in time for the Smythes' lawn tennis party. I hear that they are going to give a dance after it. Do you dance, Mr. Jeremy?"

Jeremy had to confess that he did not; indeed, as a matter of fact, no earthly power had ever been able to drag him inside a ballroom in his life.

"That is a pity; there are so few young men in these parts. Florence counted them up the other day, and the proportion is one unmarried man, between the ages of twenty and forty-five, to every nine women between eighteen and thirty."

"Then only one girl in every nine can get married," put in Dorothy, whose mind had a trick of following things to their conclusion.

"And what becomes of the other eight?" asked Jeremy.

"I suppose that they all grow into old maids like myself," answered Miss Ceswick.

Dorothy, again following the matter to its conclusion, reflected that in fifteen years or so there would, at the present rate of progression, be at least twenty-five old maids within a radius of three miles from Kesterwick. Much oppressed by this thought, she rose to take her leave.

"I know who won't be left without a husband, unless men are greater stupids than I take them for—eh, Jeremy?" said the kindly old lady, giving Dorothy a kiss.

"If you mean me," answered Dorothy, bluntly, with a slightly heightened colour, "I am not so vain as to think that anybody would care for an undersized creature whose only accomplishment is housekeeping; and I am sure it is not for anybody that I should care either."

"Ah, my dear, there are still a few men of sense in the world, who would rather get a good woman as companion than a pretty face. Good-bye, my dear."

Though Jeremy was on this occasion disappointed of seeing Eva, on the following morning he was so fortunate as to meet her and her sister walking on the beach. But when he got into her gracious presence he found somehow that he had very little to say; and the walk would, to tell the truth, have been rather dull, if it had not occasionally been enlivened by dashes of Florence's caustic wit.

On the next day, however, he returned to the charge with several hundredweight of the roots of a certain flower which Eva had expressed a desire to possess. And so it went on till at last his shyness wore off a little, and they grew very good friends.

Of course all this did not escape Florence's sharp eyes, and one day, just after Jeremy had paid her sister a lumbering compliment and departed, she summarised her observations thus:

"That moon-calf is falling in love with you, Eva."

"Nonsense, Florence! and why should you call him a moon-calf? It is not nice to talk of people so."

"Well, if you can find a better description, I am willing to adopt it."

"I think that he is an honest gentleman-like boy; and even if he were falling in love with me, I do not think there would be anything to be ashamed of—there!"

"Dear me, what a fuss we are in. Do you know, I shall soon begin to think that you are falling in love with the 'honest gentleman-like boy'—yes, that is a better title than moon-calf, though not so nervous."

Here Eva marched off in a huff.

"Well, Jeremy, and how are you getting on with the beautiful Eva?" asked Dorothy that same day.

"I say Doll," replied Jeremy, whose general appearance was that of a man plunged into the depths of misery, "don't laugh at a fellow; if you only knew what I feel—inside, you know—you wouldn't—"

"What! are you not well? have some brandy?" suggested his sister, in genuine alarm.

"Don't be an idiot, Doll; it isn't my stomach, it's here"; and he knocked his right lung, under the impression that he was indicating the position of his heart.

"And what do you feel, Jeremy?"

"Feel!" he answered with a groan; "what don't I feel? When I am away from her I feel a sort of sinking, just like one does when one has to go without one's dinner, only it's always there. When she looks at me I go hot and cold all over, and when she smiles it's just as though one had killed a couple of woodcocks right and left."

"Good gracious, Jeremy!" interposed his sister, who was beginning to think he had gone off his head; "and what happens if she doesn't smile?"

"Ah, then," he replied, sadly, "it's as though one had missed them both."

Though his similes were peculiar, it was clear to his sister that the feeling he meant to convey was genuine enough.

"Are you really fond of this girl, Jeremy dear?" she said gently.

"Well, Doll, you know, I suppose I am."

"Then why don't you ask her to marry you?"

"To marry me! Why, I am not fit to clean her shoes."

"An honest gentleman is fit for any woman, Jeremy."

"And I haven't got anything to support her on even if she said yes, which she wouldn't."

"You may get that in time. Remember, Jeremy, she is a very lovely woman, and soon she is sure to find other lovers."

Jeremy groaned.

"But if once you had secured her affection, and she is a good woman, as I think she is, that would not matter, though you might not be able to marry for some years."

"Then what am I to do?"

"I should tell her that you loved her, and ask her, if she would care for you—to wait for you awhile."

Jeremy whistled meditatively.

"I'll ask Ernest about it when he comes back on Monday.'

"If I were you I should act for myself in that matter," she said quickly.

"No good being in a hurry; I haven't known her for a fortnight—I'll ask Ernest."

"Then you will regret it," Dorothy answered, almost passionately, and rising, left the room.

"Now, what did she mean by that?" reflected her brother aloud; "she always was so deuced queer where Ernest is concerned." But his inner consciousness returned no satisfactory answer, so with a sigh the love-lorn Jeremy took up his hat and walked.

On Sunday, that was the day following his talk with Dorothy, he saw Eva again in church, where she looked, he thought, more like an angel than ever, and was quite as inaccessible. In the churchyard he did, it is true, manage to get a word or two with her, but nothing more, for the sermon had been long, and Florence was hungry, and hurried her sister home to lunch.

And then, at last, came Monday, the long-expected day of Ernest's arrival.

CHAPTER VII

ERNEST IS INDISCREET

Kesterwick is a primitive place, and has no railway station nearer than Raffham, four miles off. Ernest was expected by the midday train, and Dorothy and her brother went to meet him.

When they reached the station the train was just in sight, and Dorothy got down to await its arrival. Presently it snorted up composedly—trains do not hurry themselves on the single lines in the Eastern counties—and in due course deposited Ernest and his portmanteau.

"Hullo, Doll! so you have come to meet me. How are you, old girl?" and he embraced her on the platform.

"You shouldn't, Ernest: I am too big to be kissed like a little girl, and in public too."

"Big—h'm! Miss five-feet-nothing, and as for the public, I don't see any." The train had gone on, and the solitary porter had vanished with the portmanteau.

"Well, there is no need for you to laugh at me for being small; it is not everybody who can be a May-pole, like you, or as broad as he is long, like Jeremy."

An unearthly view halloo from this last-named personage, who had caught sight of Ernest through the door of the booking-office, put a stop to further controversy, and presently all three were driving back, each talking at the top of his or her voice.

At the door of Dum's Ness they found Mr. Cardus apparently gazing abstractedly at the ocean, but in reality waiting to greet Ernest, to whom of late years he had grown greatly attached, though his reserve seldom allowed him to show it.

"Hullo, uncle, how are you? You look pretty fresh," sang out that young gentleman before the cart had fairly come to a standstill.

"Very well, thank you, Ernest. I need not ask how you are. I am glad to see you back. You have come at a lucky moment, too, for the 'Batemania Wallisii' is in flower, and the 'Grammatophyllum speciosum' too. The last is splendid."

"Ah," said Ernest, deeply interested, for he had much of his uncle's love for orchids, "let's go and see them."

"Better have some dinner first; you must be hungry. The orchids will keep, but the dinner won't."

It was curious to see what a ray of light this lad brought with him into that rather gloomy household. Everybody began to laugh as soon as he was inside the doors. Even Grice of the beady eyes laughed when he feigned to be thunderstruck at the newly developed beauty of her person, and mad old Atterleigh's contorted features lit up with something like a smile of recognition when Ernest seized his hand and worked it like a pump-handle, roaring out his congratulations on the jollity of his looks. He was a bonny lad, the sight of whom was good for sore eyes.

After dinner he went with his uncle, and spent half an hour in going round the orchid-houses with him and Sampson the gardener. The latter was not behind the rest of the household in his appreciation of "Meester" Ernest. "'Twasn't many lads," he would say, "that knew an 'Odontoglossum' from a 'Sobralia,'" but Ernest did, and, what was more, knew whether it was well grown or not. Sampson appreciated a man who could discriminate orchids, and set his preference for Ernest down to that cause. The dour-visaged old Scotchman did not like to own that what really charmed him was the lad's openhanded, open-hearted manner, to say nothing of his ready sympathy and honest eyes.

While they were still engaged in admiring the lovely bloom of the "Grammatophyllum," Mr. Cardus saw Mr. de Talor come into his office, which, it may be remembered, was connected with the orchid blooming-house by a glass door. Ernest was much interested in observing the curious change that this man's appearance produced in his uncle. As a peaceful cat, dozing on a warm stone in summer, becomes suddenly changed into a thing of bristling wickedness and fury by the vision of the most inoffensive dog, so did the placid, bald-headed old gentleman, glowing with innocent pleasure at his horticultural masterpiece, commence to glow with very different emotions at the sight of the pompous De Talor. The ruling passion of his life asserted its sway in a moment, and his whole face changed; the upper lip began to quiver, the roving eyes glittered with a dangerous light; and then a mask seemed to gather over the features, which grew hard and almost inscrutable. It was an interesting transformation.

Although they could see De Talor, he could not see them; so for a minute they enjoyed an undisturbed period of observation.

The visitor walked round the room, and, casting a look of contempt at the flowers in the blooming-house, stopped at Mr. Cardus's desk, and glanced at the papers lying on it. Finding apparently nothing to interest him he retired to the window, and, putting his thumbs in the arm-holes of his waistcoat, amused himself by staring out of it. There was something so intensely vulgar and insolent in his appearance as he stood thus, that Ernest could not help laughing.

"Ah!" said Mr. Cardus, with a look of suppressed malignity, half to himself and half to Ernest, "I have really got a hold of you at last, and you may look out, my friend." Then he went in, and as he left the blooming-house Ernest heard him greet his visitor in that suave manner, with just a touch of deference in it, that he knew so well how to assume, and De Talor's reply of "'Ow do, Cardus? 'ow's the business getting on?"

Outside the glass houses Ernest found Jeremy waiting for him. It had for years been an understood thing that the latter was not to enter them. There was no particular reason why he should not; it was merely one of those signs of Mr. Cardus's disfavour that caused Jeremy's pride such bitter injury.

"What are you going to do, old fellow?" he asked of Ernest.

"Well, I want to go down and see Florence Ceswick, but I suppose you won't care to come."

"O yes, I'll come."

"The deuce you will! well, I never! I say, Doll," he sang out to that young lady as she appeared upon the scene, "what has happened to Jeremy—he's coming out calling?"

"I fancy he's got an attraction," said Miss Dorothy.

"I say, old fellow, you haven't been cutting me out with Florence, have you?"

"I am sure it would be no great loss if he had," put in Dorothy, with an impatient little stamp of the foot.

"You be quiet, Doll. I'm very fond of Florence, she's so clever, and nice-looking too."

"If being clever means being able to say spiteful things, and having a temper like—like a fiend, she is certainly clever enough; and as for her looks, they are a matter of taste—not that it is for me to talk about good looks."

"O, how humble we are, Doll! dust on our head and sackcloth on our back, and how our blue eyes flash!"

"Be quiet, Ernest, or I shall get angry."

"O no, don't do that; leave that to people with a temper 'like—like a fiend,' you know. There, there, don't get cross, Dolly; let's kiss and be friends."

"I won't kiss you, and I won't be friends, and you may walk by yourselves"; and before anybody could stop her she was gone.

Ernest whistled softly, reflecting that Dorothy was not good at standing chaff. Then, after waiting awhile, he and Jeremy started to pay their call.

But they were destined to be unfortunate. Eva, whom Ernest had never seen, and of whom he had heard nothing beyond that she was "good-looking"—for Jeremy, notwithstanding his expressed intention of consulting him, could not make up his mind to broach the subject—was in bed with a bad headache, and Florence had gone out to spend the afternoon with a friend. The old lady was at home, however, and received them both warmly, more especially her favourite Ernest, whom she kissed affectionately.

"I am lucky," she said, "in having two nieces, or I should never see anything of young gentlemen like you."

"I think," said Ernest, audaciously, "that old ladies are much pleasanter to talk to than young ones."

"Indeed, Master Ernest! then why did you look so blank when I told you that my young ladies were not visible?"

"Because I regretted," replied that young gentleman, who was not often at a loss, "having lost an opportunity of confirming my views."

"I will put the question again when they are present to take their own part," was the answer.

When their call was over, Ernest and Jeremy separated, Jeremy to return home, and Ernest to go to see his old master, Mr. Halford, with whom he stopped to tea. It was past seven on one of the most beautiful evenings in July when he set out on his homeward path. There were two ways of reaching Dum's Ness, either by the road that ran along the cliff, or by walking on the shingle of the beach. He chose the latter, and had reached the spot where Titheburgh Abbey frowned at its enemy, the advancing sea, when he suddenly became aware of a young lady wearing a shady hat and swinging a walking-stick, in whom he recognised Florence Ceswick.

"How do you do, Ernest?" she said, coolly, but with a slight flush upon her olive skin, which betrayed that she was not quite so cool as she looked; "what are you dreaming about? I have seen you coming for the last two hundred yards, but you never saw me."

"I was dreaming of you, of course, Florence."

"O, indeed!" she answered dryly; "I thought perhaps that Eva had got over her headache—her headaches do go in the most wonderful way—and that you had seen her, and were dreaming of her."

"And why should I dream of her, even if I had seen her?"

"For the reason that men do dream of women—because she is handsome."

"Is she better-looking than you, then, Florence?"

"Better-looking, indeed! I am not good-looking."

"Nonsense, Florence! you are very good-looking."

She stopped, for he had turned and was walking with her, and laid her hand lightly on his arm.

"Do you really think so?" she said, gazing full into his dark eyes. "I am glad you think so."

They were quite alone in the summer twilight; there was not a single soul to be seen on the beach, or on the cliffs above it. Her touch and the earnestness of her manner thrilled him; the beauty and the quiet of the evening, the sweet freshness of the air, the murmur of the falling waves, the fading purples in the sky, all these things thrilled him too. Her face looked very handsome in its own stern way, as she gazed at him so earnestly; and, remember, he was only twenty-one. He bent his dark head towards her very slowly, to give her an opportunity of escaping if she wished; but she made no sign, and in another moment he had kissed her trembling lips.

It was a foolish act, for he was not in love with Florence, and he had scarcely done it before his better sense told him that it was foolish. But it was done, and who can recall a kiss?

He saw the olive face grow pale, and for a moment she raised her arm as though to fling it about his neck, but next second she started back from him.

"Did you mean that," she said wildly, "or are you playing with me?"

Ernest looked alarmed, as well he might; the young lady's aspect at the moment was not reassuring.

"Mean it?" he said, "O yes, I meant it."

"I mean, Ernest," and again she laid her hand upon his arm and looked into his eyes, "did you mean that you loved me, as—for now I am not ashamed to tell you—I love you?"

Ernest felt that this was getting awful. To kiss a young woman was one thing—he had done that before—but such an outburst as this was more than he had bargained for. Gratifying as it was to him to learn that he possessed Florence's affection, he would at that moment have given something to be without it. He hesitated a little.

"How serious you are!" he said at last.

"Yes," she answered, "I am. I have been serious for some time. Probably you know enough of me to be aware that I am not a woman to be played with. I hope that you are serious too; if you are not, it may be the worse for us both"; and she flung his arm from her as though it had stung her.

Ernest turned cold all over, and realised that the position was positively gruesome. What to say or do he did not know; so he stood silent, and, as it happened, silence served his turn better than speech.

"There, Ernest, I have startled you. It is—it is because I love you. When you kissed me just now, everything that is beautiful in the world seemed to pass before my eyes, and for a moment I heard such music as they play in heaven. You don't understand me yet, Ernest—I am fierce, I know—but sometimes I think that my heart is deep as the sea, and I can love with ten times the strength of the shallow women round me; and as I can love, so I can hate."

This was not reassuring intelligence to Ernest.

"You are a strange girl," he said feebly.

"Yes," she answered, with a smile. "I know I am strange; but while I am with you I feel so good, and when you are away all my life is a void, in which bitter thoughts flit about like bats. But there, good-night. I shall see you at the Smythes' dance to-morrow, shall I not? You will dance with me, will you not? And you must not dance with Eva, remember—at least not too much—or I shall get jealous, and that will be bad for us both. And now good-night, my dear, good-night"; and again she put up her face to be kissed.

He kissed it—he had no alternative—and she left him swiftly. He watched her retreating form till it vanished in the shadows, and then he sat down upon a stone, wiped his forehead, and whistled.

Well might he whistle!

CHAPTER VIII

A GARDEN IDYL

Ernest did not sleep well that night: the scene of the evening haunted his dreams, and he awoke with a sense of oppression that follows impartially on the heels of misfortune, folly, and lobster-salad. Nor did the broad light of the summer day disperse his sorrows; indeed, it only served to define them more clearly. Ernest was a very inexperienced youth, but, inexperienced as he was, he could not but recognise that he had let himself in for an awkward business. He was not in the smallest degree in love with Florence Ceswick; indeed, his predominant feeling towards her was one of fear. She was, as he had said, so terribly in earnest. In short, though she was barely a year older than himself, she was a woman possessed of a strength of purpose and a rigidity of will that few of her sex ever attain to at any period of their lives. This he had guessed long ago; but what he had not guessed was that all the tide of her life set so strongly towards himself.

That unlucky kiss, as it were, had shot the bolt of the sluice-gates, and now he was in a fair way to be overwhelmed by the rush of the waters. What course of action he had best take with her now it was beyond his powers to decide. He thought of taking Dorothy into his confidence and asking her advice, but instinctively he shrank from doing so. Then he thought of Jeremy, only, however, to reject the idea. What would Jeremy know of such things? He little guessed that Jeremy was swelling with a secret of his own, of which he was too shy to deliver himself. It seemed to Ernest, the more he considered the matter, that there was only one safe course for him to follow, and that was to run away. It would be ignominious, it is true, but at any rate Florence could not run after him. He had made arrangements to meet a friend, and go for a tour with him in France towards the end of the month of August, or about five weeks from the present date. These arrangements he now determined to modify; he would go for his tour at once.

Partially comforted by these reflections, he dressed himself that evening for the dance at the Smythes', where he was to meet Florence, who, however, he reflected gratefully, could not expect him to kiss her there. The dance was to follow a lawn-tennis party, to which Dorothy, accompanied by Jeremy, had gone already, Ernest having, for reasons best known to himself, declined to go to the lawn-tennis, preferring to follow them to the dance.

When he entered the ballroom at the Smythes', the first quadrille was in progress. Making his way up the room, Ernest soon came upon Florence Ceswick, who was sitting with Dorothy, while in the background loomed Jeremy's gigantic form. Both the girls appeared to be waiting for him, for on his approach Florence, by a movement of her dress, and an almost imperceptible motion of her hand, at once made room for him on the bench beside her, and invited him to sit down. He did so.

"You are late," she said; "why did you not come to the lawn-tennis?"

"I thought that our party was sufficiently represented," he answered lamely, nodding towards Jeremy and his sister. "Why are you not dancing?"

"Because nobody asked me," she said, sharply; "and besides, I was waiting for you."

"Jeremy," said Ernest, "here is Florence saying that you didn't ask her to dance."

"Don't talk humbug, Ernest; you know I don't dance."

"No, indeed," put in Dorothy, "it is easy to see that; I never saw anybody look so miserable as you do."

"Or so big," said Florence, consolingly.

Jeremy shrank back into his corner and tried to look smaller. His sister was right, a dance was untold misery to him. The quadrille had ceased by now and presently the band struck up a waltz which Ernest danced with Florence. They both waltzed well, and Ernest kept going as much as possible perhaps in order to give no opportunity for conversation. At any rate no allusion was made to the events of the previous evening.

"Where are your aunt and sister, Florence?" he asked, as he led her back to her seat.

"They are coming presently," she answered, shortly.

The next dance was a galop, and this he danced with Dorothy, whose slim figure looked, in the white muslin dress she wore, more like that of a child than a grown woman. But child or woman, her general appearance was singularly pleasing and attractive. Ernest thought that he had never seen the quaint, puckered little face, with the two steady blue eyes in it, look so attractive. Not that it was pretty—it was not, but it was a face with a great deal of thought in it; moreover, it was a face through which the goodness of its owner seemed to shine like the light through a lamp.

"You look so nice to-night, Doll," said Ernest.

She flushed with pleasure, and answered simply, "I am glad you think so."

"Yes, I do think so; you are really pretty."

"Nonsense, Ernest! Can't you find some other butt to practise your compliments on? What is the good of wasting them on me? I am going to sit down."

"Really, Doll, I don't know what has come to you lately, you have grown so cross."

She sighed as she answered gently:

"No more do I, Ernest. I did not mean to speak crossly, but you should not make fun of me. Ah, here come Miss Ceswick and Eva."

They had rejoined Florence and Jeremy. The two ladies were seated, while Ernest and Jeremy were standing, the former in front of them, the latter against the wall behind, for they were gathered at the topmost end of the long room. At Dorothy's announcement both the lads bent forward to look down the room, and both the women fixed their eyes on Ernest's face anxiously, expectantly, something as a criminal fixes his eyes on the foreman of a jury who is about to pronounce words that will one way or another affect all his life.

"I don't see them," said Ernest carelessly. "O, here they come. By George!"

Whatever these two women were looking for in his face, they had found it, and, to all appearance, it pleased them very little. Dorothy turned pale, and leaned back with a faint smile of resignation; she had expected it, that smile seemed to say; but the blood flamed like a danger-flag into Florence's haughty features—there was no resignation there. And meanwhile Ernest was staring down the room, quite unaware of the little comedy that was going on around him; so was Jeremy, and so was every other man who was there to stare.

And this was what they were staring at. Up the centre of the long room walked, or rather swept, Miss Ceswick, for even at her advanced age she moved like a queen, and at any other time her appearance would in itself have been sufficient to excite remark. But people were not looking at Miss Ceswick, but rather at the radiant creature who accompanied her, and whose stature dwarfed her, tall as she was. Eva Ceswick—for it was she—was dressed in white soie de chiné, in the bosom of which was fixed a single rose. The dress was cut low, and her splendid neck and arms were entirely without ornament. In the masses of dark hair, which was coiled like a coronet round her head, their glistened a diamond star. Simple as was her costume, there was a grandeur about it that struck the whole room; but in truth it sprang from the almost perfect beauty of the woman who wore it. Any dress would have looked beautiful upon that noble form, that towered so high, and yet seemed to float up the room with the grace of a swan and sway like a willow in the wind. But her loveliness did not end there. From those dark eyes there shone a light that few men could look upon and forget, and yet there was nothing bold about it. It was like the light of a star.

On she came, her lips half-parted, seemingly unconscious of the admiration she was attracting, eclipsing all other women as she passed, and making their beauty, that before had seemed bright enough, look poor and mean beside her own. It took but a few seconds, ten perhaps, for her to walk up the room, and yet to Ernest it seemed long before her eyes met his own, and something passed from them into his heart that remained there all his life.

His gaze made her blush a little, it was so unmistakable. She guessed who he was, and passed him with a little inclination of her head.

"Well, here we are at last," she said, addressing her sister in her pure musical voice. "What do you think? something went wrong with the wheel of the fly, and we had to stop to get it mended!"

"Indeed!" answered Florence; "I thought that perhaps you came late in order to make a more effective entry."

"Florence," said her aunt, reprovingly, "you should not say such things."

Florence did not answer, but put her lace handkerchief to her lip. She had bitten it till the blood ran.

By this time Ernest had recovered himself. He saw several young fellows bearing down upon them, and knew what they were seeking.

"Miss Ceswick," he said, "will you introduce me?"

No sooner said than done, and at that moment the band began to play a waltz. In five seconds more Eva was floating down the room upon his arm, and the advancing young gentlemen were left lamenting, and, if the truth must be told, anathematising "that puppy Kershaw" beneath their breath.

There was a spirit in her feet; she danced divinely. Lightly leaning on his arm, they swept round the room, the incarnation of youthful strength and beauty, and, as they passed, even sour old Lady Astleigh lowered her ancient nose an inch or more, and deigned to ask who was that handsome young man dancing with the "tall girl." Presently they halted, and Ernest observed a more than usually intrepid man coming towards them, with the design, no doubt, of obtaining an introduction and the promise of dances. But again he was equal to the occasion. "Have you a card?" he asked.

"O yes."

"Will you allow me to put my name down for another dance? I think that our steps suit."

"Yes, we get on nicely. Here it is."

Ernest took it. The young man had arrived now, and was hovering round and glowering. Ernest nodded to him cheerfully, and "put his name" very much down—indeed, for no less than three dances and an extra.

Eva opened her eyes a little, but she said nothing; their steps suited so very well.

"May I ask you, Kershaw—" began his would-be rival.

"O, certainly," answered Ernest benignly, "I will be with you presently"; and they floated off again on the rising wave of the music.

When the dance ended, they stopped just by the spot where Miss Ceswick was sitting. Florence and Dorothy were both dancing, but Jeremy, who did not dance, was standing by her, looking as sulky as a bear with a sore head. Eva stretched out her hand to him with a smile.

"I hope that you are going to dance with me, Mr. Jones," she said.

"I don't dance," he answered, curtly, and walked away.

She glanced after him wonderingly; his manner was decidedly rude.

"I do not think that Mr. Jones is in a good temper," she said to Ernest, with a smile.

"O, he is a queer fellow; going out always makes him cross," he answered carelessly.

Then the gathering phalanx of would-be partners marched in and took possession and Ernest had to retire.

The ball was drawing to its close. The dancing-room, notwithstanding its open windows, was intensely hot, and many of the dancers were strolling in the gardens, among them Ernest and Eva. They had just danced their third waltz, in which they had discovered that their steps suited better than ever.

Florence, Dorothy, and her brother were also walking, all three together. It is curious how people in misfortune cling to one another. They walked in silence; they had nothing to say. Presently they caught sight of two tall figures standing by a bush, on which was fixed a dying Chinese lantern. It is sometimes unfortunate to be tall, it betrays one's identity; there was no mistaking the two figures, though it was so dark. Instinctively the three halted. And just then the expiring Chinese lantern did an unkind thing; it caught fire, and threw a lurid light upon a very pretty little scene. Ernest was bending forward towards Eva with all his soul in his expressive eyes, and begging for something. She was blushing sweetly, and looking down at the rose in her bosom; one hand, too, was raised, as though to unfasten it. The light for a moment was so strong that Dorothy afterwards remembered noticing how long Eva's curling black eyelashes looked against her cheek. In another second it had flared out, and the darkness hid the sequel; but it may here be stated that when Eva re-appeared in the ballroom she had lost her rose.

Charming and idyllic as undoubtedly was this tableau tres vivant of youth and beauty, obeying the primary laws of nature, and making love in a Garden of Eden illumined with Chinese lanterns, it did not seem to please any of the three spectators.

Jeremy actually forgot the presence of ladies, and went so far as to swear aloud. Nor did they reprove him; probably it gave their feelings some vicarious relief.

"I think we had better be going home; it is late," said Dorothy, after a pause. "Jeremy, will you go and order the carriage?"

Jeremy went.

Florence said nothing, but she took her fan in both her hands and bent it slowly, so that the ivory sticks snapped one by one with a succession of sharp reports. Then she threw it down, and set her heel upon it, and ground it into the path. There was something inexpressibly cruel about the way in which she crushed the pretty toy. The action seemed to be the appropriate and unconscious outcome of some mental process, and it is an odd proof of the excitement under which they were both labouring, that at the time the gentle-minded Dorothy saw in it nothing strange. At that moment the two girls were nearer each other than they had ever been before, or would ever be again; the common stroke of misfortune for a moment welded their opposite natures into one. At that moment, too, they knew that they both loved the same man; before, they had guessed it, and had not liked each other the better for it, but now that was forgotten.

"I think, Florence," said Dorothy, with a little tremor in her voice, "that we are 'out of the running,' as Jeremy says. Your sister is too beautiful for any woman to stand against her. He has fallen in love with her."

"Yes," said Florence, with a bitter laugh and a flash of her brown eyes; "his highness has thrown a handkerchief to a new favourite, and she has lost no time in picking it up. We always used to call her 'the sultana'"; and she laughed again.

"Perhaps," suggested Dorothy, "she only means to flirt with him a little; I hoped that Jeremy—"

"Jeremy! what chance has Jeremy against him? Ernest would make more way with a woman in two hours than Jeremy would in two years. We all love to be taken by storm, my dear. Do not deceive yourself. Flirt with him! she will love him wildly in a week. Who could help loving him?" she added, with a thrill of her rich voice.

Dorothy said nothing: she knew that it was true, and they walked a few steps in silence.

"Dorothy, do you know what generally happens to favourites and sultanas?"

"No."

"They come to a bad end; the other ladies of the harem murder them, you know."

"What do you mean?"

"Don't be frightened; I don't mean that we should murder my dear sister. What I do mean is, that I think we might manage to depose her. Will you help me if I find a plan?"

Dorothy's better self had had time to assert itself by now; the influence of the blow was over, and their natures were wide apart again.

"No, certainly not," she answered. "Ernest has a right to choose for himself, and if your sister gets the better of us, it is the fortune of war, that is all—though certainly the fight is not quite fair," she added, as she thought of Eva's radiant loveliness.

Florence glanced at her contemptuously.

"You have no spirit," she said.

"What do you mean to do?"

"Mean to do!" she answered, swinging round and facing her; "I mean to have my revenge."

"O, Florence, it is wicked to talk so! Whom are you going to be revenged on—Ernest? It is not his fault if—if you are fond of him."

"Yes, it is his fault; but whether it is his fault or not, I suffer. Remember what I say, for it will come true; he shall suffer. Why should I bear it all alone? But he shall not suffer so much as she. I told her that I was fond of him, and she promised to leave him alone—do you hear that?—and yet she is taking him away from me to gratify her vanity—she, who can have anybody she likes."

"Hush, Florence! Don't give way to your temper so, or you will be overheard. Besides, I daresay that we are making a great deal of nothing; after all, she only gave him a rose."

"I don't care if we are overheard, and it is nothing. I guessed that it would be so, I knew it would be so, and I know what is coming now. Mark my words, within a month Ernest and my sweet sister will be sitting about on the cliff with their arms around each other's necks. I have only to shut my eyes, and I can see it. O, here is Jeremy! Is the carriage there, Jeremy? That's right. Come on, Dorothy, let us go and say good-night and be off. You will drop me at the cottage, won't you?"

Half an hour later the fly that had brought Miss Ceswick and Eva came round, and with it Ernest's dog-cart. But as Miss Ceswick was rather anxious about the injured wheel, Ernest, as in duty bound, offered to see them safe home, and ordering the cart to follow, got into the fly without waiting for an answer.

Of course Miss Ceswick went to sleep, but it is not probable that either Ernest or Eva followed her example. Perhaps they were too tired to talk; perhaps they were beginning to find out what a delightful companionship is to be found in silence; perhaps his gentle pressure of the little white-gloved hand, that lay unresisting in his own, was more eloquent than any speech.

Don't be shocked, my reader; you or I would have done the same, and thought ourselves very lucky fellows!

At any rate, that drive was over all too soon.

Florence opened the door for them; she had told the servant to go to bed.

When Eva reached the door of her room she turned round to say good-night to her sister; but the latter, instead of contenting herself with a nod, as was her custom, came and kissed her on the face.

"I congratulate you on your dress and on your conquest," and again she kissed her and was gone.

"It is not like Florence to be so kind," reflected her younger sister. "I can't remember when she kissed me last."

Eva did not know that as there are some kisses that declare peace, and set the seal on love, there are others that announce war, and proclaim the hour of vengeance or treachery. Judas kissed his Master when he betrayed Him.

CHAPTER IX

EVA FINDS SOMETHING

When Ernest woke on the morning after the ball it was ten o'clock, and he had a severe headache. This—the headache—was his first impression, but presently his eye fell upon a withering red rose that lay upon the dressing table, and he smiled. Then followed reflections, those confounded reflections that always dog the heels of everything pleasant in life, and he ceased to smile.

In the end he yawned and got up. When he reached the sitting-room, which looked cool and pleasant in contrast to the hot July sunshine that beat upon the little patch of bare turf in front of the house, and the glittering sea beyond, he found that the others had done their breakfast. Jeremy had gone out, but his sister was there, looking a little pale, no doubt from the late hours of the previous night.

"Good-morning, Doll!"

"Good-morning, Ernest," she answered, rather coldly. "I have been keeping your tea as warm as I can, but I'm afraid it is getting cold."

"You are a good Samaritan, Doll. I've got such a head! perhaps the tea will make it better."

She smiled as she gave it to him; had she spoke what was in her mind, she would have answered that she had "such a heart."

He drank the tea, and apparently felt better for it, for presently he asked her, in comparatively cheerful tones, how she liked the dance.

"O, very well, thank you, Ernest: how did you like it?"

"O, awfully! I say, Doll!"

"Yes, Ernest."

"Isn't she lovely?"

"Who, Ernest?"

"Who! why, Eva Ceswick, of course."

"Yes, Ernest, she is very lovely."

There was something about her tone that was not encouraging; at any rate he did not pursue his subject.

"Where is Jeremy?" he asked next.

"He has gone out."

Presently, Ernest, having finished his second cup of tea, went out too, and came across Jeremy mooning about the yard.

"Hulloa, my hearty! and how are you after your dissipations?"

"All right, thank you," answered Jeremy, sulkily.

Ernest glanced up quickly. The voice was the voice of Jeremy, but the tones were not his tones.

"What is up, old chap?" he said, slipping his arm through his friend's.

"Nothing."

"O yes, there is, though. What is it? Out with it! I am a splendid father confessor."

Jeremy freed his arm, and remained sulkier than ever. Ernest looked hurt, and the look softened the other.

"Well, of course, if you won't tell me, there is nothing more to be said"; and he prepared to move off.

"As though you didn't know!"

"Upon my honour I don't."

"Then if you'll come in here, I will tell you"; and Jeremy opened the door of the little outhouse, where he stuffed his birds and kept his gun and collection of eggs and butterflies, and motioned Ernest majestically in.

He entered and seated himself upon the stuffing-table, gazing abstractedly at a bittern that Jeremy had shot about the time that this story opened, and which was now very moth-eaten, and waved one melancholy leg in the air in a way meant to be imposing, but only succeeded in being grotesque.

"Well, what is it?" he interrogated of the glassy eye of the decaying bittern.

Jeremy turned his broad back upon Ernest—he felt that he could speak better on such a subject with his back turned—and, addressing empty space before him, said:

"I think it was precious unkind of you."

"What was precious unkind?"

"To go and cut me out of the only girl—"

"I ever loved?" suggested Ernest, for he was hesitating.

"I ever loved!" chimed in Jeremy; for the phrase expressed his sentiments exactly.

"Well, old chap, if you would come to the point a little more, and tell me who the deuce you are talking about—"

"Why, who should I be talking about? there is only one girl—"

"You ever loved?"

"I ever loved!"

"Well, in the name of the Holy Roman Empire, who is she?"

"Why, Eva Ceswick."

Ernest whistled.

"I say, old chap," he said, after a pause, "why didn't you tell me? I didn't even know that you knew her. Are you engaged to her, then?"

"Engaged! no."

"Well, then, have you an understanding with her?"

"No, of course not."

"Look here, old fellow, if you would just slew round a bit and tell me how the matter stands, we might get on a little."

"It doesn't stand at all, but—I worship the ground she treads on; there!"

"Ah!" said Ernest, "that's awkward, for so do I—at least I think I do."

Jeremy groaned, and Ernest groaned too, by way of company.

"Look here, old chap," said the latter, "what is to be done? You should have told me, but you didn't, you see. If you had, I would have kept clear. Fact is, she bowled me over altogether, bowled me clean."

"So she did me."

"I'll tell you what, Jeremy, I'll go away and leave you to make the running. Not that I see that there is much good in either of us making the running, for we have nothing to marry on, and no more has she."

"And we are only twenty-one. We can't marry at twenty-one," put in Jeremy, "or we should have a large family by the time we're thirty. Fellows who marry at twenty-one always do."

"She's twenty-one; she told me so."

"She told me too," said Jeremy, determined to show that Ernest was not the only person favoured with this exciting fact.

"Well, shall I clear? we can't jaw about it for ever."

"No," said Jeremy, slowly, and in a way that showed that it cost him an effort to say it, "that would not be fair; besides, I expect that the mischief is done; everybody gets fond of you, old fellow, men or women. No, you shan't go, and we won't get to loggerheads over it either. I'll tell you what we will do—we will toss up."

This struck Ernest as a brilliant suggestion.

"Right you are," he said, at once producing a shilling; "singles or threes?"

"Singles, of course; it's sooner over."

Ernest poised the coin on his thumb.

"You call. But, I say, what are we tossing for? We can't draw lots for the girl like the fellows in Homer. We haven't captured her yet."

This was obviously a point that required consideration. Jeremy scratched his head.

"How will this do?" he said. "The winner to have a month to make the running in, the loser not to interfere. If she won't have anything to say to him after a month, then the loser to have his fling. If she will, loser to keep away."

"That will do. Stand clear; up you go."

The shilling spun in the air.

"Tails!" howled Jeremy.

It lit on the beak of the astonished bittern and bounded off on to the floor, finally rolling under a box full of choice specimens of petrified bones of antediluvian animals that had been washed out of the cliffs. The box was lugged out of the way with difficulty, and the shilling disclosed.

"Heads it is!" said Ernest exultingly.

"I expected as much; just my luck. Well, shake hands, Ernest. We won't quarrel about the girl, please God."

They shook hands heartily enough and parted; but from that time for many a long day there was an invisible something between them that had not been there before. Strong indeed must be the friendship of which the bonds do not slacken when the shadow of a woman's love falls upon it.

That afternoon Dorothy said that she wanted to go into Kesterwick to make some purchases, and Ernest offered to accompany her. They walked in silence as far as Titheburgh Abbey; indeed, they both suffered from a curious constraint that seemed effectually to check their usual brother-and-sister-like relations. Ernest was just beginning to feel the silence awkward when Dorothy stopped.

"What was that?" she said. "I thought I heard somebody cry out."

They listened, and presently both heard a woman's voice calling for help. The sound seemed to come from the cliff on their left. They stepped to the edge and looked over. As may be remembered, some twenty feet from the top of the cliff, and fifty or more from the bottom, there was at this spot a sandy ledge, on which were deposited many of the remains washed out of the churchyard by the sea. Now, this particular spot was almost inaccessible without ladders, because, although it was easy enough to get down to its level, the cliff bulged out on either side of it, and gave for the space of some yards little or no hold for the hands or feet of the climber.

The first thing that caught Ernest's eyes when he looked over was a lady's foot and ankle, which appeared to be resting on a tiny piece of rock that projected from the surface of the cliff; the next was the imploring face of Eva Ceswick, who was sprawling in a most undignified position on the bulge of sandstone, with nothing more between her and eternity than the very unsatisfactory and insufficient knob of rock. It was evident that she could move neither one way or the other without being precipitated to the bottom of the cliff, to which she was apparently clinging by suction like a fly.

"Great God!" exclaimed Ernest. "Hold on, I will come to you."

"I can't hold much longer."

It was one thing to say that he would come, and another to do it. The sand gave scarcely any foothold; how was he to get enough purchase to pull Eva round the bulge? He looked at Dorothy in despair. Her quick mind had taken in the situation at a glance.

"You must get down there above her, Ernest, and lie flat, and stretch out your hand to her."

"But there is nothing to hold to. When she puts her weight on to my hand we shall both go together."

"No, I will hold your legs. Be quick, she is getting exhausted."

It took Ernest but two seconds to reach the spot that Dorothy had pointed to, and to lay himself flat, or rather slanting, for his heels were a great deal higher than his head. Fortunately, he discovered a hard knob of sandstone, against which he could rest his left hand. Meanwhile, Dorothy, seating herself as securely as she could above, seized him by the ankles. Then Ernest stretched his hand downwards, and, gripping Eva by the wrist, began to put out his strength. Had the three found any time to indulge their sense of humour, they might have found the appearance they presented intensely ludicrous; but they did not, for the very good reason that for thirty seconds or so their lives were not worth a farthing's purchase. Ernest strained and strained, but Eva was a large woman, although she danced so lightly, and the bulge over which he had to pull her was almost perpendicular. Presently he felt that Dorothy was beginning to slip above him.

"She must make an effort, or we shall all go," she said in a quiet voice.

"Drive your knees into the sand and throw yourself forward, it is your only chance!" gasped Ernest to the exhausted girl beneath him.

She realised the meaning of his words, and gave a desperate struggle.

"Pull, Doll; for God's sake, pull! she's coming."

Then followed a second of despairing effort, and she was beside him on the spot where he lay; another struggle and the three sank exhausted on the top of the cliff, rescued from a most imminent death.

"By Jove!" ejaculated Ernest, "that was a near thing!"

Dorothy nodded; she was too exhausted to speak. Eva smiled and fainted.

He turned to her with a little cry and began to chafe her cold hands.

"Oh, she's dead, Doll!" he said.

"No, she has fainted. Give me your hat."

Before he could do so she had seized it, and was running as quickly as her exhaustion would allow towards a spring that bubbled up a hundred yards away, and which once had been the water supply of the old abbey.

Ernest went on rubbing for a minute or more, but without producing the slightest effect. He was in despair. The beautiful face beneath him looked so wan and death-like; all the red had left her lips. In his distress, and scarcely knowing what he did, he bent over them and kissed them, once, twice, thrice. That mode of restoration is not recommended in the medicine chest "guide," but in this instance it was not without its effect. Presently a faint and tremulous glow diffused itself over the pale cheek; in another moment it deepened to a most unmistakable blush. (Was it a half-consciousness of Ernest's new method of treatment, or merely the returning blood that produced the blush? Let us not inquire.) Next Eva sighed, opened her eyes, and sat up.

"Oh, you are not dead!"

"No, I don't think so, but I can't quite remember. What was it? Ah, I know"; and she shut her eyes, as though to keep out some horrid sight. Presently she opened them again. "You have saved my life," she said. "If it had not been for you, I should have now been lying crushed at the foot of that dreadful cliff. I am so grateful."

At that moment Dorothy came back with a little water in Ernest's black hat, for in her hurry she had spilled most of it.

"Here, drink some of this," she said.

Eva tried to do so; but a billycock hat is not a very convenient drinking vessel till you get used to it, and she upset more than she swallowed. But what she drank did her good. She put down the hat, and they all three laughed a little; it was so funny drinking out of an old hat.

"Were you long down there before we came?" asked Dorothy.

"No, not long; only about half a minute on that dreadful bulge."

"What on earth did you go there for?" said Ernest, putting his dripping hat on to his head, for the sun was hot.

"I wanted to see the bones. I am very active, and thought that I could get up quite safely; but sand is so slippery. Oh, I forgot; look here"; and she pointed to a thin cord that was tied to her wrist.

"What is that?"

"Why, it is tied to such an odd lead box that I found in the sand. Mr. Jones said the other day that he thought it was a bit of an old coffin, but it is not, it is a lead box with a rusty iron handle. I could not move it much; but I had this bit of cord with me—I thought I might want it getting down, you know—so I tied one end of it to the handle."

"Let us pull it up," said Ernest, unfastening the cord from Eva's wrist, and beginning to tug.

But the case was too heavy for him to lift alone; indeed, it proved as much as they could all three manage to drag it to the top. However, up it came at last. Ernest examined it carefully, and came to the conclusion that it was very ancient. The massive iron handle at the top of the oblong case was almost eaten through with rust, and the lead itself was much corroded, although, from fragments that still clung to it, it was evident that it had once been protected by an outer case of oak. Evidently the case had been washed out of the churchyard where it had lain for centuries.

"This is quite exciting," said Eva, who was now sufficiently interested to forget all about her escape. "What can be in it?—treasure or papers, I should think."

"I don't know," answered Ernest; "I should hardly think that they would bury such things in a churchyard. Perhaps it is a small baby."

"Ernest," broke in Dorothy, in an agitated way, "I don't like that thing. I can't tell you why, but I am sure it is unlucky. I wish that you would throw it back to where it came from, or into the sea. It is a horrid thing, and we have nearly lost our lives over it already."

"Nonsense, Doll! whoever thought that you were so superstitious? Why, perhaps it is full of money or jewels. Let's take it home and open it."

"I am not superstitious, and you can take it home if you like. I will not touch it; I tell you it is a horrid thing."

"All right Doll, then you shan't have a share of the spoil. Miss Ceswick and I will divide it. Will you help me to carry it to the house, Miss Ceswick?—that is, unless you are afraid of it, like Doll."

"Oh no," she answered, "I am not afraid; I am dying of curiosity to see what is inside."

CHAPTER X

"You are sure you are not too tired?" said Ernest, after a moment's consideration.

"No, indeed, I have quite recovered," she answered with a blush.

Ernest blushed too, from sympathy probably, and went to pick up a bough that lay beneath a stunted oak-tree which grew in the ruins of the abbey, on the spot where once the altar had stood. This he ran through the iron handle, and, directing Eva to take hold of one end, he took the other himself, Dorothy marching solemnly in front.

As it happened, Jeremy and Mr. Cardus were strolling along together smoking, when suddenly they caught sight of the cavalcade advancing, and hurried to meet it.

"What is all this?" asked Mr. Cardus of Dorothy, who was now nearly fifty yards ahead of the other two.

"Well, Reginald, it is a long story. First we found Eva Ceswick slipping down the cliff, and dragged her up just in time."

"My luck again!" thought Jeremy, groaning in spirit. "I might have sat on the edge of that cliff for ten years, and never got a chance of dragging her up."

"Then we pulled up that horrid box, which she found down in the sand, and tied a cord to."

"Yes," exclaimed Ernest, who was now arriving, "and, would you believe it, Dorothy wanted us to throw it back again!"

"I know I did; I said that it was unlucky, and it is unlucky."

"Nonsense, Dorothy! it is very interesting. I expect that it will be found to contain deeds buried in the churchyard for safety and never dug up again," broke in Mr. Cardus, much interested. "Let me catch hold of that stick, Miss Ceswick, and I daresay that Jeremy will go on and get a hammer and a cold chisel, and we will soon solve the mystery."

"Oh, very well, Reginald; you will see," said Dorothy.

Mr. Cardus glanced at her. It was curious her taking such an idea. Then they walked to the house. On reaching the sitting-room they found Jeremy already there with his hammer and chisel. He was an admirable amateur blacksmith; indeed, there were few manual trades of which he did not know a little, and, placing the case on the table, he set about the task of opening it in a most workmanlike manner.

The lead, though it was in places eaten quite away, was still thick and sound near the edges, and it took him a good quarter of an hour's hard chopping to remove what appeared to be the front of the case. Excitement was at its height as it fell forward with a bang on the table; but it was then found that what had been removed was merely a portion of an outer case, there being beneath it an inner chest, also of lead.

"Well," said Jeremy, "they fastened it up pretty well"; and then he set to work again.

This inner skin of lead was thinner and easier to cut than the first had been, and he got through the job more quickly though not nearly quickly enough for the impatience of the bystanders. At last the front fell out, and disclosed a small cabinet made of solid pieces of black oak and having a hinged door, which was fastened by a tiny latch and hasp of the common pattern that is probably as old as doors are. From this cabinet there came a strong odour of spices.

The excitement was now intense, and seemed to be shared by everybody in the house. Grice had come in through the swing-door and stationed herself in the background, Sampson and the groom were peering through the window, and even old Atterleigh, attracted by the sound of the hammering, had strolled aimlessly in.

"What can it be?" said Eva, with a gasp.

Slowly Jeremy extracted the cabinet from its leaden coverings and set it on the table.

"Shall I open it?" he said. Suiting the action to the word, he lifted the latch, and placing the chisel between the edge of the little door and its frame, prised the cabinet open.

The smell of spices became even more pronounced than ever, and for a moment the cloud of dust that came from them, as their fragments rolled out of the cabinet on to the table, prevented the spectators, who, all but Dorothy, were crowding up to the case, from seeing what it contained. Presently, however, a large whitish bundle became visible. Jeremy put in his hand, pulled it out, and laid it on the top of the box. It was heavy. But when he had done this he did not seem inclined to go any further in the matter. The bundle had, he considered, an uncanny look.

At that moment an interruption took place, for Florence Ceswick entered through the open door. She had come up to see Dorothy, and was astonished to find such a gathering.

"Why, what is it all about?" she asked.

Somebody told her in as few words as possible, for everybody's attention was concentrated on the bundle, which nobody seemed inclined to touch.

"Well, why don't you open it?" asked Florence.

"I think that they are all afraid," said Mr. Cardus, with a laugh.

He was watching the various expressions on the faces with an amused air.

"Well, I am not afraid, at any rate," said Florence. "Now, ladies and gentlemen, the Gorgon's head is about to be unveiled: look the other way, or you will all be turned to stone."

"This is getting delightfully ghastly," said Eva to Ernest.

"I know that it will be something horrid," added Dorothy.

Meanwhile Florence had drawn out a heavy pin of ancient make, with which the wrapping of the bundle was fastened, and began to unwind a long piece of discoloured linen. At the first turn another shower of spices fell out. As soon as these had been swept aside, Florence proceeded slowly with her task, and as she removed fold after fold of the linen, the bundle began to take shape and form, and the shape it took was that of a human head!

Eva saw it and drew closer to Ernest; Jeremy saw it, and felt inclined to bolt; Dorothy saw it, and knew that her presentiments as to the disagreeable nature of the contents of that unlucky case were coming true; Mr. Cardus saw it, and was more interested than ever. Only Florence and "Hard-riding Atterleigh" saw nothing. Another turn or two of the long winding-sheet, and it slipped suddenly away from whatever it enclosed.

There was a moment's dead silence as the company regarded the object thus left open to their gaze. Then one of the women gave a low cry of fear, and, actuated by some common impulse, they all turned and broke from the room in terror, and calling, "It is alive!" No, not all. Florence turned pale, but she stood there by the object, the winding-sheet in her hands; and old Atterleigh also remained staring at it, either paralysed or fascinated.

It, too, seemed to stare at him from its point of vantage on the oak chest, in which it had rested for so many centuries.

And this was what he saw there upon the box. Let the reader imagine the face and head of a lovely woman of some thirty years of age, the latter covered with rippling brown locks of great length, above which was set a roughly fashioned coronet studded with uncut gems. Let him imagine this face, all but the lips, which were coloured red, pale with the bloodless pallor of death, and the flesh so firm and fresh-looking that it might have been that of a corpse not a day old; so firm, indeed, that the head and all its pendant weight of beautiful hair could stand on the unshrunken base of the neck which, in some far-past age, cold steel had made so smooth. Then let him imagine the crowning horror of this weird sight. The eyes of a corpse are shut, but the eyes in this head were wide open, and the long black lashes, as perfect now as on the day of death, hung over what, when the light struck them, appeared to be two balls of trembling fire, that glittered and rolled and fixed themselves upon the face of the observer like living human eyes. It was these awful eyes that carried such terror to the hearts of the onlookers when they cast their first glance around, and made them not unnaturally cry out that the head was alive.

It was not until he had made a very careful examination of these fiery orbs that Mr. Cardus was afterwards able to discover what they were; and as the reader may as well understand at once that this head had nothing about it different from any other skilfully preserved head, he shall be taken into confidence without delay. They were balls of crystal fitted, probably by the aid of slender springs, into the eye-sockets with such infernal art that they shook and trembled to the slightest sound, and even on occasion rolled about. The head itself, he also discovered, had not been embalmed in the ordinary way, by extracting the brain, and filling the cavity with spices of bitumen, but had been preserved by means of the injection of silica, or some kindred substance, into the brain, veins, and arteries, which, after permeating all the flesh, had solidified and made it like marble. Some brilliant pigment had been used to give the lips their natural colour, and the hair had been preserved by means of the spices. But perhaps the most dreadful thing about this relic of forgotten ages was the mocking smile that the artist who "set it up" had managed to preserve upon the face—a smile that just drew the lips up enough to show the white teeth beneath, and gave the idea that its wearer had died in the full enjoyment of some malicious jest or triumph. It was a terrible thing to look on, that long-dead, beautiful face, with its abundant hair, its crowning coronet, its moving crystal eyes, and its smile. Yet there was something awfully fascinating about it; those who had seen it once would always long to see it again.

Mr. Cardus had fled with the rest, but as soon as he got outside the swing-door his common sense reasserted itself, and he stopped.

"Come, come," he called to the others, "don't be so silly; you are not going to run away from a dead woman's head, are you?"

"You ran too," said Dorothy, pulling up and gasping.

"Yes, I know I did; those eyes startled me; but, of course, they are glass. I am going back; it is a great curiosity."

"It is an accursed thing," muttered Dorothy.

Mr. Cardus turned and re-entered the room, and the others, comforting themselves with the reflection that it was broad daylight, and drawn by their devouring curiosity, followed him. That is, they all followed him except Grice, who was ill for two days afterwards. As for Sampson and the groom, who had seen the sight through the window, they ran for a mile or more along the cliff before they stopped.

When they got back into the room, they found old Atterleigh still standing and staring at the crystal eyes, that seemed to be returning his gaze with compound interest, while Florence was there with the long linen wrapper in her hand, gazing down at the beautiful hair that flowed from the head on to the oak box, from the box to the table, and from the table nearly to the ground. It was, oddly enough, of the same colour and texture as her own. She had taken off her hat when she began to undo the wrappings, and they all noticed the fact. Nor did the resemblance stop there. The sharp fine features of the mummied head were very like Florence's; so were the beautiful teeth and the fixed hard smile. The dead face was more lovely, indeed, but otherwise the woman of the Saxon era—for, to judge from the rude tiara on her brow, it is probable that she was Saxon—and the living girl of the nineteenth century might have been sisters, or mother and daughter. The resemblance startled them all as they entered the room, but they said nothing.

They drew near, and gazed again without a word. Dorothy was the first to break the silence.

"I think she must have been a witch," she said. "I hope that you will have it thrown away, Reginald, for she will bring us bad luck. The place where she has been buried has been unlucky; it was a great abbey once, now it is a deserted ruin. When we tried to get the case up, we were all very nearly killed. She will bring us bad luck. I am sure of it. Throw it away, Reginald, throw her into the sea. Look, she is just like Florence there."

Florence had smiled at Dorothy's words, and the resemblance became more striking than ever. Eva shuddered as she noticed it.

"Nonsense, Dorothy!" said Mr. Cardus, who was a bit of an antiquarian, and had now forgotten his start in his collector's zeal, "it is a splendid find. But I forgot," he added, in a tone of disappointment, "it does not belong to me, it belongs to Miss Ceswick."

"O, I am sure you are welcome to it, so far as I am concerned," said Eva, hastily. "I would not have it near me on any account."

"O, very well. I am much obliged to you. I shall value the relic very much."

Florence had meanwhile moved round the table, and was gazing earnestly into the crystal eyes.

"What are you doing, Florence?" asked Ernest sharply, for the scene was uncanny, and jarred upon him.

"I?" she answered with a little laugh; "I am seeking an inspiration. That face looks wise, it may teach me something. Besides, it is so like my own, I think she must be some far-distant ancestress."

"So she had noticed it too," thought Ernest.

"Put her back in the box, Jeremy," said Mr. Cardus. "I must have an airtight case made."

"I can do that," said Jeremy, "by lining the old one with lead, and putting a glass front to it."

Jeremy set about putting the head away, touching it very gingerly. When he got it back into the oak case, he dusted it, and placed it upon a bracket that jutted from the oak-panelling at the end of the room.

"Well," said Florence, "now that you have put your guardian angel on her pedestal, I think that we must be going home. Will any of you walk a little way with us?"

Dorothy said that they would all come—that is, all except Mr. Cardus, who had gone back to his office. Accordingly they started, and as they did so, Florence intimated to Ernest that she wished to speak to him. He was alarmed and disappointed, for he was afraid of Florence, and wished to walk with Eva, and presumably his face betrayed what was in his mind to her.

"Do not be frightened," she said, with a slight smile; "I am not going to say anything disagreeable."

Of course he replied that he knew that she never could say anything disagreeable at any time; at which she smiled again the same faint smile, and they dropped behind.

"Ernest," she said presently, "I want to speak to you. You remember what happened between us two evenings ago on this very beach"; for they were walking home by the beach.

"Yes, Florence, I remember," answered Ernest.

"Well, Ernest, the words I have to say are hard for a woman's lips, but I must say them. I made a mistake, Ernest, in telling you that I loved you as I did, and in talking all the wild nonsense that I talked. I don't know what made me do it—some foolish impulse, no doubt. Women are very curious, you know, Ernest, and I think that I am more curious than most. I suppose I thought that I loved you, Ernest—I know I thought it when you kissed me; but last night, when I saw you at the Smythes' dance, I knew that it was all a mistake, and that I cared for you—no more than you cared for me, Ernest. Do you understand me?"

He did not understand her in the least, but he nodded his head, feeling vaguely that things were turning out very well for him.

She looked at him and went on:

"So here, in the same place where I said them, I renounce them. We will forget all that foolish scene, Ernest. I was in error when I told you that my heart was as deep as the sea; I find that it is shallow as a brook. But will you answer me one question, Ernest, before we close this conversation?"

"Yes, Florence, if I can."

"Well, when you—you kissed me the other night, you did not really mean it, did you? I mean you only did so for a freak, or from the impulse of the moment, not because you loved me? Don't be afraid to tell me, because if it was so, I shall not be angry; you see you have so much to forgive me for. I am breaking faith, am I not?" And she looked at him straight in the face with her piercing eyes.

Ernest's glance fell under that searching gaze, and the lie that men are apt to think it no shame to use where women are concerned rose to his lips. But he could not get it out—he could not bring himself to say that he did not love her—so he compromised matters.

"I think that perhaps you were more in earnest than I was, Florence."

She laughed, a cold little laugh, that somehow made his flesh creep.

"Thank you for being candid; it makes matters so much easier, does it not? But, do you know, I suspected as much, when I was standing there by that head to-day, just at the time when you took Eva's hand?"

Ernest started visibly. "Why, your back was turned!" he said.

"Yes, but I saw what you did reflected in the crystal eyes. Well, do you know, as I stood there, it seemed to me as though I could consider the whole matter as dispassionately and with as clear a brain as though I had been that dead woman. All of a sudden I grew wise. But there are the others waiting for us."

"We shall part friends, I hope, Florence?" said Ernest, anxiously.

"O yes, Ernest, a woman always follows the career of her old admirer with the deepest interest, and for about five seconds you were my admirer—when you kissed me, you know. I shall watch all your life, and my thoughts shall follow your footsteps like a shadow. Good-night, Ernest, good-night;" and again she smiled the mocking smile which was so like that on the features of the dead woman, and fixed her piercing eyes upon his face. He bade her good-night, and made his way homewards with the others, feeling an undefinable dread heavy on his heart.

CHAPTER XI

DEEP WATERS

In due course Jeremy duly fitted up "the witch," as the mysterious head came to be called at Dum's Ness, in her air-tight cabinet, which he lengthened till it looked like a clock-case, in order to allow the beautiful hair to hang down at full length, retaining, however, the original door and ancient latch and hasp. His next step was to fit the plate-glass front, and exhaust the air as well as was feasible from the interior of the case. Then he screwed on the outside door, and stood it back on its bracket in the oak-panelled sitting-room, where, as has been said, it looked for all the world like an eight-day clock-case.

Just as he had finished the job, a visitor—it was Mr. de Talor—came in, and remarked that he had made a precious ugly clock. Jeremy, who disliked the De Talor, as he called him, excessively, said that he would not say so when he had seen the works, and at the same time unhasped the oak door of the cabinet, and turned the full glare of the dreadful crystal eyes on to his face. The results were startling. For a moment de Talor stared and gasped; then all the rich hues faded from his features, and he sank back in a sort of fit. Jeremy shut up the door in a hurry, and his visitor soon recovered; but for years nothing would induce him to enter that room again.

As for Jeremy himself, at first he was dreadfully afraid of "the witch," but as time went on—for his job took him several days—he seemed to lose his awe of her, and even to find a fearful joy in her society. He spent whole hours, as he sat in his workshop in the yard tinkering at the air-tight case, in weaving histories in which this beautiful creature, whose head had been thus marvellously recovered, played the leading-part. It was so strange to look at her lovely scornful face, and think that, long ages since, men had loved it, and kissed it, and played with the waving hair.

There it was, this relic of the dead, preserved by the consummate skill of some old monk or chemist, so that it retained all its ancient beauty long after the echoes of the tragedy with which it must have been connected had died out of the world. For, as he wrought at the case, Jeremy grew certain that here was the ghastly memento of some enormous crime; indeed, by degrees, as he tacked and hammered at the lead lining, he made up a history that was quite satisfactory to his mind, appealing on doubtful points to the witch herself, who was on the table near him, and ascertaining whether she meant "yes" or "no" by the simple process of observing whether or not her eyes trembled when he spoke. It was slow work getting the story together in this fashion, but then the manufacture of the case was slow also, and it was not without its charm, for he felt it an honour to be taken into the confidence of so lovely a lady.

But if the head had a fascination for Jeremy, it had a still greater charm for his grandfather. The old man would continually slip out of the office and cross the yard to the little room where Jeremy worked, in order to stare at this wonderful relic. One night, indeed, when the case was nearly finished, Jeremy remembered that he had not locked the door of his workshop. He was already half undressed, but slipping on his coat again, he went out by the back door, and crossed the yard, carrying the key with him. It was bright moonlight, and Jeremy, having slippers on, walked without noise. When he reached the workshop, and was about to lock the door, he thought he heard a sound in the room. This startled him, and for a moment he meditated retreat, leaving the head to look after itself. Those eyes were interesting in the daytime, but he scarcely cared to face them alone at night. It was foolish, but they did look so very much alive!

After a moment's hesitation, during which the sound, whatever it was, again made itself audible, he determined to compromise matters by going round to the other side of the room and looking in at the little window. With a beating heart he stole round, and quietly peered in. The moonlight was shining bright into the room, and struck full upon the long case he had manufactured. He had left it shut, and the head inside it. Now it was open; he could clearly see the white outlines of the trembling eyes. The sound, too—a muttering sound—was still going on. Jeremy drew back, and wiped the perspiration from his forehead, and for the second time thought of flight. But his curiosity overcame him, and he looked again. This time he discovered the cause of the muttering.

Seated upon his carpenter's bench was his grandfather, old Atterleigh, who appeared to be staring with all his might at the head, and talking incoherently to himself. This was the noise he had heard through the door. It was an uncanny sight, and made Jeremy feel cold down the back. While he was still contemplating it, and wondering what to do, old Atterleigh rose, closed the case, and left the room. Jeremy slipped round, locked up the door, and made his way back to bed much astonished. He did not, however, say anything of what he had seen, only in future he was careful never to leave the door of his workshop open.

At last the case was finished, and for an amateur, a very good job it looked. When it was done he placed it, as already narrated, back on the bracket, and showed it to Mr. de Talor.

But from the day when Eva Ceswick nearly fell to the bottom of the cliff in the course of her antiquarian researches, things began to go wrong at Dum's Ness. Everybody felt it except Ernest, and he was thinking too much of other things. Dorothy was very unhappy in those days, and began to look thin and miserable, though she sturdily alleged, when asked, that she never felt better in her life. Jeremy himself was also unhappy, and for a good reason. He had caught the fever that women like Eva Ceswick have it in their power to give to the sons of men. His was a deep self-contained nature, very gentle and tender, not admitting many things into its affections, but loving such as were admitted with all the heart and soul and strength. And it was in the deepest depths of this loyal nature that Eva Ceswick had printed her image; before he knew it, before he had time to think, it was photographed there upon his heart, and he felt that there it must stay for good or evil; that plate could never be used again.

She had been so kind to him; her eyes had grown so bright and friendly when she saw him coming! He was sure that she liked him (which indeed she did), and once he had ventured to press her little hand, and he had thought that she had returned the pressure, and had not slept all night in consequence.

But perhaps this was a mistake. And then, just as he was getting on so nicely, came Ernest, and scattered his hopes like mists before the morning sun. From the moment that those two met, he knew that it was all over with his chance. Next, to make assurance doubly sure, Providence itself, in the shape of a shilling, had declared against him, and he was left lamenting. Well, it was all fair; but still it was very hard, and for the first time in his life he felt inclined to be angry with Ernest. Indeed, he was angry, and the fact made him more unhappy than ever, because he knew that his anger was unjust, and because his brotherly love condemned it.

But for all that, the shadow between them grew darker.

Mr. Cardus, too, had his troubles, connected, needless to say—for nothing else ever really troubled him—with his monomania of revenge. Mr. de Talor, of whose discomfiture he had at last made sure, had unexpectedly slipped out of his power, nor could he at present see any way in which to draw him back again. Consequently he was distressed. As for "Hard-riding Atterleigh," ever since he had found himself fixed by "the witch's" crystal eyes, he had been madder than ever, and more perfectly convinced that Mr. Cardus was the devil in person. Indeed, Dorothy, who watched over the old man, the grandfather who never knew her, thought that she observed a marked change in him. He worked away at his writing as usual, but, it appeared to her, with more vigour, as though it were a thing to encounter and get rid of. He would cut the notches out of his stick calendar, too, more eagerly than heretofore, and altogether it seemed as though his life had become dominated by some new purpose. She called Mr. Cardus's attention to this change; but he laughed, and said that it was nothing, and would probably soon pass with the moon.

But if nobody else was happy, Ernest was—that is, except when he was sunk in the depths of woe, which was, on an average, about three days a week. On the occasion of these seizures, Dorothy, noting his miserable aspect and entire want of appetite, felt much alarmed, and took an occasion after supper to ask him what was the matter. Before many minutes were over she had cause to regret it; for Ernest burst forth with a history of his love and his wrongs that lasted for an hour. It appeared that another young gentleman, one of those who danced with the lovely Eva at the Smythes' ball, had been making the most unmistakable advances; he had called—three times; he had sent flowers—twice (Ernest sent them every morning, beguiling Sampson into cutting the best orchid-blooms for that purpose); he had been out walking—once. Dorothy listened quietly, till he ceased of his own accord. Then she spoke.

"So you really love her, Ernest?"

"Love her! I"—but we will not enter into a description of this young man's raptures. When he had done, Dorothy did a curious thing. She rose from her chair, and coming to where Ernest was sitting, bent over him and kissed him on the forehead. As she did so he noticed vaguely that she had great black rings round her eyes.

"I hope that you will be happy, my dear brother. You will have a lovely wife, and I think that she is as good as she is beautiful." She spoke quietly, but somehow her voice sounded like a sob. He kissed her in acknowledgment, and she glided away.

Ernest did not think much of the incident, however. Indeed in five minutes his thoughts were back with Eva, with whom he was seriously and earnestly in love. In sober truth, the antics that he played were enough to make the angels weep to see a human being possessing the normal weight of brain making such a donkey of himself. For instance, he would promenade for hours at night in the neighbourhood of the Cottage. Once he ventured into the garden to enjoy the perfect bliss of staring at six panes of glass, got severely bitten by the house-dog for his pains, and was finally chased for a mile or more by both the dog and the policeman, who, having heard of the mysterious figure that was to be seen mooning (in every sense of the word) round the cottage, had laid up to watch for him. Next day he had the satisfaction of hearing from his adored's own lips the story of the attempted burglary, but as she told it there was a smile playing about the corners of her mouth which almost seemed to indicate that she had her suspicions as to who the burglar was. But then Ernest walked so very lame, which, considering that the teeth of a brute called Towzer had made a big hole in his calf, was not to be wondered at.

After this he was obliged to give up his midnight sighing, but he took it out in other ways. Once indeed, without warning, he flopped down on to the floor and kissed Eva's hand, and then, aghast at his own boldness, fled from the room.

At first all this amused Eva greatly. She was pleased at her conquest, and took a malicious pleasure in leading Ernest on. When she knew that he was coming she would make herself as lovely as possible, and put on all her charming little ways and graces in order more thoroughly to enslave him. Somehow, whenever Ernest thought of her in after years as she was at that period of her life, his memory would call up a vision of her in a pretty little drawing-room at the Cottage, leaning back in a low chair in such a way as to contrive to show off her splendid figure to the best advantage, also the tiny foot and slender ankle that peeped from beneath her soft white dress. There she sat, a little Skye-terrier called "Tails" on her lap, with which his rival had presented her but a fortnight before, and—yes—actually kissing the brute at intervals, her eyes shining all the time with innocent coquetry. What would not Ernest have given to occupy for a single minute the position of that unappreciative Skye-terrier! It was agony to see so many kisses wasted on a dog, and Eva, aware that he thought so, kissed the animal more vigorously than ever.

At last he could stand it no longer. "Put that dog down!" he said, peremptorily.

She obeyed him, then, remembering that he had no right to dictate to her what she should do, made an effort to pick it up again. But "Tails," who, be it added, was not used to being kissed in private life, and thought the whole operation rather a bore, promptly bolted.

"Why should I put the dog down?" she asked, with a quick look of defiance.

"Because I hate seeing you kiss it; it is so effeminate."

He spoke in a masterful way; it was a touch of the curb, and there are few things a proud woman resents so much as the first touch of the curb.

"What right have you to dictate what I shall or shall not do?" she asked, tapping her foot upon the floor.

Ernest was very humble in those days, and he collapsed.

"None at all. Don't be angry, Eva" (it was the first time he had called her so; till now she had always been Miss Ceswick), "but the fact was I could not bear to see you kissing that dog; I was jealous of the brute."

Whereupon she blushed furiously and changed the subject. Still after a while Eva's coquettishness began to be less and less marked. When they met she no longer greeted him with a smile of mischief, but with serious eyes that once or twice, he thought, bore traces of tears. At the same time she threw him into despair by her coldness. Did he venture a tender remark, she would pretend not to hear it—alas, that the mounting blood should so obstinately proclaim that she did! Did he touch her hand, it was cold and unresponsive. She was quieter, too, and her reserve frightened him. Once he tried to break it, and began some passionate appeal, but she rose without answering and turned her face to the window. He followed her, and saw that her dark eyes were full of tears. This he felt was even more awful than her coldness, and, fearing that he had offended her, he obeyed her whispered entreaty and went. Poor boy! he was very young. Had he had a little more experience, he might have found means to brush away her tears and his own doubts. It is a melancholy thing that such opportunities should, as a rule, present themselves before people are old or experienced enough to take advantage of them.

The secret of all this change of conduct was not far to seek. Eva had toyed with edged tools till she cut her fingers to the bone. The dark-eyed boy, who danced so well and had such a handsome, happy face, had become very dear to her. She had begun by playing with him, and now, alas! she loved him better than anybody in the world. That was the sting of the thing; she had fallen in love with a boy as young as herself—a boy, too, who, so far as she was aware, had no particular prospects in life. It was humiliating to her pride to think that she, who, in the few months that she had been "out" in London, before her cousins rose up and cast her forth, had already found the satisfaction of seeing one or two men of middle age and established position at her feet, and the further satisfaction of requesting them to kneel there no more, should in the upshot have to strike her colours to a boy of twenty-one, even though he did stand six feet high, and had more wits in his young head and more love in his young heart than all her middle-aged admirers put together.

Perhaps, though she was a woman grown, she was not herself quite old enough to appreciate the great advantage it is to any girl to stamp her image upon the heart of the man she loves while the wax is yet soft and undefaced by the half worn-out marks of many shallow dies; perhaps she did not know what a blessing it is to be able really to love a man at all, young, middle-aged, or old. Many women wait till they cannot love without shame to make that discovery. Perhaps she forgot that Ernest's youth was a fault which would mend day by day, and that he had abilities which, if she would consent to inspire them, might lead him to great things. At any rate, two facts remained in her mind after much thinking: she loved him with all her heart, and of it she was ashamed.

But as yet she could not make up her mind to any fixed course. It would have been easy to crush poor Ernest, to tell him that his pretensions were ridiculous, to send him away, or to go away herself, and so to make an end of a position that she felt was growing absurd, and which we may be sure her elder sister Florence did nothing to make more pleasant. But she could not do it; that was the long and the short of the matter. The idea of living without Ernest made her feel cold all over; it seemed to her that the only hours that she really did live were the hours which they spent together, and that when he went away he took her heart with him. No, she could not make up her mind to that; the thought was too cruel. Then there was the other alternative, to encourage him a little and become engaged to him, to brave everything for his sake. But as yet she could not make up her mind to that either.

Eva Ceswick was very loving, very sweet and very good, but she did not possess a determined mind.

CHAPTER XII

DEEPER YET

While Ernest was wooing and Eva doubting, Time, whose interest in earthly affairs is that of the sickle in the growing crop, went on his way as usual.

The end of August came, as it has come so many thousand times since this globe gave its first turn in space, as it will come for many thousand times more, till at last, its appointed course run out, the world darkens, quivers, and grows still; and, behold! Ernest was still wooing, Eva still doubting.

One evening—it was a very beautiful evening—this pair were walking together on the seashore. Whether they met by appointment or by accident does not matter; they did meet, and there they were, strolling along together, as fully charged with intense feeling as a thunder-cloud with electricity and almost as quiet. The storm had not yet burst.

To listen to the talk of these two, they might have met for the first time yesterday. It was chiefly about the weather.

Presently, in the course of their wanderings, they came to a little sailing-boat drawn up upon the beach—not far up, however, just out of the reach of the waves. By this boat, in an attitude of intense contemplation, there stood an ancient mariner. His hands were in his pockets, his pipe was in his mouth, his eyes were fixed upon the deep. Apparently he did not notice their approach till they were within two yards of him. Then he turned, "dashed" himself, and asked the lady, with a pull of his grizzled forelock, if she would not take a sail.

Ernest looked surprised.

"How's the wind?" he asked.

"Straight on shore, sir; will turn with the turn of the tide, sir, and bring you back."

"Will you come for a bit of a sail, Eva?"

"O no, thank you. I must be getting home; it is seven o'clock."

"There is no hurry for you to get home. Your aunt and Florence have gone to tea with the Smythes."

"Indeed, I cannot come; I could not think of such a thing."

Her words were unequivocal, but the ancient mariner put a strange interpretation upon them. First he hauled up the little sail, and then, placing his brown hands against the stern of the boat, he rested his weight upon them, and caused her to travel far enough into the waves to float her bow.

"Now, miss."

"I am not coming, indeed."

"Now, miss."

"I will not come, Ernest."

"Come," said Ernest, quietly holding out his hand to help her in.

She took it and got in. Ernest and the mariner gave a strong shove, and as the light boat took the water the former leaped in, and at the same second a puff of wind caught the sail, and took them ten yards out or more.

"Why, the sailor is left behind!" said Eva.

"Ernest gave a twist to the tiller to get the boat's head straight off shore, and then leisurely looked round. The mariner was standing as they had found him, his hands in his pockets, his pipe in his mouth, his eyes fixed upon the deep.

"He doesn't seem to mind it," he said, meditatively.

"Yes, but I do; you must go back and fetch him."

Thus appealed to, Ernest went through some violent manoeuvres with the tiller, without producing any marked effect on the course of the boat, which by this time had got out of the shelter of the cliff, and was bowling along merrily.

"Wait till we get clear of the draught from the cliff, and I will bring her round."

But when at last they were clear from the draught of the cliff, and he slowly got her head round, lo and behold, the mariner had vanished!

"How unfortunate!" said Ernest, getting her head towards the open sea again; "he has probably gone to his tea." Eva tried hard to get angry, but somehow she could not: she only succeeded in laughing.

"If I thought that you had done this on purpose, I would never come out with you again."

Ernest looked horrified. "On purpose!" he said; and the subject dropped.

They were sitting side by side in the stern-sheets of the boat, and the sun was just dipping all red-hot into the ocean. Under the lee of the cliff there were cool shadows; before them was a path of glory that led to a golden gate. The air was very sweet, and for those two all the world was lovely; there was no sorrow on the earth, there were no storms upon the sea.

Eva took off her hat, and let the sweet breeze play upon her brow. Then she leaned over the side, and, dipping her hand into the cool water, watched the little track it made.

"Eva."

"Yes, Ernest."

"Do you know I am going away?"

The hand was withdrawn with a start.

"Going away! when?"

"The day after to-morrow; to Guernsey first, then to France."

"And when are you coming back again?"

"I think that depends upon you, Eva."

The hand went back into the water. They were a mile or more from the shore now. Ernest manipulated the sail and tiller so as to sail slowly parallel with the coast-line. Then he spoke again.

"Eva."

No answer.

"Eva, for God's sake look at me!"

There was something in his voice that forced her to obey. She took her hand out of the water and turned her eyes on to his face. It was pale, and the lips were quivering.

"I love you," he said, in a low, choked voice.

She grew angry. "Why did you bring me here? I will go home. This is nonsense; you are nothing but a boy!"

There are moments in life when the human face is capable of conveying a more intense and vivid impression than any words, when it seems to speak to the very soul in a language of its own. And so it was with Ernest now; he made no answer to her reproaches, but, if that were possible, his features grew paler yet, and his eyes, shining like stars, fixed themselves upon her, and drew her to him. What they said she and he knew alone, nor could any words convey it, for the tongue in which they talked is not spoken in this world.

A moment still she wavered, fighting against the sweet mastery of his will with all her woman's strength, and then—O Heaven! it was done, and his arms were round about her, her head upon his breast, and her voice was lost in sobs and broken words of love.

O, radiant-winged hour of more than mortal joy; the hearts which you have touched will know when their time comes that they have not been quite in vain!

And so they sat, those two, quite silent, for there seemed to be no need for speech; words could not convey half they had to say. Indeed, to tell the honest truth, their lips were, for the most part, otherwise employed.

Meanwhile the sun went down, and the sweet moon arose over the quiet sea, and turned their little ship to silver. Eva gently disengaged herself from his arms, and half rose to look at it; she had never thought it half so beautiful before. Ernest looked at it too. It is a way that lovers have.

"Do you know the lines?" he said; "I think I can say them:

"'With a swifter motion,
Out upon the ocean,
Heaven above and round us, and you along with me:
Heaven around and o'er us,
Floating on for ever, upon the flowing sea.'"

"Go on," she said, softly.

"'What time is it, dear, now?
We are in the year now
Of the New Creation, one million, two, or three;
But where are we now, love?
We are, as I trow, love,
In the Heaven of Heavens, upon the Crystal Sea.'"

"That is how I hope it may be with us, dear," she said, taking his hand, as the last words passed his lips.

"Are you happy now?" he asked her.

"Yes, Ernest, I am happy indeed. I do not think that I shall ever be so happy again; certainly I never was so happy before. Do you know, dear, I wish to tell you so, that you may see how mean I have been; I have fought so hard against my love for you."

He looked pained. "Why?" he asked.

"I will tell you quite truly, Ernest—because you are so young. I was ashamed to fall in love with a boy, and yet you see, dear, you have been too strong for me."

"Why, there is no difference in our ages!"

"Ah, Ernest, but I am a woman, and ever so much older than you. We age so much quicker, you know. I feel about old enough to be your mother," she said, with a pretty assumption of dignity.

"And I feel quite old enough to be your lover," he replied, impertinently.

"So it seems. But, Ernest, if three months ago anybody had told me that I should be in love to-day with a boy of twenty-one, I would not have believed them. Dear, I have given you all my heart; you will not betray me, will you? You know very young men are apt to change their minds."

He flushed a little as he answered, feeling that it was tiresome to have the unlucky fact that he was only twenty-one so persistently thrust before him.

"Then they are young men who have not had the honour of winning your affections. A man who has once loved you could never forget you. Indeed, it is more likely that you will forget me; you will have plenty of temptation to do so."

She saw that she had vexed him. "Don't be angry, dear; but you see the position is a very difficult one, and, if I could not be quite sure of you, it would be intolerable."

"My darling, you may be as sure of me as woman can be of man; but don't begin your doubts over again. They are settled now. Let us be quite happy just this one evening. No doubt there are plenty coming when we shall not be able."

So they kissed each other and sailed on—homeward, alas! for it was getting late—and were perfectly happy.

Presently they drew near the shore, and there, at the identical spot where they had left him, stood the ancient mariner. His hands were in his pockets, his pipe was in his mouth, his eyes were fixed upon the deep.

Ernest grounded the little boat skilfully enough, and, jumping over the bow, he and the mariner pulled it up. Then Eva got out, and as she did so she thought, in the moonlight, that she noticed something resembling a twinkle in the latter's ancient eye. She felt confused—there is nothing so confusing as a guilty conscience—and, to cover her confusion, plunged into conversation while Ernest was finding some money to pay for the boat.

"Do you often let boats?" she asked.

"No, miss, only to Mr. Ernest in a general way" (so that wicked Ernest had set a trap to catch her).

"O, then, I suppose you go out fishing?"

"No, miss, only for rikkration, like."

"Then what do you do?"—she was getting curious on the point.

"Times I does nothing; times I stands on the beach and sees things; times I runs cheeses, miss."

"Run cheeses!"

"Yes, miss, Dutch ones."

"He means that he brings cargoes of Dutch cheeses to Harwich."

"Oh!" said Eva.

Ernest paid the man, and they turned to go. She had not gone many yards when she felt a heavy hand laid upon her shoulder. Turning round in astonishment, she perceived the mariner.

"I say, miss," he said, in a hoarse whisper.

"Well, what?"

"Niver you eat the rind of a Dutch cheese! I says it as knows."

Eva did not forget his advice.

CHAPTER XIII

MR. CARDUS UNFOLDS HIS PLANS

"Ernest," said Mr. Cardus, on the morning following the events described in the previous chapter. "I want to speak to you in my office—and to you too, Jeremy."

They both followed him into his room, wondering what was the matter. He sat down and so did they, and then, as was his habit, letting his eyes stray over every part of their persons except their faces, he began:

"It is time that you two fellows took to doing something for yourselves. You must not learn to be idle men—not that most young men require much teaching in that way. What do you propose to do?"

Jeremy and Ernest stared at one another rather blankly, but apparently Mr. Cardus did not expect an answer. At any rate, he went on before either of them could frame one.

"You don't seem to know, never gave the matter any consideration probably; quite content to obey the Bible literally, and take no thought for the morrow. Well, it is lucky that you have somebody to think for you. Now I will tell you what I propose for you both. I want you, Ernest, to go to the bar. It is a foolish profession for most of young men to take to, but it will not be so in your case, because, as it happens, if you show yourself capable I shall by degrees be able to put a good deal of business in your hands—Chancery business, for I have little to do with any other. I dare say that you will wonder where the business is to come from? I don't seem to do very much here, do I? with a mad old hunting-man as a clerk, and Dorothy to copy my private letters; but I do, for all that. I may as well tell you both, in confidence, that this place is only the head centre of my business. I have another office in London, another at Ipswich, and another at Norwich, though they all work under different names; besides which I have other agencies of a different nature. But all this is neither here nor there. I have communicated with Aster, the rising Chancery man, and he will have a vacancy in his chambers next turn. Let me see—term begins on November 2nd; I propose, Ernest, to write to-day to enter you at Lincoln's Inn. I shall make you an allowance of three hundred a year, which you must clearly understand you must not exceed. I think that is all I have to say about the matter."

"I am sure I am very much obliged to you, uncle"—began Ernest, fervently, for since the previous evening he had clearly realised that it was necessary for him to make a beginning of doing something.

But his uncle cut him short.

"All right, Ernest, we will understand all that. Now, Jeremy, for you. I propose that you shall be articled to me, and if you work well and prove useful, it is my intention in time to admit you to a share of the business. In order that you may not feel entirely dependent, it is my further intention to make you an allowance also, on the amount of which I have not yet settled."

Jeremy groaned in spirit at the thought of becoming a lawyer, even with a "share of the business," but he remembered his conversation with Dorothy, and thanked Mr. Cardus with the best grace that he could muster.

"All right, then; I will have the articles prepared at once, and you can take to your stool in the office next week. I think that is all I have to say."

Acting on this hint, the pair were departing, Jeremy in the deepest state of depression, induced by the near prospect of that stool, when Mr. Cardus called Ernest back.

"I want to talk to you about something else," he said thoughtfully. "Shut the door."

Ernest turned cold down his back, and wondered if his uncle could have heard anything about Eva. He had the full intention of speaking to him about the matter, but it would be awkward to be boarded himself before he had made up his mind what to say. He shut the door, and then walking to the glass entrance to the orchid blooming-house, stood looking at the flowers, and waiting for Mr. Cardus to begin. But he did not begin; he seemed to be lost in thought.

"Well, uncle," he said at last.

"It is a delicate business, Ernest, but I may as well get it over. I am going to make a request to you, a request to which I beg you will give me no immediate answer, for from its nature it will require the most anxious and careful consideration. I want you to listen, and say nothing. You can give me your answer when you come back from abroad. At the same time, I must tell you that it is a matter which I trust you will not disappoint me in; indeed, I do not think that you could be so cruel as to do so. I must also tell you that if you do, you must prepare to be a great loser, financially speaking."

"I have not the faintest idea what you are driving at, uncle," said Ernest, turning from the glass door to speak.

"I know you have not. I will tell you. Listen; I will tell you a little story. Many years ago a great misfortune overtook me, a misfortune so great that it struck me as lightning sometimes does a tree—it left the bark sound, but turned the heart to ashes. Never mind what the details were, they were nothing out of the common; such things sometimes happen to men and women. The blow was so severe that it almost turned my brain, so from that day I gave myself to revenge. It sounds melodramatic, but there was nothing of the sort about it. I had been cruelly wronged, and I determined that those who had wronged me should taste of their own medicine. With the exception of one man they have done so. He has escaped me for a time, but he is doomed. To pass on. The woman who caused the trouble—for wherever there is trouble there is generally a woman who causes it—had children. Those children were Dorothy and her brother. I adopted them. As time went on, I grew to love the girl for her likeness to her mother. The boy I never loved; to this hour I cannot like him, though he is a gentleman, which his father never was. I can, however, honestly say that I have done my duty by him. I have told you all this in order that you may understand the request which I am going to make. I trust to you never to speak of it, and if you can to forget it. And now for my request itself."

Ernest looked up wonderingly.

"It is my most earnest desire that you should marry Dorothy."

His listener started violently, turned quite pale, and opened his lips to speak. Mr. Cardus lifted his hand and went on:

"Remember what I asked you. Pray say nothing; only listen. Of course I cannot force you into this or any other marriage. I can only beg you to give heed to my wishes, knowing that they will in every way prove to your advantage. That girl has a heart of gold; and if you marry her you shall inherit nearly all my fortune, which is now very large. I have observed that you have lately been about a great deal with Eva Ceswick. She is a handsome woman, and very likely has taken some hold upon your fancy. I warn you that any entanglement in that direction would be most disagreeable to me, and would to a great extent destroy your prospects, so far as I am concerned."

Again Ernest was about to speak, and again his uncle stopped him.

"I want no confidences, Ernest, and had much rather that no words passed between us which we might afterwards regret. And now I understand that you are going abroad with your friend Batty for a couple of months. When you return you shall give me your answer about Dorothy. In the meanwhile here is cheque for your expenses; what is over you can spend as you like. Perhaps you have some bills to pay."

He gave him a folded cheque, and then went on:

"Now leave me, as I am busy."

Ernest walked out of the room in a perfect maze. In the yard he mechanically unfolded the cheque. It was for a large sum—two hundred and fifty pounds. He put it in his pocket, and began to reflect upon his position, which was about as painful a position as can well be. Truly he was on the horns of a dilemma; probably before he was much older, one of them would have pierced him. For a moment he was about to return to his uncle and tell him all the truth, but on reflection he could not see what was to be gained by such a course. At any rate, it seemed to him that he must first consult Eva, whom he had arranged to meet on the beach at three o'clock; there was nobody else whom he could consult, for he was shy of talking about Eva to Jeremy or Dolly.

The rest of that morning went very ill for Ernest, but three o'clock came at last, and found him at the trysting-place.

About a mile on the farther side of Kesterwick, that is, two miles or so from Titheburgh Abbey, the cliff jutted out into the sea in a way that corresponded very curiously with the little promontory known as Dum's Ness, the reason of its resistance to the action of the waves being that it was at this spot composed of an upcrop of rock of a more durable nature than the sandstone and pebbles of the remainder of the line of cliff. Just at the point of this promontory the waves had worn a hollow in the rock that was locally dignified by the name of the Cave. For two hours or more at high tide this hollow was under water, and it was, therefore, impossible to pass the headland except by boat; but during the rest of the day it formed a convenient grotto or trysting-place, the more so as anybody sitting in it was quite invisible either from the beach, the cliff, or indeed, unless the boat was quite close in shore, the sea in front.

Here it was that Ernest had arranged to meet Eva, and on turning the rocky corner of the cave he found her sitting on a mass of fallen rock waiting for him. At the sight of her beautiful form he forgot all his troubles, and when rising to greet him, blushing like the dawn, she lifted her pure face for him to kiss, there was not a happier lad in England. Then she made room for him beside her—the rock was just wide enough for two—and he placed his arm round her waist, and for a minute or two she laid her head upon his shoulder, and they were very happy.

"You are early," he said at last.

"Yes; I wanted to get away from Florence and have a good think. You have no idea how unpleasant she is; she seems to know everything. For instance she knew that we went out sailing together last evening, for this morning at breakfast she said in the most cheerful way that she hoped that I enjoyed my moonlight sail last night."

"The deuce she did! and what did you say?"

"I said that I enjoyed it very much, and luckily my aunt did not take any notice."

"Why did you not say at once that we were engaged? We are engaged, you know."

"Yes—that is, I suppose so."

"Suppose so! There is no supposition about it. At least, if we are not engaged, what are we?"

"Well, you see, Ernest, it sounds so absurd to say that one is engaged to a boy! I love you Ernest, love you dearly, but how can I say that I am engaged to you?"

Ernest rose in great wrath. "I tell you what it is, Eva, if I am not good enough to acknowledge, I am not good enough to have anything to do with. A boy, indeed! I am one-and-twenty; that is my full age. Confound it all! you are always talking about my being so young, just as though I should not get old fast enough. Can't you wait for me for a year or two?" he asked, with tears of mortification in his eyes.

"O, Ernest, Ernest, do be reasonable, there's a dear; what is the good of getting angry and making me wretched? Come and sit down here, dear, and tell me, am I not worth a little patience? There is not the slightest possibility, so far as I can see, of our getting married at present; so the question is, if it is of any use to trumpet out an engagement that will only make us the object of a great deal of gossip, and which, perhaps, your uncle would not like?"

"O, by Jove!" he said, "that reminds me;" and sitting down beside her again, he told her the story of the interview with his uncle. She listened in silence.

"This is all very bad," she said, when he had finished.

"Yes, it is bad enough; but what is to be done?"

"There is nothing to be done at present."

"Shall I make a clean breast of it to him?"

"No, no, not now; it will only make matters worse. We must wait, dear. You must go abroad for a couple of months, as you had arranged, and then when you come back we will see what can be arranged."

"But, my dearest, I cannot bear to leave you; it makes my heart ache to think of it."

"Dear, I know that it is hard; but it must be done. You could not stop here now very well without speaking about—our engagement, and to do that would only be to bring your uncle's anger on you. No, you had better go away, Ernest, and meanwhile I will try to get into Mr. Cardus's good graces, and, if I fail, then when you come back we can agree upon some plan. Perhaps by that time you will take your uncle's view of the matter and want to marry Dorothy. She would make you a better wife than I shall, Ernest, my dear."

"Eva, how can you say such things! It is not kind of you!"

"O, why not? It is true. O yes, I know that I am better-looking, and that is what you men always think of; but she has more brains, more fixity of mind, and, perhaps, for all I know, more heart than I have, though, for the matter of that, I feel as if I was all heart just now. Really, Ernest, you had better transfer your allegiance. Give me up, and forget me, dear; it will save you much trouble. I know that there is trouble coming; it is in the air. Better marry Dorothy, and leave me to fight my sorrow out alone. I will release you, Ernest;" and she began to cry at the bare idea.

"I shall wait to give you up until you have given me up," said Ernest, when he had found means to stop her tears; "and as for forgetting you, I can never do that. Please, dear, don't talk so any more; it pains me."

"Very well, Ernest; then let us vow eternal fidelity instead; but, my dear, I know that I shall bring you trouble."

"It is the price that men have always paid for the smiles of women like you," he answered. "Trouble may come—so be it, let it come; at any rate, I have the consciousness of your love. When I have lost that, then, and then only, will I think that I have bought you too dear."

In the course of his after-life these words often came back to Ernest's mind.

CHAPTER XIV

GOOD-BYE

There are some scenes, trivial enough perhaps in themselves, that yet retain a peculiar power of standing out in sharp relief, as we cast our mind's eye down the long vista of our past. The group of events with which these particular scenes were connected may have long ago vanished from our mental sight, or faded into a dim and misty uniformity, and be as difficult to distinguish one from the other as the trees of a forest viewed from a height. But here and there an event, a sensation, or a face will stand out as perfectly clear as if it had been that moment experienced, felt, or seen. Perhaps it is only some scene of our childhood, such as a fish darting beneath a rustic bridge, and the ripple which its motion left upon the water. We have seen many larger fish dart in many fine rivers since then, and have forgotten them; but somehow that one little fish has kept awake in the storehouse of our brain, where most things sleep, though none are really obliterated.

It was in this clear and brilliant fashion that every little detail of the scene was indelibly photographed on Ernest's mind when, on the morning following their meeting in the cave, he said good-bye to Eva before he went abroad. It was a public good-bye, for, as it happened, there was no opportunity for the lovers to meet alone. They were all gathered in the little drawing-room at the Cottage: Miss Ceswick seated on a straight-backed chair in the bow-window; Ernest on one side of the round table, looking intensely uncomfortable; Eva on the other, a scrap-book in her hand, which she studiously kept before her; and in the background, leaning carelessly over the back of a chair in such a way that her own face could not be seen, though she could survey everybody else's, was Florence. Ernest, from where he sat, could just make out the outline of her olive face, and the quick glance of her brown eyes.

So they sat for a long time, but what was said he could not remember; it was only the scene that imprinted itself upon his memory.

Then at last the fatal moment came—he knew that it was time to go, and said good-bye to Miss Ceswick, who made some remark about his good fortune in going to France and Italy, and warned him to be careful not to lose his heart to a foreign girl. He crossed the room and shook hands with Florence, who smiled coolly in his face, and read him through with her piercing eyes; and last of all came to Eva, who dropped her album and a pocket-handkerchief in her confusion as she rose to give him her hand. He stooped and picked them up—the album he placed on the table, the little lace-edged handkerchief he crumpled up in the palm of his left hand and kept; it was almost the only souvenir he had of her. Then he took her hand, and for a moment looked into her face. It wore a smile, but beneath it the features were wan and troubled. It was so hard to part.

"Well, Ernest," said Miss Ceswick, "you two are taking leave of each other as solemnly as though you were never going to meet again."

"Perhaps they never will," said Florence, in her clear voice; and at that moment Ernest felt as though he hated her.

"You should not croak, Florence; it is unlucky," said Miss Ceswick.

Florence smiled.

Then Ernest dropped the cold hand, and turning, left the room. Florence followed him, and, snatching a hat from the pegs, passed into the garden before him. When he was halfway down the garden-walk, he found her ostensibly picking some carnations.

"I want to speak to you for a minute, Ernest," she said; "turn this way with me;" and she led him past the bow-window, down a small shrubbery-walk about twenty paces long. "I must offer you my congratulations," she went on. "I hope that you two will be happy. Such a handsome pair ought to be happy, you know."

"Why, Florence, who told you?"

"Told me! nobody told me. I have seen it all along. Let me see, you first took a fancy to one another on the night of the Smythes' dance, when she gave you a rose, and the next day you saved her life quite in the romantic and orthodox way. Well, and then events took their natural course, till one evening you went out sailing together in a boat. Shall I go on?"

"I don't think it is necessary, Florence. I am sure I don't know how you know all these things."

She had stopped, and was standing slowly picking a carnation to pieces leaf by leaf.

"Don't you?" she answered, with a laugh. "Lovers are blind; but it does not follow that other people are. I have been thinking, Ernest, that it is very fortunate that I found out my little mistake before you discovered yours. Supposing I really had cared for you, the position would have been awkward now, would it not?"

Ernest was forced to admit that it would.

"But luckily, you see, I do not. I am only your true friend now, Ernest; and it is as a friend that I wish to say a word to you about Eva—a word of warning."

"Go on."

"You love Eva, and Eva loves you, Ernest; but remember this, she is weak as water. She always was so from a child; those beautiful women often are; Nature does not give them everything, you see."

"What do you mean?"

"What I say, nothing more. She is very weak; and you must not be surprised if she throws you over."

"Good heavens, Florence! Why, she loves me with all her heart!"

"Yes; still, women often think of other things besides their hearts. But there, I don't want to frighten you, only I would not pin all my faith to Eva's constancy, however dearly you may think she loves you. Don't look so distressed, Ernest; I did not wish to pain you. And remember that if any difficulty should arise between Eva and you, you will always have me on your side. You will always think of me as your true friend, won't you, Ernest?" and she held out her hand.

He took it.

"Indeed I will," he said.

They had turned now, and again reached the bow-window, one of the divisions of which stood open. Florence touched his arm, and pointed into the room. He looked in through the open window. Miss Ceswick had gone, but Eva was still at her old place by the table. Her head was down upon the table, resting on the album he had picked up, and he could see from the motion of her shoulders that she was sobbing bitterly. Presently she lifted her face—it was all stained with tears—only, however, to drop it again. Ernest made a motion as though he would enter the house, but Florence stopped him.

"Best leave her alone," she whispered; and then, when they were well past the window, added aloud, "I am sorry that you saw her like that; if you should never meet again, or be separated for a very long time, it will leave a painful recollection in your mind. Well, good-bye. I hope that you will enjoy yourself."

Ernest shook hands in silence—there was a lump in his throat that prevented him from speaking—and then went on his way, feeling utterly miserable. As for Florence, she put up her hand to shade her keen eyes from the sun, and watched him, till he turned the corner, with a look of intense love and longing, which slowly changed into one of bitter hate. When he was out of sight she turned, and, making her way to her bedroom, flung herself upon the bed, and, burying her face in the pillow to stifle the sound of her sobbing, gave way to an outburst of jealous rage that was almost awful in its intensity.

Ernest had only just time to get back to Dum's Ness, and go through the form of eating some luncheon, before he was obliged to start to catch his train. Dorothy had packed his things, and made all those little preparations for his journey that women think of; so, after going to the office to bid good-bye to his uncle, who shook him heartily by the hand, and bade him not forget the subject of their conversation, he had nothing to do but jump into the cart and start. In the sitting-room he found Dorothy waiting for him, with his coat and gloves, also Jeremy, who was going to drive to the station with him. He put on his coat in silence; they were all quite silent; indeed, he might have been going for a long sojourn in a deadly climate, instead of two months' pleasure-tour, so depressed was everybody.

"Good-bye, Doll dear," he said, stooping to kiss her; but she shrank away from him. In another minute he was gone.

At the station a word or two about Eva passed between Jeremy and himself.

"Well, Ernest," asked the former nervously, "have you pulled it off?"

"With her?"

"Of course; who else?"

"Yes, I have. But, Jeremy—"

"Well!"

"I don't want you to say anything about it to anybody at present."

"Very good."

"I say, old fellow," Ernest went on, after a pause, "I hope you don't mind very much."

"If I said I did not mind, Ernest," he answered, slowly turning his honest eyes full on to his friend's face, "I should be telling a lie. But I do say this: as I could not win her myself, I am glad that you have, because next to her I think I love you better than anybody in the world. You always had the luck, and I wish you joy. There's the train."

Ernest wrung his hand.

"Thanks, old chap," he said; "you are a downright good fellow, and a good friend too. I know I have had the luck, but perhaps it is going to turn. Good-bye."

Ernest's plans were to sleep in London, and to leave on the following morning, a Wednesday, for Guernsey. There he was to meet his friend on Thursday, when they were to start upon their tour, first to Normandy, and thence wherever their fancy led them.

This programme he carried out to the letter—at least the first part of it. On his way from Liverpool Street Station to the rooms where he had always slept on the few occasions that he had been in London, his hansom passed down Fleet Street, and got blocked opposite No. 19. His eye caught the number, and he wondered what there was about it familiar to him. Then he remembered that 19 Fleet Street was the address of Messrs. Gosling and Sharpe, the bankers on whom his uncle had given him the cheque for £250. Bethinking himself that he might as well cash it, he stopped the cab and entered the bank. As he did so, the cashier was just leaving his desk, for it was past closing hour; but he courteously took Ernest's cheque, and though it was for a large sum, cashed it without hesitation. Mr. Cardus's name was evidently well known in the establishment. Ernest proceeded on his journey with a crisp little bundle of Bank of England notes in his breast-pocket, a circumstance that, in certain events of which at that moment he little dreamed, proved of the utmost service to him.

It will not be necessary for us to follow him in his journey to St. Peter's Port, which very much resembled other people's journeys. He arrived there safely enough on Wednesday afternoon, and proceeded to the best hotel, took a room, and inquired the hour of the table d'hôte.

In the course of the voyage from Southampton, Ernest had fallen into conversation with a quiet, foreign-looking man, who spoke English with a curious little accent. This gentleman—for there was no doubt about his being a gentleman—was accompanied by a boy about nine years of age, remarkable for his singularly prepossessing face and manners, whom Ernest rightly judged to be his son. Mr. Alston—for such he discovered his companion's name to be—was a middle-aged man, not possessed of any remarkable looks or advantages of person, nor in any way brilliant-minded. But nobody could know Mr. Alston for long without discovering that, his neutral tints notwithstanding, he was the possessor of an almost striking individuality. From his open way of talking, Ernest guessed that he was a colonial; for he had often noticed at college that colonials are much less reserved than Englishmen proper are bred up to be. He soon learned that Mr. Alston was a Natal colonist, now, for the first time, paying a visit to the old country. He had, until lately, held a high position in the Natal Government service; but having unexpectedly come into a moderate fortune through the death of an aged lady, a sister of his father in England, he had resigned his position in the service; and after his short visit "home," as colonists always call the mother country, even when they have never seen it, intended to start on a big game-shooting expedition in the country between Secocoeni's country and Delagoa Bay.

All this Ernest learned before the boat reached the harbour at St. Peter's Port, and they separated. He was, however, pleased when, having seen his luggage put into his room, he went into the little courtyard of the hotel and found Mr. Alston standing there with his son, and looking rather puzzled.

"Hullo!" said Ernest, "I am glad that you have come to this hotel. Do you want anything?"

"Well, yes, I do. The fact of the matter is, I don't understand a word of French, and I want to find my way to a place that my boy and I have come over here to see. If they talked Zulu or Sisutu, you see, I should be equal to the occasion; but to me French is a barbarous tongue, and the people about here all seem to talk nothing else. Here is the address."

"I can talk French," said Ernest, "and, if you like, I will go with you. The table d'hôte is not till seven, and it is not six yet."

"It is very kind of you."

"Not at all. I have no doubt that you would show me the way about Zululand, if ever I wandered there."

"Ay, that I would, with pleasure;" and they started.

It was with considerable difficulty that Ernest discovered the place Mr. Alston was in search of. Finally, however, he found it. It was a quaint out-of-the-way little street, very narrow and crooked, an odd mixture of old private houses and shops, most of which seemed to deal in soap and candles. At last they came to No. 36, a grey old house standing in its own grounds. Mr. Alston scanned it eagerly.

"That is the place," he said; "she often told me of the coat-of-arms over the doorway—a mullet impaled with three squirrels; there they are. I wonder if it is still a school?"

It turned out that it was still a school, and in due course they were admitted, and allowed to wander round the ancient walled garden, with every nook of which Mr. Alston seemed to be perfectly acquainted.

"There is the tree under which she used to sit," he said sadly to his boy, pointing to an old yew-tree, under which there stood a rotting bench.

"Who?" asked Ernest, much interested.

"My dead wife, that boy's mother; she was educated here," he said, with a sigh. "There, I have seen it. Let us go."

CHAPTER XV

ERNEST GETS INTO TROUBLE

When Mr. Alston and Ernest reached the hotel, there was still a quarter of an hour to elapse before the table d'hôte, so after washing his hands and putting on a black coat, Ernest went down into the coffee-room. There was only one other person in it, a tall fair Frenchwoman, apparently about thirty years of age. She was standing by the empty fireplace, her arm upon the mantelpiece, and a lace pocket-handkerchief in her hand; and Ernest's first impression of her was that she was handsome and much over-dressed. There was a newspaper upon the mantelpiece, which he desired to get possession of. As he advanced for this purpose, the lady dropped her handkerchief. Stooping down he picked it out of the grate and handed it to her.

"Mille remerciments, monsieur," she said, with a little curtsey.

"Du tout, madame?"

"Ah, monsieur parle francais?"

"Mais oui, madame."

And then they drifted into a conversation, in the course of which Ernest learned that madame thought St. Peter's Port very dull; that she had been there three days with her friends, and was nearly dead de tristesse; that she was going, however, to the public dance at the "Hall" that night. "Of course monsieur would be there;" and many other things, for madame had a considerable command of language.

In the middle of all this the door opened, and another lady of much the same cut as madame entered, followed by two young men. The first of these had a face of the commonplace English type, rather a good-humoured face; but when he saw the second, Ernest started, it was so like his own, as his would become if he were to spend half a dozen years in drinking, dicing, late hours, and their concomitants.

The man to whom this face belonged was evidently a gentleman, but he looked an ill-tempered one, and very puny and out of health; at least so thought Ernest.

"It is time for dinner, Camille," said the gentleman to madame, at the same time favouring Ernest with a most comprehensive scowl.

Madame appeared not to understand, and made some remark to Ernest.

"It is time for dinner, Camille," said the gentleman again, in a savage voice. This time she lifted her head and looked at him.

"Din-nare, dinnare! quest-que c'est que din-nare?"

"Table d'hôte," said the gentleman.

"O, pardon;" and with a little bow and most fascinating smile to Ernest, she took the gentleman's extended arm and sailed away.

"Why did you pretend not to understand me?" Ernest heard him ask, and she saw her shrug her shoulders in reply. The other gentleman followed with his companion, and after him came Ernest. When he reached the salle-a-manger he found that the only chair vacant at the table was one next to his friend of the salon. Indeed, had he thought of it, it might have struck him that madame had contrived to keep that chair vacant, for on his approach she gathered together the folds of her silk dress, which had almost hidden it, and welcomed him with a little nod.

Ernest took the chair, and forthwith madame entered into a most lively conversation with him, a course of proceeding that appeared to be extremely distasteful to the gentleman on her right, who pished and pshawed and pushed away his plate in a manner that soon became quite noticeable. But madame talked serenely on, quite careless of his antics, till at last he whispered something to her that caused the blood to mount to her fair cheek.

"Mais tais-toi, donc," Ernest heard her answer, and next moment—the subsequent history of our hero demands that the truth should be told—it was his turn to colour, for, alas! there was no doubt about it, he distinctly felt madame's little foot pressed upon his own. He took up his wine and drank a little to hide his confusion; but whether he had or had not the moral courage to withdraw from the situation, by placing his toes under the more chilly but safe guardianship of the chair-legs, history saith not; let us hope and presume that he had. But if this was so or not he did not get on very well with his dinner, for the situation was novel and not conducive to appetite. Presently Mr. Alston, who was sitting opposite, addressed him across the table.

"Are you going to the dance here to-night, Mr. Kershaw?"

To Ernest's surprise, the gentleman on the other side of madame answered, with an astonished look:

"Yes, I am going."

"I beg your pardon," said Mr. Alston, "I was speaking to the gentleman on your left."

"Oh, indeed! I thought you said Kershaw."

"Yes, I did; the gentleman's name is Kershaw, I think."

"Yes," put in Ernest, "my name is Kershaw."

"That is odd," said the other gentleman, "so is mine. I did not know that there were any other Kershaws."

"Nor did I," answered Ernest, "except Sir Hugh Kershaw;" and his face darkened as he pronounced the name.

"I am Sir Hugh Kershaw's son; my name is Hugh Kershaw," was the reply.

"Indeed! Then we are cousins, I suppose; for I am his nephew, the son of his brother Ernest."

Hugh Kershaw the elder did not receive this intelligence with even the moderate amount of enthusiasm that might have been expected; he simply lifted his scanty eyebrows, and said, "Oh, I remember, my uncle left a son;" then he turned and made some remark to the gentleman who sat next him that made the latter laugh.

Ernest felt the blood rise to his cheeks; there was something very insolent about his cousin's tone.

Shortly afterwards the dinner came to an end, and madame with another fascinating smile, retired. As for Ernest, he smoked a pipe with Mr. Alston, and about nine o'clock strolled over with him to the Hall, or Assembly Rooms, a building largely composed of glass, where thrice a week, during the season, the visitors at St. Peter's Port adjoined to dance, flirt, and make merry.

One of the first sights that caught his eye was a fair creature in evening dress, and with conspicuously white shoulders, in whom he recognised madame. She was sitting near the door, and appeared to be watching it. Ernest bowed to her, and was about to pass on; but, pursuing her former tactics, she dropped the bouquet she was carrying. He stooped, picked it up, returned it, and again made as though he would pass on, when she addressed him, just as the band struck up.

"Ah, que c'est belle, la musique! Monsieur valse, n'est-ce pas?"

In another minute they were floating down the room together. As they passed along, Ernest saw his cousin standing in the corner, looking at him with no amiable air. Madame saw his glance.

"Ah," she said, "Monsieur Hugh ne valse pas, il se grise; il a l'air jaloux, n'est-ce pas?"

Ernest danced three times with this fair enslaver, and with their last waltz the ball came to an end. Just then his cousin came up, and they all, including Mr. Alston, walked together along the steep streets, which were now quite deserted, to the door of the hotel. Here Ernest said good-night to madame, who extended her hand. He took it, and as he did so he felt a note slipped into it, which, not being accustomed to such transactions, he clumsily dropped. It was the ball programme, and there was something written across it in pencil. Unfortunately, he was not the only one who saw this; his cousin,

Hugh, who had evidently been drinking, saw it too, and tried to pick up the programme, but Ernest was too quick for him.

"Give me that," said his cousin, hoarsely.

Ernest answered by putting it into his pocket.

"What is written on that programme?"

"I don't know."

"What have you written on that programme, Camille?"

"Mon Dieu, mais vous m'ennuyez!" was the answer.

"I insist upon your giving me that!" with an oath.

"Monsieur est 'gentleman.' Monsieur ne la rendra pas," said madame, with a meaning glance; and then turning, she entered the hotel.

"I am not going to give it to you," said Ernest.

"You shall give it to me."

"Is this lady your wife?" asked Ernest.

"That is my affair; give me that note."

"I shall not give it to you," said Ernest, whose temper was rapidly rising. "I don't know what is on it, and I don't wish to know; but whatever it is, the lady gave it to me, and not to you. She is not your wife, and you have no right to ask for it."

His cousin Hugh turned livid with fury. At the best of times he was an evil-tempered man; and now, inflamed as he was by drink and jealousy, he looked a perfect fiend.

"Damn you!" he hissed, "you half-bred cur; I suppose that you get your—manners from your—of a mother!"

He did not get any further; for at this point Ernest knocked him into the gutter, and then stood over him, very quiet and pale, and told him that if ever he dared to let a disrespectful word about his mother pass his lips again, he (Ernest) would half-kill him (Hugh). Then he let him get up.

Hugh Kershaw rose, and turning, whispered something to his friend, who had sat next him at dinner, a man about thirty years of age, and with a military air about him. His friend listened and pulled his large moustache thoughtfully. Then he addressed Ernest with the utmost politeness:

"I am Captain Justice, of the — Hussars. Of course, Mr. Kershaw, you are aware that you cannot indulge yourself in the luxury of knocking people down without hearing more about it. Have you any friend with you?"

Ernest shook his head as he answered: "This," indicating Mr. Alston, who had been an attentive observer of everything that had passed, "is the only gentleman I know in the town, and I cannot ask him to mix himself up in my quarrels." Ernest was beginning to understand that this quarrel was a very serious business.

"All right, my lad," said Mr. Alston quietly, "I will stand by you."

"Really, I have no right—" began Ernest.

"Nonsense! It is one of our colonial customs to stick by one another."

"Mr. Justice—"

"Captain Justice," put in that gentleman, with a bow.

"Captain Justice, my name is Alston. I am very much at your service."

Captain Justice turned to Hugh Kershaw, whose clothes were dripping from the water in the gutter, and after whispering with him for a moment, said aloud, "If I were you, Kershaw, I should go and change those clothes; you will catch cold." And then, addressing Mr. Alston, "I think the smoking-room is empty. Shall we go and have a chat?"

Mr. Alston assented, and they went in together. Ernest followed; but having lit his pipe, sat down in a far corner of the room. Presently, Mr. Alston called him.

"Look here, Kershaw, this is a serious business, and as you are principally concerned, I think you had better give your own answer. To be brief, your cousin, Mr. Hugh Kershaw, demands that you should apologise in writing for having struck him."

"I am willing to do that if he will apologise for the terms he used in connection with my mother."

"Ah!" said the gallant Captain, "the young gentleman is coming to reason."

"He also demands that you should hand over the note you received from the lady."

"That I certainly shall not do," he answered; and drawing the card from his pocket, he tore it into fragments unread.

Captain Justice bowed and left the room. In a few minutes he returned, and, addressing Mr. Alston and Ernest, said:

"Mr. Kershaw is not satisfied with what you offer to do. He declines to apologise for any expression that he may have used with reference to your mother, and he now wishes you to choose between signing an apology, which I shall dictate, or meeting him to-morrow morning. You must remember that we are in Guernsey, where you cannot insult a man on the payment of forty shillings."

Of course, this view was an entirely incorrect one. Although Guernsey has a political constitution of its own, many of its laws being based upon the old Norman-French customs, and judicial proceedings being carried on in French, &c., it is quite as criminal an act to fight a duel there as in England, as Captain Justice himself afterwards found out to his cost. But they none of them knew that.

Ernest felt the blood run to his heart. He understood now what Captain Justice meant. He answered simply:

"I shall be very happy to meet my cousin in whatever place and way you and Mr. Alston may agree upon;" and then he returned to his chair, and gave himself up to the enjoyment of his pipe and an entirely new set of sensations.

Captain Justice gazed after him pityingly. "I am sorry for him," he said to Mr. Alston. "Kershaw is, I believe, a good shot with pistols. I suppose you will choose pistols. It would be difficult to get swords in such a hurry. He is a fine young fellow. Took it coolly, by George! Well, I don't think that he will trouble the world much longer."

"This is a silly business, and likely to land us all in a nasty mess. Is there no way out of it?"

"None that I know of, unless your young friend will eat dirt. He is a nasty-tempered fellow, Kershaw, and wild about that woman, over whom he has spent thousands. Nor is he likely to forgive being rolled in the gutter. You had better get your man to give in, for if you don't, Kershaw will kill him."

"It is no good talking of it. I have lived a rough life, and know what men are made of. He is not of that sort. Besides, your man is in the wrong, not that boy. If anybody spoke of my mother like that I would shoot him."

"Very good, Mr. Alston. And now about the pistols; I have none."

"I have a pair of Smith & Wesson revolvers that I bought yesterday to take out to Africa with me. They throw a very heavy bullet, Captain Justice."

"Too heavy. If one of them is hit anywhere in the body—" He did not finish the sentence.

Mr. Alston nodded. "We must put them twenty paces apart, to give them a chance of missing. And now about the place and the time?"

"I know a place on the beach, about a mile and a half from here, that will do very well. You go down that street till you strike the beach, then turn to your right, and follow the line of the sea till you come to a deserted hut or cottage. There we will meet you."

"At what time?"

"Let me see; shall we say a quarter to five. It will be light enough for us then."

"Very good. The Weymouth boat leaves at half-past six. I am going to see about getting my things ready to go to meet it. I should advise you to do the same, Captain Justice. We had better not return here after it is over."

"No."

Then they parted.

Luckily the manager of the hotel had not gone to bed; so the various parties concerned were able to pay their bills, and make arrangements about their luggage being sent to meet the early boat, without exciting the slightest suspicion. Ernest wrote a note, and left it to be given to his friend when he should arrive on the morrow, in which he stated mysteriously that business had called him away. He could not help smiling to himself sadly when he thought that his business might be of a sort that it would take all eternity to settle.

Then he went to his room and wrote two letters, one to Eva and one to Dorothy. Mr. Alston was to post them if anything happened to him. The first was of a passionate nature, and breathed hopes of reunion in another place—ah, how fondly the poor human heart clings to that idea!—the second collected and sensible enough. The letters finished, following Mr. Alston's advice, he undressed and took a bath; then he said his prayers—the prayers his mother had taught him—put on a quiet dark suit of clothes, and went and sat by the open window. The night was very still and fragrant with the sweet strong breath of the sea. Not a sound came from the quaint old town beneath—all was at peace. Ernest, sitting there, wondered whether he would live to see another night, and, if not, what the nights were like in the land whither he was journeying. As he thought of it the grey damps that hide that unrisen world from our gaze struck into his soul and made him feel afraid. Not afraid of death, but afraid of the empty loneliness beyond it—of the cold air of an infinite space in which nothing human can live. Would his mother meet him there, he wondered, or would she put him from her, coming with blood upon his hands? Next he thought of Eva, and in his solitude a tear gathered in his dark eyes, it seemed so hard to go to that other place without her.

CHAPTER XVI

MADAME'S WORK

Presently the eastern sky began to be barred with rays of light, and Ernest knew that the dawn was near.

Rising with a sigh, he made his last preparations, inwardly determining that, if he was to die, he would die in a way befitting all English gentlemen. There should be no sign of his fears on his face when he looked at his adversary's pistol.

Presently there came a soft knock at the door, and Mr. Alston entered with his shoes off. In his hand he held the case containing the two Smith & Wessons.

"We must be off presently," he said. "I just heard Captain Justice go down. Look here, Kershaw, do you understand anything about these?" and he tapped the Smith & Wessons.

"Yes; I have often practised with a pair of old duelling pistols at home. I used to be a very fair shot with them."

"That is lucky. Now take one of these revolvers; I want to give you a lesson, and accustom you to handle it."

"No, I will not. It would not be fair to the other man. If I did, and killed him, I should feel like a murderer."

"As you like; but I am going to tell you something, and give you a bit of advice. These revolvers are hair-triggered; I had the scears filed. When the word is given, bring the barrel of your pistol down till you get the sight well on to your antagonist, somewhere about his chest, then press the trigger, do not pull it, remember that. If you do as I tell you, he will never hear the report. Above all, do not lose your nerve; and don't be sentimental and fire in the air, or any such nonsense, for that is a most futile proceeding, morally, and in every other way. Mark my words, if you do not kill him, he will kill you. He intends to kill you, and you are in the right. Now we must be going. Your luggage is in the hall, is it not?"

"All except this bag."

"Very good; bring it down with you. My boy will bring it to the boat with my own. If you are not hit, you will do well to get out of this as soon as possible. I mean to make for Southampton as straight as I can. There is a vessel sailing for South Africa on Friday morning; I shall embark in her. We will settle what you are to do afterwards."

"Yes," said Ernest, with a smile, "there is no need to talk of that at present."

Five minutes afterwards they met in the hall, and slipped quietly out through the door that always stood open all night for the accommodation of visitors addicted to late hours. Following the street that Captain Justice had pointed out, they descended to the beach, and, turning to the right, walked along it leisurely. The early morning air was very sweet, and all nature smiled dimly upon them as they went, for the sun was not yet up; but at that moment Ernest did not think much of the beauty of the morning. It all seemed like a frightful dream. At last they came to the deserted hut, looming large in the grey mist. By it stood two figures.

"They are there already," said Mr. Alston.

As they approached, the two figures lifted their hats, a compliment which they returned. Then Mr. Alston went to Captain Justice, and fell into conversation with him, and together they paced off a certain distance on the sand, marking its limits with their walking sticks. Ernest noticed that it was about the length of a short cricket pitch.

"Shall we place them?" he heard Captain Justice say.

"Not just yet," was the reply; "there is barely light enough."

"Now, gentlemen," said Mr. Alston presently, "I have prepared in duplicate a paper setting forth as fairly as I can the circumstances under which this unhappy affair has come about. I propose to read it to you, and to ask you all to sign it, as a protection to—to us all. I have brought a pen and a pocket ink-pot with me for that purpose."

Nobody objected, so he read the paper. It was short, concise, and just, and they all signed it as it stood. Ernest's hand shook a good deal as he did so.

"Come, that won't do," said Mr. Alston, encouragingly, as he pocketed one copy of the document after handing the other to Captain Justice. "Shake yourself together, man!"

But for all his brave words he looked the more nervous of the two.

"I wish to say," began Ernest, addressing himself to all the other three, "that this quarrel is none of my seeking. I could not in honour give up the note the lady wrote to me. But I feel that this is a dreadful business; and if you," addressing his cousin, "are ready to apologise for what you said about my mother, I am ready to do the same for attacking you."

Mr. Hugh Kershaw smiled bitterly, and, turning, said something to his second. Ernest caught the words "white feather."

"Mr. Hugh Kershaw refuses to offer any apology; he expects one," was Captain Justice's ready answer.

"Then if any blood is shed, on his head be it!" said Mr. Alston solemnly. "Come let us get it over."

Each took his man and placed him by one of the sticks, and then handed him a revolver.

"Stand sideways, and remember what I told you," whispered Mr. Alston.

"Are you ready, gentlemen?" asked Captain Justice presently.

There was no answer; but Ernest felt his heart stand still, and a mist gathered before his eyes. At that moment he heard a lark rise into the air near him and begin to sing. Unless he could get his sight back he felt that he was lost.

"One:" The mist cleared away from his eyes; he saw his adversary's pistol-barrel pointing steadily at him.

"Two:" A ray broke from the rising sun, and caught a crystal pin Hugh Kershaw incautiously wore. Instinctively Ernest remembered Mr. Alston's advice, and lowered the sight of his long barrel till it was dead on the crystal pin. Curiously enough, it reminded him at that moment of the eyes in the witch's head at Dum's Ness. His vital forces rose to the emergency, and his arm grew as steady as a rock. Then came a pause that seemed hours long.

"Three:" There was a double report, and Ernest became aware of a commotion in his hair. Hugh Kershaw flung up his arms wildly, sprang a few inches off the ground, and fell backwards. Great God, it was over!

Ernest staggered a moment from the reaction, and then ran with the others towards his cousin—nay, towards what had been his cousin. He was lying on his back upon the sand, his wide-opened eyes staring up at the blue sky, as though to trace the flight of the spirit, his arms extended. The heavy revolver-ball had struck near the crystal pin, and then passed upwards through the throat and out at the base of the head, shattering the spinal column.

"He is dead," said Captain Justice, solemnly.

Ernest wrung his hands.

"I have killed him," he said—"I have killed my own cousin!"

"Young man," said Mr. Alston, "do not stand there wringing your hands, but thank providence for your own escape. He was very near killing you, let me tell you. Is your head cut?"

Instinctively Ernest took off his hat, and as he did so some fragments of his curly hair fell to the ground. There was a neat hole through the felt, and a neat groove along his thick hair. His cousin had meant to kill him; and he was a good shot—so good that he thought that he could put a ball through Ernest's head. But he forgot that a heavy American revolver, with forty grains of powder behind the ball, is apt to throw a trifle high.

They all stood silent and looked at the body; and the lark, that had been frightened by the noise, began to sing again.

"This will not do," said Mr. Alston presently. "We had better move the body in there," and he pointed to the deserted hut. "Captain Justice, what do you intend to do?"

"Give myself up to the authorities, I suppose," was the gallant Captain's scared answer.

"Very well. I don't advise you to do that, but it you are determined to, there is no need for you to be in a hurry about it. You must give us time to get clear first."

They lifted the corpse, reverently bore it into the deserted hut, and laid it on the floor. Ernest remained standing looking at the red stain where it had been. Presently they came out again, and Mr. Alston kicked some sand over the stain and hid it.

"Now," he said, "we had better make an addition to those documents, to say how this came about."

They all went back to the hut, and the addition was made, standing there by the body. When it came to Ernest's turn to sign, he almost wished that his signature was the one missing from the foot of that ghastly postscriptum. Mr. Alston guessed his thoughts.

"The fortune of war," he said, coolly. "Now, Captain Justice, we are going to catch the early boat, and we hope that you will not give yourself up before midday, if you can help it. The inquiry into the affair will not then be held before to-morrow; and by eleven to-morrow morning I hope to have seen the last of England for some years to come."

The Captain was a good fellow at bottom, and had no wish to see others dragged into trouble.

"I shall certainly give myself up," he said; "but I don't see any reason to hurry about it. I don't think that they can do much to me here. Poor Hugh! he can well afford to wait," he added, with a sigh, glancing down at the figure that lay so still, with a coat thrown over the face. "I suppose that they will lock me up for six months—pleasant prospect! But I say, Mr. Kershaw, you had better keep clear; it will be more awkward for you. You see, he was your cousin, and by his death you become, unless I am mistaken, next heir to the title."

"Yes, I suppose so," said Ernest, vaguely.

Here it may be stated that Captain Justice found himself sadly mistaken. Instead of the six months he expected, he was arraigned for murder, and finally sentenced to a term of penal servitude. He received a pardon, however, after serving about a year of his time.

"Come, we must be off," said Mr. Alston, "or we shall be late for the boat;" and, bowing to Captain Justice, he left the hut.

Ernest followed his example, and, when he had gone a few yards, glanced round at the hateful spot. There stood Captain Justice in the doorway of the hut, looking much depressed, and there, a few yards to the left, was the impress in the sand that marked where his cousin had fallen. He never saw either the man or the place again.

"Kershaw," said Mr. Alston, "what do you propose doing?"

"I don't know."

"But you must think; remember, you are in an awkward fix. You know by English law duelling is murder; and now I come to think of it, I expect that this place is subject to the English law in criminal matters, or at least that the law is identical."

"I think I had better give myself up, like Captain Justice."

"Nonsense. You must hide away somewhere for a year or two till the row blows over."

"Where am I to hide?"

"Have you any money, or can you get any?"

"Yes, I have nearly two hundred and fifty pounds on me now."

"My word, that is fortunate! Well, now, what I have to suggest is, that you should assume a false name, and sail for South Africa with me. I am going up country on a shooting expedition, outside British territory, so there will be little fear of your being caught and extradited. Then, in a year or so, when the affair is forgotten, you can come back to England. What do you say to that?"

"I suppose I may as well go there as anywhere else. I shall be a marked man all my life, anyhow. What does it matter where I go?"

"Ah, you are down on your luck now; by-and-by you will cheer up again."

Just then they met a fisherman, who gazed at them, wondering what the two gentlemen were doing out walking at that hour; but concluding that, after the mad fashion of Englishmen, they had been to bathe, he passed them with a civil "Bonjour." Ernest coloured to the eyes under the scrutiny; he was beginning to feel the dreadful burden of his secret. Presently they reached the steamer, and found Mr. Alston's little boy Roger, who, though he was only nine years old was as quick and self-reliant as many English lads of fourteen, waiting for them by the bridge.

"Oh, here you are, father; you have been walking so long that I thought you would miss the boat. I have brought the luggage down all right, and this gentleman's too."

"That's right, my lad. Kershaw, do you go and take the tickets; I want to get rid of this;" and he tapped the revolver-case, that was concealed beneath his coat.

Ernest did so, and presently met Mr. Alston on the boat. A few minutes more and, to his intense relief, she cast off and stood out to sea. There were not very many passengers on board, and those there were, were too much taken up in making preparations to be sea-sick to take any notice of Ernest. Yet he could not shake himself free from the idea that everybody knew that he had just killed a man. His own self-consciousness was so intense that he saw his guilt on the faces of all he met. He gazed around him in awe, expecting every moment to be greeted as a murderer. Most people who have ever done anything they should not are acquainted with this sensation.

Overcome with this idea, he took refuge in his berth, nor did he emerge therefrom till the boat reached Weymouth. There both he and Mr. Alston bought some rough clothes, and, to a great extent, succeeded in disguising themselves; then made their way across country to Southampton in the same train, but in separate compartments. Reaching Southampton without let or hindrance, they agreed to take passages in the Union Company's R.M.S. Moor, sailing on the following morning. Mr. Alston obtained a list of the passengers; fortunately there was no one among them whom he knew. For greater security, however, they took steerage passages, and booked themselves under assumed names. Ernest took his second Christian name, and figured on the passenger list as E. Beyton, while Mr. Alston and his boy assumed the name of James. They took their passages at different times, and feigned to be unknown to each other. These precautions they found to be doubly necessary, inasmuch as at Southampton Mr. Alston managed to get hold of a book on English criminal law, from which it appeared that the fact of the duel having been fought in Guernsey did not in the least clear them from the legal consequences of the act, as they had vaguely supposed would be the case, on the insufficient authority of Captain Justice's statement.

At last the vessel sailed, and it was with a sigh of relief that Ernest saw his native shores fade from view. As they disappeared a fellow-passenger, valet to a gentleman going to the Cape for his health, politely offered him a paper to read. It was the Standard of that day's date. He took it and glanced at the foreign intelligence. The first thing that caught his eye was the following paragraph, headed "A fatal Duel":

"The town of St. Peter's in Guernsey has been thrown into a state of consternation by the discovery of an English gentleman, who was this morning shot dead in a duel. Captain Justice, of the — Hussars, who was the unfortunate gentleman's second, has surrendered himself to the authorities. The other parties, who are at present unknown, have absconded. It is said that they have been traced to Weymouth; but there all trace of them has been lost. The cause of the duel is unknown, and in the present state of excitement it is difficult to obtain authentic information."

By the pilot who left the vessel Ernest despatched two letters, one to Eva Ceswick, and the other—which contained a copy of the memoranda drawn up before and after the duel, and attested by Mr. Alston—to his uncle. To both he told the story of his misfortune, fully and fairly, imploring the former not to forget him and to wait for happier times, and asking the forgiveness of the latter for the trouble that he had brought upon himself and all belonging to him. Should they wish to write to him, he gave his address as Ernest Beyton, Post-office, Maritzburg.

The pilot-boat hoisted her brown sail with a huge white P. upon it and vanished into the night; and Ernest, feeling that he was a ruined man, and with the stain of blood upon his hands, crept to his bunk and wept like a child.

Yesterday he had been loved, prosperous, happy, with a bright career before him. To-day he was a nameless outcast, departing into exile, and his young life shadowed by a cloud in which he could see no break.

Well might he weep; it was a hard lesson.

BOOK II

CHAPTER I

MY POOR EVA

Two days after the pilot-boat, flitting away from the vessel's side like some silent-flighted bird, had vanished into the night, Florence Ceswick happened to be walking past the village post-office on her way to pay a visit to Dorothy, when it struck her that the afternoon post must be in, and that she might as well ask if there were any letters for Dum's Ness. There was no second delivery at Kesterwick, and she knew that it was not always convenient to Mr. Cardus to send in. The civil old postmaster gave her a little bundle of letters, remarking at the same time that he thought that there was one for the Cottage.

"Is it for me, Mr. Brown?" asked Florence.

"No, miss; it is for Miss Eva."

"O, then, I will leave it; I am going up to Dum's Ness. No doubt Miss Eva will call."

She knew that Eva watched the arrival of the posts very carefully. When she got outside the office she glanced at the bundle of letters in her hand, and noticed with a start that one of them, addressed to Mr. Cardus, was in Ernest's handwriting. It bore a Southampton post-mark. What, she wondered, could he be doing at Southampton? He should have been in Guernsey.

She walked on briskly to Dum's Ness, and on her arrival found Dorothy sitting working in the sitting-room. After she had greeted her she handed over the letters.

"There is one from Ernest," she said.

"O, I am so glad!" answered Dorothy. "Who is it for?"

"For Mr. Cardus. O, here he comes."

Mr. Cardus shook hands with her, and thanked her for bringing the letters, which he turned over casually, after the fashion of a man accustomed to receive large quantities of correspondence of an uninteresting nature. Presently his manner quickened, and he opened Ernest's letter. Florence fixed her keen eyes upon him. He read the letter; she read his face.

Mr. Cardus was accustomed to conceal his emotions, but on this occasion it was clear that they were too strong for him. Astonishment and grief pursued each other across his features as he proceeded. Finally he put the letter down and glanced at an enclosure.

"What is it, Reginald, what is it?" asked Dorothy.

"It is," answered Mr. Cardus solemnly, "that Ernest is a murderer and a fugitive."

Dorothy sank into a chair with a groan, and covered her face with her hands. Florence turned ashy pale.

"What do you mean?" she said.

"Read the letter for yourself, and see. Stop, read it aloud, and the enclosure too. I may have misunderstood."

Florence did so in a quiet voice. It was wonderful how her power came out in contrast to the intense disturbance of the other two. The old man of the world shook like a leaf, the young girl stood firm as a rock. Yet, in all probability, her interest in Ernest was more intense than his.

When she had finished, Mr. Cardus spoke again.

"You see," he said, "I was right. He is a murderer and an outcast. And I loved the boy, I loved him. Well, let him go."

"O, Ernest, Ernest!" sobbed Dorothy.

Florence glanced from one to the other with contempt.

"What are you talking about?" she said at last. "What is there to make all this fuss about? 'Murderer,' indeed! Then our grandfathers were often murderers. What would you have had him do? Would you have had him give up the woman's letter to save himself? Would you have had him put up with this other man's insults about his mother? If he had, I would never have spoken to him again. Stop that groaning, Dorothy. You should be proud of him; he behaved as a gentleman should. If I had the right I should be proud of him;" and her breast heaved and the proud lips curled as she said it.

Mr. Cardus listened attentively, and it was evident that her enthusiasm moved him.

"There is something in what Florence says," he broke in. "I should not have liked the boy to show the white feather. But it is an awful business to kill one's own first cousin, especially when one is next in the entail. Old Kershaw will be furious at losing his only son, and Ernest will never be able to come back to this country while he lives, or he will set the law on him."

"It is dreadful!" said Dorothy; "just as he was beginning life, and going into a profession, and now to have to go and wander in that far-off country under a false name!"

"O, yes, it is sad enough," said Mr. Cardus; "but what is done cannot be undone. He is young, and will live it down, and if the worst comes to the worst, must make himself a home out there. But it is hard upon me, hard upon me;" and he went to his office, muttering, "hard upon me."

When Florence started upon her homeward way, the afternoon had set in wet and chilly, and the sea was hidden in wreaths of grey mist. Altogether the scene was depressing. On arrival at the Cottage she found Eva standing, the picture of melancholy, by the window, and staring out at the misty sea.

"O, Florence, I am glad that you have come home; I really began to feel inclined to commit suicide."

"Indeed! and may I ask why?"

"I don't know; the rain is so depressing, I suppose."

"It does not depress me."

"No, nothing ever does; you live in the land of perpetual calm."

"I take exercise, and keep my liver in good order. Have you been out this afternoon?"

"No."

"Ah, I thought not. No wonder you feel depressed, staying indoors all day. Why don't you go for a walk?"

"There is nowhere to go."

"Really, Eva, I don't know what has come to you lately. Why don't you go along the cliff, or stop—have you been to the post-office? I called for the Dum's Ness letters, and Mr. Brown said that there was one for you."

Eva jumped up with remarkable animation, and passed out of the room with her peculiarly light tread. The mention of that word "letter" had sufficed to change the aspect of things considerably.

Florence watched her go with a dark little smile.

"Ah," she said aloud, as the door closed, "your feet will soon fall heavily enough."

Presently Eva went out, and Florence, having thrown off her cloak, took her sister's place at the window and waited. It was seven minute's walk to the post-office. She would be back in about a quarter of an hour. Watch in hand, Florence waited patiently. Seventeen minutes had elapsed when the garden-gate was opened, and Eva re-entered, her face quite grey with pain, and furtively applying a handkerchief to her eyes. Florence smiled again.

"I thought so," she said.

From all of which it will be seen that Florence was a very remarkable woman. She had scarcely exaggerated when she said that her heart was as deep as the sea. The love that she bore Ernest was the strongest thing in all her strong and vigorous life; when every other characteristic and influence crumbled away and was forgotten, it would still remain over-mastering as ever. And when she discovered that her high love, the greatest and best part of her, had been made a plaything of by a thoughtless boy, who kissed girls on the same principle that a duck takes to water, because it came natural to him, the love in its mortal agonies gave birth to a hate destined to grow as great as itself. But, with all a woman's injustice, it was not directed towards the same object. On Ernest, indeed, she would wreak vengeance if she could, but she still loved him as dearly as at first. The revenge would be a mere episode in the history of her passion. But to her sister, the innocent woman who, she chose to consider had robbed her, she gave all that bountiful hate. Herself the more powerful character of the two, she determined upon the utter destruction of the weaker. Strong as Fate, and unrelenting as Time, she dedicated her life to that end. Everything, she said, comes to those who can wait. She forgot that the Providence above us can wait the longest of us all. In the end it is Providence that wins.

Eva came in, and Florence heard her make her way up the stairs to her room. Again she spoke to herself:

"The poor fool will weep over him and renounce him. If she had the courage she would follow him and comfort him in his trouble, and so tie him to her for ever. Oh, that I had her chance! But the chances always come to fools."

Then she went upstairs and listened outside Eva's door. She was sobbing audibly. Turning the handle, she walked casually in.

"Well, Eva, did you— Why, my dear girl, what is the matter with you?"

Eva, who was lying sobbing on her bed, turned her head to the wall and went on sobbing.

"What is the matter, Eva? If you only knew how absurd you look!"

"No-no-nothing!"

"Nonsense! People do not make such a scene as this for nothing."

No answer.

"Come, my dear, as your affectionate sister, I really must ask what has happened to you."

The tone was commanding, and half unconsciously Eva obeyed it. "Ernest!" she ejaculated.

"Well, what about Ernest? He is nothing to you, is he?"

"No—that is, yes. O, it is so dreadful! It was the letter;" and she touched a sheet of closely written paper that lay on the bed beside her.

"Well, as you do not seem to be in a condition to explain yourself, perhaps you had better let me read the letter."

"O no."

"Nonsense! Give it me; perhaps I may be able to help you;" and she took the paper from her unresisting grasp and, turning her face from the light, read it deliberately through.

It was very passionate in its terms, and rather incoherent; such a letter, in short, as a lad almost wild with love and grief would write under the circumstances.

"So," said Florence, as she coolly folded it up, "it appears that you are engaged to him."

No answer, unless sobs can be said to constitute one.

"And it seems that you are engaged to a man who has just committed a frightful murder, and run away from the consequences."

Eva sat up on the bed.

"It was not a murder; it was a duel."

"Precisely, a duel about another woman; but the law calls it murder. If he is caught he will be hanged."

"O Florence! how can you say such dreadful things?"

"I only say what is true. Poor Eva, I do not wonder that you are distressed."

"It is all so dreadful!"

"You love him, I suppose?"

"O yes, dearly."

"Then you must get over it; you must never think of him any more."

"Never think of him! I shall think of him all my life."

"That is as it may be. You must never have anything more to do with him. He has blood upon his hands, blood shed for some bad woman."

"I cannot desert him, Florence, because he has got into trouble."

"Over another woman."

A peculiar expression of pain passed over Eva's face.

"How cruel you are, Florence! He is only a boy, and boys will go wrong sometimes. Anybody can make a fool of a boy."

"And it seems that boys can make fools of some people who should know better."

"O Florence, what is to be done? You have such a clear head; tell me what I must do. I cannot give him up; I cannot indeed."

Florence seated herself on the bed beside her sister, and put an arm round her neck and kissed her. Eva was much touched at her kindness.

"My poor Eva," she said, "I am so sorry for you! But tell me, when did you get engaged to him—that evening you went out sailing together?"

"Yes."

"He kissed you, I suppose, and all that?"

"Yes. Oh, I was so happy!"

"My poor Eva!"

"I tell you I cannot give him up."

"Well, perhaps there will be no need for you to do so. But you must not answer that letter."

"Why not?"

"Because it will not do. Look at it which way you will, Ernest has just killed his own cousin in a quarrel about another woman. It is necessary that you should mark your disapproval of that in some way or other. Do not answer his letter. If in time he can wash himself clear of the reproach, and remains faithful to you, then it will be soon enough to show that you still care for him."

"But if I leave him like that, he will fall into the hands of other women, though he loves me all the time. I know him well; his is not a nature that can stand alone."

"Well, let him."

"But, Florence, you forget that I love him, too. I cannot bear to think of it. O, I love him, I love him!" and she dropped her head upon her sister's shoulder and began to sob again.

"My dear, it is just because you do love him so that you should prove him; and besides, my dear, you have your own self-respect to think of. Be guided by me, Eva; do not answer that letter; I am sure that you will regret it if you do. Let matters stand for a few months, then we can arrange a plan of action. Above all, do not let your engagement transpire to anybody. There will be a dreadful scandal about this business, and it will be most unpleasant for you, and, indeed, for us all, to have our name mixed up in the matter. Hark! there is aunt coming in. I will go and talk to her; you can stop here and recover yourself a little. You will follow my advice, will you not, dearest?"

"I suppose so," answered Eva, with a heavy sigh, as she buried her face in the pillow.

Then Florence left her.

And so it came to pass that Ernest's letter remained unanswered. But Mr. Cardus, Dorothy, and Jeremy all wrote. Mr. Cardus's letter was very kind and considerate. It expressed his deep grief at what had happened, and told him of the excitement that the duel had caused, and of the threatening letters which he had received from Sir Hugh Kershaw, who was half-wild with grief and fury at the loss of his son. Finally, it commended his wisdom in putting the seas between himself and the avengers of blood, and told him that he should not want for money, as his drafts would be honoured to the extent of a thousand a year, should he require so much—Mr. Cardus was very open-handed where Ernest was concerned; also if he required any particular sum of money for any purpose, such as to buy land or start a business, he was to let him know.

Dorothy's letter was like herself, sweet and gentle, and overflowing with womanly sympathy. She bade him not to be downhearted, but to hope for a time when all this dreadful business would be forgotten, and he would be able to return in peace to England. She bade him also, shyly enough, to remember that there was only one Power that could really wash away the stain of blood upon his hands. Every month she said she would write him a letter, whether he answered it or not. This promise she faithfully kept.

Jeremy's letter was characteristic. It is worth transcribing:

"My dear old Fellow,—Your news has knocked us all into the middle of next week. To think of your fighting a duel, and my not being there to hold the sponge! And I will tell you what it is, old chap; some of these people round here, like that old de Talor, call it murder, but that is gammon, and don't you trouble your head about it. It was he who got up the row, not you, and he tried to shoot you into the bargain. I am awfully glad that you kept your nerve and plugged him; it would have been better if you could have nailed him through the right shoulder, which would not have killed him; but at the best of times you were never good enough with a pistol for that. Don't you remember when we used to shoot with the old pistols at the man I cut out on the cliff, you were always just as likely to hit him on the head or in the stomach as through the heart? It is a sad pity that you did not practise a little more, but it is no use crying over spilt milk—and after all the shot seems to have been a very creditable one. So you are going on a shooting expedition up in Secocoeni's country. That is what I call glorious. To think of a rhinoceros makes my mouth water; I would give one of my fingers to shoot one. Life here is simply wretched now that you have gone—Mr. Cardus as glum as Titheburgh Abbey on a cloudy day, and Doll always looking as though she had been crying, or were going to cry. Old Grandfather Atterleigh is quite lively compared to those two. As for the office, I hate it, everlastingly copying deeds which I don't in the slightest understand, and adding up figures in which I make mistakes. Your respected uncle told me the other day, in his politest way, that he considered I sailed as near being a complete fool as any man he ever knew. I answered that I quite agreed with him.

"I met that young fellow Smithers the other day, the one who gave Eva that little brute of a dog. He said something disagreeable about wondering if they would hang you. I told him that I didn't know if they would or not, but unless he dropped his infernal sneer I was very sure that I would break his neck. He concluded to move on. By the way, I met Eva Ceswick herself yesterday. She looked pale, and asked if we had heard anything of you. She said that she had got a letter from you. Florence came up here, and spoke up well for you; she said that she was proud of you, or would be if she had a right to. I never liked her before, but now I think that she is a brick. Good-bye, old chap; I never wrote such a long letter before. You don't know how I miss you; life doesn't seem worth having. Yesterday was the First; I went out and killed twenty brace to my own gun—fired forty-six cartridges. Not bad, eh! And yet somehow I didn't seem to care a twopenny curse about the whole thing, though if you had been there you would have duffed them awfully. I feel sure you would have set my teeth on edge with letting them off—the birds, I mean. Mind you write to me often. Good-bye, old fellow. God bless you!

"Your affectionate friend,
"Jeremy Jones."

"P.S.—In shooting big game, a fellow told me that the top of the flank raking forward is a very deadly shot, as it either breaks the back or passes through the kidneys to the lungs and heart. I should have thought that the shot was very apt to waste itself in the flesh of the flank. Please try it, and take notes of the results."

About a fortnight after these letters, addressed Ernest Beyton, Esq., Post Office, Maritzburg, Natal, had been despatched, Kesterwick and its neighbourhood was thrown into a state of mild excitement by the announcement that Mr. Halford, the clergyman, whose health had of late been none of the best, purposed to take a year's rest, and that the Bishop had consented to the duties of his parish being carried on by a locum tenens, named the Reverend James Plowden. Mr. Halford was much liked and respected, and the intelligence was received with general regret, which was, however, tempered with curiosity as to the new-comer. Thus, when it became known that Mr. Plowden was to preach in the parish church at the evening service on the third Sunday in September, all Kesterwick was seized with profound religious fervour, and went to hear him.

The parish church at Kesterwick was unusually large and beautiful, being a relic of an age when, whatever men's lives may have been, they spared neither their money nor their thought in rearing up fitting habitations to the Deity, whom they regarded perhaps with more of superstitious awe than true religious feeling. Standing as it did somewhat back from the sea, it alone had escaped the shock of the devouring waves, and remained till this day a monument of architectural triumph. Its tall tower, pointing like a great finger up to heaven, looked very solemn on that quiet September evening as the crowd of church-goers passed beneath its shadow into the old doorway, through which most of them had been carried to their christening, and would in due time be carried to their burial. At least so thought Eva and Dorothy, as they stood for a moment by the monument to "five unknown sailors," washed ashore after a great gale, and buried in a common grave. How many suffering, erring human beings had stood upon the same spot and thought the same thoughts! How many more now sleeping in the womb of time would stand there and think them, when these two had suffered and erred their full, and been long forgotten!

They formed a strange contrast, those two sweet women, as they passed together into the sacred stillness of the church—the one stately, dark, and splendid, with an unrestful trouble in her eyes; the other almost insignificant in figure, but pure and patient of face, and with steady blue eyes which never wavered. Did they guess, those two, as they walked thus together, how closely their destines were linked? Did they know that each at heart was striving for the same prize—a poor one indeed, but still all the world to them? Perhaps they did, very vaguely, and it was the pressure of their common trouble that drew them closer together in those days. But if they did, they never spoke of it; and as for little Dorothy, she never dreamed of winning. She was content to be allowed to toil along in the painful race.

When they reached the pew that the Ceswicks habitually occupied, they found Miss Ceswick and Florence already there. Jeremy had refused to come; he had a most unreasonable antipathy to parsons. Mr. Halford he liked, but of this new man he would have none. The general curiosity to see him was to Jeremy inexplicable, his opinion being that he should soon see a great deal more of him than he liked. "Just like a pack of girls running after a new doll," he growled; "well, there is one thing, you will soon be tired of hearing him squeak."

As the service went on, the aisles of the great church grew dim except where the setting sun shot a crimson shaft through the west window, which wandered from spot to spot and face to face, and made them glorious. When it came to the hymn before the sermon, Eva could scarcely see to read, and with the exception of the crimson pencil of sunlight that came through the head of the Virgin Mary, and wavered restlessly about, and the strong glow of the lights upon the pulpit, the church was almost dark.

When the new clergyman, Mr. Plowden, ascended the steps of the ancient pulpit and gave out his text, Eva looked at him in common with the rest of the congregation. Mr. Plowden was a large man of a somewhat lumbering make. His head, too, was large, and covered with masses of rather coarse-textured black hair. The forehead was prominent, and gave signs of intellectual power; the eyebrows thick and strongly-marked, and in curious contrast to the cold light-grey eyes that played unceasingly beneath them. All the lower part of the face, which, to judge from the purple hue of the skin, Nature had intended should be plentifully clothed with hair, was clean shaven, and revealed a large jaw, square chin, and pair of thick lips. Altogether Mr. Plowden was considered a fine man, and his face was generally spoken of as "striking." Perhaps the most curious thing about it, however, was a species of varicose vein on the forehead, which was generally quite unnoticeable, but whenever he was excited or nervous stood out above the level of the skin in the form of a perfect cross. It was thus visible when Eva looked at him, and it struck her as being an unpleasant mark to have on one's forehead. She turned her eyes away—the man did not please her fastidious taste—and listened for his voice. Presently it came; it was powerful and even musical, but coarse.

"He is not a gentleman," thought Eva to herself; and then dismissing him and his sermon too from her mind, she leaned back against the poppy-head at the end of the pew, half-closed her eyes, and let her thoughts wander in the way that thoughts have the power to do in church. Far cross the sea they flew, to where a great vessel, labouring in a heavy gale, was ploughing her steady way along—to where a young man stood clinging to the iron stanchions, and gazed out into the darkness with sorrow in his eyes.

Wonderfully soft and tender grew her beautiful face as the vision passed before her soul; the ripe lips quivered, and there was a world of love in the half-opened eyes. And just then the wandering patch of glory perceived her, settled on her like a butterfly upon a flower, and for a while wandered no longer.

Suddenly she became aware of a momentary pause in the even flow of the clergyman's eloquence, and waking from her reverie, glanced up at that spot of light surrounding him, and as she did so it struck her that she herself was illuminated with a more beautiful light—that he and she alone were distinguishable out of all the people beneath that roof.

The same thought had evidently struck Mr. Plowden, for he was gazing intently at her.

Instinctively she drew back into the shadow, and Mr. Plowden went on with his sermon. But he had driven away poor Eva's vision; there only remained of it the sad reproachful look of those dark eyes.

Outside the church Dorothy found Jeremy waiting to escort her home. They all went together as far as the Cottage. When they got clear of the crowd Florence spoke:

"What a good-looking man Mr. Plowden is, and how well he preached!"

"I did not like him much," said Dorothy.

"What do you think of him, Eva?" asked Florence.

"I? Oh, I do not know. I do not think he is a gentleman."

"I am sure that he is not," put in Jeremy. "I saw him by the post-office this morning. He is a cad."

"Rather a sweeping remark that, is it not, Mr. Jones?" said Florence.

"I don't know if it is sweeping or not," answered Jeremy sententiously, "but I am sure that it is true."

Then they said good-night, and went their separate ways.

CHAPTER III

EVA TAKES A DISTRICT

The Reverend James Plowden was born of rich but honest parents in the sugar-broking way. He was one of a large family, who were objects of anxious thought to Mr. and Mrs. Plowden. These worthy people, aware of the disadvantages under which they laboured in the matter of education, determined that neither trouble nor money should be spared to make their children "genteel." And so it came to pass that the "mansion" near Bloomsbury was overrun with the most expensive nurses, milliners, governesses, and tutors, all straining every nerve to secure the perfect gentility of the young Plowdens. The result was highly ornamental, but scarcely equivalent to the vast expense incurred. The Plowden youth of both sexes may be said to have been painted, and varnished, and gilded into an admirable imitation of gentlefolks; but if the lacquer-work would stand the buffetings of the world's weather was another question, and one which does not concern us, except in so far as it has to do with a single member of the family.

Master James Plowden came about halfway down the family list, but he might just as well have stood at the head of it, for he ruled his brothers and sisters—old and young—with a heavy rod. He was the strong one of the family, strong both in mind and body, and he had a hand of iron.

For his misdeeds were his brothers thrashed, preferring to take those ills they knew of from the hands of the thrasher rather than endure the unimagined horrors brother James would make ready for them should they venture to protest.

Thus it was that he became to be considered par excellence the good boy of the family, as he was certainly the clever one, and bore every sort of blushing honour thick upon him.

It was to an occurrence in his boyhood that Mr. Plowden owed his parents' determination to send him into the Church. His future career had always been a matter of much speculation to them, for they belonged to that class of people who love to arrange their infants' destines when the infants themselves are still in the cradle, and argue their fitness for certain lines of life from remarks which they make at three years old.

Now, James's mamma had a very favourite parrot with a red tail, and out of this tail it was James's delight to pull the feathers, having discovered that so doing gave a parrot a lively twinge of pain. The onus of the feather-pulling, if discovered, was shouldered on to a chosen brother, who was promptly thrashed.

But on one occasion things went wrong with Master James. The parrot was climbing up the outside of his cage, presenting the remainder of his tail to the hand of the spoiler in a way that was irresistibly seductive. But, aware of the fact that his enemy was in the neighbourhood, he kept a careful lookout from the corner of his eye, and the moment that he saw James's stealthy hand draw near his tail made a sudden dart at it, and actually succeeded in making its powerful beak meet through its forefinger. James shrieked with pain and fury, and shaking the bird on to the floor, stunned it with a book. But he was not satisfied with this revenge, for, as soon as he saw that it could no longer bite, he seized it and twisted its neck.

"There, you devil!" he said, throwing the creature into the cage. "Hullo, something has burst in my forehead!"

"O James, what have you done?" said his little brother Montague, well knowing that he had a lively personal interest in James's misdoings.

"Nonsense! what have you done? Now remember, Montague, you killed the parrot."

Just then Mr. and Mrs. Plowden came in from a drive, and a very lively scene ensued, into which we need not enter. Suffice it to say that, all evidence to the contrary notwithstanding, James was acquitted on the ground of general good character, and Montague, howling and protesting his innocence, was led off to execution. Justly fearful lest something further should transpire, James was hurriedly leaving the room, when his mother called him back.

"Why, what is that on your forehead?"

"Don't know," answered James; "something went snap there just now."

"Well I never! Just look at the boy, John; he has got a cross upon his forehead."

Mr. Plowden papa examined the phenomenon very carefully, and then, solemnly removing his spectacles, remarked with much deliberation:

"Elizabeth, that settles the point."

"What point, John?"

"What point! Why, the point of the boy's profession. It is, as you remark, a cross upon his forehead. Good!—he shall go into the Church. Now, I must decline to be argued with, Elizabeth. The matter is settled."

And so in due course James Plowden, Esq., went to Cambridge, and became the Reverend James Plowden.

Shortly after the Reverend James had started in life as a curate—having first beguiled his parents into settling on himself a portion just twice as large as that to which he was entitled—he found it convenient to cut off his connection with a family he considered vulgar, and a drag upon his professional success. But somehow, with all his gifts—and undoubtedly he was by nature well-endowed, especially as regards his mind, that was remarkable for a species of hard cleverness and persuasive power—and with all the advantages which he derived from being in receipt of an independent income, the Reverend James had not hitherto proved a conspicuous success. He had held some important curacies, and of late had acted as the locum tenens of several gentlemen who, like Mr. Halford, through loss of health or other reasons, had been called away from their livings for a length of time.

But from all these places the Reverend James had departed without regret, nor had there been any very universal lamentations over his going. The fact of the matter was that the Reverend James was not a popular man. He had ability in plenty, and money in plenty, and would expend both without stint if he had an end to gain. He was more or less of a good companion, too, in the ordinary sense of the word; that is, he could make himself agreeable in a rough, exaggerated kind of way to both men and women. Indeed, by the former he was often spoken of carelessly as a good "fellow"; but women, or rather ladies, following their finer instincts, disliked him intensely. He jarred upon them.

Of course, it is impossible to lay down any fixed rule about men, but there are two tokens by which they may be known. The first is by their friends; the second by the degree of friendship and affection to which they are admitted by women. The man to whom members of the other sex attach themselves is in ninety-nine cases out of a hundred a good fellow, and women's instinct tells them so, or they would not love him. It may be urged that women often love blackguards. To this the answer is, that there must be a good deal of good mixed up with the blackguardism. Show me the man whom two or three women of his own rank love or have loved with all their honest hearts, and I will trust all I have into his hands and not be a penny the poorer.

But women did not love the Reverend James Plowden, although he had for several years come to the conclusion that it was desirable that they should, or rather that one of them should. In plain language he had for some years past thought that he would improve his position by getting married. He was a shrewd man, and he could not disguise from himself the fact that so far he was not altogether a success. He had tried his best, but, with all his considerable advantages, he had failed. There was only one avenue to success which he had not tried, and that was marriage. Marriage with a woman of high caste, quick intellect, and beauty, might give him the tone that his social position so badly needed. He was a man in a good position, he had money, he had intelligence of a robust if of a coarse order, he had fairly good looks, and he was only thirty-five; why should he not marry blood, brains, and beauty, and shine with a reflected splendour?

Such were the thoughts which were simmering in the astute brain of the Reverend James Plowden when he first set eyes upon Eva Ceswick in the old church at Kesterwick.

Within a week or so of his arrival, Mr. Plowden, in his character of spiritual adviser to the motley Kesterwick flock, paid a ceremonious call on the Misses Ceswick. They were all at home.

Miss Ceswick and Florence welcomed him graciously; Eva politely, but with an air that said plainly that he interested her not at all. Yet it was to Eva that he chiefly directed himself. He took this opportunity to inform them all, especially Eva, that he felt the responsibilities of his position as locum tenens to weigh heavily upon him. He appealed to them all, especially Eva, to help him bear his load. He was going to institute a new system of district visiting. Would they all, especially Eva, assist him? If they would, the good work was already half done. There was so much for young ladies to do. He could assure them, from his personal experience, that one visit from a young lady, however useless she might be in a general way, which his instinct assured him these particular young ladies before him were not, had more influence with a distressed and godless family than six from well-meaning but unsympathetic clergymen like himself. Might he rely on their help?

"I am afraid that I am too old for that sort of thing, Mr. Plowden," answered Miss Ceswick. "You might see what you can do with my nieces."

"I am sure that I shall be delighted to help," said Florence, "if Eva will bear me company. I always feel a shyness about intruding myself into cottages unsupported."

"Your shyness is not surprising, Miss Ceswick. I suffered from it myself for many years, but at last I have, I am thankful to say, got the better of it. But I am sure that we shall not appeal to your sister in vain."

"I shall be glad to help if you think that I can do any good," put in Eva, thus directly appealed to; "but I must tell you I have no great faith in myself."

"Do the work, Miss Ceswick, and the faith will come; sow the seed and the tree will spring up, and bear fruit too in due season."

There was no reply, so he continued: "Then I have your permission to put you down for a district?"

"O yes, Mr. Plowden," answered Florence. "Will you take some more tea?"

Mr. Plowden would take no more tea, but went on his way to finish the day's work he had mapped out for himself—for he worked hard and according to a strict rule—reflecting that Eva Ceswick was the loveliest woman he had ever seen.

"I think that we must congratulate you on a conquest, Eva," said Miss Ceswick, cheerfully, as the front door closed. "Mr. Plowden never took his eyes off you, and really, my dear, I do not wonder at it; you look charming."

Eva flushed up angrily.

"Nonsense, aunt!" she said, and left the room.

"Really," said Miss Ceswick, "I don't know what has come to Eva lately, she is so very strange."

"I expect that you have touched her on a sore point. I rather fancy that she has taken a liking to Mr. Plowden," said Florence, dryly.

"O, indeed!" answered the old lady, nodding her head wisely.

In due course a district was assigned to the two Miss Ceswicks, and for her part Eva was glad of the occupation. It brought her a good deal into contact with Mr. Plowden, which was not altogether pleasant to her, for she cherished a vague dislike of the clergyman, and did not admire his shifty eyes. But, as she got to know him better, she could find nothing to justify her dislike. He was not, it is true, quite a gentleman, but that was his misfortune. His manner to herself was subdued and almost deferential; he never obtruded himself upon her society, though somehow he was in it almost daily. Indeed, he even succeeded in raising her to some enthusiasm about her work, a quality in which poor Eva had of late been sadly lacking. She thought him a very good clergyman, with his heart in his duty. But she disliked him all the same.

Eva never answered Ernest's letter. Once she began an answer, but bethought her of Florence's sage advice, and changed her mind. "He will write again," she said to herself. She did not know Ernest; his was not a nature to humble itself before a woman. Could she have seen her lover hanging about the steps of the Maritzburg post-office when the English mail was being delivered, in order to go back to the window when the people had dispersed, and ask the tired clerk if he was "sure" that there were no more letters for Ernest Beyton, and get severely snubbed for his pains, perhaps her heart would have relented. And yet it was a performance which poor Ernest went through once a week out there in Natal.

One mail-day Mr. Alston went with him.

"Well, Ernest, has it come?" he asked, as he came down the steps, a letter from Dorothy in his hand.

"No, Alston, and never will. She has thrown me over."

Mr. Alston took his arm, and walked away with him across the market-square.

"Look here, my lad," he said; "the woman who deserts a man in trouble, or as soon as his back is turned, is worthless. It is a sharp lesson to learn, but, as most men have cause to know, the world is full of sharp lessons and worthless women. You know that she got your letter?"

"Yes, she told my friend so."

"Then I tell you that your Eva, or whatever her name is, is more worthless than most of them. She has been tried and found wanting. Look," he went on, pointing to a shapely Kafir girl passing with a pot of native beer on her head, "you had better take that Intombi to wife than such a woman as this Eva. She at any rate would stand by you in trouble, and if you fell would stop to be killed over your dead body. Come, be a man, and have done with her."

"Ay, by Heaven I will!" answered Ernest.

"That's right; and now, look here, the waggons will be at Lydenburg in a week. Let us take the post-cart to-morrow and go up. Then we can have a month's vilderbeeste and koodoo shooting until it is safe to go into the fever country. Once you get among the big game you won't think any more about that woman. Women are all very well in their way, but if it comes to choosing between them and big game shooting, give me the big game."

CHAPTER IV

JEREMY'S IDEA OF A SHAKING

Two months or so after Ernest's flight there came a letter from him to Mr. Cardus in answer to the one sent by his uncle. He thanked his uncle warmly for his kindness, and more especially for not joining in the hue and cry against him. As regarded money, he hoped to be able to make a living for himself, but if he wanted any he would draw. The letter, which was short, ended thus:

"Thank Doll and Jeremy for their letters. I would answer them, but I am too down on my luck to write much; writing stirs up so many painful memories, and makes me think of all the dear folks at home more than is good for me. The fact is, my dear uncle, what between one thing and another, I never was so miserable in my life, and as for loneliness, I never knew what it meant before. Sometimes I wish that my cousin had hit me instead of my hitting him, and that I was dead and buried, clean out of the way. Alston, who was my second in that unhappy affair, and with whom I am going up-country shooting, has been most kind to me, and has introduced me to a good many people here. They are very hospitable—everybody is hospitable in a colony; but somehow a hundred new faces cannot make up for one old one, and I should think old Atterleigh a cheerful companion beside the best of them. What is more, I feel myself an impostor intruding myself on them under an assumed name. Good-bye, my dear uncle. It would be difficult for me to explain how grateful I am for your goodness to me. Love to dear Doll and Jeremy.

"Ever your affectionate nephew,
"E. K."

All the party at Dum's Ness were much touched by this letter, more especially Dorothy, who could not bear to think of Ernest all alone out there in that strange far-off land. Her tender little heart grew alive with love and sorrow as she lay awake at night and thought of him travelling over the great African plains. She got all the books that were to be had about South Africa and read them, so that she might be the better able to follow his life in her thoughts. One day when Florence came to see her she read her part of Ernest's letter, and when she had finished she was astonished to see a tear in her visitor's keen eyes. She liked Florence the better for that tear. Could she have seen the conflict that was raging in the fierce heart of the woman before her, she would have started from her as though she had been a poisonous snake. The letter touched Florence—touched her to the quick. The tale of Ernest's loneliness almost overcame her resolution, for she alone knew why he was so utterly lonely, and what it was that crushed him. Had Ernest alone been concerned, it is probable that she would then and there have thrown up her cruel game; but he was not alone concerned. There was her sister who had robbed her of her lover—her sister whose loveliness was a standing affront to her as her sweetness was a standing reproach. She was sorry for Ernest, and would have been glad to make him happier, but as that could only be done by foregoing revenge upon her sister, Ernest must continue to suffer. And after all why should he not suffer? she argued. Did not she suffer?

When Florence got home she told Eva about the letter from her love, but she said nothing of his evident distress. He was making friends, he expected great pleasure from his shooting—altogether he was getting on well.

Eva listened, hardened her heart, and went out district visiting with Mr. Plowden.

Time went on, and no letters came from Ernest. One month, two months, six months passed, and there was no intelligence of him. Dorothy grew very anxious, and so did Mr. Cardus, but they did not speak of the matter much except to remark that the reason no doubt was that he was away on his shooting excursion.

Jeremy also, in his slow way, grew intensely preoccupied with the fact that they never heard from Ernest now, and that life was consequently a blank. He sat upon the stool in his uncle's outer office and made pretence to copy deeds and drafts, but in reality he occupied his time in assiduously polishing his nails and thinking. As for the deeds and drafts, he gave them to his grandfather to copy. "It kept the old gentleman employed," he would explain to Dorothy, "and from indulging in bad thoughts about the devil."

But it was one night out duck-shooting that his great inspiration came. It was a bitter night, a night on which no sane creature except Jeremy would ever have dreamed of going to shoot ducks or anything else. The marshes were partially frozen, and a fierce east wind was blowing across them; but utterly regardless of the cold, there sat Jeremy under the ice of a dike bank, listening for the sound of the ducks' wings as they passed to their feeding-grounds, and occasionally getting a shot at them as they crossed the moon above him. There were not many ducks, and the solitude and silence were inductive to contemplation. Ernest did not write. Was he dead? Not probable, or they would have heard of it. Where was he, then? Impossible to say, impossible to discover. Was it impossible? "Swish, swish, bang!" and down came a mallard at his feet. A quick shot, that! Yes, it was impossible; they had no means of inquiry here. The inquiry, if any, must be made, on the other side of the water. But who was to make it? Ah! an idea struck him. Why should not he, Jeremy, make that inquiry? Why should he not go to South Africa and look for Ernest? A flight of duck passed over his head unheeded. What did he care for duck? He had solved the problem which had been troubling him all these months. He would go to South Africa and look for Ernest. If Mr. Cardus would not give him the money, he would work his way out. Anyhow he would go. He could bear the suspense no longer.

Jeremy rose in the new-found strength of his purpose, and gathering up the slain—there were only three—whistled to his retriever, and made his way back to Dum's Ness.

He found Mr. Cardus and Dorothy by the fire in the sitting-room. "Hard-riding Atterleigh" was there too, in his place in the inglenook, a riding-whip in his ink-stained hand, with which he was tapping his top-boot. They turned as he entered, except his grandfather, who did not hear him.

"What sport have you had, Jeremy?" asked his sister, with a sad little smile. Her face had grown very sad of late.

"Three ducks," he answered shortly, advancing his powerful form out of the shadows into the firelight. "I came home just as they were beginning to fly."

"You found it cold, I suppose?" said Mr. Cardus, absently. They had been talking of Ernest, and he was still thinking of him.

"No, I did not think of the cold. I came home because I had an idea."

Both his hearers looked up surprised. Ideas were not very common to Jeremy, or if they were he kept them to himself.

"Well, Jeremy?" said Dorothy, inquiringly.

"Well, it is this. I cannot stand it about Ernest any longer and I am going to look for him. If you won't give me the money," he went on, addressing Mr. Cardus almost fiercely, "I will work my way out. It is no credit to me," he added; "I lead a dog's life while I don't know where he is."

Dorothy flushed a pale pink with pleasure. Rising, she went up to her great strong brother, and standing on tip-toe, managed to kiss him on the chin.

"That is like you, Jeremy dear," she said softly.

Mr. Cardus looked up too, and after his fashion let his eyes wander round Jeremy before he spoke.

"You shall have as much money as you like, Jeremy," he said presently; "and if you bring Ernest back safe, I will leave you twenty thousand pounds;" and he struck his hand down upon his knee, an evidence of excitement which it was unusual for him to display.

"I don't want your twenty thousand pounds—I want Ernest," answered the young man, gruffly.

"No. I know you don't, my lad; I know you don't. But find him and keep him safe, and you shall have it. Money is not to be sneezed at, let me tell you. I say keep him, for I forgot you cannot bring him back till this accursed business has blown over. When will you go?"

"By the next mail, of course. They leave every Friday; I will not waste a day. To-day is Saturday; I will sail next Friday."

"That is right; you shall go at once. I will give you a cheque for five hundred pounds to-morrow, and mind, Jeremy, you are not to spare money. If he has gone to the Zambesi, you must follow him. Never think of the money; I will think of that."

Jeremy soon made his preparations. They consisted chiefly of trifles. He was to leave Dum's Ness early on the Thursday. On the Wednesday afternoon it occurred to him that he might as well tell Eva Ceswick that he was going in search of Ernest, and ask if she had any message. Jeremy was the only person, or thought that he was the only person, in the secret of Ernest's affection for Eva. Ernest had asked him to keep it secret, and he had kept it secret as the dead, never breathing a word of it, even to his sister.

It was about five o'clock on a windy March afternoon when he set out for the Cottage. On the edge of the hamlet of Kesterwick, some three hundred yards from the cliff, stood two or three little hovels, turning their naked faces to the full fury of the sea-blast. He was drawing near to these when he came to a stile which gave passage over a sod wall that ran to the edge of the cliff, marking the limits of the village common. As he approached the stile the wind brought him the sound of voices—a man's and a woman's—engaged apparently in angry dispute on the farther side of the wall. Instead of getting over the stile, he stepped to the right and looked over the wall, and saw the new clergyman, Mr. Plowden, standing with his back towards him, and, apparently very much against her will, holding Eva Ceswick by the hand. Jeremy was too far off to overhear his words, but from his voice it was clear that Plowden was talking in an excited, masterful tone. Just then Eva turned her head a little, and he did hear what she said, her voice being so much clearer:

"No, Mr. Plowden, no! Let go my hand. Ah! why will you not take an answer?"

Just at that moment she succeeded in wrenching her imprisoned hand from his strong grasp, and without waiting for any more words, set off towards Kesterwick almost at a run.

Jeremy was a man of slow mind, though when once his mind was made up, it was of a singularly determined nature. At first he did not quite take in the full significance of the scene, but when he did a great red flush spread over his honest face, and the big grey eyes sparkled dangerously. Presently Mr. Plowden turned and saw him. Jeremy noticed that the "sign of the cross" was remarkably visible on his forehead, and that his face wore an expression by no means pleasant to behold—anything but a Christian, in short.

"Hullo!" he said to Jeremy; "what are you doing there?"

Before answering, Jeremy put his hand on the top of the sod wall, and vaulting over, walked straight up to the clergyman.

"I was watching you," he said, looking him straight in the eyes.

"Indeed!—an honourable employment: eavesdropping I think it is generally called."

Whatever had passed between Mr. Plowden and Eva Ceswick, it had clearly not improved the former's temper.

"What do you mean?"

"I mean what I say."

"Well, Mr. Plowden, I may as well tell you what I mean; I am not good at talking, but I know that I shall be able to make you understand. I saw you just now assaulting Miss Ceswick."

"It is a lie!"

"That is not a gentlemanlike word, Mr. Plowden, but as you are not a gentleman I will overlook it." Jeremy, after the dangerous fashion of the Anglo-Saxon race, always got wonderfully cool as a row thickened. "I repeat that I saw you holding her, notwithstanding her struggles to get away."

"And what is that to you, confound you!" said Mr. Plowden, shaking with fury, and raising a thick stick he held in his hand in a suggestive manner.

"Don't lose your temper, and you shall hear. Miss Eva Ceswick is engaged to my friend Ernest Kershaw, or something very like it, and, as he is not here to look after his own interests, I must look after them for him."

"Ah, yes," answered Mr. Plowden, with a ghastly smile, "I have heard of that. The murderer, you mean."

"I recommend you, Mr. Plowden, in your own interest, to be a little more careful in your terms."

"And supposing that there has been something between your—your friend—"

"Much better term, Mr. Plowden."

"And Miss Eva Ceswick, what, I should like to know, is there to prevent her having changed her mind?"

Jeremy laughed aloud, it must be admitted rather insolently, and in a way calculated to irritate people of meeker mind than Mr. Plowden.

"To any one, Mr. Plowden, who has the privilege of your acquaintance, and who also knows Ernest Kershaw, your question would seem absurd. You see, there are some people between whom there can be no comparison. It is not possible that, after caring for Ernest, any woman could care for you;" and Jeremy laughed again.

Mr. Plowden's thick lips turned quite pale, the velnous cross upon his forehead throbbed until Jeremy thought that it would burst, and his eyes shone with the concentrated light of hate. His vanity was his weakest point. He controlled himself with an effort, however; though if there had been any deadly weapon at hand it might have gone hard with Jeremy.

"Perhaps you will explain the meaning of your interference and your insolence, and let me go on?"

"Oh, with pleasure," answered Jeremy, with refreshing cheerfulness. "It is just this: if I catch you at any such tricks again, you shall suffer for it. One can't thrash a clergyman, and one can't fight him, because he won't fight; but look here, one can shake him, for that leaves no marks; and if you go on with these games, so sure as my name is Jeremy Jones, I will shake your teeth down your throat! Good-night!" and Jeremy turned to go.

It is not wise to turn one's back upon an infuriated animal and at that moment Mr. Plowden was nothing more. Even as he turned, Jeremy remembered this, and gave himself a slew to one side. It was fortunate for him that he did so, for at that moment Mr. Plowden's heavy blackthorn stick, directed downwards with all the strength of Mr. Plowden's powerful arm, passed within a few inches of his head, out of which, had he not turned, it would have probably knocked the brains. As it was, it struck the ground with such force that the jar sent it flying out of its owner's hands.

"Ah, you would!" was Jeremy's reflection as he sprang at his assailant.

Now Mr. Plowden was a very powerful man, but he was no match for Jeremy, who in after days came to be known as the strongest man in the east of England, and so was destined to find him out. Once Jeremy got a grip of him—for his respect for the Church prevented him from trying to knock him down—he seemed to crumple up like a piece of paper in his iron grasp. Jeremy could easily have thrown him, but he would not; he had his own ends in view. So he just held the Reverend James tight enough to prevent him from doing him any serious injury, and let him struggle frantically till he thought he was sufficiently exhausted for his purpose. Then Jeremy suddenly gave him a violent twist, got behind him, and set to work with a will to fulfil his promise of a shaking. O, what a shake that was! First of all he shook him backwards and forwards for Ernest's sake, then he alternated the motion and shook him from side to side for his own sake, and finally he shook him every possible way for the sake of Eva Ceswick.

It was a wonderful sight to see the great burly clergyman, his hat off, his white tie undone, and his coat-tails waving like streamers, bounding and gambolling on the breezy cliffs, his head, legs, and arms jerking in every possible direction, like those of a galvanised frog; while behind him, his legs slightly apart to get a better grip of the ground, and his teeth firmly clinched, Jeremy shook away with the fixity of Fate.

At last, getting exhausted, he stopped, and holding Mr. Plowden still, gave him a drop-kick—only one. But Jeremy's leg was very strong, and he always wore thick boots, and the result was startling. Mr. Plowden rose some inches off the ground, and went on his face into a furze-bush.

"He will hardly like to show that honourable wound," reflected Jeremy, as he wiped the perspiration from his brow with every sign of satisfaction.

He went and picked his fallen enemy out of the bush, where he had nearly fainted, smoothed his clothes, tied the white tie as nearly as he could, and put the wide hat on the dishevelled hair. Then he sat him down on the furze to recover himself.

"Good-night, Mr. Plowden, good-night. Next time you wish to hit a man with a big stick, do not wait till his back is turned. Ah, I daresay your head aches. I should advise you to go home and have a nice sleep."

And Jeremy departed on his way, filled with a fearful joy.

When he reached the Cottage, he found everything in a state of confusion. Miss Ceswick, it appeared, had been suddenly taken very seriously ill; indeed, it was feared that she had got a stroke of apoplexy. He managed, however, to send up a message to Eva to say that he wished to speak to her for a minute. Presently she came down, crying.

"O, my poor aunt is so dreadfully ill," she said. "We think that she is dying!"

Jeremy offered some awkward condolences, and indeed was much distressed. He liked old Miss Ceswick.

"I am going to South Africa to-morrow, Miss Eva," he said.

She started violently, and blushed up to her hair.

"Going to South Africa! What for?"

"I am going to look for Ernest. We are afraid that something must have happened to him."

"O, don't say that!" she said. "Perhaps he has—amusements which prevent his writing."

"I may as well tell you that I saw something of what passed between you and Mr. Plowden."

Again Eva blushed.

"Mr. Plowden was very rude," she said.

"So I thought; but I think that he is sorry for it now."

"What do you mean?"

"I mean that I nearly shook his ugly head off for him."

"O, how could you?" Eva asked, severely; but there was no severity on her face.

Just then Florence's voice was heard calling imperatively.

"I must go," said Eva.

"Have you any message for Ernest, if I find him?"

Eva hesitated.

"I know all about it," said Jeremy, considerately turning his head.

"O no, I have no message—that is—O, tell him that I love him dearly!" and she turned and fled upstairs.

CHAPTER V

FLORENCE ON MARRIAGE

Miss Ceswick's seizure turned out to be even worse than was anticipated. Once she appeared to regain consciousness, and began to mutter something; then she sank back into a torpor, out of which she never woke again.

It was fortunate that her condition was not such as to require the services of the clergyman, because, for some time after the events described in the last chapter, Mr. Plowden was not in any condition to give them. Whether it was the shaking or the well-planted kick or the shock to his system it is impossible to say, but in the upshot he was constrained to keep his bed for several days. Indeed, the first service that he took was on the occasion of the opening of the ancient Ceswick vault to receive the remains of the recently deceased lady. The only territorial possession which remained to the Ceswicks was their vault. Indeed, as Florence afterwards remarked to her sister, there was a certain irony in the reflection that of all their wide acres there remained only the few square feet of soil which for centuries had covered the bones of the race.

When their aunt was dead and buried the two girls went back to the Cottage, and were very desolate. They had both of them loved the old lady in their separate ways, more especially Florence, both because she possessed the deeper nature of the two and because she had lived the longest with her.

But the grief of youth at the departure of age is not inconsolable, and after a month or so they had conquered the worst of their sorrow. Then it was that the question what they were to do came prominently to the fore. Such little property as their aunt had possessed was equally divided between them, and the Cottage left to their joint use. This gave them enough to live on in their quiet way, but it undoubtedly left them in a very lonely and unprotected position. Such as it was, however, they, or rather Florence—for she managed all the business—decided to make the best of it. At Kesterwick, at any rate, they were known, and it was, they felt, better to stay there than to float away and become waifs and strays on the great sea of English life. So they settled to stay.

Florence, moreover, had her own reasons for staying. She had come to the conclusion that it would be desirable that her sister Eva should marry Mr. Plowden. Not that she liked Mr. Plowden—her lady's instincts rose up in rebellion against the man—but if Eva did not marry him, it as probable that she would in the long-run marry Ernest, and Ernest, Florence swore, she should not marry. To prevent such a marriage was the main purpose of her life. Her jealousy and hatred of her sister had become a part of herself; the gratification of her revenge was the evil star by which she shaped her course. It may seem a terrible thing that so young a woman could give the best energies of her life to such a purpose, but it was none the less the truth.

Hers was a wild strange nature, a nature capable of violent love and violent hate; the same pendulum could swing with equal ease to each extreme. Eva had robbed her of her lover; she would rob Eva, and put the prize out of her reach too. Little she recked of the wickedness of her design; for where in the long record of human suffering is there a wickedness to surpass the deliberate separation, for no good reason, of two people who love each other with all their hearts? Surely there is none. She knew this, but she did not hesitate on that account. She was not hypocritical. She made no excuses to herself. She knew well that on every ground it was best that Eva should marry Ernest, and pursue her natural destiny, happy in his love and in her own. But she would have none of it. If once they should meet again, the game would pass out of her hands; for the weakest woman grows strong of purpose when she has her lover's arm to lean on. Florence realised this, and determined that they should never set eyes on each other until an impassable barrier, in the shape of Mr. Plowden, had been raised between the two. Having thus finally determined on the sacrifice, she set about whetting the knife.

One day, a month or so after Miss Ceswick was buried, Mr. Plowden called at the Cottage on some of the endless details of which district-visiting was the parent. He had hardly seen Eva since that never-to-be-forgotten day when he had learned what Jeremy's ideas of a shaking were, for the very good reason that she had carefully kept out of his way.

So it came to pass that when, looking out of the window on the afternoon in question, she saw the crown of a clerical hat coming along the road, Eva promptly gathered up her work and commenced a hasty retreat to her bedroom.

"Where are you going to, Eva?" asked her sister.

"Upstairs—here he comes."

"'He'! who is 'he'?"

"Mr. Plowden, of course."

"And why should you run away because Mr. Plowden is coming?"

"I do not like Mr. Plowden."

"Really, Eva, you are too bad. You know what a friendless position we are in right now, and you go and get up a dislike to one of the few men we know. It is very selfish of you, and most unreasonable."

At that moment the front-door bell rang, and Eva fled.

Mr. Plowden on entering looked round the room with a somewhat disappointed air.

"If you are looking for my sister," said Florence, "she is not very well."

"Indeed, I am afraid that her health is not good; she is so often indisposed."

Florence smiled, and they dropped into the district-visiting. Presently, however, Florence dropped out again.

"By the way, Mr. Plowden, I want to tell you of something I heard the other day, and which concerns you. Indeed, I think that it is only right that I should do so. I heard that you were seen talking to my sister, not very far from the Titheburgh Abbey cottages, and that she—she ran away from you. Then Mr. Jones jumped over the wall, and also began to talk with you. Presently he also turned, and, so said my informant, you struck at him with a heavy stick, but missed him. Thereupon a tussle ensued, and you got the worst of it."

"He irritated me beyond all endurance," broke in Mr. Plowden excitedly.

"O, then the story is true?"

Mr. Plowden saw that he had made a fatal mistake; but it was too late to deny it.

"To a certain extent," he said, sulkily. "That young ruffian told me that I was not a gentleman."

"Really! Of course that was unpleasant. But how glad you must feel that you missed him, especially as his back was turned! It would have looked so bad for a clergyman to be had up for assault, or worse, wouldn't it?"

Mr. Plowden turned pale, and bit his lip. He began to feel that he was in the power of this quiet, dignified young woman, and the feeling was not pleasant.

"And it would not look well if the story got round here, would it? I mean even if it was not known that you hit at him with the stick when he was not looking, because, you see, it would seem so absurd!"

Mr. Plowden winced beneath her mockery, and rising, seized his hat; but she motioned him back to his chair.

"Don't go yet," she said. "I wanted to tell you that you ought to be much obliged to me for thinking of all this for you. I thought that it would be painful for you to have the story all over the country-side, so I nipped it in the bud."

Mr. Plowden groaned in spirit. If these were the results of a story nipped in the bud, what would its uninjured bloom be like?

"Who told you?" he asked, brusquely. "Jones went away."

"Yes. How glad you must be, by the way, that he is gone! But it was not Mr. Jones, it was a person who oversaw the difference of opinion. No, never mind who it was; I have found means to silence that person."

Little did Mr. Plowden guess that during the whole course of his love-scene, and the subsequent affair with Jeremy, there had leaned gracefully in an angle of the sod wall, not twenty yards away, a figure uncommonly resembling that of an ancient mariner in an attitude of the most intense and solemn contemplation; but so it was.

"I am grateful to you, Miss Ceswick."

"Thank you, Mr. Plowden, it is refreshing to meet with true gratitude, it is a scarce flower in this world; but really I don't deserve any. The observer who oversaw the painful scene between you and Mr. Jones also oversaw a scene preceding it, that, so far as I can gather, seems to have been hardly less painful in its way."

Mr. Plowden coloured, but said nothing.

"Now you see, Mr. Plowden, I am left in a rather peculiar position as regards my sister; she is younger than I am, and has always been accustomed to look up to me, so, as you will easily understand, I feel my responsibilities to weigh upon me. Consequently, I feel bound to ask you what I am to understand from the report of my informant?"

"Simply this, Miss Ceswick: I proposed to your sister, and she refused me."

"Indeed! you were unfortunate that afternoon."

"Miss Ceswick," went on Mr. Plowden, after a pause, "if I could find means to induce your sister to change her verdict, would my suit have your support?"

Florence raised her piercing eyes from her work, and for a second fixed them on the clergyman's face.

"That depends, Mr. Plowden."

"I am well off," he went on, eagerly, "and I will tell you a secret. I have bought the advowson of this living; I happened to hear that it was going, and got it at a bargain. I don't think that Halford's life is worth five years' purchase."

"Why do you want to marry Eva, Mr. Plowden," asked Florence, ignoring this piece of information; "you are not in love with her?"

"In love! No, Miss Ceswick. I don't think that sensible men fall in love; they leave that to boys and women."

"Oh! Then why do you want to marry Eva? It will be best to tell me frankly, Mr. Plowden."

He hesitated, and then came to the conclusion that, with a person of Florence's penetration, frankness was the best game.

"Well, as you must know, your sister is an extraordinarily beautiful woman."

"And would therefore form a desirable addition to your establishment?"

"Precisely," said Mr. Plowden. "Also," he went on, "she is a distinguished-looking woman, and quite the lady."

Florence shuddered at the phrase.

"And would therefore give you social status, Mr. Plowden?"

"Yes. She is also sprung from an ancient family."

Florence smiled, and looked at Mr. Plowden with an air that said more plainly than any words, "Which you clearly are not."

"In short, I am anxious to get married, and I admire your sister Eva more than anybody I ever saw."

"All of which are very satisfactory reasons, Mr. Plowden; all you have to do is convince my sister of the many advantages you have to offer her, and—to win her affections."

"Ah, Miss Ceswick, that is just the point. She told me that her affections were already irredeemably engaged, and that she had none to give. If only I have the opportunity however, I shall hope to be able to outdistance my rival."

Florence looked at him scrutinisingly as she answered:

"You do not know Ernest Kershaw, or you would not be so confident."

"Why am I not as good as this Ernest?" he asked; for Florence's remark, identical as it was with that of Jeremy, wounded his vanity intensely.

"Well, Mr. Plowden, I do not want to be rude, but it is impossible for me to conceive a woman's affections being won away from Ernest Kershaw by you. You are so very different."

If Mr. Plowden wanted a straightforward answer, he had certainly got it. For some moments he sat in sulky silence, and then he said:

"I suppose, if that is the case, there is nothing to be done."

"I never said that. Women are frequently married whose affections are very much engaged elsewhere. You know how they win their wives in savage countries, Mr. Plowden: they catch them. Marriage by capture is one of the oldest institutions in the world."

"Well!"

"Well, the same institution still obtains in England, only we don't call it by that name. Do you suppose that no women are hunted down nowadays? Ah, very many are; the would-be husband heads the pack, and all the loving relatives swell its cry."

"You mean that your sister can be hunted down," he said bluntly.

"I! I mean nothing, except that the persistent suitor on the spot often has a better chance than the lover at a distance, however dear he may be."

Then Mr. Plowden took his leave. Florence watched him walking down the garden-path.

"I am glad Jeremy shook you soundly," she said aloud. "Poor Eva!"

CHAPTER VI

MR. PLOWDEN GOES A-WOOING

Mr. Plowden was not a suitor to let the grass grow under his feet. As he once took the trouble to explain to Florence, he considered that there was nothing like boldness in wooing, and he acted up to his convictions. Possessing no more delicacy of feeling than a bull-elephant, and as much consideration for the lady as the elephant has for a lily it tramples underfoot, figuratively speaking, he charged at Eva every time he saw her. He laid wait for her round corners, and asked her to marry him; he dropped in on her at odd hours, and insisted upon her marrying him. It was quite useless for her to say, "No, no, no," or to appeal to his better feelings or compassion, for he had none. He simply would not listen to her; but encouraged thereto by the moral support which he had received from Florence, he crushed the poor girl with his amorous eloquence.

It was a merry chase that Florence sat and watched with a dark smile on her scornful lip. In vain did the poor white doe dash along at her best speed; the great black hound was ever at her flank, and each time she turned came bounding at her throat. This idea of a chase, and a hound, and a doe took such a strong possession of Florence's saturnine imagination, that she actually made a drawing of it, for she was a clever artist, and not without training, throwing, by a few strokes of her pencil, a perfect likeness of Mr.

Plowden into the fierce features of the hound. The doe she drew with Eva's dark eyes, and when she had done them there was such agony in her tortured gaze that she could not bear to look at them, and tore the picture up.

One day Florence came in, and found her sister weeping.

"Well, Eva, what is it now?" she asked, contemptuously.

"Mr. Plowden," sobbed Eva.

"Oh, Mr. Plowden again! Well, my dear, if you will be so beautiful, and encourage men, you must take the consequences."

"I never encouraged Mr. Plowden."

"Nonsense, Eva! you will not get me to believe that. If you did not encourage him he would not go on making love to you. Gentlemen are not fond of being snubbed."

"Mr. Plowden is not a gentleman," exclaimed Eva.

"What makes you say that?"

"Because a gentleman would not persecute one as he does. He will not take No for an answer, and to-day he kissed my hand. I tried to get it away from him, but I could not. Oh, I hate him!"

"I tell you what it is, Eva; I have no patience with you and your fancies. Mr. Plowden is a very respectable man; he is a clergyman, and well off, altogether quite the sort of man to marry. Ah, Ernest—I am sick of Ernest! If he wanted to marry you, he should not go shooting people, and then running off to South Africa. He was all very well to flirt with while he was here; now he has made a fool of himself and gone, and there is an end of him."

"But, Florence, I love Ernest. I think I love him more dearly every day, and I detest Mr. Plowden."

"Very likely. I don't ask you to love Mr. Plowden; I ask you to marry him. What have love and marriage got to do with each other, I should like to know? If people were always to marry the people they loved, things would soon get into a pretty mess. Look here, Eva, as you know I do not often obtrude myself or my interests, but I think that I have a right to be considered a little in this matter. You have now got an opportunity of making a home for both of us. There is nothing against Mr. Plowden. Why should you not marry him as well as anybody else? Of course, if you choose to sacrifice your own ultimate happiness and the comfort of us both to a silly whim, I cannot prevent you; you are your own mistress. Only I beg you to disabuse your mind of the idea that you could not be happy with Mr. Plowden, because you happen to fancy yourself in love with Ernest. Why, in six months you will have forgotten all about him."

"But I don't want to forget about him."

"I daresay not. That is your abominable egotism again. But whether you want to or not, you will. In a year or two, when you have your own interests and your children—"

"Florence, you may talk to midnight if you like; but, once and for all, I will not marry Mr. Plowden;" and she swept out of the room in her stately way.

Florence laughed softly to herself as she said after her:

"Oh yes, you will, Eva. I shall be pinning a bride's veil on to that pretty head of yours before you are six months older, my dear."

Florence was quite right; it was only a question of time and cunningly applied pressure. Eva yielded at last.

But there is no need for us to follow the hateful story through its various stages. If by chance any of the readers of this history are curious about them, let them go and study from the life. Such cases exist around them, and, so far as the victims are concerned, there is a painful monotony in the development of their details and their conclusion.

And so it came to pass that one afternoon in the early summer, Florence, coming in from walking, found Mr. Plowden and her sister together in the little drawing-room. The latter was very pale, and shrinking with scared eyes and trembling limbs up against the mantelpiece, near which she was standing. The former, looking big and vulgar, was standing over her and trying to take her hand.

"Congratulate me, Miss Florence," he said. "Eva has promised to be mine."

"Has she?" said Florence, coldly. "How glad you must be that Mr. Jones is out of the way!"

It was not a kind speech, but the fact was that there were few people in the world for whom Florence had such a complete contempt, or whom she regarded with such intense dislike, as she did Mr. Plowden. The mere presence of the man irritated her beyond all bearing. He was an instrument suited to her purposes, so she used him; but she could find it in her heart to regret that the instrument was not more pleasant to handle.

Mr. Plowden turned pale at her taunt, and even in the midst of her fear and misery Eva smiled, and thought to herself that it was lucky for her hateful lover that somebody else was "out of the way."

Poor Eva!

"Poor Eva!" you think to yourself, my reader. "There was nothing poor about her. She was weak; she was wicked and contemptible."

Oh, pause awhile before you say so. Remember that circumstances were against her; remember that the ideas of duty and of gain drilled into her breast and the breasts of her ancestresses from generation to generation, and fated as often as not to prove more of a bane than a blessing, were against her; remember that her sister's ever-present influence over-shadowed her, and that her suitor's vulgar vitality crushed her to the ground.

"Yet with it all she was weak," you say. Well, she was weak, as weak as you must expect some women to be after centuries of custom have bred weakness into their very nature. Why are women weak? Because men have made them so. Because the law that was framed by men, and the public opinion which it has been their privilege to direct, have from age to age drilled into women the belief—in which, it must be admitted, they for the most part readily acquiesce—that they are chattels, to be owned and played with, existing for man's pleasure and the gratification of his passion. Because men have systematically stunted their mental grown and denied them their natural rights, and that equality which is theirs. Weak!—women have become weak because weakness is the passport to the favour of our sex. They have become foolish because education has been withheld from them and ability discouraged; they have become frivolous because frivolity has been declared to be the natural mission of women. There is no male simpleton who does not like to find a bigger simpleton than he is to lord it over. Truly, the triumph of the stronger sex has been complete, for it has even succeeded in enlisting its victims to its service. The great instruments in the suppression of women, and in their retention at their present level, are women themselves. And yet let us be for a minute just. Which is the superior of the two—the woman or the man? In strength we have the advantage, but in intellect she is almost our equal, if only we will give her fair-play. And in purity, in tenderness, in long-suffering, in fidelity, in all the Christian virtues, which is the superior in these things? Oh man, whoever you are, think of your mother and your sisters; think of her who nursed you in sickness, of her who stood by you in trouble when all others would have none of you, and then answer.

Poor Eva! Yes, give her all your pity, but, if you can, purge it of your contempt. It requires that a woman should possess a mind of unusual robustness to stand out against circumstances such as hemmed her in, and this she did not possess. Nature, which had showered physical gifts upon her with such a lavish hand, had not given her that most useful of all gifts, the power of self-defence. She was made to yield; but this was her only, if an absolutely fatal, fault. For the rest she was pure as the mountain snow, and with a heart of gold. Herself incapable of deceit, it never occurred to her to imagine it in others. She never suspected that Florence could have a motive in her advocacy of Mr. Plowden's cause. On the contrary, she was possessed to the full with that idea of duty and self-sacrifice which in some women amounts almost to madness. The notion so cleverly started by Florence, that she was bound to take this opportunity of giving her sister a home and the permanent protection of a brother-in-law, had taken a firm hold of her mind. As for the cruel wrong and injustice which her marriage with Mr. Plowden would work to Ernest, strange though it may seem, as is usual in such cases it never occurred to her to consider the matter in that light. She knew what her own sufferings were and always must be; she thought that she would rather die than be false to Ernest; but somehow she never looked at the other side of the picture, never considered the matter from Ernest's point of view. After the true womanly fashion she was prepared to throw herself under her Juggernaut called Duty, and let her inner life, the life of her heart, be crushed out of her; but she never thought of the other life which was welded with her own, and which must be crushed too.

How curious it is that when women talk so much of their duties they often think so little of the higher duty which they owe to the unlucky man whose love they have won, and whom they cherish in their misguided hearts! The only feasible explanation of the mystery—outside of that of innate selfishness—is, that one of the ideas which has been persistently drilled into the female breast is that men have not any real feelings. It is vaguely supposed that they will "get over it." However this may be, when a woman decides to do violence to her natural feelings, and because of pressure or profit contracts herself into an unholy marriage, the lover whom she deserts is generally the last person to be considered. Poor wretch! he will, no doubt, "get over it."

Fortunately, many do.

Mr. Alston and Ernest carried out their plans as regarded sport. They went up to Lydenburg and had a month's vilderbeeste and blesbok shooting within three day's "trek" with an ox-waggon from that curious little town. The style of life was quite new to Ernest, and he enjoyed it much. They owned an ox-waggon and a span of sixteen "salted" oxen, that is, oxen which will not die of lung-sickness, and in this lumbering vehicle they travelled about wherever fancy or the presence of buck took them. Mr. Alston and his boy Roger slept in the waggon, and Ernest in a little tent which was pitched every night alongside, and never did he sleep sounder. There was a freshness and freedom about the life which charmed him. It is pleasant after the day's shooting or travelling to partake of a hearty meal, of which the piece de resistance generally consists of a stew compounded indiscriminately of vilderbeeste beef, bustard, partridges, snipe, rice, and compressed vegetables—a dish, by the way, which is, if properly cooked, fit to set before a king. Then comes the pipe, or rather a succession of pipes, and the talk over the day's sport, and the effect of that long shot, and the hunting-yarn of which it "reminds me." And after the yarn the well-known square bottle is produced, and the tin pannikins, out of which you have been drinking tea, are sent to the spring down in the hollow to be washed by the Zulu "voorlooper," who objects to going because of the "spooks" (ghosts) which he is credibly informed inhabit that hollow; and you indulge in your evening "tot," and smoke your pipes, and talk or ruminate as the fancy takes you. At last comes the splendid African moon like a radiant queen rising from a throne of inky cloud, flooding the whole wide veld with mysterious light, and reveals the long lines of game slowly travelling to their feeding-grounds along the ridges of the rolling plain.

Well "one more drop," and so to bed, having come to the admirable decision—so easy to make overnight, so hard to adhere to when the time comes—to "trek from the yoke" at dawn. Having undressed yourself outside the tent, all except the flannel shirt in which you are going to sleep—for there is no room to do so inside—you stow your clothes and boots away under your mackintosh sheet—for clothes wet through with dew are unpleasant to wear before the sun is up—creep on your hands and knees into your little tenement, and wriggle between the blankets.

For awhile, perhaps, you lie so, your pipe still between your lips, gazing up through the opening of the little tent at two bright particular stars shining in the blue depths above, or watching the waving of the tall tambouki-grass as the night-wind goes sighing through it. Behold! the cold far stars draw near, grow warm with life, and change to Eva's eyes—if unluckily, you have an Eva—and the yellow tambouki-grass is her waving hair, and the sad whispering of the wind her voice, which speaks and tells you that she has come from far across the great seas to tell you that she loves you, to lull you to your rest.

What was it that frightened her so soon? The rattling of chains and the deep lowing of the oxen, rising to be ready for the dawn. It has not come yet; but it is not far off. See, the grey light begins to gleam upon the oxen's horns, and far away, there in the east, the grey is streaked with primrose. Away with dreams, and up to pull the shivering Kafirs from their snug lair beneath the waggon, and to give the good nags, which must gallop vilderbeeste all to-day, a double handful of mealies before you start.

Ah neu-yak-trek! the great waggon strains and starts, and presently the glorious sun comes up, and you eat a crust of bread as you sit on the waggon-box, and wash it down with a mouthful of spirit, and feel that it is a splendid thing to get up early.

Then, about half-past eight, comes the halt for breakfast, and the welcome tub in the clear spring that you have been making for, and, after breakfast, saddle up the nags, take your bearings by the kopjé, and off after that great herd of vilderbeeste.

So, my reader, day adds itself to day, and each day will find you healthier, happier, and stronger than the last. No letters, no newspapers, no duns, no women, and no babies. Think of the joy of it, effete Caucasian, then go buy an ox-waggon and do likewise.

After a month of this life, Mr. Alston came to the conclusion that there would now be no danger in descending into the low country towards Delagoa Bay in search of large game. Accordingly, having added to their party another would-be Nimrod, a gentleman just arrived from England in search of sport, they started. For the first month or so, things went very well with them. They killed a good quantity of buffalo, koodoo, eland, and water-buck, also two giraffes; but to Ernest's great disappointment did not come across any rhinoceros, and only got a shot at one lion, which he missed, though there were plenty round them.

But soon the luck turned. First their horses died of the terrible scourge of all this part of South Africa, the horse-sickness. They had given large prices for them, about seventy pounds each, as "salted" animals—that is, animals that, having already had the sickness and recovered from it, were supposed to be proof against its attacks. Still they died one after another. This was only the beginning of evils. The day after the last horse died, the companion who had joined them at Lydenburg was taken ill of the fever. Mr. Jeffries—for that was his name—was a very reserved English gentleman of good fortune, something over thirty years of age. Like most people who came into close relationship with Ernest he had taken a considerable fancy to him, and the two were, comparatively speaking, intimate. During the first stages of his fever, Ernest nursed him like a brother, and was at length rewarded by seeing him in a fair way to recovery. On one unlucky day, however, Mr. Alston and Ernest went out to try and shoot a buck, as they were short of meat, leaving the camp in charge of the boy Roger. For a long while they could find no game, but at last Ernest came across a fine bull-eland standing rubbing himself against a mimosa thorn-tree. A shot from his express, planted well behind the shoulder, brought the noble beast down quite dead, and having laden the two Kafirs with them with the tongue, liver, and as much of the best meat as they could carry, they started back for camp.

Meanwhile one of the sudden and tremendous thunderstorms peculiar to South Africa came swiftly up against the wind, heralding its arrival by a blast of ice-cold air, and presently they were staggering along in the teeth of a fearful tempest. The whole sky was lurid with lightning, the hills echoed with the continuous roll of thunder, and the rain came down in sheets. In the thick of it all exhausted, bewildered, and wet to the skin, they reached the camp. There a sad sight awaited them. In front of the tent which served as a hospital for Jeffries, was a large ant-heap, and on this ant-heap, clad in nothing but a flannel shirt, sat Jeffries himself. The rain was beating on his bare head and emaciated face, and the ice-cold breeze was tossing his dripping hair. One hand he kept raising to the sky to let the cold water fall upon it; the other the boy Roger held, and by it vainly attempted to drag him back to the tent. But Jeffries was a man of large build, and the little lad might as well have tried to drag an ox.

"Isn't it glorious?" shouted the delirious man, as they came up. "I've got cool at last!"

"Yes, and you will soon be cold, poor fellow!" muttered Mr. Alston, as they hurried up.

They got him back into the tent, and in half an hour he was beyond all hope. He did not rave much, but kept repeating a single word in every possible tone. That word was:

"Alice!"

At dawn on the following morning he died with it on his lips. Ernest often wondered afterwards who "Alice" could be.

Next day they dug a deep grave under an ancient thorn-tree, and reverently laid him to his rest. On his breast they piled great stones to keep away the jackals, filling in the cracks with earth.

Then they left him to his sleep. It is a sad task that, burying a comrade in the lonely wilderness.

As they were approaching the waggon again, little Roger sobbing bitterly—for Mr. Jeffries had been very kind to him, and a first experience of death is dreadful to the young—they met the Zulu voorlooper, a lad called Jim, who had been out all day watching the cattle as they grazed. He saluted Mr. Alston after the Zulu fashion by lifting the right arm and saying the word "Inkoos," then stood still.

"Well, what is it, boy?" asked Mr. Alston. "Have you lost the oxen?"

"No, Inkoos, the oxen are safe at the yoke. It is this. When I was sitting on the kopjé yonder, watching that the oxen of the Inkoos should not stray, an Intombi (young girl) from the kraal under the mountain yonder came to me. She is the daughter of a Zulu mother who fell into the hands of a Basuto dog, and my half-cousin."

"Well!"

"Inkoos, I have met this girl before, I have met her when I have been sent to buy 'maas' (buttermilk) at the kraal."

"Good!"

"Inkoos, the girl came to bring heavy news, such as will press upon your heart. Secocoeni, chief of the Bapedi, who lives over yonder under the Blue Mountains, has declared war against the Boers."

"I hear."

"Sikukuni wants rifles for his men, such as the Boers use. He has heard of the Inkosis hunting here. To-night he will send an Impi to kill the Inkosis and take their guns."

"These are the words of the Intombi?"

"Yes, Inkoos, these are her very words. She was sitting outside the hut, grinding 'imphi' (Kafir corn) for beer, when she heard Secocoeni's messenger order her father to call the men together to kill us to-night."

"I hear. At what time of the night was the killing to be?"

"At the first break of dawn, so that they may have light to take the waggon away by."

"Good! we shall escape them. The moon will be up in an hour, and we can trek away."

The lad's face fell.

"Alas!" he said, "it is impossible; there is a spy watching the camp now. He is up there among the rocks; I saw him as I brought the oxen home. If we move he will report it, and we shall be overtaken in an hour."

Mr. Alston thought for a moment, and then made up his mind with the rapidity that characterises men who spend their lives in dealing with savage races.

"Mazooku!" he called to a Zulu, who was sitting smoking by the camp fire, a man whom Ernest had hired as his particular servant. The man rose and came to him, and saluted.

He was not a very tall man; but, standing there nude except for the "moocha" round his centre, his proportions, especially those of the chest and the lower limbs, looked gigantic. He had been a soldier in one of Cetywayo's regiments, but having been so indiscreet as to break through some of the Zulu marriage laws, had been forced to fly for refuge to Natal, where he had become a groom, and picked up a peculiar language which he called English. Even among a people where all the men are fearless he bore a reputation for bravery. Leaving him standing awhile, Mr. Alston rapidly explained the state of the case to Ernest, and what he proposed to do. Then turning, he addressed the Zulu:

"Mazooku, the Inkoos here, your master, whom you black people have named Mazimba, tells me that he thinks you a brave man."

The Zulu's handsome face expanded into a smile that was positively alarming in its extent.

"He says that you told him that when you were Cetywayo's man in the Undi Regiment, you once killed four Basutos, who set upon you together."

Mazooku lifted his right arm and saluted, by way of answer, and then glanced slightly at the assegai-wounds on his chest.

"Well, I tell your master that I do not believe you. It is a lie you speak to him; you ran away from Cetywayo because you did not like to fight and be killed as the king's ox, as a brave man should."

The Zulu coloured up under his dusky skin, and again glanced at his wounds.

"Ow-w!" he said.

"Bah! there is no need for you to look at those scratches; they were left by women's nails. You are nothing but a woman. Silence! who told you to speak? If you are not a woman, show it. There is an armed Basuto among those rocks. He watches us. Your master cannot eat and sleep in peace when he is watched. Take that big stabbing assegai you are so fond of showing, and kill him, or die a coward! He must make no sound, remember."

Mazooku turned towards Ernest for confirmation of the order. A Zulu always likes to take his orders straight from his own chief. Mr. Alston noticed it, and added:

"I am the Inkoosi's mouth, and speak his words."

Mazooku saluted again, and turning, went to the waggon to fetch his assegai.

"Tread softly, or you will wake him; and he will run from so great a man," Mr. Alston called after him sarcastically.

"I go among the rocks to seek 'mouti'" (medicine), the Zulu answered with a smile.

"We are in a serious mess, my boy," said Mr. Alston to Ernest, "and it is a toss-up if we get out of it. I taunted that fellow so that there may be no mistake about the spy. He must be killed, and Mazooku would rather die himself than not kill him now."

"Would it not have been safer to send another man with him?"

"Yes; but I was afraid that if the scout saw two men coming towards him he would make off, however innocent they might look. Our horses are dead, and if that fellow escapes we shall never get out of this place alive. It would be folly to expect Basutos to distinguish between Boers and Englishmen when their blood is up; and besides, Secocoeni has sent orders that we are to be killed, and they would not dare to disobey. Look, there goes Mr. Mazooku with an assegai as big as a fire-shovel."

The kopjé, or stony hill, where the spy was hid, was about three hundred yards from the little hollow in which the camp was formed, and across the stretch of bushy plain between the two Mazooku was quietly strolling, his assegai in one hand and two long sticks in the other. Presently he vanished into the shadow, for the sun was setting rapidly. After what seemed a long pause to Ernest, who was watching his movements through a pair of field-glasses, he reappeared walking along the shoulder of the hill right against the sky-line, his eyes fixed upon the ground as though he were searching among the crevices of the rocks for the medical herbs which Zulus prize.

All of a sudden Ernest saw the stalwart form straighten itself and spring down into a dip, which hid it from sight, with the assegai in its hand raised to the level of its head. Then came a pause, lasting perhaps for twenty seconds. On the farther side of the dip was a large flat rock, which was straight in a line with the fiery ball of the setting sun. Suddenly a tall figure sprang up out of the hollow on to this rock, followed by another figure, in whom Ernest recognised Mazooku. For a moment the two men, looking from their position like people afire, struggled together on the top of the flat stone, and Ernest could clearly distinguish the quick flash of their spears as they struck at each other; then they vanished together over the edge of the stone.

"By Jove!" said Ernest, who was trembling with excitement, "I wonder how it has ended?"

"We shall know presently," answered Mr. Alston coolly. "At any rate, the die is cast one way or another, and we may as well make a bolt for it. Now, you Zulus, down with those tents and get the oxen inspanned, and look quick about it, if you don't want a Basuto assegai to send you to join the spirit of Chaka."

The voorlooper had by this time communicated his alarming intelligence to the driver and other Kafirs, and Mr. Alston's exhortation to look sharp was quite unnecessary. Ernest never saw camp struck or oxen inspanned with such rapidity before. But before the first tent was fairly down, they were all enormously relieved to see Mazooku coming trotting cheerfully across the plain, droning a little Zulu song as he ran. His appearance, however, was by no means cheerful, for he was perfectly drenched with blood, some of it flowing from a wound in his left shoulder, and the rest till recently the personal property of somebody else. Arrived in front of where Mr. Alston and Ernest were standing, he raised his broad assegai, which was still dripping blood, and saluted.

"I hear," said Mr. Alston.

"I have done the Inkoosi Mazimba's bidding. There were two of them; the first I killed easily in the hollow, but the other, a very big man, fought well for a Basuto. They are dead, and I threw them into a hole, that their brothers might not find them easily."

"Good! go wash yourself and get your master's things into the waggon. Stop! let me sew up that cut. How came you to be so awkward as to get touched by a Basuto?"

"Inkoos, he was very quick with his spear, and he fought like a cat."

Mr. Alston did not reply, but, taking a stout needle and some silk from a little housewife he carried in his pocket, he quickly stitched up the assegai-gash, which, fortunately, was not deep. Mazooku stood without flinching till the job was finished, and then retired to wash himself at the spring.

The short twilight faded rapidly into darkness, or rather into what would have been darkness, had it not been for the half-grown moon, which was to serve to light them on their path. Then a large fire having been lit on the site of the camp to make it appear as though it were still pitched there, the order was given to start. The oxen, obedient to the voice of the driver, strained at the trek-tow, the waggon creaked and jolted, and they began their long flight for life. The order of march was as follows: Two hundred yards ahead of the waggon walked a Kafir, with strict orders to keep his eyes very wide open indeed, and report in the best way possible, under the circumstances, if he detected any signs of an ambush. At the head of the long line of cattle, leading the two front oxen by a "reim," or strip of buffalo-hide, was the Zulu boy Jim, to whose timely discovery they owed their lives, and by the side of the waggon the driver, a Cape Hottentot, plodded along in fear and trembling. On the waggon-box itself, each with a Winchester repeating rifle on his knees, and keeping a sharp look-out into the shadows, sat Mr. Alston and Ernest. In the hinder part of the waggon, also armed with a rifle and keeping a keen look-out, sat Mazooku. The other servants marched alongside, and the boy Roger was asleep inside, on the "cartle," or hide bed.

So they travelled on hour after hour. Now they bumped down terrific hills strewn with boulders, which would have smashed anything less solid than an African ox-waggon to splinters; now they crept along a dark valley, that looked spiritual and solemn in the moonlight, expecting to see Secocoeni's Impi emerge from every clump of bush; and now again they waded through mountain-steams. At last, about midnight, they reached a plain dividing two stretches of mountainous country, and here they halted for a while to give the oxen, which were fortunately in good condition and fat after their long rest, a short breathing-time. Then on again through the long, quiet night, on, still on, till the dawn found them the other side of the wide plain at the foot of the mountain-range.

Here they rested for two hours, and let the oxen fill themselves with the lush grass. They had travelled thirty miles since the yokes were put upon their necks—not far according to our way of journeying, but very far for cumbersome oxen over an almost impassable country. As soon as the sun was well up they inspanned again, and hurried forwards, bethinking them of the Basuto horde who would now be pressing on their spoor; on with brief halt through all that day and the greater part of the following night, till the cattle began to fall down in the yokes—till at last they crossed the boundary and were in Transvaal territory.

When dawn broke, Mr. Alston took the glasses and examined the track over which they had fled. There was nothing to be seen except a great herd of hartebeest.

"I think that we are safe now," he said, at last, "and thank God for it. Do you know what those Basuto devils would have done if they had caught us?"

"What?"

"They would have skinned us, and made our hearts and livers into 'mouti' (medicine), and eaten them to give them the courage of the white man."

"By Jove!" said Ernest.

CHAPTER VIII

A HOMERIC COMBAT

When Mr. Alston and Ernest found themselves safe upon Transvaal soil, they determined to give up the idea of following any more big game for the present, and to content themselves with the comparatively humble vilderbeeste, blesbok, springbok, and other small antelopes. The plan they pursued was to slowly journey from one point of the country to another, stopping wherever they found the buck particularly plentiful. In this way they got excellent sport, and spent several months very agreeably, with the further advantage that Ernest obtained considerable knowledge of the country and its inhabitants, the Boers.

It was a wild rough life that they led, but by no means a lowering one. The continual contact with Nature in all her moods, and in her wildest shapes, to a man of impressionable mind like Ernest, was an education in itself. His mind absorbed something of the greatness round him, and seemed to grow wider and deeper during those months of lonely travel. The long struggle, too, with the hundred difficulties which arise in waggon-journeys, and the quickness of decision necessary to avoid danger or discomfort in such a mode of life, were of great service to him in shaping his character. Nor was he left without suitable society, for in his companion he found a friend for whose talents and intelligence he had the highest respect.

Mr. Alston was a very quiet individual; he never said a thing unless he had first considered it in all its bearings; but when he did say it, it was always well worth hearing. He was a man who had spent his life in the closest observation of human nature in the rough. Now you, my reader, may think that there is a considerable difference between human nature "in the rough," as exemplified by a Zulu warrior stalking out of his kraal in a kaross and brandishing an assegai, and yourself, say, strolling up the steps of your club in a frock-coat, and twirling one of Brigg's umbrellas. But, as a matter of fact, the difference is of a most superficial character, bearing the same proportion to the common substance that the furniture polish does to the table. Scratch the polish, and there you have best raw Zulu human nature. Indeed, to anybody who has taken the trouble to study the question, it is simply absurd to observe how powerless high civilisation has been to do anything more than veneer that raw material, which remains identical in each case.

To return. The result of Mr. Alston's observations had been to make him an extremely shrewd companion, and an excellent judge of men and their affairs. There were few subjects which he had not quietly considered during all the years that he had been trading or shooting or serving the Government in one capacity or another; and Ernest was astonished to find, although he had only spent some four months of his life in England, how intimate was his knowledge of the state of political parties, of the great social questions of the day, and even of matters connected with literature and art. It is not too much to say that it was from Mr. Alston that Ernest imbibed principles on all these subjects which he never deserted in after-life, and that subsequent experience proved to be for the most part sound.

Thus, between shooting and philosophical discussion, the time passed on pleasantly enough, till at length they drew near to Pretoria, the capital of the Transvaal, where they had decided to rest the oxen for a month or two before making arrangements for a real big-game excursion up towards Central Africa. They struck into the Pretoria road just above a town called Heidelberg, about sixty miles from the former place, and proceeded by easy stages towards their destination.

As they went on, they generally found it convenient to outspan at spots which it was evident had been used for the same purpose by some waggon that was travelling one stage ahead of them. So frequently did this happen, that during their first five or six outspans they were able on no less than three occasions to avail themselves of the dying fires of their predecessors' camp. This was a matter of lively interest to Ernest, who always did cook; and a very good cook he became. One of the great bothers of South African travelling is the fire question. Indeed, how to make sufficient fire to boil a kettle when you have no fuel to make it of is the great question of South African travel. A ready-made fire is, therefore, peculiarly acceptable; and for the last half-hour of the trek was Ernest always in a great state of expectation as to whether the waggon before them had or had not been considerate enough to leave theirs burning.

Thus it came to pass that one morning, when they were about fifteen miles from Pretoria, which they expected to reach the same evening, and the waggon was slowly drawing up to the outspan-place, Ernest, accompanied by Mazooku, who lounged after him like a black shadow, ran forward to see if their predecessors had or had not been considerate. In this instance energy was rewarded, for the fire was still burning.

"Hoorah!" said Ernest. "Get the sticks, Mazooku, and go and fill the kettle. By Jove! there's a knife."

There was a knife, a many-bladed knife, with a buckhorn handle and a corkscrew in it, left by the dying fire. Ernest took it up and looked at it; somehow it seemed familiar to him. He turned it round, examined the silver plate upon it, and suddenly started.

"What is the matter, Ernest?" said Mr. Alston, who had joined them.

"Look here," he answered, pointing to two initials on the knife.

"Well, I see some fellow has left his knife; so much the better for the finder."

"You have heard me speak of my friend Jeremy. That is his knife; I gave it to him years ago. Look—J. J."

"Nonsense! it is some knife like it; I have seen hundreds of that make."

"I believe that it is the same. He must be here."

Mr. Alston shrugged his shoulders.

"Not probable," he said.

Ernest made no answer. He stood staring at the knife.

"Have you written to your people lately, Ernest?"

"No; the last letter I wrote was down there in Secocoeni's country; you remember I sent it by the Basuto who was going to Lydenburg, just before Jeffries died."

"Like enough he never got to Lydenburg. He would not have dared to go to Lydenburg after the war broke out. You should write."

"I mean to, from Pretoria; but somehow I have had no heart for writing."

Nothing more was said about the matter, and Ernest put the knife into his pocket.

That evening they trekked down through the "Poort" that commands the most charming view of the South African towns, and, on the plain below, Pretoria, bathed in the bright glow of the evening sunshine, smiled its welcome to them. Mr. Alston, who knew the town, determined to trek straight through it and outspan the waggon on the farther side, where he thought there would be better grazing for the cattle. Accordingly, they rumbled on past the gaol, past the pleasant white building which was at that moment occupied by the English Special Commissioner and his staff, about whose doings all sorts of rumours had reached them during their journey, and on to the market-square. This area was at the moment crowded with Boer waggons, whose owners had trekked in to celebrate their "nachtmaal" (communion), of which it is their habit, in company with their wives and children, to partake four times a year. The "Volksraad," or local Parliament, was also in special session to consider the proposals made to it on behalf of the Imperial Government, so that the little town was positively choked with visitors. The road down which they were passing ran past the buildings used as Government offices, and between this and the Dutch church a considerable crowd was gathered, which, to judge from the shouts and volleys of oaths—Dutch and English—that proceeded from it, was working itself up into a state of excitement.

"Hold on," shouted Ernest to the voorlooper; and then, turning to Mr. Alston, "There is a jolly row going on there; let us go and see what it is."

"All right, my boy; where the fighting is, there will the Englishmen be gathered together;" and they climbed down off the waggon and made for the crowd.

The row was this. Among the Boers assembled for the "nachtmaal" festival was a well-known giant of the name of Van Zyl. This man's strength was a matter of public notoriety all over the country, and many were the feats which were told of him. Among others it was said that he could bear the weight of the after-part of an African buck waggon on his shoulders, with a load of three thousand pounds of corn upon it, while the wheels were greased. He stood about six feet seven high, weighed eighteen stone and a half, and had a double row of teeth. On the evening in question this remarkable specimen of humanity was sitting on his waggon-box with a pipe, of which the size was proportionate to his own, clinched firmly between his double row of teeth. About ten paces of him stood a young Englishman, also of large size, though he looked quite small beside the giant, who was contemplating the phenomenon on the waggon-box, and wondering how many inches he measured round the chest. That young Englishman had just descended from a newly-arrived waggon, and his name was Jeremy Jones.

To these advances a cringing Hottentot boy of small size. The Hottentot is evidently the servant or slave of the giant, and a man standing by Jeremy, who understands Dutch, informs him that he is telling his master than an ox has strayed. Slowly the giant rouses himself, and, descending from the waggon-box, seizes the trembling Tottie with one hand, and, taking a reim of buffalo-hide, lashes him to the waggon-wheel.

"Now," remarked Jeremy's acquaintance, "you will see how a Boer deals with a nigger."

"You don't mean to say that great brute is going to beat that poor little devil?"

Just then a small fat woman put her head out of a tent pitched by the waggon, and inquired what the matter was. She was the giant's wife. On being informed of the straying of the ox, her wrath knew no bounds.

"Slaat em! slaat de swartsel!" (Thrash him! thrash the black creature!) she cried out in a shrill voice, running to the waggon, and with her own fair hands drawing out a huge "sjambock," that is, a strip of prepared hippopotamus-hide used to drive the after-oxen with, and giving it to her spouse. "Cut the liver out of the black devil!" she went on, "but mind you don't hit his head, or he won't be able to go to work afterwards. Never mind about making the blood come; I have got lots of salt to rub in."

Her harangue, and the sight of the Hottentot tied to the wheel, had by this time attracted quite a crowd of Boers and Englishmen who were idling about the market-square.

"Softly, Vrouw, softly; I will thrash enough to satisfy even you, and we all know that must be very hard where a black creature is in question."

A roar of laughter from the Dutch people round greeted this sally of wit, and the giant, taking the sjambock with a good-humoured smile—for, like most giants, he was easy-tempered by nature—lifted it, whirled his great arm, as thick as the leg of an average man, round his head, and brought the whip down on the back of the miserable Hottentot. The poor wretch yelled with pain, and no wonder, for the greasy old shirt he wore was divided clean in two, together with the skin beneath it, and the blood was pouring from the gash.

"Allamachter! dat is een lecker slaat" (Almighty! that was a nice one), said the old woman; at which the crowd laughed again.

But there was one man who did not laugh, and that man was Jeremy. On the contrary, his clear eyes flashed and his brown cheek burned with indignation. Nor did he stop at that. Stepping forward he placed himself between the giant and the howling Hottentot, and said to the former, in the most nervous English:

"You are a damned coward!"

The Boer stared at him, and smiled, and then, turning, asked what the "English fellow" was saying. Somebody translated Jeremy's remark, whereupon the Boer, who was not a bad-natured fellow, smiled again, and remarked that Jeremy must be madder than the majority of "accursed Englishmen." Then he turned to continue thrashing the Hottentot, but, lo! the mad Englishman was still there. This put the Dutchman out.

"Footsack, carl; ik is Van Zyl!" (Get out, fellow; I am Van Zyl!) This was interpreted to Jeremy by the bystanders.

"All right; and tell him that I am Jones, a name he may have heard before," was the reply.

"What does this brain-sick fellow want?" shouted the giant.

Jeremy explained that he wanted him to stop his brutality.

"And what will the little man do if I refuse?"

"I shall try to make you," was the answer.

This remark was received with a shout of laughter from the crowd which had now collected, in which the giant joined very heartily when it was interpreted to him.

Giving Jeremy a shove to one side, he again lifted the great sjambock, with the purpose of bringing it down on the Hottentot. Another second, and Jeremy had snatched the whip from his hand, and sent it flying fifty yards away. Then, realising that his antagonist was really in earnest, the great Dutchman solemnly set himself to crush him. Doubling a fist which was the size of a Welsh leg of mutton, he struck with all his strength straight at the Englishman's head. Had the blow caught Jeremy, it would in all probability have killed him; but he was a practised boxer, and, without moving his body, he swung his head to one side. The Boer's fist passed him harmlessly, and, striking the panel of the waggon, went clean through it. Next instant several of the giant's double row of teeth were rolling loose in his mouth. Jeremy had returned the stroke by a righthander, into which he put all his power, and which would have knocked any other man backwards.

A great shout from the assembled Englishmen followed this blow, and a counter-shout from the crowd of Dutchmen, who pointed triumphantly to the hole in the stout yellow-wood panel made by their champion's fist, and asked who the madman was who dared to stand against him.

The Boer turned and spat out some of his superfluous teeth, and at the same instant a young Englishman came and caught hold of Jeremy by the arm.

"For Heaven's sake, my dear fellow, be careful! That man will kill you; he is the strongest fellow in the Transvaal. You are a fellow to be proud of, though!"

"He may try," said Jeremy laconically, stripping off his coat and waistcoat. "Will you hold these for me?"

"Hold them?" answered the young fellow, who was a good sort; "ay, that I will, and I would give half I have to see you lick him. I saw him stun an ox once with a blow of his fist."

Jeremy smiled.

"Stop," he said. "Ask that miserable coward, if I best him, if he will let off that miserable beggar?" and he pointed to the trembling Hottentot.

The question was put, and the great man answered. "Yah, yah! I will make you a present of him!" ironically, and then expressed his intention of knocking Jeremy into small pieces in the course of the next two minutes.

Then they faced one another. The giant was a trifle over six feet seven high; Jeremy was a trifle under six feet two and a half, and looked short beside him. But one or two critical observers, looking at the latter now that he was stripped for the encounter, shrewdly guessed that the Dutchman would have his work cut out. Jeremy did not, it is true, scale more than fourteen stone six, but his proportions were perfect. The great deep chest, the brawny arms—not very large, but a mass of muscle—the short strong neck, the quick eye, and massive leg, all bespoke the strength of a young Hercules. It was evident, too, that though he was so young, and not yet come to his full power, he was in the most perfect training. The Boer, on the other hand, was enormous, but his flesh was somewhat soft. Still, knowing his feats, the Englishmen present sighed for their champion, feeling that he had no chance.

For a moment they stood facing each other; then Jeremy made a feint, and, getting in, planted a heavy blow with his left hand on his adversary's chest. But he was to pay for it, for the next second the Dutchman got in his right hand, and Jeremy was lifted clean off his feet, and sent flying backwards among the crowd.

The Boers cheered, the giant smiled, and the Englishmen looked sad. They knew how it would be.

But Jeremy picked himself up little the worse. The stroke had struck the muscles of his chest, and had not hurt him greatly. As he advanced, the gradually increasing crowd of Englishmen cheered him warmly, and he swore in his heart that he would justify those cheers, or die for it.

It was at this juncture that Ernest and Mr. Alston came up.

"Good heavens!" exclaimed the former; "it is Jeremy."

Mr. Alston took in the situation at a glance.

"Don't let him see you; you will put him off," he said. "Get behind me."

Ernest obeyed, overwhelmed. Mr. Alston shook his head. He recognised that Jeremy had a poor chance, but he did not say so to Ernest.

Meanwhile Jeremy came up and faced the Dutchman. Encouraged by his late success, presently his adversary struck a tremendous blow at him. Jeremy dodged, and next instant succeeded in landing such a fearful right and left full on the giant's face that the latter went reeling backwards.

A yell of frantic excitement arose from the English portion of the crowd. This was indeed a David.

The Dutchman soon recovered, however, and, rendered more cautious, in his turn, kept out of Jeremy's reach, trying to strike him down from a distance. For a round or two no important blow was struck, till at last a brilliant idea took possession of the young fellow who had charge of Jeremy's coat.

"Hit him about the body," he whispered; "he's soft."

Jeremy took the advice, and next round succeeded in getting in two or three blows straight from the shoulder, every one of which bruised the Boer's huge body sadly, and made him rather short of wind.

Next round he repeated the same tactics, receiving himself a stroke on the shoulder from Van Zyl's right hand that for a moment rendered his left arm helpless. Before another second was over, however, Jeremy had his revenge, and the blood was pouring from his adversary's lips.

Now the popular excitement on both sides grew intense, for to the interest attaching to the encounter was added that of national feeling, which was then at a high state of tension. Englishmen, Dutchmen, and a mob of Kafirs yelled and shouted, and each of the former two felt that the honour of his people was on the issue. And yet it was an unequal fight.

"I believe that your friend will be a match for Van Zyl," said Mr. Alston, coolly, but the flash of his eye belied his coolness; "and, I tell you what, he's a devilish fine fellow, too."

At that moment, however, an untoward thing happened. The giant struck out his strongest, and Jeremy could not succeed in entirely warding off the blow, though he broke its force. Crashing through his guard, it struck him on the forehead, and for a moment he dropped senseless. His second rushed up and dashed some water over him, and in another instant he was on his legs again; but for the rest of that round he contented himself with dodging his adversary's attack, at which the Dutchmen cheered, thinking that his iron strength was broken.

But presently, when for the sixth time Jeremy came up with the same quiet look of determination in his eyes, and, except for the gaping of the nostrils and the twitching of the lip showed a certain measure of distress, looking but little the worse, they turned with anxiety to examine the condition of the giant. It was not very promising. He was perspiring profusely, and his enormous chest rose and fell in jerks. Wherever Jeremy's strokes had fallen, also, a great blue bruise had risen on his flesh. It was evident that his condition was the worse of the two, but still the Boers had little doubt of the issue. It could not be that the man would be worsted by an English lad, who, for a bet, with one hand had once quelled the struggles of a wild ox, holding it for the space of five minutes by the horn. So they called on him to stop playing with the English boy, and crush him.

Thus encouraged, the giant man came on, striking out with fearful force, but wildly, for he could not box. For thirty seconds or more Jeremy contented himself with avoiding the blows; then, seeing an opportunity, he planted a heavy one on his adversary's chest. This staggered Van Zyl and threw him off his guard, and, taking the offensive, Jeremy dodged in right under the huge fists that beat the air above him and hit upwards with all his power. Thud, thud! The sound of the blows could be heard fifty yards off. Nor were they without their effect. The giant staggered, threw up his arms, and, amidst fearful shouts and groans, fell like an ox struck with a pole-axe. But it was not over yet. In another moment he was on his legs again, and spitting out blood and teeth, whirling his hands like the sails of a windmill, reeled straight at Jeremy, a fearful and alarming spectacle. As he came, again Jeremy hit him in the face, but it did not stop him, and in another second the huge arms had closed round him and held him like a vice.

"Not fair! no holding!" shouted the Englishmen; but the Boer held on. Indeed, he did more. Putting all his vast strength into the effort, he strained and tugged, meaning to lift Jeremy up and dash him on the ground. But lo! amid frantic shouts from the crowd, Jeremy stood firm, moving not an inch. Whereupon the Boers called out, saying that he was not a mortal, but a man possessed with a devil! Again the Dutchman gripped him, and this time succeeded in lifting him a few inches from the ground.

"By George, he will throw him next time!" said Mr. Alston to Ernest, who was shaking like a leaf with the excitement; "look!—he is turning white; the grip is choking him."

And, indeed, Jeremy was in evil case; his senses were fast being crushed out of him in that fearful embrace, and he was thinking with bitter sorrow that he must fail after all, for an Englishman does not like to be beaten even when he has fought his best. Just then it was, when things were beginning to swim around him, that a voice he loved, and which he had been listening for these many months, rang in his ears; whether it was fancy or whether he really heard it he knew not.

"Remember 'Marsh Joe,' Jeremy, and lift him. Don't be beat. For God's sake, lift him!" said the voice.

Now there was a trick, which I will not tell you, that a famous Eastern Counties' wrestler, known as Marsh Joe, had taught to Jeremy. So well had he taught him, indeed, that at the age of seventeen Jeremy had hoisted his teacher with his own trick.

Just at the moment that Jeremy heard the voice, the giant shifted his hold a little, preparatory to making a fresh effort, and thus enabled his antagonist to fill his lungs with air. Ernest saw the broad white chest heave with relief, for by this time most of the upper clothing of the combatants had been wrenched away, and the darkening eye grow bright again, and he knew that Jeremy had heard him, and that he would conquer or die where he was.

And then—lo, and behold! just as the Boer, feeling that at last he was master of the situation, leisurely enough prepared himself for the final struggle, suddenly the Englishman advanced his right leg a few inches, and with the rapidity of lightning entirely shifted his grip. Then he gathered himself for the effort. What secret reserve of strength he drew on, who can say? But Ernest's voice had excited it, and it came at his call: and he did a thing that few living men could have done, the fame of which will go down in South Africa from generation to generation. For the Englishman's lithe arms had found their hold; they tightened and gripped till they sunk in almost level with the flesh of his mighty foe. Then slowly Jeremy began to gather purchase, swaying backwards and forwards, and the Dutchman swayed with him.

"Make an end of him! make an end of him!" shouted the Boers. But behold! their champion's eyes are starting from his blackened face; his head sinks lower and lower, his buttocks rise; he cannot stir.

To and fro sways Jeremy, and now the giant's feet are lifted from the ground. Then one slow and mighty effort—oh, gallant Jeremy!—up, still up above the gasping of the wonder-stricken crowd, up to his shoulder—by Heaven, over it! Crash!

Van Zyl fell, to be carried away by six strong men a cripple for life.

CHAPTER IX

ERNEST'S LOVE-LETTER

Cheer after cheer rose from the Englishmen around, and angry curses from the Dutchmen, as Jeremy turned to look at the senseless carcase of the giant. But, even as he turned, exhausted Nature gave out, and he fell fainting into Ernest's arms.

Then did selected individuals of his fellow-countrymen come forward and bear him reverently to a restaurant called the "European," where the proprietor—himself an old Eton fellow—met him, and washed and clothed and restored him, and vowed with tears in his eyes that he, Jeremy, should live at his expense for as long as he liked—ay, even if he chose to drink nothing meaner than champagne all day long; for thus it is that Englishmen greet one who ministers to that deepest rooted of all their feelings—national pride. When at length he had been brought to, and refreshed with a tumblerful of dry Monopole, and wonderingly shaken Ernest by the hand, the enthusiasm of the crowd outside burst its bounds. They poured into the restaurant, and, seizing Jeremy and the chair whereon he sat, they bore him in triumph round the market-square to the tune of "God save the Queen." This was a proceeding that would have ended in provoking a riot had not an aide-de-camp from his Excellency the Special Commissioner, who sent in a message begging that they would desist, succeeded in persuading them to return to the restaurant. Here they all dined, and forced Jeremy to drink a good deal more dry Monopole than was good for him, with the result that for the first and last time in his life he was persuaded into making an after-dinner speech. As far as it was reported it ran something like this:

"Dear friends" (cheers) "and Englishmen" (renewed cheers)—pause—"all making great fuss about nothing" (cheers and shouts of "No, no!"). "Fight the Dutchman again to-morrow—very big, but soft as putty—anybody fight him" (frantic cheering). "Glad I wasn't thrashed, as you all seem so pleased; 'spose you don't like the Dutchman. 'Fraid he hurt himself over my shoulder. Wonder what he did it for? Sit down now. Dear friends, dear old Ernest—been looking for you for long while;" and he turned his glassy eye on to Ernest, who cheered frantically, under the impression that Jeremy had just said something very much to the point. "Sit down now" ("No, no; go on"). "Can't go on—quite pumped—very thirsty, too." ("Give him some more champagne; open a fresh case"). "Wish Eva and Doll were here, don't you?" (loud cheers). "Gemman" (cheers)—"no, not gemman—friends" (louder cheers)—"no, not gemman—friends—English brothers" (yet louder cheers), "I give you a toast. Eva and Doll: you all know 'em and love 'em, or if you don't you would, you see, if you did, you know." (Frantic outburst of cheering, during which Jeremy tries to resume his seat, but gracefully drops on to the floor, and begins singing "Auld lang syne" under the table; whereupon the whole company rise, and with the exception of

Ernest and a jovial member of the Special Commissioner's staff, who get upon the table to lead the chorus, join hands and sing that beautiful old song with all the solemnity of intoxication. After which they drink more champagne, and jointly and severally swear eternal friendship, especially Ernest and the member of his Excellency's staff, who shake hands and bless each other, till the warmth of their emotions proves too much for them, and they weep in chorus there upon the table.)

For the rest, Ernest had some vague recollection of helping to drive his newly-found friend home in a wheelbarrow that would persist in upsetting in every "sluit" or ditch, especially if it had running water in it; and that was about all he did remember.

In the morning he woke up, or rather first became conscious of pain in his head, in a little double-bedded room attached to the hotel. On the pillow of the bed opposite to him lay Jeremy's battered face.

For a while Ernest could make nothing of all this. Why was Jeremy there? Where were they? Everything turned round and seemed phantasmagorial; the only real, substantial thing was that awful pain in the head. But presently things began to come back to him, and the sight of Jeremy's bruised face recalled the fight, and the fight recalled the dinner, and the dinner brought back a vague recollection of Jeremy's speech and of something he had said about Eva. What could it have been? Ah, Eva! Perhaps, Jeremy knew something about her; perhaps he had brought the letter that had been so long in coming. O, how his heart went out towards her. But how came Jeremy there in bed before him? how came he to be in South Africa at all.

At that moment his reflections were interrupted by the entry of Mazooku, bearing the coffee which it is the national habit in South Africa to drink early in the morning.

The martial-looking Zulu—who seemed curiously out of place carrying cups of coffee—seeing that his master was awake, saluted him with the customary "Koos," lifting one of the cups of coffee to give emphasis to the word, and nearly upsetting it in the effort.

"Mazooku," said Ernest, severely, "how did we get here?"

The substance of the retainer's explanation was as follows: When the moon was getting low—vanishing, indeed, behind the "horned house" yonder (the Dutch church with pinnacles on it), it occurred to him, waiting on the verandah, that his master must be weary; and as most had departed from the "dance" in the "tin house" (restaurant), evidently made happy by the "twala" (drink), he entered into the tin house to look for him, and found him overcome by sleep under the table, lying next to the "Lion-who-threw-oxen-over-his-shoulder" (i.e. Jeremy), so overcome by sleep, indeed, that it was quite impossible to conduct him to the waggon. This being so, he (Mazooku) considered what was his duty under the circumstances, and he came to the accurate conclusion that the best thing to do was to put them in the white man's bed, since he knew that his master did not love the floor to lie on. Accordingly, having discovered that this was a room of beds, he and another Zulu entered, but were perplexed to find the beds already occupied by two white men, who had lain down to rest with their clothes on. But, under all these circumstances, he and the other Zulu, considering that their first thought should be towards their own master, had taken the liberty of lifting up the two white men, who were slumbering profoundly after the "dance," by the head and by the heels, and putting them out in the sweet cool air of the night. Having thus "made a place," they then conveyed first Ernest, and next, in consideration of his undoubted greatness, they ventured to take the "Lion-who, &c.," himself, and put him in the other. He was a very great man, the "Lion," and his art of throwing greater men over his shoulder could only be attributed to witchcraft. He himself (Mazooku) had tried it on that morning with a Basuto with whom he had a slight difference of opinion, but the result had not been all that could be desired, inasmuch as the Basuto had kicked him in the stomach, and forced him to drop him.

Ernest laughed as heartily as his headache would allow at this story, and in doing so woke up Jeremy, who at once clapped his hands to his head and looked round; whereupon Mazooku, having saluted the awakened "Lion-who, &c.," with much fervour, and spilled a considerable quantity of hot coffee over him in doing so, took his departure abashed, and at length the two friends were left alone. Thereupon, rising from their respective pallets, they took a step in all the glory of their undress uniform into the middle of the little room, and, after the manner of Englishmen, shook hands and called each other "old fellow." Then they went back to bed and began to converse.

"I say, old fellow, what on earth brought you out here?"

"Well, you see, I came out to look you up. You did not write any letters, and they began to get anxious about you at home, so I packed up my duds and started. Your uncle stands unlimited tin, so I am travelling like a prince in a waggon of my own. I heard of you down in Maritzburg, and guessed that I had best make for Pretoria; and here I am and there you are, and I am devilish glad to see you again, old chap! By Jove, what a head I have! But, I say, why didn't you write? Doll half broke her heart about it, so did your uncle, only he would not say so."

"I did write. I wrote from Secocoeni's country, but I suppose the letter did not fetch," answered Ernest, feeling very guilty. "The fact is, old fellow, I had not the heart to write much; I have been so confoundedly down on my luck ever since that duel business."

"Ah!" interposed Jeremy, "that shot was a credit to you. I didn't think you could have done it."

"A credit! I'll tell you what, it is an awful thing to kill a man like that, I often see his face as he fell, at night in my sleep."

"I was merely looking at it as a shot," replied Jeremy, innocently. "I don't trouble myself with moral considerations, which are topsy-turvy things; and, considered as a shot at twenty paces and under trying circumstances, it was a credit to you."

"Then you see, Jeremy, there was another thing, you know—about—about Eva. Well, I wrote to her, and she has never answered my letter, unless," with a gleam of hope, "you have brought an answer."

Jeremy shook his aching head.

"Ah! no such luck. Well, it put me off, and that's the fact. Since she has chucked me up, I don't care twopence about anything. I don't say but what she is right; I daresay that I am not worth sticking to. She can do much better elsewhere;" and Ernest groaned, and thought that his head was very bad indeed. "But there it is. I hadn't the heart to write any more letters, and I was too proud to write again to her. Confound her! let her go! I am not going to grovel to any woman under heaven, no, not even to her!" and he kicked the bedclothes viciously.

"I haven't learned much Zulu yet," replied Jeremy, sententiously; "but I know two words—'hamba gachlé.'"

"Well, what of them?" said Ernest, testily.

"They mean, I am told, 'take it easy,' or 'look before you leap,' or 'never jump to conclusions,' or 'don't be in a confounded hurry'; very fine mottoes, I think."

"Of course they are; but what have they got to do with Eva?"

"Well, just this: I said I had got no letter; I never said—"

"What?" shouted Ernest.

"Hamba gachlé," replied Jeremy the imperturbable, gazing at Ernest out of his blackened eyes. "I never said that I had not got a message."

Ernest sprang clean out of the little truckle-bed, shaking with excitement. "What is it, man?"

"Just this. She told me to tell you that 'she loved you dearly.'"

Slowly Ernest sat down on the bed again, and, throwing a blanket over his head and shoulders, remarked, in a tone befitting a sheeted ghost:

"The devil she did! Why couldn't you say so before?"

Then he got up again and commenced walking, blanket and all, up and down the room with long strides, and knocking over the water-jug in his excitement.

"Hamba gachlé," again remarked Jeremy, rising and picking up the water-jug. "How are we going to get any more water? I'll tell you all about it."

And he did, including the story of Mr. Plowden's shaking, at which Ernest chuckled fiercely.

"I wish I had been there to kick him," he remarked parenthetically.

"I did that too; I kicked him hard," put in Jeremy; at which Ernest chuckled again.

"I can't make it all out," said Ernest, at length, "but I will go home at once."

"You can't do that, old fellow. Your respected uncle, Sir Hugh, will have you run in."

"Ah, I forgot! Well, I will write to her to-day."

"That's better; now let's dress. My head is rather clearer. By George, though, I am stiff! It is no joke fighting a giant."

But Ernest answered not a word. He was already, after his quick-brained fashion, employed in concocting his letter to Eva.

In the course of the morning he drafted it. It, or rather part of it with which we need concern ourselves, ran thus:

"Such then, my dearest Eva, was the state of my mind towards you. I thought—God forgive me for the treason!—that perhaps you were, as so many women are, a fair-weather lover, and that now that I am in trouble you wished to slip the cable. If that was so, I felt that it was not for me to remonstrate. I wrote to you, and I knew that the letter came safely to your hands. You did not answer it, and I could only come to one conclusion. Hence my own silence. And to be plain I do not at this moment quite understand why you have never written. But Jeremy has brought me your message, and with that I must be content; for no doubt you have reasons which are satisfactory to yourself, and if that is so, no doubt, too, they would be equally satisfactory to me if I only knew them. You see, my dearest love, the fact is that I trust and believe in you utterly and entirely. What is right and true, what is loyal and sincere to me and to yourself—those are the things that you will do. Jeremy tells me a rather amusing story about the new clergyman who has come to Kesterwick, and who is, it appears, an aspirant for your hand. Well, Eva, I am sufficiently conceited not to be jealous; although I am in the unlucky position of an absent man, and worse still, an absent man under a cloud, I do not believe that he will cut me out. But on the day that you can put your hand on your heart, and look me straight in the eyes, and tell me, on your honour as a lady, that you love this or any other man better than you do me, on that day I shall be ready to resign you to him. But till that day comes—and there is something which tells me that it is as impossible for it to come as for the mountain-range I look on as I write to move towards the town and bury it—I am free from jealousy, for I know that it is impossible that you should be faithless to your love.

"Oh, my sweet, the troth we plighted was not for days, or years, or times—it was for ever. I believe that nothing can dissolve it, and that Death himself will be powerless against it. I believe that with each new and progressive existence it will re-arise as surely as the flowers in spring, only, unlike them, more fragrant and beautiful than before. Sometimes I think that it has already existed through countless ages. Strange thoughts come into a man's mind out there on the great veld, riding alone hour after hour, and day after day, through sunlight and through moonlight, till the spirit of nature broods upon him, and he begins to learn the rudiments of truth. Some day I shall tell them all to you. Not that I have ever been quite alone, for I can say honestly that you have always been at my side since I left you; there has been no hour of the day or night when you have not been in my thoughts, and I believe that, till death blots out my senses, no such hour will ever come.

"Day by day, too, my love has grown stronger even in its despair. Day by day it has taken shape and form and colour, and become more and more a living thing, more and more an entity, as distinct as soul and body, and yet as inextricably blended and woven into the substance of each. If ever a woman was beloved, you are that woman, Eva Ceswick; if ever a man's life, present and to come, lay in a woman's hands, my life lies in yours. It is a germ which you can cast away or destroy, or which you can nourish till it bursts into bloom, and bears fruit beautiful beyond imagining. You are my fate, my other part. With you my destiny is intertwined, and you can mould it as you will. There is no height to which I cannot rise by your side; there is no depth to which I may not sink without you.

"And now, what does all this lead up to? Will you make a sacrifice for me, who am ready to give up all my life to you—no, who have already given it? That sacrifice is this: I want you to come out here and marry me; for, as you know, circumstances prevent me from returning to you. If you will come, I will meet you at the Cape, and marry you there. Ah, surely you will come! As for money, I have plenty from home, and can make as much more as we shall want here, so that need be no obstacle. It is long to wait for your answer—three months—but I hope that the faith that will, as the Bible tells us, enable people to move mountains—and my faith in you is as great as that—will also enable me to bear the suspense, and in the end prove its own reward."

Ernest read selected portions of this exalted composition to Mr. Alston and Jeremy. Both listened in solemn silence, and at the conclusion Jeremy scratched his head and remarked that it was deep enough to "fetch" any girl, though for his part he did not quite understand it. Mr. Alston relit his pipe, and for a while said nothing; but to himself he thought that it was a remarkable letter for so young a man to have written, and revealed a curious turn of mind. One remark he did make, however, and that was rather a rude one:

"The girl won't understand what you are driving at, Master Ernest; she will think that you have gone off your head in these savage parts. All you say may or may not be true—on that point I express no opinion; but to write such things to a woman is to throw your pearls before swine. You should ask her about her bonnets, my boy, and tell her what sort of dresses she should bring out, and that the air is good for the complexion. She would come then."

Here Ernest fired up.

"You are beastly cynical, Alston, and you should not speak of Miss Ceswick like that to me. Bonnets, indeed!"

"All right, my lad—all right. Time will show. Ah, you boys! you go building up your ideals of ivory and gold and fine linen, only to find them one day turned into the commonest of clay, draped in the dirtiest of rags. Well, well, it is the way of the world; but you take my advice Ernest; burn that letter, and go in for an Intombi. It is not too late yet, and there is no mistake about the sort of clay of which a Kafir girl is made."

Here Ernest stamped out of the room in a passion.

"Too cock-sure, wanted cooling down a little," remarked Mr. Alston to Jeremy; "should never be cock-sure where a woman is concerned; women are fond of playing dirty tricks, and saying they could not help it. I know them; for, though you mightn't think it, I was once young myself. Come on; let us find him, and go for a walk."

They found Ernest sitting on the box of the waggon, which was outspanned, together with Jeremy's, just outside the town, and looking rather sulky.

"Come on, Ernest," said Mr. Alston, apologetically; "I will throw no more mud at your ideal. In the course of the last thirty years I have seen so many fall to pieces of their own accord that I could not help warning you. But perhaps they make them of better stuff in England than we do in these parts."

Ernest descended and soon forgot his pique. It was but rarely that he bore malice for more than half an hour. As they walked along one of the by-streets they met the young fellow who had acted as second to Jeremy in the big fight of the previous day. He informed them that he had just been to inquire how the giant was. It appeared that he had received an injury to the spine, the effect of Jeremy's "lift," from which there was little hope of his recovery. He was not, however, in much pain. This intelligence distressed Jeremy not a little. He had earnestly desired to thrash the giant, but he had felt no wish to injure him. With his usual promptitude he announced his intention of going to see his fallen enemy.

"You are likely to meet with a warm reception if you do," said Mr. Alston.

"I'll risk it. I should like to tell him that I am sorry."

"Very good; come along—that is the house."

The injured man had been carried to the house of a relative just outside the town, a white thatched building that had been built five-and-thirty years before, when the site of Pretoria was a plain, inhabited only by quaggas, eland, and vilderbeeste. In front of the door was a grove of orange-trees, which smelled sweet and looked golden with hanging fruit.

The house itself was a small white building, with a double-swinging door, like those used in stables in this country. The top half of the door was open, and over the lower portion of it leaned a Boer, a rough-looking customer, smoking a huge pipe.

"'Dagh, Oom'" (Good-day, uncle), said Mr. Alston, stretching out his hand.

The other looked at him suspiciously, and then held out a damp paw to each in turn, at the same time opening the door. As Ernest passed the threshold he noticed that the clay flooring was studded with peach-stones well trodden into its substance to prevent wear and tear from passing feet. The door opened into a fair-sized room with whitewashed walls called the "sit-kamé" or sitting-room, and furnished with a settee, a table, and several chairs seated with "rimpi," or strips of hide. On the biggest of these chairs sat a woman of large size, the mother of the family. She did not rise on their entry, but without speaking held out a limp hand, which Mr. Alston and the others took, addressing her affectionately as "tanta," or aunt. Then they shook hands with six or seven girls and young men, the latter sitting about in an aimless sort of way, the former clearing off the remains of the family meal, which had consisted of huge bones of boiled fresh beef. So fresh was it, indeed, that on the floor by the side of the table lay the gory head and skin of a newly-killed ox, from which the beef had been cut. Ernest, noticing this, wondered at the super-human strength of stomach that could take its food under such circumstances.

The preliminary ceremony of hand-shaking having been got through, Mr. Alston, who spoke Dutch perfectly, explained the object of their visit. The faces of the Dutchmen darkened as he did so, and the men scowled at Jeremy with hatred not unmingled with terror. When he had done, the oldest man said that he would ask his cousin if he would see them, adding, however, that he was so ill that he did not think it likely. Raising a curtain, which served as a door, he passed from the sitting-room into the bedroom, or "slaap-kamé."

Presently he returned and beckoned to the Englishmen to enter. They passed into a small chamber about ten feet square, which was hermetically sealed from air, after the fashion of these people in cases of any illness. On a large bed that blocked up most of the room, and on which it was the usual habit of the master of the house and his wife to sleep in their clothes, lay the fallen giant. So much as could be seen of his face was a mass of hideous bruises, and one of his hands, which lay on the bed, was in splints; the chief injury, however, was to his back, and from this he could never expect to recover. By his side sat his little wife, who had on the previous day urged the thrashing of the Hottentot. She glared fiercely at Jeremy, but said nothing. On catching sight of his victor, the giant turned his face to the wall and asked what he wanted.

"I have come," said Jeremy, Mr. Alston interpreting for him, "to say that I am sorry that you are injured so much; that I wanted to beat you, but had no idea that I should hurt you so. I know that the trick of throwing a man as I threw you is dangerous, and I only used it as a last resource, and because you would have killed me if I had not."

The Boer muttered something in reply about its being very bitter to be beaten by such a little man.

It was evident to Ernest that the man's pride was utterly broken. He had believed himself the strongest man, white or black, in Africa, and now an English lad had thrown him over his shoulder like a plaything.

Jeremy next said that he hoped that he bore no malice, and would shake hands.

The giant hesitated a little, then stretched out his uninjured hand, which Jeremy shook.

"Englishman," he said, "you are a wonderful man, and you will grow stronger yet. You have made a baby of me for life, and turned my heart to a baby's too. Perhaps one day some man will do the same for you. Till then you can never know what I feel. They will give you the Hottentot outside. No, you must take him; you won him in fair fight. He is a good driver, though he is so small. Now go."

The sight was a painful one, and they were not sorry to get away from it. Outside they found one of the young Boers waiting with the Hottentot boy, whom he insisted in handing over to Jeremy.

Any scruples the latter had about accepting him were overcome by the look of intense satisfaction on the features of the poor wretch himself when he learnt that he was to be handed over.

His name was "Aasvögel" (vulture), and he made Jeremy an excellent and most faithful servant.

CHAPTER X

A WAY OF ESCAPE

When Mr. Alston, Jeremy and Ernest emerged from the back street in which was the house they had visited into one of the principal thoroughfares of Pretoria, they came upon a curious sight. In the middle of the street stood, or rather danced, a wiry Zulu, dressed in an old military great-coat and the ordinary native "moocha," or scanty kilt, and having a red worsted comforter tied round one arm. He was shouting out something at the top of his voice, and surrounded by a crowd of other natives, who at intervals expressed their approval of what he was saying in deep guttural exclamations.

"What is that lunatic after?" asked Jeremy.

Mr. Alston listened for a minute, and answered:

"I know the man well. His name is Goza. He is the fleetest runner in Natal, and can go as fast as a horse; indeed, there are few horses that he cannot tire out. By profession he is a 'praiser.' He is now singing the praises of the Special Commissioner—'bongering' they call it. This is what he is saying:

"'Listen to the foot of the great elephant Somptseu (Sir T. Shepstone). Feel how the earth shakes beneath the tread of the white t'Chaka,[*] father of the Zulus, foremost among the great white people. Ou! he is coming; ou! he is here. See how the faces of the "Amaboona" (the Boers) turn pale before him. He will eat them up; he will swallow them, the huge vulture, who sits still till the ox is dead, who fights the fight of "sit down." Oh! he is great, the lion; where he turns his eye the people melt away, their hearts turn to fat. Where is there one like Somptseu, the man who is not afraid of Death; who looks at Death and it runs from him; who has the tongue of honey; who reigns like the first star at night; who is beloved and honoured of the great white mother, the Queen; who loves his children, the Amazulu, and shelters them under his wide wing; who lifted Cetywayo out of the dirt, and can put him back in the dirt again? Abase yourselves, you low people, doctor yourself with medicine, lest his fierce eyes should burn you up. O! hark! he comes, the father of kings, the Chaka; O! be still; O! be silent; O! shake in your knees. He is here, the elephant, the lion, the fierce one, the patient one, the strong one! See he deigns to talk to little children; he teaches them wisdom; he gives light like the sun—he is the sun—he is t'Somptseu.'"

[*] The Zulu Napoleon, great-uncle to the last King of Zululand, Cetywayo.

At this juncture a quiet-looking, oldish gentleman, entirely unlike either an elephant, a lion, or a vulture, of medium height, with grey whiskers, a black coat, and a neat black tie fastened in a bow, came round the corner, leading a little girl by the hand. As he came the praiser lifted up his right hand, and in the most stentorian tones gave the royal salute, "Bayète," which was re-echoed by all the other natives.

The oldish gentleman, who was none other than the Special Commissioner himself, turned upon his extoller with a look of intense annoyance, and addressed him very sharply in Zulu.

"Be still," he said. "Why do you always annoy me with your noise? Be still, I say, you loud-tongued dog, or I will send you back to Natal. My head aches with your empty words."

"O, elephant! I am silent as the dead: Bayète. O, Somptseu! I am quiet: Bayète."

"Go! Begone!"

With a final shout of Bayète the Zulu turned and fled down the street with the swiftness of the wind, shouting praises as he went.

"How do you do, sir?" said Mr. Alston, advancing. "I was just coming up to call upon you."

"Ah, Alston, I am delighted to see you. I heard that you were gone on a hunting trip. Given up work and taken to hunting, eh? Well, I should like to do the same."

"If I could have found you when I came up here, I should have been tempted to ask you to come with us."

At this point Mr. Alston introduced Ernest and Jeremy. The Special Commissioner shook hands with them.

"I have heard of you," he said to Jeremy; "but I must ask you not to fight any more giants here just at present; the tension between Boer and Englishman is too great to allow of its being stretched any more. Do you know, you nearly provoked an outbreak last night with your fighting? I trust that you will not do it again."

He spoke rather severely, and Jeremy coloured. Presently, however, he made amends by asking them all to dinner.

On the following morning Ernest sent off his letter to Eva. He also wrote to his uncle and to Dorothy, explaining his long silence as best he could. The latter, too, he for the first time took into his confidence about Eva. At a distance he no longer felt the same shyness in speaking to her about another woman that had overpowered him when he was by her side.

Now that he had been away from England for a year or so, many things connected with his home life had grown rather faint amid the daily change and activity of his new life. The rush of fresh impressions had to a great extent overlaid the old ones, and Dorothy and Mr. Cardus and all the old Kesterwick existence and surroundings seemed faint and far away. They were indeed rapidly assuming that unreality which in time the wanderer finds will gather round his old associations. He feels that they know him no more; very likely he imagines that they have forgotten him, and so they become like the shades of the dead. It is almost a shock to such an one to come back and find, after an absence of many years, that though he has been living his rapid vigorous life, and storing his time with many acts, good, bad, and indifferent; though he thinks that he has changed so completely, and developed greatly in one direction or another, yet the old spots, the old familiar surroundings, and the old dear faces have changed hardly one whit. They have been living their quiet English life, in which sensation, incident, and excitement are things unfamiliar, and have varied not at all.

Most people, as a matter of fact, change very little except in so far as they are influenced by the cyclic variations of their life, the passage from youth to maturity, and from maturity to age, and the attendant modes of thought and action befitting each period. But even then the change is superficial rather than real. What the child is, that the middle-aged person and the old man will be also. The reason of this appears to be sufficiently obvious: the unchanging personality that grows not old, the animating spiritual "ego," is there, and practically identical at all periods of life. The body, the brain, and the subtler intellect may all vary according to the circumstances, mostly physical, of personal existence; but the effect that the passage of a few years, more or less active or stormy, can produce upon a principle so indestructible, so immeasurably ancient, and the inheritor of so far-reaching a destiny as some of us believe the individual human soul to be, surely must be small.

Already Ernest began to find it something of a labour to indite epistles to people in England, and yet he had the pen of a ready writer. The links that bound them together were fast breaking loose. Eva, and Eva alone, remained clear and real to the vision of his mind. She was always with him; and to her, at any period of his life, he never found difficulty in writing. For, in truth, their very natures were interwoven and the rapport between them was not produced merely by the pressure of external circumstances, or by the fact of continual contact and mutual attraction arising from physical causes, such as the natural leaning of youth to youth and beauty to beauty.

These causes, according to Ernest's creed, no doubt, had to do with its production, and perhaps were necessary to its mundane birth, as the battery is necessary to the creation of the electric spark. Thus, had Eva been old, instead of a young and lovely girl, the rapport would perhaps never have come into being here. In short, they formed the cable along which the occult communication could pass, but there their function ended. Having once established that communication, and provided a means by which the fusion of spirit could be effected, youth and beauty and the natural attraction of sex to sex had done their part. The great dividing river that rolls so fast and wide between our souls in their human shape had been safely passed, and the two fortunate travellers had been allowed before their time to reap advantages—the measureless advantage of real love, so rare on earth, and at its best so stained by passion, which will only come to most of us, and then perhaps imperfectly, in a different world from this.

Yes, the bridge might now be broken down; it had served its purpose. Come age, or loss of physical attraction, or separation and icy silence, or the change called death itself, and the souls thus subtly blended can and will and do defy them. For the real life is not here; here only is the blind beginning of things, maybe the premature beginning.

And so Ernest posted his letters, and then, partly to employ his thoughts, and partly because it was his nature to throw himself into whatever stream of life was flowing past him, he set himself to master the state of political affairs in the country in which he found himself.

This need not be entered into here, further than to say that it was such as might with advantage have employed wiser heads than his, and indeed did employ them. Suffice it to say that he contrived to make himself of considerable use to the English party, both before and after the annexation of the Transvaal to the dominions of the Crown. Among other things he went on several missions in conjunction with Mr. Alston, with a view of ascertaining the real state of feeling among the Boers. Also, together with Jeremy, he joined a volunteer corps which was organised for the defence of Pretoria when it was still a matter of doubt whether or not the contemplated annexation would or would not result in an attack being made upon the town by the Boers. It was a most exciting time, and once or twice Ernest and Jeremy had narrow escapes of being murdered. However, nothing worthy of note happened to them, and at last the long-expected annexation came off successfully, to the intense joy of all the Englishmen in the country, and to the great relief of the vast majority of the Boers.

Now, together with the proclamation by which the Transvaal was annexed to her Majesty's dominions, was issued another that was to have a considerable bearing upon Ernest's fortunes. This was none other than a promise of her Majesty's gracious pardon to all such as had been resident in the Transvaal for a period of six months previous to the date of annexation, being former British subjects and offenders against the English criminal law, who would register their name and offence within a given time. The object of this proclamation was to give immunity from prosecution to many individuals, former deserters from the English army, and other people who had in some way transgressed the laws, but were now occupying respectable positions in their adopted country.

Mr. Alston read this proclamation attentively when it came out in a special number of the Gazette. Then, after thinking for a while, he handed it to Ernest.

"You have read this amnesty proclamation?" he said.

"Yes," answered Ernest; "what of it?"

"What of it? Ah, the stupidity of youth! Go down, go down on your knees, young man, and render thanks to the Power that inspired Lord Carnarvon with the idea of annexing the Transvaal. Can't you very well see that it takes your neck out of the halter? Off with you, and register your name and offence with the secretary to Government, and you will be clear for ever from any consequences that might ensue from the slight indiscretion of having shot your own first cousin in a duel on British soil."

"By Jove, Alston! you don't mean that!"

"Mean it? Of course I do. The proclamation does not specify any particular offence to which the pardon is to be denied, and you have lived more than six months on Transvaal territory. Off you go!"

Ernest went like an arrow.

CHAPTER XI

FOUND WANTING

Ernest reached the Government office and registered his name, and in due course received "her Majesty's gracious pardon and indemnity from and against all actions, proceedings, and prosecutions at law, having arisen, arising, or to arise, by whomsoever undertaken, &c., conveyed through his Excellency the Administrator of Our said territory of the Transvaal."

When this precious document was in his pocket, Ernest thought that he now for the first time fully realised what must be the feelings of a slave unexpectedly manumitted. Had it not been for this fortunate accident, the consequences of that fatal duel must have continually overshadowed him. Had he returned to England, he would have been liable at any period of his life to a prosecution for murder. Indeed, the arm of the law is long, and he lived in continual apprehension of an application for his extradition being made to the authorities of whatever country he was in. But now all this was gone from him, and he felt that he would not be afraid to have words with an attorney-general, or shudder any more at the sight of a policeman.

His first idea on getting his pardon was to return straightway to England; but that silent Fate which directs men's lives, driving them whither they would not, and forcing their bare and bleeding feet to stumble along the stony paths of its hidden purpose, came into his mind, and made him see that it would be better to delay a while. In a few weeks Eva's answer would surely reach him. If he were to go now, it was even possible that he might pass her in mid-ocean, for in his heart he never doubted but that she would come.

And indeed the very next mail there came a letter from Dorothy, written in answer to that which he had posted on the same day that he had written to Eva. It was only a short letter—the last post that could catch the mail was just going out, and his welcome letter had only just arrived; but she had twenty minutes, and she would send one line. She told him how grateful they were to hear that he was well and safe, and reproached him gently for not writing. Then she thanked him for making her his confidante about Eva Ceswick. She had guessed it long before, she said; and she thought they were both lucky in each other, and hoped and prayed that when the time came they would be as completely happy as it was possible for people to be. She had never spoken to Eva about him; but she should no longer feel any diffidence in doing so now. She should go and see her very soon, and plead his cause: not that it wanted any pleading, however, she was sure of that. Eva looked sad now that he was gone. There had been some talk a while back of Mr. Plowden, the new clergyman; but she supposed that Eva had given him his quietus, as she heard no more of it now; and so on, till "the postman is at the door waiting for this letter."

Little did Ernest guess what it cost poor Dorothy to write her congratulations and wishes of happiness. A man—the nobler animal, remember—could hardly have done it; only the inferior woman would show such unselfishness.

This letter filled Ernest with a sure and certain hope. Eva, he clearly saw, had not had time to write by that mail; by the next her answer would come. It can be imagined that he waited for its advent with some anxiety.

Mr. Alston, Ernest, and Jeremy had taken a house in Pretoria, and for the past month or two had been living in it very comfortably. It was a pleasant one-storied house, with a verandah and a patch of flower-garden in front of it, in which grew a large gardenia-bush covered with hundreds of sweet-scented blooms, and many rose-trees, that in the divine climate of Pretoria flourish like thistles in our own. Beyond the flowers was a patch of vines, covered at this season of the year with enormous bunches of grapes, extending down to the line of waving willow-trees, interspersed with clumps of bamboo that grew along the edge of the sluit and kept the house private from the road. On the other side of the narrow path which led to the gate was a bed of melons, now rapidly coming to perfection. This garden was Ernest's especial pride and occupation, and just then he was much troubled in his mind about the melons, which were getting scorched by the bright rays of the sun. To obviate this he had designed cunning frameworks of little willow twigs, which he stuck over the melons and covered with dry grass—"parasols" he called them.

One morning—it was a particularly lovely morning—Ernest was standing after breakfast on this path, smoking, and directing Mazooku as to the erection of the "parasols" over his favourite melons. It was not a job at all suited to the capacity of the great Zulu, whose assegai, stuck in the ground behind him in the middle of a small bundle of knob-sticks, seemed a tool ominously unlike those used by gardeners of other lands. However, "needs must when the devil drives," and there was the brawny fellow on his knees, puffing and blowing, and trying to fix the tuft of grass to Ernest's satisfaction.

"Mazooku, you lazy hound," said the latter, at last, "if you don't put that tuft right in two shakes, by the heaven you will never reach, I'll break your head with your own kerrie!"

"Ow, Inkoos," replied the Zulu sulkily, again trying to prop up the tuft, and muttering to himself meanwhile.

"Do you catch what that fellow of yours is saying?" asked Mr. Alston. "He is saying that all Englishmen are mad, and that you are the maddest of the mad. He considers that nobody who was not a lunatic would bother his head with those 'weeds that stink' (flowers), or those fruits which, even if you succeed in growing them—and surely the things are bewitched, or they would grow without 'hats'" (Ernest's parasols)—"must lie very cold on the stomach."

At that moment the particular "hat" which Mazooku was trying to arrange fell down again, whereupon the Zulu's patience gave out, and, cursing it for a witch in the most vigorous language, he emphasised his words by bringing his fist straight down on the melon, smashing it to pieces. Whereupon Ernest made for him, and he vanished swiftly.

Mr. Alston stood by laughing at the scene, and awaited Ernest's return. Presently he came strolling back, not having caught Mazooku. Indeed, it would not have greatly mattered if he had; for, as that swarthy gentleman very well knew, great indeed must be the provocation that could induce Ernest to touch a native. It was a thing to which he had an almost unconquerable aversion, in the same way that he objected to the word "nigger" as applied to a people who, whatever their faults may be, are, as a rule, gentlemen in the truest sense of the word.

As he came strolling down the path towards him, his face a little flushed with the exertion, Mr. Alston thought to himself that Ernest was growing into a very handsome fellow. The tall frame, narrow at the waist and broad at the shoulders, the eloquent dark eyes, which so far surpass the loveliest grey or blue, the silken hair, which curled over his head like that on a Grecian statue, the curved lips, the quick intelligence and kindly smile that lit the whole face—all these things helped to make his appearance not so much handsome as charming, and to women captivating to a dangerous extent. His dress, too—which consisted of riding-breeches, boots and spurs, a white waistcoat and linen coat, with a very broad soft felt hat looped up at one side, so as to throw the face into alternate light and shadow—helped the general effect considerably. Altogether Ernest was a pretty fellow in those days.

Jeremy was lounging on an easy-chair in the verandah, in company with the boy Roger Alston, and intensely interested in watching a furious battle between two lines of ants, black and red, who had their homes somewhere in the stonework. For a long while the issue of the battle remained doubtful, victory inclining, if anything, to the side of the thin red line, when suddenly, from the entrance to the nest of the black ants, there emerged a battalion of giants—great fellows, at least six times the size of the others—who fell upon the red ants and routed them, taking many prisoners. Then followed the most curious spectacle, namely, the deliberate execution of the captive red ants, by having their heads bitten off by the great black soldiers. Jeremy and Roger knew what was coming very well, for these battles were of frequent occurrence, and the casualties among the red ants simply frightful. On this occasion they determined to save the prisoners, which was effected by dipping a match in some of the nicotine at the bottom of a pipe, and placing it in front of the black giants. The ferocious insects would thereupon abandon their captives, and, rushing at the strange intruder, hang on like bulldogs till the poison did its work, and they dropped off senseless, to recover presently and stagger off home, holding their legs to their antenné and exhibiting every other symptom of a frightful headache.

Jeremy was sitting on a chair, oiling the matches, and Roger, kneeling on the pavement, was employed in beguiling the giants into biting them, when suddenly they heard the sound of galloping horses and the rattle of wheels. The lad, lowering his head still more, looked out towards the market-square through a gap between the willow-stems.

"Hurrah, Mr. Jones," he said, "here comes the mail!"

Next minute, amid loud blasts from the bugle, and enveloped in a cloud of dust, the heavy cart, to the sides and seats of which the begrimed and worn-out passengers were clinging like drowning men to straws, came rattling along as fast as the six greys reserved for the last stage could gallop, and vanished towards the post-office.

"There's the mail, Ernest," hallooed Jeremy; "she will bring the English letters."

Ernest nodded, turned a little pale, and nervously knocked out his pipe. No wonder: that mail-cart carried his destiny, and he knew it. Presently he walked across the square to the post-office. The letters were not sorted, and he was the first person there. Very soon one of his Excellency's staff came riding down to get the Government House bag. It was the same gentleman with whom he had sung "Auld lang syne" so enthusiastically on the day of Jeremy's encounter with the giant, and had afterwards been carted home in the wheelbarrow.

"Hullo, Kershaw, here we are, 'primos inter omnes,' 'primos primi primores,' which is it? Come, Kershaw, you are the last from school—which is it? I don't believe you know—ha! ha! ha! What are you doing down here so soon? Does the 'expectant swain await the postmen's knock?' Why, my dear fellow, you look pale; you must be in love or thirsty. So am I—the latter, not the former. Love, I do abjure thee. 'Quis separabit,' who will have a split? I think that the sun can't be far from the line. Shall we, my dear Kershaw, shall we take an observation? Ha! ha! ha!"

"No, thank you, I never drink anything between meals."

"Ah! my boy, a bad habit; give it up before it is too late. Break it off, my dear Kershaw, and always wet your whistle in the strictest moderation, or you will die young. What says the poet?—

"'He who drinks strong beer, and goes to bed mellow,
Lives as he ought to live, lives as he ought to live,
Lives as he ought to live, and dies a jolly good fellow.'

"Byron, I think, is it not? Ha! ha! ha!"

Just then some others came up, and, somewhat to Ernest's relief, his friend turned the light of his kindly countenance to shine elsewhere, and left him to his thoughts.

At last the little shutter of the post-office was thrown up, and Ernest got his own letters, together with those belonging to Mr. Alston and Jeremy. He turned into the shade of a neighbouring verandah, and rapidly sorted the pile. There was no letter in Eva's handwriting. But there was one in that of her sister Florence. Ernest knew the writing well; there was no mistaking its peculiar upright, powerful-looking characters. This he opened hurriedly. Enclosed in the letter was a note, which was in the writing he had expected to see. He rapidly unfolded it, and as he did so, a flash of fear passed through his brain.

"Why did she write in this way?"

The note could not have been a long one, for in another minute it was lying on the ground, and Ernest, pale-faced and with catching breath, was clinging to the verandah-post with both hands to save himself from falling. In a few seconds he recovered, and, picking up the note, walked quickly across the square towards the house. Half-way across he was overtaken by his friend on the Staff cantering gaily along on a particularly wooden-looking pony, from the sides of which his legs projected widely, and waving in one hand the Colonial Office bag addressed to the administrator of the Government.

"Hallo, my abstemious friend!" he hallooed, as he pulled up the wooden pony with a jerk that sent each of its stiff legs sprawling in a different direction. "Was patience rewarded? Is Chloe over the water kind? If not, take my advice, and don't trouble your head about her. Quant on n'a pas ce qu'on aime, the wise man aimes ce qu'il a. Kershaw, I have conceived a great affection for you, and I will let you into a secret.

Come with me this afternoon, and I will introduce you to two charming specimens of indigenous beauty. Like roses they bloom upon the veld, and waste their sweetness on the desert air. 'Mater pulchra, puella pulcherrima,' as Virgil says. I, as befits my years, will attach myself to the mater, for your sweet youth shall be reserved the puella. Ha! ha! ha!" And he brought the despatch-bag down with a sounding whack between the ears of the wooden pony, with the result that he was nearly sent flying into the sluit, being landed by a sudden plunge well on the animal's crupper.

"Woho, Bucephaluas, woho! or your mealies shall be cut off."

Just then he for the first time caught sight of the face of his companion, who was plodding along in silence by his side.

"Hullo! what's up, Kershaw?" he said, in an altered tone; "you don't look well. Nothing wrong, I hope?"

"Nothing, nothing," answered Ernest quietly; "that is, I have got some bad news, that is all. Nothing to speak of, nothing."

"My dear fellow, I am so sorry, and I have been troubling you with my nonsense. Forgive me. There, you wish to be alone. Good-bye."

A few seconds later Mr. Alston and Jeremy, from their point of vantage on the verandah, saw Ernest coming with swift strides up the garden path. His face was drawn with pain, and there was a fleck of blood upon his lip. He passed them without a word, and, entering the house, slammed the door of his own room. Mr. Alston and Jeremy looked at one another.

"What's up?" said the laconic Jeremy.

Mr. Alston thought a while before he answered, as was his fashion.

"Something gone wrong with 'the ideal,' I should say," he said at length; "that is the way of ideals."

"Shall we go and see?" said Jeremy, uneasily.

"No, give him a minute or two to pull himself together. Lots of time for consultation afterwards."

Meanwhile Ernest, having got into his room, sat down upon the bed, and again read the note which was enclosed in Florence's letter. Then he folded it up and put it down, slowly and methodically. Next he opened the other letter, which he had not yet looked at, and read that too. After he had done it he threw himself face downwards on the pillow, and thought a while. Presently he arose, and, going to the other side of the room, took down a revolver-case which hung to a nail, and drew out a revolver, which was loaded. Returning, he again sat down upon the bed, and cocked it. So he remained for a minute or two, and then slowly lifted the pistol towards his head. At that moment he heard footsteps approaching, and, with a quick movement, threw the weapon under the bed. As he did so Mr. Alston and Jeremy entered.

"Any letters, Ernest?" asked the former.

"Letters! O yes, I beg your pardon; here they are;" and he took a packet from the pocket of his white coat, and handed them to him.

Mr. Alston took them, looking all the while fixedly at Ernest, who avoided his glance.

"What is the matter, my boy?" he said kindly, at last; "nothing wrong, I hope."

Ernest looked at him blankly.

"What is it, old chap?" said Jeremy, seating himself on the bed beside him, and laying his hand on his arm.

Then Ernest broke out into a paroxysm of grief painful to behold. Fortunately for all concerned, it was brief. Had it lasted much longer, something must have given way. Suddenly his mood changed, and he grew hard and bitter.

"Nothing, my dear fellow, nothing," he said; "that is, only the sequel to a pretty little idyl. You may remember a letter I wrote—to a woman—some months back. There, you both of you know the story. Now you shall hear the answer, or, to be more correct, the answers.

"That—woman has a sister. Both she and her sister have written to me. My—her sister's letter is the longest. We will take it first. I think that we may skip the first page, there is nothing particular in it, and I do not wish to—waste your time. Now listen:

"'By the way, I have a piece of news for you which will interest you, and which you will, I am sure, be glad to hear; for, of course, you will have by this time got over any little tendresse you may have had in that direction. Eva' (that is the woman to whom I wrote, and to whom I thought I was engaged) 'is going to be married to a Mr. Plowden, a gentleman who has been acting as locum tenens for Mr. Halford.'"

Here Jeremy sprang up, and swore a great oath. Ernest motioned him down, and went on:

"'I say I am certain that you will be glad to hear this, because the match is in every respect a satisfactory one, and will, I am sure, bring dear Eva happiness. Mr. Plowden is well off, and, of course, a clergyman—two great guarantees for the success of their matrimonial venture. Eva tells me that she had a letter from you last mail' (the letter I read you, gentlemen), 'and asks me to thank you for it. If she can find time, she will send you a line shortly; but, as you will understand, she has her hands very full just at present. The wedding is to take place at Kesterwick Church on the 17th of May' (that is to-morrow, gentlemen), 'and, if this letter reaches you in time, I am sure you will think of us all on that day. It will be very quiet owing to our dear aunt's death being still so comparatively recent. Indeed, the engagement has, in obedience to Mr. Plowden's wishes—for he is very retiring—been kept quite secret, and you are absolutely the first person to whom it has been announced. I hope that you will feel duly flattered, sir. We are very busy about the trousseau and just now the burning question is, of what colour the dress in which Eva is to go away in after the wedding shall be. Eva and I are all for grey. Mr. Plowden is for olive-green, and, as is natural under the circumstances, I expect that he will carry the day. They are together in the drawing-room setting it now. You always admired Eva (rather warmly once; do you remember how cut up you both were when you went away? Alas for the fickleness of human nature!); you should see her now. Her happiness makes her look lovely; but I hear her calling me. No doubt they have settled the momentous question. Good-bye. I am not clever at writing, but I hope that my news will make up for my want of skill.—Always yours,

"'Florence Ceswick.'

"Now for the enclosure," said Ernest.

"'Dear Ernest,—I got your letter. Florence will tell you what there is to tell. I am going to be married. Think what you will of me; I cannot help myself. Believe me, this has cost me great suffering; but my duty seems clear. I hope that you will forget me, Ernest, as henceforth it will be my duty to forget you. Good-bye, my dear Ernest; Oh, good-bye!

"'E.'"

"Humph!" murmured Alston beneath his breath. "As I thought—clay, and damned bad clay, too!"

Slowly Ernest tore the letter into small fragments, threw them down, and stamped upon them with his foot as though they were a living thing.

"I wish I had shaken the life out of that devil of a parson!" groaned Jeremy, who was in his way as much affected by the news as his friend.

"Curse you!" said Ernest, turning on him fiercely; "why didn't you stop where you were and look after her, instead of coming humbugging after me?"

Jeremy only groaned humbly by way of answer. Mr. Alston, as was his way when perplexed, filled his pipe and lit it. Ernest paced swiftly up and down the little room, the white walls of which he had decorated with pictures cut from illustrated papers, Christmas cards, and photographs. Over the head of the bed was a photograph of Eva herself, which he had framed in some beautiful native wood. He reached it down.

"Look," he said, "that is the lady herself. Handsome, isn't she, and pleasant to look on? Who would have thought that she was such a devil? Tells me to forget her, and talks about 'her duty'! Women love a little joke!"

He hurled the photograph on to the floor, and treated it as he had treated the letter, grinding it to pieces with his heel.

"They say," he went on, "that a man's curses are sometimes heard wherever it is they arrange these pleasant surprises for us. Now, you fellows, bear witness to what I say, and watch that woman's life. I curse her before God and man! May she lay down her head in sorrow night by night and year by year! May her—"

"Stop, Ernest," said Mr. Alston, with a shrug; "you might be taken at your word, and you wouldn't like that, you know. Besides, it is cowardly to go on cursing at a woman."

Ernest paused, standing for a moment with his clenched fist still raised above his head, his pale lips quivering with intense excitement, and his dark eyes flashing and blazing like stars.

"You are right," he said, dropping his fist on to the table. "It is with the man that I have to deal."

"What man?"

"This Plowden. I fear that I shall disturb his honeymoon."

"What do you mean?"

"I mean that I am going to kill him, or he is going to kill me; it does not matter which."

"Why, what quarrel have you with the man? Of course he looked after himself. You could not expect him to consider your interests, could you?"

"If he had cut me out fairly, I should not have a word to say. Every man for himself in this pleasant world. But, mark my words, this parson and Florence have forced Eva into this unholy business, and I will have his life in payment. If you don't believe me, ask Jeremy. He saw something of the game before he left."

"Look here, Kershaw, the man's a parson. He will take shelter behind his cloth; he won't fight. What shall you do then?"

"I shall shoot him," was the cool reply.

"Ernest, you are mad; it won't do. You shall not go, and that is all about it. You shall not ruin yourself over this woman, who is not fit to black an honest man's shoes."

"Shall not! shall not! Alston, you use strong language. Who will prevent me?"

"I will prevent you," he answered, sternly. "I am your superior officer, and the corps you belong to is not disbanded. If you try to leave this place you shall be arrested as a deserter. Now don't be a fool, lad; you have killed one man, and got out of the mess. If you kill another you will not get out of it. Besides, what will the satisfaction be? If you want revenge, be patient. It will come. I have seen something of life; at least, I am old enough to be your father, and I know that you think me a cynic because I laugh at your 'high-falutin' about women. How justly I warned you, you see now. But, cynic or not, I believe in the God above us, and I believe, too, that there is a rough justice in this world. It is in the world principally that people expiate the sins of the world; and if this marriage is such a wicked thing as you think, it will bring its own trouble with it, without any help from you. Time will avenge you. Everything comes to him who can wait."

Ernest's eyes glittered coldly as he answered:

"I cannot wait. I am a ruined man already; all my life is laid waste. I wish to die, but I wish to kill him before I die."

"So sure as my name is Alston, you shall not go!"

"So sure as my name is Kershaw, I will go!"

For a moment the two men faced one another; it would have been hard to say which looked the most determined. Then Mr. Alston turned and left the room and the house. On the verandah he paused and considered for a moment.

"The boy means business," he thought to himself. "He will try and bolt. How can I stop him? Ah, I have it!" And he set off briskly towards Government house, saying aloud as he went, "I love that lad too well to let him destroy himself over a jilt."

CHAPTER XII

ERNEST RUNS AWAY

When Alston left the room, Ernest sat down on the bed again.

"I am not going to be domineered over by Alston," he said excitedly; "he presumes upon his friendship."

Jeremy came in and sat beside him, and took hold of his arm.

"My dear fellow, don't talk like that. You know he means kindly by you. You are not yourself just yet. By-and-by you will see things in a different light."

"Not myself, indeed! Would you be yourself, I wonder, if you knew that the woman who had pinned all your soul to her bosom, as though it were a ribbon, was going to marry another man to-morrow?"

"Old fellow, you forget, though I can't talk of it in as pretty words as you can, I loved her too. I could bear to give her up to you, especially as she didn't care a brass farthing about me; but when I think about this other fellow, with his cold grey eye, and that mark on his confounded forehead—ah, Ernest, it makes me sick!"

And they sat on the bed together and groaned in chorus, looking, to tell the truth, rather absurd.

"I tell you what it is, Jeremy," said Ernest, when he had finished groaning at the vision of his successful rival as painted by Jeremy; "you are a good fellow, and I am a selfish beast. Here have I been kicking up all this devil's delight, and you haven't said a word. You are a more decent chap than I am, Jeremy, by a long chalk. And I daresay you are as fond of her as I am. No, I don't think you can be that, though."

"My dear fellow, there is no parallel between our cases. I never expected to marry her. You did, and had every right to do so. Besides, we are differently made. You feel things three times as much as I do."

Ernest laughed bitterly.

"I don't think that I shall ever feel anything again," he said. "My capacities for suffering will be pretty nearly used up. O, what a sublime fool is the man who gives all his life and heart to one woman! No man would have done it; but what could you expect of a couple of boys like we were? That is why women like boys: it is so easy to take them in—like puppies going to be drowned, in love and faith they lick the hand that will destroy them. It must be amusing—to the destroyers. By Jove, Alston was right about his ideals! Do you know, I am beginning to see all these things in quite a different light. I used to believe in women, Jeremy—actually I used to believe in them. I thought they were better than we are," and he laughed hysterically. "Well, we buy our experience; I shan't make the mistake again."

"Come, come, Ernest, don't go on talking like that. You have got a blow as bad as death, and the only thing to do is to meet it as you would death—in silence. You will not go after that fellow, will you? It will only make things worse, you see. You won't have time to kill him before he marries her, and it really would not be worth while getting hanged about it when the mischief is done. There is literally nothing to be done except grin and bear it. We won't go back to England at all, but right up to the Zambesi, and hunt elephants; and as things have turned out, if you should get knocked on the head, why, you won't so much mind it, you know."

Ernest made no answer to this consolatory address, and Jeremy left him alone, thinking that he had convinced him. But the Ernest of midday was a very different man from the Ernest of the morning, directing the erection of "parasols" over melons. The cruel news that the mail had brought him, and which from force of association caused him for years afterwards to hate the sight of a letter, had, figuratively speaking, destroyed him. He could never recover from it, though he would certainly survive it. Sharp indeed must be the grief which kills. But all the bloom and beauty had gone from his life; the gentle faith which he had placed in women was gone (for so narrow-minded are we all, that we cannot help judging a class by our salient experience of individuals), and, from that day forward, for many years, he was handed over to a long-drawn-out pain, which never quite ceased, though it frequently culminated in paroxysms, and to which death itself would have been almost preferable.

But as yet he did not realise all these things; what he did realise was an intense and savage thirst for revenge, so intense, indeed, that he felt as though he must put himself in a way to gratify it, or his brain would go. To-morrow, he thought, was to see the final act of his betrayal. To-day was the eve of her marriage, and he as powerless to avert it as a child. O, great God! And yet through it all he knew she loved him.

Ernest, like many other pleasant, kindly-tempered men, if once stung into action by the sense of overpowering wrong was extremely dangerous. Ill indeed would it have fared with Mr. Plowden if he could have come across him at that moment. And he honestly meant that it should fare ill with that reverend gentleman. So much did he mean it, that before he left his room he wrote his resignation of membership of the volunteer corps to which he belonged, and took it up to the Government office. Then, remembering that the Potchefstroom post-cart left Pretoria at dawn on the following morning, he made his way to the office, and ascertained that there were no passengers booked to leave by it. But he did not take a place; he was too clever to do that. Leaving the office, he went to the bank, and drew one hundred and fifty pounds in gold. Then he went home again. Here he found a Kafir messenger, dressed in the Government white uniform, waiting for him with an official letter.

The letter acknowledged receipt of his resignation, but "regretted that, in the present unsettled state of affairs, his Excellency was, in the interest of the public service, unable to dispense with his services."

Ernest dismissed the messenger, and tore the letter across. If the Government could not dispense with him, he would dispense with the Government. His aim was to go to Potchefstroom, and thence to the Diamond Fields. Once there, he could take the post-cart to Cape Town, where he would meet the English mail steamer, and in one month from the present date be once more in England.

That evening he dined with Mr. Alston, Jeremy, and Roger as usual, and no allusion was made to the events of the morning. About eleven o'clock he went to bed, but not to sleep. The post-cart left at four. At three he rose very quietly, and put a few things into a leather saddle-bag, extracted his revolver from under the bed where he had thrown it when, in the first burst of his agony, he had been interrupted in this contemplated act of self-destruction, and buckled it round his waist. Then he slipped out through the window of his room, crept stealthily down the garden-path, and struck out for the Potchefstroom road. But, silently and secretly as he went, there went behind him one more silent and secret than he—one to whose race, through long generations of tracking foes and wild beasts, silence and secrecy had become an instinct. It was the Hottentot boy, Aasvögel.

The Hottentot followed him in the dim light, never more than fifty paces behind him, sometimes not more than ten, and yet totally invisible. Now he was behind a bush or a tuft of rank grass; now he was running down a ditch; and now again creeping over the open on his belly like a two-legged snake. As soon as Ernest got out of the town, and began to loiter along the Potchefstroom road, the Hottentot halted, uttering to himself a guttural expression of satisfaction. Then, watching his opportunity, he turned and ran swiftly back to Pretoria. In ten minutes he was at Ernest's house.

In front of the door were five horses, three with white riders, two being held by Kafirs. On the verandah, as usual, smoking, was Mr. Alston, and with him Jeremy, the latter armed and spurred.

The Hottentot made his report and vanished.

Mr. Alston turned and addressed Jeremy in the tone of one giving an order.

"Now go," he said at last, handing him a paper; and Jeremy went, and, mounting one of the led horses, a powerful cream-coloured animal with a snow-white mane and tall, galloped off in the twilight, followed by the three white men.

Meanwhile Ernest walked quietly along the road. Once he paused, thinking that he heard the sound of galloping horses, half a mile or so to the left. It passed, and he went on again. Presently the mist began to lift, and the glorious sun came up; then came a rumble of wheels running along the silent road, and the post-cart with six fresh horses was upon him. He halted, and held up his hand to the native driver. The man knew him, and stopped the team at once.

"I am going with you to Potchefstroom, Apollo," he said.

"All right, sar; plenty of room inside, sar. No passenger this trip, sar, and damn good job too."

Ernest got up, and off they went. He was safe now. There was no telegraph to Potchefstroom, and nothing could catch the post-cart if it had an hour's start.

A mile further on there was a hill, up which the unlovely Apollo walked his horses. At the top of the hill was a clump of mimosa-bush, out of which, to the intense astonishment of both Ernest and Apollo, there emerged four mounted men with a led horse. One of these men was Jeremy; it was impossible to mistake his powerful form, sitting on his horse with the grip of a centaur.

They rode up to the post-cart in silence. Jeremy motioned to Apollo to pull up. He obeyed, and one of the men dismounted and seized the horse's head.

"Tricked, by Heaven!" said Ernest.

"You must come back with me, Ernest," said Jeremy quietly. "I have a warrant for your arrest as a deserter, signed by the Governor."

"And if I refuse?"

"Then my orders are to take you back."

Ernest drew his revolver.

"This is a trick," he said, "and I shall not go back."

"Then I must take you," was the reply; and Jeremy coolly dismounted.

Ernest's eyes flashed dangerously, and he lifted the pistol.

"O yes, you can shoot me if you like; but if you do, the others will take you;" and he continued to walk towards him.

Ernest cocked his revolver and pointed it.

"At your peril!" he said.

"So be it," said Jeremy, and he walked up to the cart.

Ernest dropped his weapon.

"It is mean of you, Jeremy," he said. "You know I can't fire at you."

"Of course you can't, old fellow. Come, skip out of that; you are keeping the mail. I have a horse ready for you, a slow one; you won't be able to run away on him."

Ernest obeyed, feeling rather small, and in half an hour was back at his own house.

Mr. Alston was waiting for him.

"Good-morning, Ernest," he said, cheerfully. "Went out driving and came back riding, eh?"

Ernest looked at him, and his brown cheek flushed.

"You have played me a dirty trick," he said.

"Look here, my boy," answered Mr. Alston, sternly, "I am slow at making a friend; but when once I take his hand I hold it till one of the two grows cold. I should have been no true friend to you if I had let you go on this fool's errand, this wicked errand. Will you give me your word that you will not attempt to escape, or must I put you under arrest?"

"I give you my word," answered Ernest, humbled; "and I ask your forgiveness."

Thus it was that, for the first time in his life, Ernest tried to run away.

That morning Jeremy, missing Ernest, went into his room to see what he was doing. The room was shuttered to keep out the glare of the sun; but when he got used to the light he discovered Ernest sitting at the table, and staring straight before him with a wild look in his eyes.

"Come in, old fellow, come in," he called out, with bitter jocularity, "and assist in this happy ceremony. Rather dark, isn't it? but lovers like the dark. Look!" he went on, pointing to his watch, which lay upon the table before him, "by English time it is now about twenty minutes past eleven. They are being married now, Jeremy, my boy, I can feel it. By Heaven, I have only to shut my eyes, and I can see it!"

"Come, come, Ernest," said Jeremy, "don't go on like that. You are not yourself, man."

He laughed and answered:

"I am sure I wish I wasn't. I tell you I can see it all. I can see Kesterwick Church full of people, and before the altar, in her white dress, is Eva; but her face is whiter than her dress, Jeremy, and her eyes are very much afraid. And there is Florence, with her dark smile, and your friend Mr. Plowden, too, with his cold eyes and the cross upon his forehead. Oh, I assure you, I can see them all. It is a pretty wedding, very. There, it is over now, and I think I will go away before the kissing."

"O, hang it all, Ernest, wake up!" said Jeremy, shaking him by the shoulder. "You will drive yourself mad if you give your imagination too much rein."

"Wake up, my boy! I feel more inclined to sleep. Have some grog. Won't you? Well, I will."

He rose and went to the mantelpiece, on which stood a square bottle of hollands and a tumbler. Rapidly filling the tumbler with raw spirit, he drank it as fast as the contractions of his throat would allow. He filled it again, and drank that too. Then he fell insensible upon the bed.

It was a strange scene, and in some ways a coarse one, yet not without a pathos of its own.

"Ernest," said Mr. Alston, three weeks later, "you are strong enough to travel now; what do you say to six months or a year among the elephants? The oxen are in first-rate condition, and we ought to get to our ground in six or seven weeks."

Ernest, who was lying back in a low cane-chair, looking very thin and pale, thought for a moment before he answered:

"All right, I'm your man; only let's get off soon. I am tired of this place, and want something to think about."

"You have given up any idea of returning to England?"

"Yes, quite."

"And what do you say, Jeremy?"

"Where Ernest goes, there will I go also. Besides, to shoot an elephant is the one ambition of my life."

"Good! then we will consider that settled. We shall want to pick up another eight-bore; but I know of one a fellow wants to sell, a beauty, by Riley. I will begin to make arrangements at once."

CHAPTER XIII

MR. PLOWDEN ASSERTS HIS RIGHTS

When last we saw Eva she had just become privately engaged to the Reverend James Plowden. But the marriage was not to take place till the following spring, and the following spring was a long way off. Vaguely she hoped something might occur to prevent it, forgetting that, as a rule, in real life it is only happy things which accidents occur to prevent. Rare, indeed, is it that the Plowdens of this world are prevented from marrying the Evas; Fate has sufficient to do in thwarting the Ernests. And, meanwhile, her position was not altogether unendurable, for she had made a bargain with her lover that the usual amenities of courtship were to be dispensed with. There were to be no embracings or other tender passages; she was not even to be forced to call him James. "James!" how she detested the name! Thus did the wretched girl try to put off the evil day, much as the ostrich is supposed to hide her head in a bush and indulge in dreams of fancied security. Mr. Plowden did not object; he was too wary a hunter to do so. While his stately prey was there with her head in the thickest of the bush he was sure of her. She would never wake from her foolish dream till the ripe moment came to deliver the fatal blow, and all would be over. But if, on the contrary, he startled her now, she might take flight more swiftly than he could follow, and leave him alone in the desert.

So when Eva made her little stipulations he acquiesced in them, after only just so much hesitation as he thought would seem lover-like. "Life, Eva," he said, sententiously, "is a compromise. I yield to your wishes." But in his heart he thought that a time would come when she would have to yield to him, and his cold eye gleamed. Eva saw the gleam, and shuddered prophetically.

The Reverend Mr. Plowden did not suffer much distress at the coldness with which he was treated. He knew that his day would come, and was content to wait for it like a wise man. He was not in love with Eva. A nature like his is scarcely capable of any such feeling as that, for instance, which Eva and Ernest bore to each other. True love, crowned with immortality, veils his shining face from such men as Mr. Plowden. He was fascinated by her beauty, that was all. But his cunning was of a superior order, and he was quite content to wait. So he contrived to extract a letter from Eva, in which she talked of "our engagement," and alluded to "our forthcoming marriage," and waited.

And thus the time went on all too quickly for Eva. She was quietly miserable, but she was not acutely unhappy. That was yet to come, with other evil things. Christmas came and went, the spring came too, and with the daffodils and violets came Ernest's letter.

Eva was down the first one morning, and was engaged in making the tea in the Cottage dining-room, when that modern minister to the decrees of Fate, the postman, brought the letter. She recognised the writing in a moment, and the tea-caddy fell with a crash on to the floor. Seizing the sealed letter, she tore it open and read it swiftly. O, what a wave of love surged up in her heart as she read! Pressing the senseless paper to her lips, she kissed it again and again.

"O Ernest!" she murmured; "O my love, my darling!"

Just then Florence came down, looking cool and composed, and giving that idea of quiet strength which is the natural attribute of some women.

Eva pushed the letter into her bosom.

"What is the matter, Eva?" said Florence, quietly, noting her flushed face, "and why have you upset the tea?"

"Matter!" she answered, laughing happily—she had not laughed so for months; "O, nothing—I have heard from Ernest, that is all."

"Indeed!" answered her sister, with a troubled smile on her dark face; "and what has our runaway to say for himself?"

"Say! O, he has a great deal to say, and I have something to say too. I am going to marry him."

"Indeed! And Mr. Plowden?"

Eva turned pale.

"Mr. Plowden! I have done with Mr. Plowden."

"Indeed!" said Florence, again; "really this is quite romantic. But please pick up that tea. Whoever you marry, let us have some breakfast in the meanwhile. Excuse me for one moment, I have forgotten my handkerchief."

Eva did as she was bid, and made the tea after a fashion.

Meanwhile Florence went to her room and scribbled a note, enclosed it in an envelope, and rang the bell.

The servant answered.

"Tell John to take this to Mr. Plowden's lodgings at once; and if he should be out, to follow him till he finds him, and deliver it."

"Yes, miss."

Ten minutes later Mr. Plowden got the following note:

"Come here at once. Eva has heard from Ernest Kershaw, and announces her intention of throwing you over and marrying him. Be prepared for a struggle, but do not show that you have heard from me. You must find means to hold your own. Burn this."

Mr. Plowden whistled as he laid the paper down. Going to his desk, he unlocked it, and extracted the letter he had received from Eva, in which she acknowledged her engagement to him, and then, seizing his hat, walked swiftly towards the Cottage.

Meanwhile Florence made her way downstairs again, saying to herself as she went, "An unlucky chance. If I had seen the letter first, I would have burned it. But we shall win yet. She has not the stamina to stand out against that brute."

As soon as she reached the dining-room Eva began to say something more about her letter, but her sister stopped her quickly.

"Let me have my breakfast in peace, Eva. We will talk of the letter afterwards. He does not interest me, your Ernest, and it takes away my appetite to talk business at meals."

Eva ceased, and sat silent; breakfast had no charms for her that morning.

Presently there was a knock at the door, and Mr. Plowden entered with a smile of forced gaiety on his face.

"How do you do, Florence?" he said; "how do you do, dear Eva? You see I have come to see you early this morning. I want a little refreshment to enable me to get though my day's duty. The early suitor has come to pick up the worm of his affections," and he laughed at his joke.

Florence shuddered at the simile, and thought to herself that there was a fair chance of the affectionate worm disagreeing with the early suitor.

Eva said nothing. She sat quite still and pale.

"Why, what is the matter with you both? Have you seen a ghost?"

"Not exactly; but I think that Eva has received a message from the dead," said Florence, with a nervous laugh.

Eva rose. "I think, Mr. Plowden," she said, "that I had better be frank with you at once. I ask you to listen to me for a few moments."

"Am I not always at your service, dear Eva?"

"I wish," began Eva, and broke down—"I wish," she went on again, "to appeal to your generosity and to your feelings as a gentleman."

Florence smiled.

Mr. Plowden bowed with mock humility and smiled too—a very ugly smile.

"You are aware that, before I became engaged to you, I had had a previous affair."

"With the boy who committed a murder," put in Mr. Plowden.

"With a gentleman who had the misfortune to kill a man in a duel," explained Eva.

"The Church and the law call it murder."

"Excuse me, Mr. Plowden, we are dealing neither with the Church nor the law; we are dealing with the thing as it is called among gentlemen and ladies."

"Go on," said Mr. Plowden.

"Well, misunderstandings, which I need not now enter into, arose with reference to that affair, though, as I told you, I loved the man. To-day I have heard from him, and his letter puts everything straight in my mind, and I see how wrong and unjust has been my behaviour to him, and I know that I love him more than ever."

"Curse the fellow's impudence!" said the clergyman, furiously; "if he were here I would give him a bit of my mind!"

Eva's spirit rose, and she turned on him with flashing eyes, looking like a queen in her imperial beauty.

"If he were here, Mr. Plowden, you would not dare to look him in the face. Men like you only take advantage of the absent."

The clergyman ground his teeth. He felt his furious temper rising and did not dare to answer, though he was a bold man, in face of a woman. He feared lest it should get beyond him; but beneath his breath he muttered, "You shall pay for that, my lady!"

"Under these circumstances," went on Eva, "I appeal to you as a gentleman to release me from an engagement into which, as you know, I have been drawn more by force of circumstances than by my own wish. Surely it is not necessary for me to say any more."

Mr. Plowden rose and came and stood quite close to her, so that his face was within a few inches of her eyes.

"Eva," he said, "I am not going to be trifled with like this. You have promised to marry me, and I shall keep you to your promise. You laid yourself out to win my affection, the affection of an honest man."

Again Florence smiled, and Eva made a faint motion of dissent.

"Yes, but you did, you encouraged me. It is very well for you to deny it now, when it suits your purpose, but you did, and you know it, and your sister there knows it."

Florence bowed her head in assent.

"And now you wish, in order to gratify an unlawful passion for a shedder of blood—you wish to throw me over, to trample upon my holiest feelings, and to rob me of the prize which I have won. No, Eva, I will not release you."

"Surely, surely, Mr. Plowden," said Eva, faintly, for she was a gentle creature, and the man's violence overwhelmed her, "you will not force me into a marriage which I tell you is repugnant to me? I appeal to your generosity to release me. You can never oblige me to marry you when I tell you that I do not love you, and that my whole heart is given to another man."

Mr. Plowden saw that his violence was doing its work, and determined to follow it up. He raised his voice till it was almost a shout.

"Yes," he said, "I will; I will not submit to such wickedness. Love! that will come. I am quite willing to take my chance of it. No, I tell you fairly that I will not let you off; and if you try to avoid fulfilling your engagement to me I will do more: I will proclaim you all over the country as a jilt; I will bring an action for breach of promise of marriage against you—perhaps you did not know that men can do that as well as women—and cover your name with disgrace! Look, I have your written promise of marriage"; and he produced her letter.

Eva turned to her sister.

"Florence," she said, "cannot you say a word to help me? I am overwhelmed."

"I wish I could, Eva dear," answered her sister, kindly; "but how can I? What Mr. Plowden says is just and right. You are engaged to him, and are in honour bound to marry him. O, Eva, do not bring trouble and disgrace upon us all by your obstinacy! You owe something to your name as well as to yourself, and something to me too. I am sure that Mr. Plowden will be willing to forget all about this if you will undertake never to allude to it again."

"O yes, certainly, Miss Florence. I am not revengeful; I only want my rights."

Eva looked faintly from one to the other; her head sank, and great black rings painted themselves beneath her eyes. The lily was broken at last.

"You are very cruel," she said, slowly; "but I suppose it must be as you wish. Pray God I may die first, that is all!" and she put her hands to her head and stumbled from the room, leaving the two conspirators facing each other.

"Come, we got over that capitally," said Mr. Plowden, rubbing his hands. "There is nothing like taking the high hand with a woman. Ladies must sometimes be taught that gentlemen have rights as well as themselves."

Florence turned on him with bitter scorn.

"Gentlemen! Mr. Plowden, why is the word so often on your lips? Surely, after the part you have just played, you do not presume to rank yourself among gentlemen? Listen! it suits my purposes that you should marry Eva, and you shall marry her; but I will not stoop to play the hypocrite with a man like you.

You talk of yourself as a gentleman, and do not scruple to force an innocent girl into a wicked marriage, and to crush her spirit with your cunning cruelty. A gentleman, forsooth!—a satyr, a devil in disguise!"

"I am only asserting my rights," he said furiously, "and whatever I have done, you have done more."

"Do not try your violence on me, Mr. Plowden; it will not do. I am not made of the same stuff as your victim. Lower your voice, or leave the house and do not enter it again."

Mr. Plowden's heavy under-jaw fell a little; he was terribly afraid of Florence.

"Now," she said, "listen! I do not choose that you should labour under any mistake. I hold your hand in this business, though to have to do with you in any way is in itself a defilement," and she wiped her delicate fingers on a pocket-handkerchief as she said the word, "because I have an end of my own to gain. Not a vulgar end like yours, but a revenge which shall be almost divine or diabolical, call it which you will, in its completeness. Perhaps it is a madness, perhaps it is an inspiration, perhaps it is a fate. Whatever it is, it animates me body and soul, and I will gratify it, though to do so I have to use a tool like you. I wished to explain this to you. I wished, too, to make it clear to you that I consider you contemptible. I have done both, and I have now the pleasure to wish you good-morning."

Mr. Plowden left the house white with fury, and cursing in a manner remarkable in a clergyman.

"If she wasn't so handsome, hang me if I would not throw the whole thing up!" he said.

Needless to say, he did nothing of the sort; he only kept out of Florence's way.

CHAPTER XIV

THE VIRGIN MARTYR

Dorothy, in her note to Ernest that he received by the mail previous to the one that brought the letters which at a single blow laid the hope and promise of his life in the dust, it may be remembered, had stated her intention of going to see Eva in order to plead Ernest's cause; but what with one thing and another, her visit was considerably delayed. Twice she was on the point of going, and twice something occurred to prevent her. The fact of the matter was, the errand was distasteful, and she was in no hurry to execute it. She loved Ernest herself, and, however deep that love might be trampled down, however fast it might be chained in the dungeons of her secret thoughts, it was still there, a living thing, an immortal thing. She could tread it down and chain it; she could not kill it. Its shade would rise and walk in the upper chambers of her heart, and wring its hands and cry to her, telling what it suffered in those subterranean places, whispering how bitterly it envied the bright and happy life which moved in the free air, and had usurped the love it claimed. It was hard to have to ignore those pleadings, to disregard those cries for pity, and to say that there was no hope, that it must always be chained, till time ate away the chains. It was harder still to have to be one of the actual ministers to the suffering. Still, she meant to go. Her duty to Ernest was not to be forsaken because it was a painful duty.

On two or three occasions she met Eva, but got no opportunity of speaking to her. Either her sister Florence was with her, or she was obliged to return immediately. The truth was that, after the scene described in the last chapter, Eva was subjected to the closest espionage. At home, Florence watched her as a cat watches a mouse; abroad, Mr. Plowden seemed to be constantly hovering on her flank, or, if he was not there, then she became aware of the presence of the ancient and contemplative mariner who traded in Dutch cheeses. Mr. Plowden feared lest she should run away, and so cheat him of his prize; Florence, lest she should confide in Dorothy, or possibly Mr. Cardus, and, supported by them, find the courage to assert herself and defraud her of her revenge. So they watched her every movement.

At last Dorothy made up her mind to wait no longer for opportunities, but to go and see Eva at her own home. She knew nothing of the Plowden imbroglio; but it did strike her as curious that no one had said anything about Ernest. He had written; it was scarcely likely the letter had miscarried. How was it that Eva had not said anything on the subject? Little did Dorothy guess that, even as these thoughts were passing through her mind, a great vessel was steaming out of Southampton docks, bearing those epistles of final renunciation which Ernest, very little to his satisfaction, received in due course.

Full of these reflections, Dorothy found herself one lovely spring afternoon knocking at the door of the Cottage. Eva was at home, and she was at once ushered into her presence. She was sitting in a low chair—the same on which Ernest always pictured her with that confounded Skye terrier she was so fond of kissing—an open book upon her knee, and looking out at the little garden and the sea beyond. She looked pale and thin, Dorothy thought.

On her visitor's entrance, Eva rose and kissed her.

"I am so glad to see you," she said; "I was feeling lonely."

"Lonely!" answered Dorothy, in her straightforward way; "why, I have been trying to find you alone for the last fortnight, and have never succeeded."

Eva coloured. "One may be lonely with ever so many people round one."

Then for a minute or so they talked about the weather; so persistently did they discuss it, indeed, that the womanly instinct of each told her that the other was fencing.

After all, it was Eva who broke the ice first.

"Have you heard from Ernest lately?" she said, nervously.

"Yes; I got a note by last mail."

"Oh," said Eva, clasping her hands involuntarily, "what did he say?"

"Nothing much. But I got a letter by the mail before that, in which he said a good deal. Among other things, he said he had written to you. Did you get the letter?"

Eva coloured to her eyes. "Yes," she whispered.

Dorothy rose, and seated herself again on a footstool by Eva's feet, and wondered at the trouble in her eyes. How could she be troubled when she had heard from Ernest—"like that?"

"What did you answer him, dear?"

Eva covered her face with her hands.

"Do not talk about it," she said; "it is too dreadful to me!"

"What can you mean? He tells me you are engaged to him."

"Yes—that is, no. I was half engaged. Now I am engaged to Mr. Plowden."

Dorothy gave a gasp of horrified astonishment.

"Engaged to that man when you were engaged to Ernest! You must be joking."

"O Dorothy, I am not joking; I wish to Heaven I were. I am engaged to him. I am to marry him in less than a month. O, pity me, I am wretched."

"You mean to tell me," said Dorothy, rising, "that you are engaged to Mr. Plowden when you love Ernest?"

"Yes, oh yes; I cannot help—"

At that moment the door opened, and Florence entered, attended by Mr. Plowden.

Her keen eyes saw at once that something was wrong, and her intelligence told her what it was. After her bold fashion, she determined to take the bull by the horns. Unless something were done, with Dorothy at her back, Eva might prove obdurate after all

Advancing, she shook Dorothy cordially by the hand.

"I see from your face," she said, "that you have just heard the good news. Mr. Plowden is so shy that he would not consent to announce it before; but here he is to receive your congratulations."

Mr. Plowden took the cue, and advanced effusively on Dorothy with outstretched hand. "Yes, Miss Jones, I am sure you will congratulate me; and I ought to be congratulated. I am the luckiest—"

Here he broke off. It really was very awkward. His hand remained limply hanging in the air before Dorothy, but not the slightest sign did that dignified little lady show of taking it. On the contrary, she drew herself up to her full height—which was not very tall—and fixing her steady blue eyes on the clergyman's shifty orbs, deliberately placed her right hand behind her back.

"I do not shake hands with people who play such tricks," she said, quietly.

Mr. Plowden's hand fell to his side, and he stepped back. He did not expect such courage in anything so small. Florence however, sailed in to the rescue.

"Really, Dorothy, we do not quite understand."

"O yes, I think you do, Florence, or if you do not, then I will explain. Eva here was engaged to marry Ernest Kershaw. Eva here has just with her own lips told me that she still loves Ernest, but that she is obliged to marry—that man"; and she pointed with her little forefinger at Mr. Plowden, who recoiled another step. "Is not that true, Eva?"

Eva bowed her head by way of answer. She still sat in the low chair, with her hands over her face.

"Really, Dorothy, I fail to see what right you have to interfere in this matter," said Florence.

"I have the right of common justice, Florence—the right a friend has to protect the absent. Are you not ashamed of such a wicked plot to wrong an absent man? Is there no way" (addressing Mr. Plowden) "in which I can appeal to your feelings, to induce you to free this wretched girl you have entrapped?"

"I only ask my own," said Mr. Plowden, sulkily.

"For shame, for shame! And you a minister of God's Word! And you too, Florence! Oh, now I can read your heart, and see the bad thoughts looking from your eyes!"

Florence for a moment was abashed, and turned her face aside.

"And you, Eva—how can you become a party to such a shameful thing? You, a good girl, to sell yourself away from dear Ernest to such a man as that"; and again she pointed contemptuously at Mr. Plowden.

"Oh, don't, Dorothy, don't; it is my duty. You don't understand."

"Yes, Eva, I do understand. I understand that it is your duty to drown yourself before you do such a thing. I am a woman as well as you, and though I am not beautiful, I have a heart and a conscience, and I understand only too well."

"You will be lost if you drown yourself—I mean it is very wicked," said Mr. Plowden to Eva, suddenly assuming his clerical character as most likely to be effective. The suggestion alarmed him. He had bargained for a live Eva.

"Yes, Mr. Plowden," went on Dorothy, "you are right: it would be wicked, but not so wicked as to marry you. God gave us women our lives, but He put a spirit in our hearts which tells us that we should rather throw them away than suffer ourselves to be degraded. Oh, Eva, tell me that you will not do this shameful thing. No, do not whisper to her, Florence."

"Dorothy, Dorothy," said Eva, rising and wringing her hands, "it is all useless. Do not break my heart with your cruel words. I must marry him. I have fallen into the power of people who do not know what mercy is."

"Thank you," said Florence.

Mr. Plowden scowled darkly.

"Then I have done"; and Dorothy walked towards the door. Before she reached it she paused and turned. "One word, and I will trouble you no more. What do you all expect will come of this wicked marriage?"

There was no answer. Then Dorothy went.

But her efforts did not stop there. She made her way straight to Mr. Cardus's office.

"O Reginald," she said, "I have such dreadful news for you. There, let me cry a little first, and I will tell you."

And she did, telling him the whole story from beginning to end. It was entirely new to him, and he listened with some astonishment, and with a feeling of something like indignation against Ernest. He had intended that young gentleman to fall in love with Dorothy, and behold, he had fallen in love with Eva. Alas for the perversity of youth!

"Well," he said, when she had done, "and what do you wish me to do? It seems that you have to do with a heartless scheming woman, a clerical cad, and a beautiful fool. One might deal with the schemer and the fool, but no power on earth can soften the cad. At least, that is my experience. Besides, I think the whole thing is much better left alone. I should be very sorry to see Ernest married to a woman so worthless as this Eva must be. She is handsome, it is true, and that is about all she is, as far as I can see. Don't distress yourself, my dear; he will get over it, and after he has had his fling out there, and lived down that duel business, he will come home, and if he is wise, I know where he will look for consolation."

Dorothy tossed her head and coloured.

"It is not a question of consolation," she said; "it is a question of Ernest's happiness in life."

"Don't alarm yourself, Dorothy; people's happiness is not so easily affected. He will forget all about her in a year."

"I think that men always talk of each other like that, Reginald," said Dorothy, resting her head upon her hands, and looking straight at the old gentleman. "Each of you likes to think that he has a monopoly of feeling, and that the rest of his kind are as shallow as a milk-pan. And yet it was only last night that you were talking to me about my mother. You told me, you remember, that life had been a worthless thing to you since she was torn from you, which no success had been able to render pleasant. You said more: you said that you hoped that the end was not far off; that you had suffered enough and waited enough; and that, though you had not seen her face for five-and-twenty years, you loved her as wildly as you did the day when she first promised to become your wife."

Mr. Cardus had risen, and was looking through the glass door at the blooming orchids. Dorothy got up, and following him, laid her hand upon his shoulder.

"Reginald," she said, "think! Ernest is about to be robbed of his wife under circumstances curiously like those by which you were robbed of yours. Unless it is prevented, what you have suffered all your life he will suffer also. Remember you are of the same blood, and, allowing for the difference between your ages, of very much the same temperament too. Think how different life would have been to you if any one had staved off your disaster, and then I am sure you will do all you can to stave off his."

"Life would have been non-existent for you," he answered, "for you would never have been born."

"Ah, well," she said, with a little sigh, "I am sure I should have got on every well without. I could have spared myself."

Mr. Cardus was a keen man, and could see as far into the human heart as most.

"Girl," he said, contracting his white eyebrows and suddenly turning round upon her, "you love Ernest yourself. I have often suspected it; now I am sure you do."

Dorothy flinched.

"Yes," she answered, "I do love him. What then?"

"And yet you are advocating my interference to secure his marriage with another woman, a worthless creature who does not know her own mind. You cannot really care about him."

"Care about him!" and she turned her sweet blue eyes upwards. "I love him with all my heart and soul and strength. I have always loved him; I always shall love him. I love him so well that I can do my duty to him, Reginald. It is my duty to strain every nerve to prevent this marriage. I had rather that my heart should ache than Ernest's. I implore of you to help me."

"Dorothy, it has always been my dearest wish that you should marry Ernest. I told him so just before that unhappy duel. I love you both. All the fibres of my heart that are left alive have wound themselves around you. Jeremy I could never care for. Indeed, I fear that I used sometimes to treat the boy harshly. He reminds me so of his father. And do you know, my dear, I sometimes think that on that point I am not quite sane. But because you have asked me to do it, and because you have quoted your dear mother—may peace be with her!—I will do what I can. This girl Eva is of age, and I will write and offer her a home. She need fear no persecution here."

"You are kind and good, Reginald, and I thank you."

"The letter shall go by to-night's post. But run away, now; I see my friend De Talor coming to speak to me"; and the white eyebrows drew near together in a way that it would have been unpleasant for the great De Talor to behold. "That business is drawing towards its end."

"O Reginald," answered Dorothy, shaking her forefinger at him in her old childish way, "haven't you given up those ideas yet? They are very wrong."

"Never mind, Dorothy. I shall give them up soon, when I have squared accounts with De Talor. A year or two more—a stern chase is a long chase, you know—and the thing will be done, and then I shall become a good Christian again."

The letter was written. It offered Eva a home and protection.

In due course an answer, signed by Eva herself, came back. It thanked him for his kindness, and regretted that circumstances and "her sense of duty" prevented her from accepting the offer.

Then Dorothy felt that she had done all that in her lay, and gave the matter up.

It was about this time that Florence drew another picture. It represented Eva as Andromeda gazing hopelessly in the dim light of a ghastly dawn out across a glassy sea; and far away in the oily depths there was a ripple, and beneath the ripple a form travelling towards the chained maiden. The form had a human head and cold grey eyes, and its features were those of Mr. Plowden.

And so, day by day, Destiny, throned in space, shot her flaming shuttle from darkness into darkness, and the time passed on, as time must pass, till the inevitable end of all things is attained.

Eva existed and suffered, and that was all she did. She scarcely ate, or drank, or slept. But still she lived; she was not brave enough to die, and the chains were riveted too tight round her tender wrists to let her flee away. Poor nineteenth-century Andromeda! No Perseus shall come to save you.

The sun rose and set in his appointed course, the flowers bloomed and died, children were born, and the allotted portion of mankind passed onwards to its rest; but no godlike Perseus came flying out of the golden east.

Once more the sun rose. The dragon heaved his head above the quiet waters, and she was lost. By her own act, of her own folly and weakness, she was undone. Behold her! the wedding is over. The echoes of the loud mockery of the bells have scarcely died upon the noonday air, and in her chamber, the chamber of her free and happy maidenhood, the virgin martyr stands alone.

It is done. There lie the sickly scented flowers; there, too, the bride's white robe. It is done. Oh, that life were done too, that she might once more press her lips to his and die!

The door opens, and Florence stands before her, pale, triumphant, awe-inspiring.

"I must congratulate you, my dear Eva. You really went through the ceremony very well; only you looked like a statue."

"Florence, why do you come to mock me?"

"Mock you, Eva, mock you! I come to wish you joy as Mr. Plowden's wife. I hope that you will be happy."

"Happy! I shall never be happy. I detest him!"

"You detest him, and you marry him; there must be some mistake."

"There is no mistake. O Ernest, my darling!"

Florence smiled.

"If Ernest is your darling, why did you not marry Ernest?"

"How could I marry him when you forced me into this?"

"Forced you! A free woman of full age cannot be forced. You married Mr. Plowden of your own will. You might have married Ernest Kershaw if you chose—he is in many ways a more desirable match than Mr. Plowden—but you did not choose."

"Florence, what do you mean? You always said it was impossible. Is this all some cruel plot of yours?"

"Impossible! there is nothing impossible to those who have courage. Yes," and she turned upon her sister fiercely, "it was a plot, and you shall know it, you poor weak fool! I loved Ernest Kershaw, and you robbed me of him, although you promised to leave him alone; and so I have revenged myself upon you. I despise you, I tell you; you are quite contemptible, and yet he could prefer you to me. Well, he has got his reward. You have deserted him when he was absent and in trouble, and you have outraged his love and your own. You have fallen very low indeed, Eva, and presently you will fall lower yet. I know you well. You will sink till at last you even lose the sense of your own humiliation. Don't you wonder what Ernest must think of you now? There is Mr. Plowden calling you. Come, it is time for you to be going."

Eva listened aghast, and then sank against the wall, sobbing despairingly.

CHAPTER XV

HANS'S CITY OF REST

Mr. Alston, Ernest, and Jeremy had very good sport among the elephants, killing in all nineteen bulls. It was during this expedition that an incident occurred which in its effect endeared Ernest to Mr. Alston more than ever.

The boy Roger, who always went wherever Mr. Alston went, was the object of his father's most tender solicitude. He believed in the boy as he believed in little else in the world—for at heart Mr. Alston was a sad cynic—and to a certain extent the boy justified his belief. He was quick, intelligent, and plucky, much such a boy as you may pick up by the dozen out of any English public school, except that his knowledge of men and manners was more developed, as is usual among young colonists. At the age of twelve Master Roger Alston knew many things denied to most children of his age. On the subject of education Mr. Alston had queer ideas. "The best education for a boy," he would say, "is to mix with grown-up gentlemen. If you send him to school, he learns little except mischief; if you let him live with gentlemen, he learns, at any rate, to be a gentleman."

But whatever Master Roger knew, he did not know much about elephants, and on this point he was destined to gain some experience.

One day—it was just after they had got into the elephant country—they were all engaged in following the fresh spoor of a solitary bull. But though an elephant is a big beast, it is hard work catching him up because he never seems to get tired, and this was exactly what our party of hunters found. They followed that energetic elephant for hours, but they could not catch him, though the spoorers told them that he was certainly not more than a mile or so ahead. At last the sun began to get low, and their legs had already grown weary; so they gave it up for that day, determining to camp where they were.

This being so, after a rest, Ernest and the boy Roger started out of camp to see if they could not shoot a buck or some birds for supper. Roger had a repeating Winchester carbine, Ernest a double-barrelled shot-gun. Hardly had they left the camp, when Aasvögel, Jeremy's Hottentot, came running in, and reported that he had seen the elephant, an enormous bull with a white spot upon his trunk, feeding in a clump of mimosa, not a quarter of a mile away. Up jumped Mr. Alston and Jeremy, as fresh as though they had not walked a mile, and, seizing their double-eight elephant rifles, started off with Aasvögel.

Meanwhile Ernest and Roger had been strolling towards this identical clump of mimosa. As they neared it, the former saw some guinea-fowl run into the shelter of the trees.

"Capital!" he said. "Guinea-fowl are first-class eating. Now, Roger, just you go into the bush and drive the flock over me. I'll stand here, and make believe they are pheasants."

The lad did as he was bid. But in order to get well behind the covey of guinea-fowl, which are dreadful things to run, he made a little circuit through the thickest part of the clump. As he did so his quick eye was arrested by a most unusual performance on the part of one of the flat-crowned mimosa-trees. Suddenly, and without the slightest apparent reason, it rose into the air, and then, behold! where its crown had been a moment before, appeared its roots.

Such an "Alice in Wonderland" sort of performance on the part of a tree could not but excite the curiosity of an intelligent youth. Accordingly, Roger pushed forwards, and slipped round an intervening tree. This was what he saw. In a little glade about ten paces from him, flapping its ears, stood an enormous elephant with great white tusks, looking as large as a house and as cool as a cucumber. Nobody, to look at the brute, would have believed that he had given them a twenty miles' trot under a burning sun. He was now refreshing himself by pulling up mimosa-trees as easily as though they were radishes, and eating the sweet fibrous roots.

Roger saw this, and his heart burned with ambition to kill that elephant—the mighty great beast, about a hundred times as big as himself, who could pull up a large tree and make his dinner off the roots. Roger was a plucky boy, and, in his sportsmanlike zeal, he quite forgot that a repeating carbine is not exactly the weapon one would choose to shoot elephants with. Indeed, without giving the matter another thought, he lifted the little rifle, aimed it at the great beast's head, and fired. He hit it somewhere, that was very clear, for next moment the air resounded with the most terrific scream of fury that it had ever been his lot to hear. That scream was too much for him; he turned and fled swiftly. Elephants were evidently difficult things to kill.

Fortunately for Roger, the elephant could not for some seconds make out where his tiny assailant was. Presently, however, he winded him, and came crashing after him, screaming shrilly, with his trunk and tail well up. On hearing the shot and the scream of the elephant, Ernest, who was standing some way out in the open, in anticipation of a driving shot of the guinea-fowl, had run towards the spot where Roger had entered the bush; and, just as he got opposite to it, out he came, scuttling along for his life, with the elephant not more than twenty paces behind him.

Then Ernest did a brave thing.

"Make for the bush!" he yelled to the boy, who at once swerved to the right. On thundered the elephant, straight towards Ernest. But with Ernest it was evident that he considered he had no quarrel, for presently he tried to swing himself round after Roger. Then Ernest lifted his shot-gun, and sent a charge of No. 4 into the brute's face, stinging him sadly. It was, humanly speaking, certain death which he courted, but at the moment his main idea was to save the boy. Screaming afresh, the elephant abandoned the pursuit of Roger, and made straight for Ernest, who fired the other barrel of small-shot, in the vain hope of blinding him. By now the boy had pulled up, being some forty yards off, and seeing Ernest just about to be crumpled up, wildly fired the repeating rifle in their direction. Some good angel must have guided the little bullet; for, as it happened, it struck the elephant in the region of the knee, and, forcing its way in, slightly injured a tendon, and brought the great beast thundering to the ground. Ernest had only just time to dodge to one side as the huge mass came to the earth; indeed, as it was, he got a tap from the tip of the elephant's trunk which knocked him down, and, though he did not feel it at the time, made him sore for days afterwards. In a moment, however, he was up again, and away at his best speed, legging it as he had never legged it before in his life; and so was the elephant. People have no idea at what a pace an elephant can go when he is out of temper, until they put it to the proof. Had it not been the slight injury to the knee, and the twenty-yards' start he got, Ernest would have been represented by little pieces before he was ten seconds older. As it was, when, a hundred and fifty yards farther on, elephant and Ernest broke upon the astonished view of Mr. Alston and Jeremy, who were hurrying up to the scene of action, they were almost one flesh; that is, the tip of the elephant's trunk was now up in the air, and now about six inches off the seat of Ernest's trousers, at which it snapped, convulsively.

Up went Jeremy's rifle, which luckily he had in his hand.

"Behind the shoulder, half-way down the ear," said Mr. Alston, beckoning to a Kafir to bring his rifle, which he was carrying. The probability of Jeremy's stopping the beast at that distance—they were quite sixty yards off—was infinitesimal.

There was a second's pause. The snapping tip touched the retreating trousers, but did not get hold of them, and the contact sent a magnetic thrill up Ernest's back.

"Boom—thud—crash!" and the elephant was down dead as a door-nail. Jeremy had made no mistake: the bullet went straight through the great brute's heart, and broke the shoulder on the other side. He was one of those men who not only rarely miss, but always seem to hit their game in the right place.

Ernest sank exhausted on the ground, and Mr. Alston and Jeremy rushed up rejoicing.

"Near go that, Ernest," said the former.

Ernest nodded in reply. He could not speak.

"By Jove! where is Roger?" he went on, turning pale as he missed his son for the first time.

But at this moment that young gentleman hove in sight, and, recovering from his fright when he saw that the great animal was stone-dead, rushed up with yells of exultation, and, climbing on to the upper tusk, began to point out where he had hit him.

Meanwhile Mr. Alston had extracted the story of the adventure from Ernest.

"You young rascal," he said to his son, "come off that tusk. Do you know that if it had not been for Mr. Kershaw here, who courted almost certain death to save you from the results of your own folly, you would be as dead as that elephant and as flat as a biscuit? Come down, sir, and offer up your thanks to Providence and Mr. Kershaw that you have a sound square inch of skin left on your worthless young body!"

Roger descended accordingly, considerably crestfallen.

"Never you mind, Roger; that was a most rattling good shot of yours at his knee," said Ernest, who had now got his breath back again. "You would not do it again if you fired at elephants for a week."

And so the matter passed off; but afterwards Mr. Alston thanked Ernest with tears in his eyes for saving his son's life.

This was the first elephant they killed, and also the largest. It measured ten feet eleven inches at the shoulder, and the tusks weighed, when dried out, about sixty pounds each.

They remained in the elephant country for nearly four months, when the approach of the unhealthy season forced them to leave it—not, however, before they had killed a great quantity of large game of all sorts. It was a most successful hunt, so successful, indeed, that the ivory they brought down paid all the expenses of the trip, and left a handsome surplus over.

It was on the occasion of their return to Pretoria that Ernest made the acquaintance of a curious character in a curious way.

As soon as they reached the boundaries of the Transvaal, Ernest bought a horse from a Boer, on which he used to ride after the herds of buck which swarmed upon the high veld. They had none with them, because in the country where they had been shooting no horse would live. One day as they were travelling slowly along a little before midday, a couple of bull-vilderbeeste galloped across the waggon-track about two hundred yards in front of the oxen. The voorlooper stopped the oxen in order to give Ernest, who was sitting on the waggon-box with a rifle by his side, a steady shot. Ernest fired at the last of the two galloping bulls. The line was good; but he did not make sufficient allowance for the pace at which the bull was travelling, with the result that instead of striking it forwards and killing it, the bullet shattered its flank, and did not stop its career.

"Dash it!" said Ernest, when he saw what he had done, "I can't leave the poor beast like that. Bring me my horse; I will go after him, and finish him."

The horse, which was tied already saddled behind the waggon, was quickly brought, and Ernest, mounting, told them not to keep the waggons for him, as he would strike across country and meet them at the outspan place, about a mile or so on. Then he started after his wounded bull, which could be plainly discerned standing with one leg up on the crest of a rise about a thousand yards away. But if ever a vilderbeeste was possessed by a fixed determination not to be finished off, it was that particular vilderbeeste. The pace at which a vilderbeeste can travel on three legs when he is not too fat is perfectly astonishing, and Ernest had traversed a couple of miles of great rolling plain before he even got within fair galloping distance of him.

He had a good horse, however, and at last he got within fifty yards, and then away they went at a merry pace, Ernest's object being to ride alongside and put a bullet through him. Their gallop lasted a good two miles or more. On the level, Ernest gained on the vilderbeeste, but whenever they came to a patch of ant-bear holes or a ridge of stones, the vilderbeeste had the pull, and drew away again. At last they came to a dry pan or lake about half a mile broad, crowded with hundreds of buck of all sorts, which scampered away as they came tearing along. Here Ernest at length drew up level with his quarry, and grasping the rifle with his right hand, tried to get it so that he could put a bullet through the beast, and drop him. But it was no easy matter, as any one who has ever tried it will know, and, while he was still making up his mind, the vilderbeeste slewed round, and came at him bravely. Had his horse been unused to the work, he must have had his inside ripped out by the crooked horns; but he was an old hunter, and equal to the occasion. To turn was impossible, the speed was too great, but he managed to slew, with the result that the charging animal brushed his head, instead of landing himself in his belly. At the same moment Ernest stretched out his rifle and pulled the trigger, and, as it chanced, put the bullet right through the vilderbeeste and dropped him dead.

Then he pulled up, and, dismounting, cut off some of the best of beef with his hunting-knife, stowed it away in a saddle-bag, and set off on his horse, now pretty well fagged, to find the waggons. But to find a waggon-track on the great veld, unless you have in the first instance taken the most careful bearings, is almost as difficult as it would be to return from a distance to any given spot on the ocean without a compass. There are no trees or hills to guide the travellers; nothing but a vast wilderness of land resembling a sea petrified in a heavy swell.

Ernest rode on for three or four miles, as he thought, retracing his steps over the line of country he had traversed, and at last, to his joy, struck the path. There were waggon-tracks on it; but he thought they did not look quite fresh. However, he followed them faute de mieux for some five miles. Then he became convinced that they could not have been made by his waggons. He had overshot the mark, and must hark back. So he turned his weary horse's head, and made his way along the road to the spot where his spoor struck into it. The waggons must be out-spanned, waiting for him a little farther back. He went on, one mile, two, three—no waggons. A little to the left of the road was an eminence. He rode to it, and up and scanned the horizon. O joy! there far away, five or six miles off, was the white cap of a waggon. He rode to it straight across country. Once he got bogged in a vlei or swamp, and had to throw himself off, and drag his horse out by the bridle. He struggled on, and at last came to the dip in which he had seen the waggon-tent. It was a great white stone perched on a mound of brown ones.

By this time he had utterly lost his reckoning. Just then, to make matters worse, a thunder-shower came up with a bitter wind, and drenched him to the skin. The rain passed, but the wind did not. It blew like ice, and chilled his frame, enervated with the tropical heat in which he had been living through and through. He wandered on aimlessly, till suddenly his tired horse put his foot in a hole and fell heavily, throwing him on to his head and shoulder. For a few minutes his senses left him; but he recovered, and, mounting his worn-out horse, wandered on again. Luckily, he had broken no bones. Had he done so, he would probably have perished miserably in that lonely place.

The sun was sinking now, and he was faint for want of food, for he had eaten nothing that day but a biscuit. He had not even a pipe of tobacco with him. Just as the sun vanished he hit a little path, or what might once have been a path. He followed it till the pitchy darkness set in; then he got off his horse and took off the saddle, which he put down on the bare black veld, for a fire had recently swept off the dry grass, and wrapping the saddle-cloth round his feet, laid his aching head upon the saddle. The reins he hitched round his arm, lest the horse should stray away from him to look for food. The wind was bitterly cold, and he was wet through; the hyenas came and howled at him. He cut off a piece of the raw vilderbeeste-beef and chewed it, but it turned his stomach and he spat it out. Then he shivered and sank into a torpor from which there was a poor chance of his awakening.

How long he lay so he did not know—it seemed a few minutes; it was really an hour—when suddenly he was awakened by feeling something shaking him by the shoulder.

"What is it?" he said wearily.

"Wat is it? Ach Himmel! wat is it? dat is just wat I wants to know. Wat do you here? You shall die so."

The voice was the voice of a German, and Ernest knew German well.

"I have lost my way," he said, in that language; "I cannot find the waggons."

"Ah, you can speak the tongue of the Vaterland," said his visitor, still addressing him in English. "I will embrace you;" and he did so.

Ernest sighed. It is a bore to be embraced in the dark by an unknown male German when you feel that you are not far off dissolution.

"You are hungered?" said the German.

Ernest signified that he was.

"And athirsted?"

Again he signified assent.

"And perhaps you have no 'gui' (tobacco)?"

"No, none."

"Good! my little wife, my Wilhelmina, shall find you all these things."

"What the devil," thought Ernest to himself, "can a German be doing with his little wife in this place?"

By this time the stars had come out, and gave some light.

"Come, rouse yourself, and come and see my little wife. O, the pferd!" (horse)—"we will tie him to my wife. Ah, she is beautiful, though her leg shakes. O yes, you will love her."

"The deuce I shall!" ejaculated Ernest; and then, mindful of the good things the lady in question was to provide him with, he added solemnly, "Lead on, Macduff."

"Macduffer! my name is not so, my name is Hans; all ze great South Africa know me very well, and all South Africa love my wife."

"Really!" said Ernest.

Although he was so miserable, he began to feel that the situation was interesting. A lady to whom his horse was to be tied, and whom all South Africa was enamoured of, could hardly fail to be interesting. Rising, he advanced a step or two with his friend, who he could now see was a large burly man with white hair, apparently about sixty years of age. Presently they came to something that in the dim light reminded him of the hand-hearse in Kesterwick Church, only it had two wheels instead of four, and no springs.

"Behold my beautiful wife," said the German. "Soon I will show you how her leg shakes; it shakes, O, horrid!"

"Is—is the lady inside?" asked Ernest. It occurred to him that his friend might be carting about a corpse.

"Inside! no, she is outside, she is all over"; and stepping back, the German put his head on one side in a most comical fashion, and, regarding the unofficial hearse with the deepest affection, said in a low voice, "Ah, liebe vrouw, ah, Wilhelmina, is you tired, my dear? and how is your poor leg?" and he caught hold of a groggy wheel and shook it.

Had Ernest been a little less wretched, and one degree further off starvation, it is probable that he would have exploded with laughter, for he had a keen sense of the ludicrous; but he had not got a laugh left in him, and, besides, he was afraid of offending the German. So he merely murmured, "Poor, poor leg!" sympathetically, and then alluded to the question of eatables.

"Ah, yes, of course. Let us see what Wilhelmina shall give us;" and he trotted round to the back end of the cart, which, in keeping with its hearse-like character, opened by means of two little folding-doors, and pulled out, first, two blankets, one of which he gave to Ernest to put round his shoulders; second, a large piece of biltong, or sun-dried game flesh, and some biscuits; and, third, a bottle of peach-brandy. On these viands they fell to, and though they were not in themselves of an appetising nature, Ernest never enjoyed anything more in his life. Their meal did not take very long, and after it his friend Hans produced some excellent Boer tobacco, and over their pipes Ernest told him how he had lost his way. Hans asked him what road he had been travelling on.

"The Rustenburg road."

"Then, my friend, you are not more than one thousand paces off it. My wife and I we travel along him all day, till just now Wilhelmina she think she would like to come up here, and so I come, and now you see the reason why. She know you lie here and die in the cold, and she turn up to save your life. Ah, the good woman!"

Ernest was greatly relieved to hear that he was so near the road, as, once upon it, he would have no difficulty in falling in with the waggons. Clearly, during the latter part of his wanderings, he must have unknowingly approached it. His mind, relieved upon this point, was at liberty to satisfy its curiosity about his friend. He soon discovered that he was a harmless lunatic, whose craze it was to wander all over South Africa, dragging his hand-cart after him. He made no fixed point, nor had he any settled round. The beginning of the year might find him near the Zambesi, and the end near Cape Town, or anywhere else. By the natives he was looked upon as inspired, and invariably treated with respect, and he lived upon what was given to him, or what he shot as he walked along. This mode of life he had pursued for years, and though he had many adventures, he never came to harm.

"You see, my friend," said the simple man, in answer to Ernest's inquiries, "I make my wife down there in Scatterdorp, in the old colony. The houses are a long way off each other there, and the church it is in the middle. And the good volk there, they die very fast, and did get tired of carrying each other to be buried. And so they come to me and say, 'Hans, you are a carpenter, you must make a beautiful black cart to put us in when we die.' And so I set to, and I work, and work, and work at my cart till I gets quite—what do you call him?—stoopid. And then one night, just as my cart was finished, I dreams that she and I are travelling along a wide straight road, like the road on the high veld, and I knows that she is my wife, and that we must travel always together till we reach the City of Rest. And far, far away, above the top of a high mountain like the Drakensberg, I see a great wide tree, rooted on a cloud and covered all over with beautiful snow, that shined in the sunlight like the diamonds at Kimberley. And I know that under that tree is the gate of the real Rustenburg, the City of Rest, and my wife and I, we must journey on, on, on till we find it."

"Where do you come from now?"

"From Utrecht, from out of the east, where the sun rises so red every morning over Zululand, the land of bloodshed. O, the land will run with blood there. I know it; Wilhelmina told me as we came along; but I don't know when. But you are tired. Good! you shall sleep with Wilhelmina; I will sleep beneath her. No, you shall, or she will be—what you call him?—offended."

Ernest crept into the cavity, and at once fell asleep, and dreamed that he had been buried alive. Suddenly in the middle of the night there was a most fearful jolt, caused by his horse, which was tied to the pole of Wilhelmina, having pulled the prop aside and let the pole down with a run. This Ernest mistook for the resurrection, and was extremely relieved to find himself in error. At dawn he emerged, bade his friend farewell, and gaining the road, rejoined the waggons in safety.

CHAPTER XVI

ERNEST ACCEPTS A COMMISSION

A young man of that ardent, impetuous, intelligent mind which makes him charming and a thing to love, as contrasted with the young man of the sober, cautious, money-making mind (infinitely the more useful article), which makes him a "comfort" to his relatives and a thing to respect, avoid, and marry your daughter to, has two great safeguards standing between him and the ruin which dogs the heels of the ardent, the impetuous, and the intelligent. These are, his religion and his belief in women. It is probable that he will start on his erratic career with a full store of both. He has never questioned the former; the latter, so far as his own class in life is concerned, are to him all sweet and good, and perhaps there is one particular star who only shines for him, and is the sweetest and best of them all.

But one day the sweetest and best of all throws him over, being a younger son, and marries his eldest brother, or a paralytic cotton-spinner of enormous wealth and uncertain temper, and then a sudden change comes over the spirit of the ardent, intelligent, and impetuous one. Not being of a well-balanced mind, he rushes to the other extreme, and believes in his sore heart that all women would throw over such as he and marry eldest brothers or superannuated cotton-spinners. He may be right or he may be wrong. The materials for ascertaining the fact are wanting, for all women engaged to impecunious young gentlemen to not get the chance. But, right or wrong, the result upon the sufferer is the same—his faith in women is shaken, if not destroyed. Nor does the mischief stop there; his religion often follows his belief in the other sex, for in some mysterious way the two things are interwoven. A young man of the nobler class of mind in love is generally for the time being a religious man; his affection lifts him more or less above the things of earth, and floats him on its radiant wings a day's journey nearer heaven.

The same thing applies conversely. If a man's religious belief is emasculated, he becomes suspicious of the "sweetest and best"; he grows cynical, and no longer puts faith in superlatives. From atheism there is but a small step to misogyny, or rather to that disbelief in humanity which embraces a profounder constituent disbelief in its feminine section, and in turn, as already said, the misogynist walks daily along the edge of atheism. Of course there is a way out of these discouraging results. If the mind that suffers and falls through its suffering be of the truly noble order, it may in time come to see that this world is a world not of superlatives, but of the most arid positives, with here and there a little comparative oasis to break the monotony of its general outline. Its owner may learn that the fault lay with him, for believing too much, for trusting too far, for setting up as an idol a creature exactly like himself, only several degrees lower beneath proof; and at last he may come to see that though "sweetest and bests" are chimerical, there are women in the world who may fairly be called "sweet and good."

Or, to return to the converse side of the picture, it may occur to our young gentleman that although Providence starts us in the world with a full inherited or indoctrinated belief in a given religion, that is not what Providence understands by faith. Faith, perfect faith, is only to be won by struggle, and in most cultivated minds by the passage through the dim, mirage-clad land of disbelief. The true believer is he who has trodden down disbelief, not he who has run away from it. When we have descended from the height of our childhood, when we have entertained Apollyon, and having considered what he has to say, given him battle and routed him in the plain, then, and not till then, can we say with guileless hearts, "Lord, I believe," and feel no need to add the sadly qualifying words, "help Thou mine unbelief."

Now these are more or less principles of human nature. They may not be universally true, probably nothing is—that is, as we define and understand truth. But they apply to the majority of those cases which fall strictly within their limits. Among others they applied rather strikingly to Ernest Kershaw. Eva's desertion struck his belief in womanhood to the ground, and soon his religion lay in the dust beside it. Of this his life for some years after that event gave considerable evidence. He took to evil ways, he forgot his better self. He raced horses, he devoted himself with great success to love-affairs that he would have done better to leave alone. Sometimes, to his shame be it said, he drank—for the excitement of drinking, not for the love of it. In short, he gave himself and all his fund of energy up to any and every excitement and dissipation he could command, and he managed to command a good many. Travelling rapidly from place to place in South Africa, he was well known and well liked in all. Now he was at Kimberley, now at King William's Town, now at Durban. In each of these places he kept race-horses; in each there was some fair woman's face that grew the brighter for his coming.

But Ernest's face did not grow brighter; on the contrary, his eyes acquired a peculiar sadness which was almost pathetic in one so young. He could not forget. For a few days or a few months he might stifle thought, but it always re-rose. Eva, pale queen of women, was ever there to haunt his sleep, and though in his waking hours he might curse her memory, when night drew the veil from truth the words he murmured were words of love eternal.

He no longer prayed, he no longer reverenced woman, but he was not the happier for having freed his soul from these burdens. He despised himself. Occasionally he would take stock of his mental condition, and at each stocktaking he would notice that he had receded, not progressed. He was growing coarse, his finer sense was being blunted; he was no longer the same Ernest who had written that queer letter to his betrothed before disaster overwhelmed him. Slowly and surely he was sinking. He knew it, but he did not try to save himself. Why should he? He had no object in life. But at times a great depression and weariness of existence would take possession of him. It has been said that he never prayed; that is not strictly true. Once or twice he did throw himself upon his knees and pray with all his strength that he might die. He did more: he persistently courted death, and, as is usual in such cases, it persistently avoided him. About taking his own life he had scruples, or perhaps he would have taken it. In those dark days he hated life, and in his calmer and more reflective moments he loathed the pleasures and excitements by means of which he strove to make it palatable. His was a fine strung mind, and, in spite of himself, he shuddered when it was set to play such coarse music.

During those years Ernest seemed to bear a charmed existence. There was a well-known thoroughbred horse in the Transvaal which had killed two men in rapid succession. Ernest bought it and rode it, and it never hurt him. Disturbances broke out in Secocoeni's country, and one of the chief strongholds was ordered to be stormed. Ernest rode down from Pretoria with Jeremy to see the fun, and, reaching the fort the day before the attack, got leave to join the storming party. Accordingly, next day at dawn they attacked in the teeth of a furious fusillade, and in time took the place, though with very heavy loss to themselves. Jeremy's hat was shot off with one bullet and his hand cut by another; Ernest, as usual, came off scathless; the man next to him was killed, but he was not touched. After that he insisted upon going buffalo-shooting towards Delagoa Bay in the height of the fever-season, having got rid of Jeremy by persuading him to go to New Scotland to see about a tract of land they had bought. He started with a dozen bearers and Mazooku. Six weeks later he, Mazooku, and three bearers returned—all the rest were dead of fever.

On another occasion, Alston, Jeremy, and himself were sent on a political mission to a hostile chief, whose stronghold lay in the heart of almost inaccessible mountains. The "indaba" (palaver) took all day, and was purposely prolonged in order to enable the intelligent native to set an ambush in the pass through which the white chiefs must go back, with strict instructions to murder all three of them. When they left the stronghold the moon was rising, and, as they neared the pass, up she came behind the mountains in all her splendour, flooding the wide valley behind them with her mysterious light, and throwing a pale, sad lustre on every stone and tree. On they rode steadily through the moonlight and the silence, little guessing how near death was to them. The faint beauty of the scene sank deep into Ernest's heart, and presently, when they came to a spot where a track ran out loopwise from the main pass, returning to it a couple of miles farther on, he half insisted on their taking it, because it passed over yet higher ground, and would give them a better view of the moon-bathed valley. Mr. Alston grumbled at "his nonsense" and complied, and meanwhile a party of murderers half a mile farther on played with their assegais, and wondered why they did not hear the sound of the white men's feet. But the white men had already passed along the higher path three-quarters of a mile to their right. Ernest's love of moonlight effects had saved them all from a certain and perhaps from a lingering death.

It was shortly after this incident that Ernest and Jeremy were seated together on the verandah of the same house at Pretoria where they had been living before they went on the elephant hunt, and which they had now purchased. Ernest had been in the garden, watering a cucumber-plant he was trying to develop from a very sickly seedling. Even if he only stopped a month in a place he would start a little garden; it was a habit of his. Presently he came back to the verandah, where Jeremy was as usual watching the battle of the red and black ants, which after several years' encounter was not yet finally decided.

"Curse that cucumber-plant!" said Ernest emphatically, "it won't grow. I tell you what it is, Jeremy, I am sick of this place; I vote we go away."

"For goodness' sake, Ernest, let us have a little rest; you do rattle one about so in those confounded post-carts," replied Jeremy, yawning.

"I mean, go away from South Africa altogether."

"Oh," said Jeremy, dragging his great frame into an upright position, "the deuce you do! And where do you want to go to—England?"

"England! no, I have had enough of England. South America, I think. But perhaps you want to go home. It is not fair to keep dragging you all over the world."

"My dear fellow, I like it, I assure you. I have no wish to return to Mr. Cardus's stool. For goodness' sake, don't suggest such a thing; I should be wretched."

"Yes, but you ought to be doing something with your life. It is all very well for me, who am a poor devil of a waif and stray, to go on with this sort of existence, but I don't see why you should; you should be making your way in the world."

"Wait a bit, my hearty!" said Jeremy, with his slow smile; "I am going to read you a statement of our financial affairs which I drew up last night. Considering that we have been doing nothing all this time except enjoy ourselves, and that all our investments have been made out of income, which no doubt your respected uncle fancies we have dissipated, I do not think that the total is so bad." And Jeremy read:

```
"Landed property in Natal and the Transvaal, estimated value £2,500
This house                                                      940
Stocks—waggons, etc., say                                       300
Race-horses
```

"I have left that blank."

"Put them at £800," said Ernest, after thinking. "You know I won £500 with Lady Mary on the Cape Town Plate last week."

Jeremy went on:

```
"Race-horses and winnings              £1,300
Sundries—cash, balance, &c.              180
Total                                  £5,220
```

"Now, of this we have actually saved and invested about twenty-five hundred, the rest we have made or it has accumulated. Now, I ask you, where could we have done better than that, as things go? So don't talk to me about wasting my time."

"Bravo, Jeremy! My uncle was right, after all: you ought to have been a lawyer; you are first-class at figures. I congratulate you on your management of the estates."

"My system is simple," answered Jeremy. "Whenever there is any money to spare I buy something with it, then you are not likely to spend it. Then, when I have things enough—waggons, oxen, horses, what not—I sell them and buy some land; that can't run away. If you only do that sort of thing long enough, you will grow rich at last."

"Sweetly simple, certainly. Well, five thousand will go a long way towards stocking a farm or something in South America, or wherever we make up our minds to go, and then I don't think that we need draw on my uncle any more. It is hardly fair to drain him so. Old Alston will come with us, I think, and will put in another five thousand. He told me some time ago that he was getting tired of South Africa, with its Boers and blacks, in his old age, and had a fancy to make a start in some other place. I will write to him to-night. What hotel is he staying at in Maritzburg? the Royal, isn't it? And then I vote we clear in the spring."

"Right you are, my hearty!"

"But I say, Jeremy, I really should advise you to think twice before you come. A fine, upstanding young man like you should not waste his sweetness on the desert air of Mexico, or any such place. You should go home and be admired of the young women—they appreciate a great big chap like you—and make a good marriage, and rear up a large family in a virtuous, respectable, and Jones-like fashion. I am a sort of wandering comet without the shine; but, I repeat, I see no reason why you should play tail to a second class comet."

"Married! get married! I! No, thank you, my boy. Look you, Ernest, in the words of the prophet, 'When a wise man openeth his eye, and seeth a thing, verily he shutteth it not up again.' Now, I opened my eye and saw one or two things in the course of our joint little affair—Eva, you know."

Ernest winced at the name.

"I beg your pardon," said Jeremy, noticing it; "I don't want to allude to painful subjects, but I must to make my meaning clear. I was very hard hit, you know, over that lady, but I stopped in time, and, not having any imagination to speak of, did not give it rein. What is the consequence? I have got over it; sleep well at night, have a capital appetite, and don't think about her twice a week. But with you it is different. Hard hit, too, large amount of imagination galloping about loose, so to speak—rapturous joy, dreams of true love and perfect union of souls, which no doubt would be well enough if the woman could put in her whack of soul, which she can't, not having it to spare, but in a general way is gammon. Results, when the burst-up comes: want of sleep, want of appetite, a desire to go buffalo-shooting in the fever-season, and to be potted by Basutos from behind rocks. In short, a general weariness and disgust of life—O yes, you needn't deny it, I have watched you—most unwholesome state of mind. Further results: horse-racing, a disposition to stop away from church, and nip Cape sherry; and, worse sign of all, a leaning to ladies' society. Being a reasoning creature I notice this, and draw my own deductions, which amount to the conclusion that you are in a fair way to go to the deuce, owing to trusting your life to a woman. And the moral of all this, which I lay to heart for my own guidance, is, never speak to a woman if you can avoid it, and when you can't, let your speech be yea, yea, and nay, nay, more especially 'nay.' Then you stand a good chance of keeping your appetite and peace of mind, and of making your way in the world. Marriage, indeed!—never talk to me of marriage again;" and Jeremy shivered at the thought.

Ernest laughed out loud at this lengthy disquisition.

"And I'll tell you what, old fellow," he went on, drawing himself up to his full height, and standing right over Ernest, so that the latter's six feet looked very insignificant beside him, "never you speak to me about leaving you again, unless you want to put me clean out of temper, because, look here, I don't like it. We have lived together since we were twelve, or thereabouts, and, so far as I am concerned, I mean to go on living together to the end of the chapter, or till I see I am not wanted. You can go to Mexico, or the North Pole, or Acapulto, or wherever you like, but I shall go too, and so that is all about it."

"Thank you, old fellow," said Ernest, simply; and at that moment their conversation was interrupted by the arrival of a Kafir messenger with a telegram addressed to Ernest. He opened it and read it. "Hullo," he said, "here is something better than Mexico; listen.

"'Alston, Pieter Maritzburg, to Kershaw, Pretoria. High Commissioner has declared war against Cetywayo. Local cavalry urgently required for service in Zululand. Have offered to raise a small corps of about seventy mounted men. Offer has been accepted. Will you accept post of second in command?—you would hold the Queen's commission. If so, set about picking suitable recruits. Terms ten shillings a day, all found. Am coming up Pretoria by this post-cart. Ask Jones if he will accept sergeant-majorship.'

"Hurrah!" sang out Ernest, with flashing eyes. "Here is some real service at last. Of course you will accept."

"Of course," said Jeremy, quietly; "but don't indulge in rejoicings yet; this is going to be a big business, unless I am mistaken."

CHAPTER XVII

HANS PROPHESIES EVIL

Ernest and Jeremy did not let the grass grow under their feet. They guessed that there would soon be a good deal of recruiting for various corps, and so set to work at once to secure the best men. The stamp of man they aimed at getting was the colonial-born Englishman, both because such men have more self-respect, independence of character, and "gumption," than the ordinary drifting sediment from the diamond fields and seaports, and also because they were practically ready-made soldiers. They could ride as well as they could walk, they were splendid rifle-shots, and they had, too, from childhood, been trained in the art of travelling without baggage, and very rapidly.

Ernest did not find much difficulty in the task. Mr. Alston was well known, and had seen a great deal of service as a young man in the Basuto wars, and stories were still told of his nerve and pluck. He was known, too, to be a wary man, not rash or over-confident, but of a determined mind; and, what is more, to possess a perfect knowledge of Zulu warfare and tactics. This went a long way with intending recruits, for the first thing a would-be colonial volunteer inquires into is the character of his officers. He will not trust his life to men in whom he puts no reliance. He is willing to lose it in the way of duty, but he has a great objection to having it blundered away. Indeed, in many South African volunteer corps it is a fundamental principle that the officers should be elected by the men themselves. Once elected, however, they cannot be deposed except by competent authority.

Ernest, too, was by this time well known in the Transvaal, and universally believed in. Mr. Alston could not have chosen a better lieutenant. He was known to have pluck and dash, and to be ready-witted in emergency; but it was not those qualities only which made him acceptable to the individuals whose continued existence would very possibly depend upon his courage and discretion. Indeed, it would be difficult to say what it was; but there are some men who are by nature born leaders of their fellows, and who inspire confidence magnetically. Ernest had this great gift. At first sight he was much like any other young man, rather careless-looking than otherwise in appearance, and giving the observer the impression that he was thinking of something else; but old hands at native warfare, looking into his dark eyes, saw something there which told them that this young fellow, boy as he was, comparatively speaking, would not show himself wanting in the moment of emergency, either in courage or discretion. Jeremy's nomination, too, as sergeant-major, a very important post in such a corps, was popular enough. People had not forgotten his victory over the Boer giant, and besides, a sergeant-major with such a physique would have been a credit to any corps.

All these things helped to make recruiting an easy task, and when Alston and his son Roger, weary and bruised, stepped out of the Natal post-cart four days later, it was to be met by Ernest and Jeremy with the intelligence that his telegram had been received, the appointments accepted, and thirty-five men provisionally enrolled subject to his approval.

"My word, young gentlemen," he said, highly pleased, "you are lieutenants worth having."

The next fortnight was a busy one for all concerned. The organisation of a colonial volunteer corps is no joke, as anybody who has ever tried it can testify. There were rough uniforms to be provided, arms to be obtained, and a hundred and one other wants to be satisfied. Then came some delay about the horses, which were to be served out by Government. At last these were handed over, a good-looking lot, but apparently very wild. Matters were at this point, when one day Ernest was seated in the room he used as an office in his house, enrolling a new recruit previous to his being sworn, interviewing a tradesman about flannel shirts, making arrangements for a supply of forage, filling up the endless forms which the imperial authorities required for transmission to the War Office, and a hundred other matters. Suddenly his orderly announced that two privates of the corps wished to see him.

"What is it?" he asked of the orderly, testily; for he was nearly worked to death.

"A complaint, sir."

"Well, send them in."

The door opened, and a curious couple entered. One was a great, burly sailorman, who had been a quartermaster on board one of her Majesty's ships at Cape Town, got drunk, overstayed his leave, and deserted rather than face the punishment; the other a quick, active little fellow, with a face like a ferret. He was a Zululand trader, who had ruined himself by drink, and a peculiarly valuable member of the corps on account of his knowledge of the country in which they were going to serve. Both men saluted and stood at ease.

"Well, my men, what is it?" asked Ernest, going on filling up his forms.

"Nothing, so far as I am concerned, sir," said the little man.

Ernest looked up sharply at the quondam tar.

"Now, Adam, your complaint; I have no time to waste."

Adam hitched up his breeches and began:

"You see, sir, I brought he here by the scruff of the neck."

"That's true, sir," said the little man, rubbing that portion of his body.

"Because he and I, sir, as is messmates, sir, 'ad a difference of opinion. It was his day, you see, sir, to cook for our mess, and instead of putting on the pot, sir, he comes to me he does, and he says, 'Adam, you blooming father of a race of fools'—that's what he says, sir, a-comparing of me to the gent who lived in a garden—'why don't you come and take the skins off the — taters, instead of a-squatting of yourself down on that there — bed!'"

"Slightly in error, sir," broke in the little man, suavely; "our big friend's memory is not as substantial as his form. What I said was, 'My dear Adam, as I see you have nothing to occupy your time, except sit and play a jew's-harp upon your couch, would you be so kind as to come and assist me to remove the outer integument of these potatoes?'"

Ernest began to explode, but checked himself, and said sternly:

"Don't talk nonsense, Adam; tell me your complaint or go."

"Well, sir," answered the big sailor, scratching his head, "if I git it a name, it is this—this here man, sir, be too infarnal sargustic."

"Be off with you both," said Ernest, sternly, "and don't trouble me with any such nonsense again, or I will put you both under arrest, and stop your pay. Come, march!" and he pointed to the door. As he did so he observed a Boer gallop swiftly past the house, and take the turn to Government House.

"What is up now?" he wondered.

Half an hour afterwards another man passed the window, also at full gallop, and also turned up towards Government House. Another half-hour passed, and Mr. Alston came hurrying in.

"Look here, Ernest," he said, "here is a pretty business. Three men have come in to report that Cetywayo has sent an Impi (army) round by the back of Secocoeni's country to burn Pretoria, and return to Zululand across the high veld. They say that the Impi is now resting in the Saltpan Bush, about twenty miles off, and will attack the town to-night or to-morrow night. All these three, who have, by the way, had no communication with each other, state that they have actually seen the captains of the Impi, who came to tell them to bid the other Dutchmen to stand aside, as they are now fighting the Queen, and the Boers would not be hurt."

"It seems incredible," said Ernest; "do you believe it?"

"I don't know. It is possible, and the evidence is strong. It is possible; I have known the Zulus make longer marches than that. The Governor has ordered me to gallop to the spot, and report if I can see anything of this Impi."

"Am I to go too?"

"No, you will remain in the corps. I take Roger with me—he is a light weight—and two spare horses. If there should be an attack and I should not be back, or if anything should happen, you will do your duty."

"Yes."

"Good-bye. I am off. You had better muster the men to be ready for an emergency;" and he was gone.

Ten minutes afterwards, down came an orderly from the officer commanding, with a peremptory order that the officer commanding Alston's Horse was to mount and parade his men in readiness for immediate service.

"Here is a pretty go," thought Ernest, "and the horses not served out yet!"

Just then Jeremy came in, saluted, and informed him that the men were mustered.

"Serve out the saddlery. Let every man shoulder his saddle. Tell Mazooku to bring out the 'Devil' (Ernest's favourite horse), and march the men up to the Government stables. I will be with you presently."

Jeremy saluted again with much ceremony and vanished. He was the most punctilious sergeant-major who ever breathed.

Twenty minutes later, a long file of men, each with a carbine slung to his back, and a saddle on his head, which, at a distance, gave them the appearance of a string of gigantic mushrooms, were to be seen proceeding towards the Government stables a mile away.

Ernest, mounted on his great black stallion, and looking, in his military uniform and the revolver slung across his shoulders, a typical volunteer officer, was there before them.

"Now, my men," he said, as soon as they were paraded, "go in, and each man choose the horse which he likes best, bridle him, bring him out and saddle him. Sharp!"

The men broke their ranks and rushed to the stables, each anxious to secure a better horse than his neighbours. Presently from the stables there arose a sound of kicking, plunging, and "wo-hoing" impossible to describe.

"There will be a pretty scene soon, with these unbroken brutes," thought Ernest.

He was not destined to be disappointed. The horses were dragged out, most of them lying back upon their haunches, kicking, bucking, and going through every other equine antic.

"Saddle up!" shouted Ernest, as soon as they were all out.

It was done with great difficulty.

"Now mount."

Sixty men lifted their legs and swung themselves into the saddle, not without sad misgivings. A few seconds passed, and at least twenty of them were on the broad of their backs; one or two were being dragged by the stirrup-leather; a few were clinging to their bucking and plunging steeds; and the remainder of Alston's Horse was scouring the plain in every possible direction. Never was there such a scene.

In time, however, most of the men got back again, and some sort of order was restored. Several men were hurt, one or two badly. These were sent to the hospital, and Ernest formed the rest into half-sections, to be marched to the place of rendezvous. Just then, to make matters better, down came the rain in sheets, soaking them to the skin, and making confusion worse confounded. So they rode to the town, which was by this time in an extraordinary state of panic.

All business was suspended; women were standing about on verandahs, hugging their babies and crying, or making preparations to go into laager; men were hiding deeds and valuables, or hurrying to defence meetings on the market-square, where the Government were serving out rifles and ammunition to all able-bodied citizens; frightened mobs of Basutos and Christian Kafirs were jabbering in the streets, and telling tales of the completeness of Zulu slaughter, or else running from the city to pass the night among the hills. Altogether the scene was most curious, till dense darkness came down over it like an extinguisher, and put it out.

Ernest took his men to a building which the Government had placed at their disposal, and had the horses stabled, but not unsaddled. Presently orders came down to him to keep the corps under arms all night; to send out four patrols to be relieved at midnight, to watch the approaches to the town; and at dawn to saddle up and reconnoitre the neighbouring country.

Ernest obeyed these orders as well as he could; that is, he sent the patrols out, but so dense was the darkness that they never got back again till the following morning, when they were collected, and, in one instance, dug out of the various ditches, quarry-holes, etc., into which they had fallen.

About eleven o'clock Ernest was seated in a little room that opened out of the main building where they were quartered, consulting with Jeremy about matters connected with the corps, and wondering if Alston had found a Zulu Impi, or if it was all gammon, when suddenly they heard the sharp challenge of the sentry outside:

"Who goes there?"

"Whoever it is had better answer sharp," said Ernest; "I gave the sentry orders to be quick with his rifle to-night."

Bang!—crash! followed by loud howls of "Wilhelmina, my wife! Ah, the cruel man has killed my Wilhelmina!"

"Heavens, it is that lunatic German! Here, orderly, run up to the Defence Committee and the Government offices, and tell them that it is nothing; they will think the Zulus are here. Tell two men to bring the man in here, and to stop his howls."

Presently Ernest's old friend of the high veld, looking very wild and uncouth in the lamplight, with his long beard and matted hair, from which the rain was dripping, was bundled rather unceremoniously into the room.

"Ah, there you are, dear sir; it is two—three years since we met. I look for you everywhere, and they tell me you are here, and I come on quick all through the dark and the rain; and then before I know if I am on my head or my heel, the cruel man he ups a rifle, and do shoot my Wilhelmina, and make a great hole through her poor stomach. O sir, what shall I do?" and the great child began to shed tears; "you, too, will weep: you, too, love my Wilhelmina, and sleep with her one night—bo-hoo!"

"For goodness' sake stop that nonsense! This is no time or place for such fooling."

He spoke sharply, and the monomaniac pulled up, only giving vent to an occasional sob.

"Now, what is your business with me?"

The German's face changed from its expression of idiotic grief to one of refined intelligence. He glanced towards Jeremy, who was exploding in the corner.

"You can speak before this gentleman, Hans," said Ernest.

"Sir, I am going to say a strange thing to you this night."

He was speaking quite quietly and composedly now, and might have been mistaken for a sane man.

"Sir, I hear that you go down to Zululand to help to fight the fierce Zulus. When I hear it, I was far away, but something come into my head to travel as quick as Wilhelmina can, and come and tell you not to go."

"What do you mean?"

"How can I say what I do mean? This I know—many shall go down to Zululand who rest in this house to-night, few shall come back."

"You mean that I shall be killed?"

"I know not. There are things as bad as death, and yet not death."

He covered his eyes with his hand, and continued:

"I cannot see you dead, but do not go; I pray you do not go."

"My good Hans, what is the use of coming to me with such an old wives' tale? Even if it were true, and I knew that I must be killed twenty times, I should go; I cannot run away from my duty."

"That is spoken as a brave man should," answered his visitor, in his native tongue. "I have done my duty, and told you what Wilhelmina said. Now go, and when the black men are leaping up at you like the sea-waves round a rock, may the God of Rest guide your hand, and bring you safe from the slaughter!"

Ernest gazed at the old man's pale face; it wore a curious rapt expression, and the eyes were looking upwards.

"Perhaps, old friend," he said addressing him in German, "I, as well as you, have a City of Rest which I would reach, and care not if I pass thither on an assegai."

"I know it," replied Hans, in the same tongue; "but useless is it to seek rest till God gives it. You have sought and passed through the jaws of many deaths, but you have not found. If it be not God's will, you will not find it now. I know you too seek rest, my brother, and had I known that you would find that only down there"—and he pointed towards Zululand—"I had not come down to warn you, for blessed is rest, and happy is he who gains it. But no, it is not that; I am sure now that you will not die; your evil, whatever it is, will fall from heaven."

"So be it," said Ernest; "you are a strange man. I thought you a common monomaniac, and now you speak like a prophet."

The old man smiled.

"You are right; I am both. Mostly I am mad. I know it. But sometimes my madness has its moments of inspiration, when the clouds lift from my mind, and I see things none others can see, and hear voices to which your ears are deaf. Such a moment is on me now; soon I shall be mad again. But before the cloud settles I would speak to you. Why, I know not, save that I loved you when first I saw your eyes open there upon the cold veld. Presently I must go, and we shall meet no more, for I draw near to the snowclad tree that marks the gate of the City of Rest. I can look into your heart now and see the trouble in it, and the sad, beautiful face that is printed on your mind. Ah, she is not happy; she, too, must work out her rest. But the time is short, the cloud settles, and I would tell you what is in my mind. Even though trouble, great trouble, close you in, do not be cast down, for trouble is the key of heaven. Be good; turn to the God you have neglected; struggle against the snares of the senses. Oh, I can see now! For you and for all you love there is joy and there is peace!"

Suddenly he broke off; the look of inspiration faded from his face, which grew stupid and wild-looking.

"Ah, the cruel man; he made a great hole in the stomach of my Wilhelmina!"

Ernest had been bending forwards, listening with parted lips to the old man's talk. When he saw that the inspiration had left him, he raised his head and said:

"Gather yourself together, I beg you, for a moment. I wish to ask one question. Shall I ever—"

"How shall I stop de bleeding from the witals of my dear wife?—who will plug up the hole in her?"

Ernest gazed at the man. Was he putting all this on?—or was he really mad? For the life of him he could not tell.

Taking out a sovereign, he gave it to him.

"There is money to doctor Wilhelmina with," he said. "Would you like to sleep here?—I can give you a blanket."

The old man took the money without hesitation, and thanked Ernest for it, but said he must go on at once.

"Where are you going to?" asked Jeremy, who had been watching him with great curiosity, but had not understood that part of the conversation which had been carried on in German.

Hans turned upon him with a quick look of suspicion.

"Rustenburg" (Anglicè, the town of rest), he answered.

"Indeed! the road is bad, and it is far to travel."

"Yes," he replied, "the road is rough and long. Farewell!" And he was gone.

"Well, he is a curious old buster, and no mistake, with his cheerful anticipations and his Wilhelmina," reflected Jeremy aloud. "Just fancy starting for Rustenburg at this hour of the night, too! Why, it is a hundred miles off!"

Ernest only smiled. He knew that it was no earthly Rustenburg that the old man sought.

Some while afterwards he heard that Hans had attained the rest which he desired. Wilhelmina got fixed in a snowdrift in a pass of the Drakensberg. He was unable to drag her out.

So he crept underneath, and fell asleep, and the snow came down and covered them.

CHAPTER XVIII

MR. ALSTON'S VIEWS

The Zulu attack on Pretoria ultimately turned out only to have existed in the minds of two mad Kafirs, who dressed themselves up after the fashion of chiefs and personating two Zulu nobles of repute, who were known to be in the command of regiments, rode from house to house, telling the Dutch inhabitants that they had an Impi of thirty thousand men lying in the bush, and bidding them stand aside while they destroyed the Englishmen. Hence the scare.

The next month was a busy one for Alston's Horse. It was drill, drill, drill, morning, noon, and night. But the results soon became apparent. In three weeks from the day they got their horses, there was not a smarter, quicker corps in South Africa, and Mr. Alston and Ernest were highly complimented on the soldier-like appearance of the men, and the rapidity and exactitude with which they executed all the ordinary cavalry manoeuvres.

They were to march from Pretoria on the 10th of January, and expected to overtake Colonel Glynn's column, with which was the General, about the 18th, by which time Mr. Alston calculated the real advance upon Zululand would begin.

On the 8th, the good people of Pretoria gave the corps a farewell banquet, for most of its members were Pretoria men; and colonists are never behindhand when there is an excuse for conviviality and good-fellowship.

Of course, after the banquet, Mr.—or, as he was now called, Captain—Alston's health was drunk. But Alston was a man of few words, and had a horror of speech-making. He contented himself with a few brief sentences of acknowledgment and sat down. Then somebody proposed the health of the other commissioned and non-commissioned officers, and to this Ernest rose to respond, making a very good speech in reply. He rapidly sketched the state of political affairs, of which the Zulu war was the outcome, and, without any opinion on the justice or wisdom of that war, of which, to speak the truth, he had grave doubts, he went on to show, in a few well-chosen, weighty words, how vital were the interests involved in its successful conclusion, now that it once had been undertaken. Finally he concluded thus:

"I am well aware, gentlemen, that with many of those who are your guests here to-night, and my own comrades, this state of affairs, and the conviction of the extreme urgency of the occasion, has been the cause of their enlistment. It is impossible for me to look down these tables, and see so many in our rough-and-ready uniform, whom I have known in other walks of life, as farmers, store-keepers, Government clerks, and what not, without realising most clearly the extreme necessity that can have brought these peaceable citizens together on such an errand as we are bent on. Certainly it is not the ten shillings a day, or the mere excitement of savage warfare, that has done this" (cries of "No, no!"); "because most of them can well afford to despise the money, and many more have seen enough of native war, and know well that few rewards and plenty of hard work fall to the lot of colonial volunteers. Then what is it? I will venture to reply. It is that sense of patriotism which is a part and parcel of the English mind" (cheers), "and which from generation to generation has been the root of England's greatness, and, so long as the British blood remains untainted, will from unborn generation to generation be the mainspring of the greatness that is yet to be of those wider Englands, of which I hope this continent will become not the least." (Loud cheers).

"That, gentlemen, and men of Alston's Horse, is the bond which unites us together; it is the sense of a common duty to perform, of a common danger to combat, of a common patriotism to vindicate. And for that reason, because of the patriotism and the duty, I feel sure that when the end of this campaign comes, whatever that end may be, no one, be he imperial officer or newspaper correspondent, or Zulu foe, will be able to say that Alston's Horse shirked its work, or was mutinous, or proved a broken reed, piercing the side of those who leaned on it." (Cheers.) "I feel sure, too, that, though there may be a record of brave deeds such as become brave men, there will be none of a comrade deserted in the time of need, or of a failure in the moment of emergency, my brethren in arms," and here Ernest's eyes flashed and his strong clear voice went ringing down the great hall, "whom England has called, and who have not failed to answer the call, I repeat, however terrible may be that emergency, even if it should involve the certainty of death—I speak thus because I feel I am addressing brave men, who do not fear to die, when death means duty, and life means dishonour—I know well that you will rise to it, and, falling shoulder to shoulder, will pass as heroes should on to the land of shades—on to that Valhalla of which no true heart should fear to set foot upon the threshold."

Ernest sat down amid ringing cheers. Nor did these noble words, coming as they did straight from the loyal heart of an English gentleman, fail of their effect. On the contrary, when, a fortnight later, Alston's Horse formed that fatal ring on Isandhlwana's bloody field, they flashed through the brain of more than one despairing man, so that he set his teeth and died the harder for them.

"Bravo, my young Viking!" said Mr. Alston to Ernest, while the roof was still echoing to the cheers evoked by his speech, "the old Berserker spirit is cropping up, eh?" He knew that Ernest's mother's family, like so many of the old Eastern County stocks, were of Danish extraction.

It was a great night for Ernest.

Two days later Alston's Horse, sixty-four strong, marched out of Pretoria with a military band playing before. Alas! they never marched back again.

At the neck of the poort or pass the band and the crowd of ladies and gentlemen who had accompanied them halted, and, having given them three cheers, turned and left them. Ernest, too, turned and gazed at the pretty town, with its white houses and rose-hedges red with bloom, nestling on the plain beneath, and wondered if he would ever see it again. He never did.

The troop was then ordered to march at ease in half-sections, and Ernest rode up to the side of Alston; on his other side was the boy Roger, now about fourteen years of age, who acted as Alston's aide-de-camp, and was in high spirits at the prospect of the coming campaign. Presently Alston sent his son back to the other end of the line on some errand.

Ernest watched him as he galloped off, and a thought struck him.

"Alston," he said, "do you think that it is wise to bring that boy into this business?"

His friend slewed himself round sharply in the saddle.

"Why not?" he asked, in his deliberate way.

"Well, you know there is a risk."

"And why should not the boy run risks as well as the rest of us? Look here, Ernest, when I first met you there in Guernsey I was going to see the place where my wife was brought up. Do you know how she died?"

"I have heard she died a violent death; I do not know how."

"Then I will tell you, though it costs me something to speak of it. She died by a Zulu assegai, a week after the boy was born. She saved his life by hiding him under a heap of straw. Don't ask me particulars; I can't bear to talk of it. Perhaps now you will understand why I am commanding a corps enrolled to serve against the Zulus. Perhaps, too, you will understand why the lad is with me. We go to avenge my wife and his mother, or to fall in the attempt. I have waited long for the opportunity; it has come."

Ernest relapsed into silence, and presently fell back to his troop.

On the 20th of January, Alston's Horse, having moved down by easy marches from Pretoria, camped at Rorke's Drift, on the Buffalo River, not far from a store and a thatched building being used as a hospital, which were destined to become historical. Here orders reached them to march on the following day and join No. 3 column, with which was Lord Chelmsford himself, and which was camped about nine miles from the Buffalo River at a spot called Isandhlwana, or the "Place of the Little Hand." Next day, the 21st of January, the corps moved on accordingly, and following the waggon-track that runs past the Inhlazatye Mountain, by midday came up to the camp, where about twenty-five hundred men of all arms were assembled under the immediate command of Colonel Glynn. Their camp, which was about eight hundred yards square, was pitched facing a wide plain, with its back towards a precipitous, slab-sided hill, of the curious formation sometimes to be seen in South Africa. This was Isandhlwana.

"Hullo!" said Alston, as, on reaching the summit of the neck over which the waggon-road runs, they came in sight of the camp, "they are not entrenched. By Jove," he added, after scanning the camp carefully, "they haven't even got a waggon-laager!" and he whistled expressively.

"What do you mean?" asked Ernest.

Mr. Alston so rarely showed surprise that he knew there must be something very wrong.

"I mean, Ernest, that there is nothing to prevent the camp from being destroyed, and every soul in it, by a couple of Zulu regiments, if they choose to make a night attack. How they are to be kept out, I should like to know, in the dark, when you can't see to shoot them, unless there is some barrier? These officers, fresh from home, don't know what a Zulu charge is, that is very clear. I only hope they won't have occasion to find out. Look there," and he pointed to a waggon lumbering along before them, on the top of which, among a lot of other miscellaneous articles, lay a bundle of cricketing bats and wickets, "they think that they are going on a picnic. What is the use, too, I should like to know, of sending four feeble columns sprawling over Zululand, to run the risk of being crushed in detail by a foe that can move from point to point at the rate of fifty miles a day, and which can at any moment slip past them and turn Natal into a howling wilderness? There, it is no use grumbling; I only hope I may be wrong. Get back to your troop, Ernest, and let us come into camp smartly. Form fours—trot!"

On arrival in the camp, Mr. Alston learned, on reporting himself to the officer commanding, that two strong parties of mounted men under the command of Major Dartnell were out on a reconnaissance towards the Inhlazatye Mountain, in which direction the Zulus were supposed to be in force. The orders he received were to rest his horses, as he might be required to join the mounted force with Major Dartnell on the morrow.

That night, as Alston and Ernest stood together at the door of their tent, smoking a pipe before turning in, they had some conversation. It was a beautiful night, and the stars shone brightly. Ernest looked at them, and thought on how many of man's wars those stars had looked.

"Star-gazing?" asked Mr. Alston.

"I was contemplating our future homes," said Ernest, laughing.

"Ah, you believe that, do you? think you are immortal, and that sort of thing?"

"Yes; I believe that we shall live many lives, and that some of them will be there," and he pointed to the stars. "Don't you?"

"I don't know. I think it rather presumptuous. Why should you propose that for you is reserved a bright destiny among the stars more than for these?" and he put out his hand and clasped several of a swarm of flying-ants which were passing at the time. "Just think how small must be the difference between these ants and us in the eyes of a Power who can produce both. These have their homes, their government, their colonies, their drones and workers. They enslave and annex, lay up riches, and, to bring the argument to an appropriate conclusion, make peace and war. What then is the difference? We are bigger, walk on two legs, have a larger capacity for suffering, and, we believe, a soul. Is it so great that we should suppose that for us is reserved a heaven, or all the glorious worlds which people space—for these, annihilation? Perhaps we are at the top of the tree of development, and for them may be the future, for us the annihilation. Who knows? There, fly away, and make the most of the present, for nothing else is certain."

"You overlook religion entirely."

"Religion? Which religion? There are so many. Our Christian God, Buddha, Mohammed, Brahma, all number their countless millions of worshippers. Each promises a different thing, each commands the equally intense belief of his worshippers, for with them all blind faith is a condition precedent; and each appears to satisfy their spiritual aspirations. Can all of these be true religions? Each holds the other false and outside the pale; each tries to convert the other, and fails. There are many lesser ones of which the same thing may be said."

"But the same spirit underlies them all."

"Perhaps. There is much that is noble in all religions, but there is also much that is terrible. To the actual horrors and wearing anxieties of physical existence, religion bids us add on the vaguer horrors of a spiritual existence, which are to be absolutely endless. The average Christian would be uncomfortable if you deprived him of his hell and his personal devil. For myself, I decline to believe in such things. If there is a hell, it is this world; this world is a place of expiation for the sins of the world; and the only real devil is the devil of man's evil passions."

"It is possible to be religious and be a good man without believing in hell," said Ernest.

"Yes, I think so, otherwise my chance is a poor one. Besides, I do not deny the Almighty Power. I only deny the cruelty that is attributed to Him. It may be that, from the accumulated mass of the wrong and bloodshed and agony of this hard world, that Power is building up some high purpose. Out of the bodies of millions of living creatures Nature worked out her purpose and made the rocks, but the process must have been unpleasant to the living creatures by whose humble means the great strata were reared up. They lived, to die in billions, that tens of thousands of years afterwards there might be a rock. It may be so with us. Our tears and blood and agony may produce some solid end that now we cannot guess; their volume, which cannot be wasted, for nothing is wasted, may be building up one of the rocks of God's far-off purpose. But that we shall be tortured here for a time in order that we may be indefinitely tortured there," and he pointed to the stars, "that I will never believe. Look at the mist rising from that hollow; so does the reek of the world's misery rise as an offering to the world's gods. The mist will cease to rise, and fall again in rain, and bring a blessing; but the incense of human suffering rises night and day for so long as the earth shall endure, nor does it fall again in dews of mercy. And yet Christians, who declare that God is love, declare, too, that for the vast majority of their fellow-creatures this process is to continue from millennium to millennium."

"It depends on our life, they say."

"Look here, Ernest, a man can do no more than he can. When I got to the age of discretion, which I put at eight-and-twenty—you have hardly reached it yet, my boy, you are nothing but a babe—I made three resolutions: always to try and do my duty, never to turn my back on a poor man or a friend in trouble, and, if possible, not to make love to my neighbour's wife. Those resolutions I have often broken more or less, either in the spirit or the letter, but in the main I have stuck to them, and I can put my hand upon my heart to-night and say, 'I have done my best!' And so I go my path, turning neither to the right nor to the left, and when Fate finds me, I shall meet him, fearing nothing, for I know he has wreaked his worst upon me, and can only at the utmost bring me eternal sleep; and hoping nothing, because my experience here has not been such as to justify the hope of any happiness for man, and my vanity is not sufficiently strong to allow me to believe in the intervention of a superior Power to save so miserable a creature from the common lot of life. Good-night."

On the following day his fate found him.

CHAPTER XIX

ISANDHLWANA

Midnight came, and the camp was sunk in sleep. Up to the sky, whither it was decreed their spirits should pass, before the dark closed in again and hit their mangled corpses, floated the faint breath of some fourteen hundred men. There they lay, sleeping the healthy sleep of vigorous manhood, their brains busy with the fantastic madness of a hundred dreams, and little recking of the inevitable morrow. There, in his sleep, the white man saw his native village, with its tall, wind-swayed elms, and the grey old church that for centuries had watched the last slumber of his race; the Kafir, the sunny slope of fair Natal, with its bright light dancing on his cattle's horns, and the green of the gardens, where, for his well-being, his wives and children toiled. To some that night came dreams of high ambition, of brave adventure, crowned with the perfect triumph we never reach; to some, visions of beloved faces, long since passed away; to some, the reflected light of a far-off home, and echoes of the happy laughter of little children. And so their lamps wavered hither and thither in the spiritual breath of sleep, flickering wildly, ere they went out for ever.

The night-wind swept in sad gusts across Isandhlwana's plain, tossing the green grass, which to-morrow would be red. It moaned against Inhlazatye's Mountain and died upon Upindo, fanning the dark faces of a host of warriors who rested there upon their spears, sharpened for the coming slaughter. And as it breathed upon them, they turned, those brave soldiers of U'Cetywayo—"born to be killed," as their saying runs, at Cetywayo's bidding—and, grasping their assegais, raised themselves to listen. It was nothing, death was not yet; death for the morrow, sleep for the night.

A little after one o'clock on the morning of the 22nd of January, Ernest was roused by the sound of a horse's hoofs and the hard challenge of the sentries. "Despatch from Major Dartnell," was the answer, and the messenger passed on. Half an hour more and the reveille was sounded, and the camp hummed in the darkness like a hive of bees making ready for the dawn.

Soon it was known that the General and Colonel Glynn were about to move out to the support of Major Dartnell, who reported a large force of the enemy in front of him, with six companies of the second battalion of the 24th Regiment, four guns, and the mounted infantry.

At dawn they left.

At eight o'clock a report arrived from a picket, stationed about a mile away on a hill to the north of the camp, that a body of Zulus was approaching from the north-east.

At nine o'clock the enemy showed over the crest of the hills for a few minutes, and then disappeared.

At ten o'clock Colonel Durnford arrived from Rorke's Drift with a rocket battery and two hundred and fifty mounted native soldiers, and took over the command of the camp from Colonel Pulleine. As he came up he stopped for a minute to speak to Alston, whom he knew, and Ernest noticed him. He was a handsome, soldier-like man, with his arm in a sling, a long, fair moustache, and a restless, anxious expression of face.

At 10.30 Colonel Durnford's force, divided into two portions, was, with the rocket battery, pushed some miles towards to ascertain the enemy's movements, and a company of the 24th was directed to take up a position on the hill about a mile to the north of the camp. Meanwhile, the enemy, which they afterwards heard consisted of the Undi Corps, the Nokenke and Umcitu Regiments, and the Nkobamakosi and Imbonambi Regiments, in all about twenty thousand men, were resting about two miles from Isandhlwana, with no intention of attacking that day. They had not yet been "moutied" (doctored), and the condition of the moon was not propitious.

Unfortunately, however, Colonel Durnford's mounted Basutos, in pushing forwards, came upon a portion of the Umcitu Regiment, and fired on it; whereupon the Umcitu came into action, driving Durnford's Horse before them, and then engaged the company of the 24th, which had been stationed on the hill to the north of the camp, and, after a stubborn resistance, annihilating it. It was followed by the Nokenke, Imbonambi, and Nkobamakosi Regiments, who executed a flanking movement, and threatened the front of the camp. For a while the Undi Corps, which formed the chest of the army, held its ground. Then it marched off to the right, and directed its course to the north of Isandhlwana Mountain, with the object of turning the position.

Meanwhile, the remaining companies of the 24th were advanced to various positions in front of the camp, and engaged the enemy, for a while holding them in check; the two guns under Major Smith shelling the Nokenke Regiment, which formed the Zulu left centre, with great effect. The shells could be seen bursting amid the dense masses of Zulus, who were coming on slowly and in perfect silence, making large gaps in their ranks, which instantly closed up over the dead.

At this point the advance of the Undi Regiment to the Zulu right and the English left was reported; and Alston's Horse were ordered to proceed, and, if possible, to check it. Accordingly they left, and, riding behind the company of the 24th on the hill, to the north of the camp, which was now hotly engaged with the Umcitu, and Durnford's Basutos, who, fighting splendidly, were slowly being pushed back, made for the north side of Isandhlwana. As soon as they got on to the high ground they caught sight of the Undi, who, something over three thousand strong, were running swiftly in a formation of companies, about half a mile to the northward.

"By Heaven, they mean to turn the mountain, and seize the waggon-road!" said Mr. Alston. "Gallop!"

The troop dashed down the slope towards a pass in a stony ridge, which would command the path of the Undi, as they did so breaking through and killing two or three of a thin line of Zulus that formed the extreme point of one of the horns or nippers, by means of which the enemy intended to enclose the camp and crush it.

After this Alston's Horse saw nothing more of the general fight; but it may be as well to briefly relate what happened. The Zulus of the various regiments pushed slowly on towards the camp, notwithstanding their heavy losses. Their object was to give time to the horns or nippers to close round it. Meanwhile, those in command realised too late the extreme seriousness of the position, and began to concentrate the various companies. Too late! The enemy saw that the nippers had closed. He knew, too, that the Undi could not be far off the waggon-road, the only way of retreat; and so, abandoning his silence and his slow advance, he raised the Zulu war-shout, and charged it from a distance of from six to eight hundred yards.

Up to this time the English loss had been small, for the shooting of the Zulus was vile. The enemy, on the contrary, had, especially during the last half-hour before they charged lost heavily. But now the tables were turned. First the Natal Contingent, seeing that they were surrounded, bolted and laid open the right and rear flank of the troops. In poured the Zulus, so that most of the soldiers had not even time to fix bayonets. In another minute, our men were being assegaied right and left, and the retreat on the camp had become a fearful rout. But even then there was nowhere to run to. The Undi Corps (which afterwards passed on and attacked the post at Rorke's Drift) already held the waggon-road, and the only practical way of retreat was down a gully to the south of the road. Into this the broken fragments of the force plunged wildly, and after them and mixed up with them, went their Zulu foes massacring every living thing they came across.

So the camp was cleared. When a couple of hours afterwards, Commandant Lonsdale, of Londsdale's Horse, was sent back by General Chelmsford to ascertain what the firing was about, he could see nothing wrong. The tents were sanding, the waggons were there; there were even soldiers moving about. It did not occur to him that it was the soldiers' coats which were moving on the backs of Kafirs, and that the soldiers themselves would never move again. So he rode quickly up to the headquarters tents; out of which, to his surprise, there suddenly stalked a huge naked Zulu, smeared all over with blood, and waving in his hand a bloody assegai.

Having seen enough, he then rode back again to tell the General that his camp was taken.

To God's good providence and Cetywayo's clemency, rather than to our own wisdom, do we owe it that all the outlying homesteads in Natal were not laid in ashes, and men, women, and children put to the assegai.

Alston's Horse soon reached the ridge, past which the Undi were commencing to run, at a distance of about three hundred and fifty yards, and the order was given to dismount and line it. This they did, one man in every four keeping a few paces back to hold the horses of his section. Then they opened fire; and next second came back the sound of the thudding of the bullets on the shields and bodies of the Zulu warriors.

Ernest, seated up high on his great black horse "The Devil," for the officers did not dismount, could see how terrible was the effect of that raking fire, delivered as it was, not by raw English boys, who scarcely knew one end of a rifle from the other, but by men, all of whom could shoot, and many of whom were crack shots. All along the line of the Undi companies men threw up their arms and dropped dead, or staggered out of the ranks wounded. But the main body never paused. By and by they would come back and move the wounded, or kill them if they were not likely to recover.

Soon, as the range got longer, the fire began to be less deadly, and Ernest could see that fewer men were dropping.

"Ernest," said Alston, galloping up to him, "I am going to charge them. Look, they will soon cross the donga, and reach the slopes of the mountain, and we shan't be able to follow them on the broken ground."

"Isn't it rather risky?" asked Ernest, somewhat dismayed at the idea of launching their little clump of mounted men at the moving mass before them.

"Risky? yes, of course it is, but my orders were to delay the enemy as much as possible, and the horses are fresh. But, my lad"—and he bent towards him and spoke low—"it doesn't much matter whether we are killed charging or running away. I am sure that the camp must be taken; there is no hope. Good-bye, Ernest; if I fall, fight the corps as long as possible, and kill as many of those devils as you can; and if you survive, remember to make off well to the left. The regiments will have passed by then. God bless you, my boy! Now order the bugler to sound the 'cease fire,' and let the men mount."

"Yes, sir."

They were the last words Alston ever spoke to him, and Ernest often remembered, with affectionate admiration, that even at that moment he thought more of his friend's safety than he did of his own. As to their tenor, Ernest had already suspected the truth, though, luckily, the suspicion had not as yet impregnated the corps. Mazooku, too, who as usual was with him, mounted on a Basuto pony, had just informed him that, in his (Mazooku's) opinion, they were all as good as ripped up (alluding to the Zulu habit of cutting a dead enemy open), and adding a consolatory remark to the effect that man can die but once, and "good job too."

But, strangely enough, he did not feel afraid; indeed, he never felt quieter in his life than he did in that hour of death. A wild expectancy thrilled his nerves and looked out of his eyes. "What would it be like?" he wondered. In another minute all such thoughts were gone, for he was at the head of his troop, ready for the order.

Alston, followed by the boy Roger, galloped swiftly round, seeing that the formation was right, and then gave the word to unsheath the short swords with which he had insisted upon the corps being armed. Meanwhile, the Undi were drawing on to a flat plain, four hundred yards or more broad, at the foot of the mountain, a very suitable spot for a cavalry manoeuvre.

"Now, men of Alston's Horse, there is the enemy before you. Let me see how you can go through them. Charge!"

"Charge!" re-echoed Ernest.

"Charge!" roared Sergeant-Major Jones, brandishing his sword.

Down the slope they go, slowly at first; now they are on the plain, and the pace quickens to a hand-gallop.

Ernest feels his great horse gather himself together and spring along beneath him; he hears the hum of astonishment rising from the dense black mass before them as it halts to receive the attack; he glances round, and sees the set faces and determined look upon the features of his men, and his blood boils up with a wild exhilaration, and for a while he tastes the fierce joy of war.

Quicker still grows the pace; now he can see the white round the dark eyeballs of the Zulus.

"Crash!" They are among them, trampling them down, hewing them down, thrusting, slashing, stabbing, and being stabbed. The air is alive with assegais, and echoes with the savage Zulu war-cries and with the shouts of the gallant troopers, fighting now as troopers have not often fought before. Presently, as in a dream, Ernest sees a huge Zulu seize Alston's horse by the bridle, jerk it on to its haunches, and raise his assegai. Then the boy Roger, who is by his father's side, makes a point with his sword, and runs the Zulu through. He falls, but next moment the lad is attacked by more, is assegaied, and falls fighting bravely. Then Alston pulls up, and, turning, shoots with his revolver at the men who have killed his son. Two fall, another runs up, and with a shout drives a great spear right through Alston, so that it stands out a hand-breadth behind his back. On to the body of his son he, too, falls and dies. Next second the Zulu's head is cleft in twain down to the chin. That was Jeremy's stroke.

All this time they are travelling on, leaving a broad red line of dead and dying in their track. Presently it was done; they had passed right through the Impi. But out of sixty-four men they had lost their captain and twenty troopers. As they emerged, Ernest noticed that his sword was dripping blood, and his sword-hand stained red. Yet he could not at the moment remember having killed anybody.

But Alston was dead, and he was now in command of what remained of the corps. They were in no condition to charge again, for many horses and some men were wounded. So he led them round the rear of the Impi, which, detaching a company of about three hundred men to deal with the remnants of the troop, went on its way with lessened numbers, and filled with admiration at the exhibition of a courage in no way inferior to their own.

This company, running swiftly, took possession of the ridge down which the troop had charged, and by which alone it would be possible for Ernest to retreat, and taking shelter behind stones, began to pour in an inaccurate but galling fire on the little party of whites. Ernest charged up through them, losing two more men and several horses in the process; but what was his horror, on reaching the crest of the ridge, to see about a thousand Zulus drawn up, apparently in reserve, in the neck of the pass leading to the plain beyond! To escape through them would be almost impossible, for he was crippled with wounded and dismounted men, and the pace of a force is the pace of the slowest. Their position was desperate, and looking round at his men, he could see that they thought so too.

His resolution was soon taken. A few paces from where he had for a moment halted the remainder of the corps was a little eminence, something like an early British tumulus. To this he rode, and, dismounting, turned his horse loose, ordering this men to do the same. So good was the discipline, and so great his control over them, that there were no wild rushes to escape; they obeyed, realising their desperate case, and formed a ring round the rise.

"Now, men of Alston's Horse," said Ernest, "we have done our best, let us die our hardest."

The men set up a cheer, and next minute the Zulus, creeping up under shelter of the rocks which were strewed around, attacked them with fury.

In five minutes, in spite of the withering fire which they poured in upon the surrounding Zulus, six more of the little band were dead. Four were shot, two were killed in a rush made by about a dozen men, who, reckless of their own life, determined to break through the white man's ring. They perished in the attempt, but not before they had stabbed two of Alston's Horse. The remainder, but little more than thirty men, retired a few paces farther up the little rise so as to contract their circle and kept up a ceaseless fire upon the enemy. The Zulus, thanks to the accurate shooting of the white men, had by this time lost more than fifty of their number, and, annoyed at being put to such loss by a foe numerically so insignificant, they determined to end the matter with a rush. Ernest saw their leader, a big almost naked fellow, with a small shield and a necklace of lion's claws, walking utterly regardless of the pitiless rifle fire from group to group and exhorting them. Taking up a rifle which had just fallen from the hand of a dead trooper—for up to the present Ernest had not joined in the firing—he took a fine sight at about eighty yards at the Zulu chief's broad chest and pulled. The shot was a good one; the great fellow sprang into the air and dropped. Instantly another commander took his place and the final advance began.

But the Zulus had to come up-hill with but little cover, and scores were mown down by the scorching and continuous fire from the breech-loaders. Twice, when within twenty yards, were they driven back, twice did they come on again. Now they were but twelve paces or so away, and a murderous fire was kept up upon them. For a moment they wavered, then pushed forwards up the slope.

"Close up!" shouted Ernest, "and use your swords and pistols."

His voice was heard above the din. Some of the men dropped the now useless rifles, and the revolvers began to crack.

Then the Zulus closed in upon the doomed band, with a shout of "Bulala umlungo!" (Kill the white man!)

Out rang the pistol-shots, and fire flew from the clash of swords and assegais; and still the little band, momentarily growing fewer, fought on with labouring breath. Never did hope-forsaken men make a more gallant stand. Still they fought, and still they fell, one by one, and as they fell were stabbed to death; but scarcely one of them was there whose death-wound was in his back.

At last the remaining Zulus drew back; they thought that it was done.

But no; three men yet stood together upon the very summit of the mound, holding six foes at bay. The Zulu captain laughed aloud when he saw it, and gave a rapid order. Thereupon the remaining Zulus formed up, and stabbing the wounded as they went, departed swiftly over the dead, after the main body of the corps, which had now vanished round the mountain.

They left the six to finish the three.

Three hundred had come to attack Alston's Horse; not more than one hundred departed from the attack. The overpowered white men had rendered a good account of their foes.

The three left alive on the summit of the little hill, were, as Fate would have it, Ernest, Jeremy, and the ex-sailor, who had complained of the "sargustic" companion, who, it happened, had just died by his side.

Their revolvers were empty; Ernest's sword had broken off short in the body of a Zulu; Jeremy still had his sword, and the sailor a clubbed carbine.

Presently one of the six Zulus dodged in under the carbine and ran the sailor through. Glancing round, Ernest saw his face turn grey. The honest fellow died as he had lived, swearing hard.

"Ah, you — black mate," he sang out, "take that, and be damned to you!" The clubbed rifle came down upon the Zulu's skull and cracked it to bits, and both fell dead together.

Now there were five Zulus left, and only Ernest and Jeremy to meet them. But stay; suddenly from under a corpse up rises another foe. No, it is not a foe, it is Mazooku, who has been shamming dead, but suddenly and most opportunely shows himself to be very much alive. Advancing from behind, he stabs one of the attacking party, and kills him. That leaves four. Then he engages another, and after a long struggle kills him too, which leaves three. And still the two white men stand back to back with flashing eyes and gasping breath, and hold their own. Soaked with blood, desperate, and expecting death, they were yet a gallant sight to see. Two of the remaining Zulus rush at the giant Jeremy, one at Ernest. Ernest, having no effective weapon left, dodges the assegai-thrust and closes with his antagonist, and they roll, over and over, down the hill together, struggling for the assegai the Zulu holds. It snaps in two, but the blade and about eight inches of the shaft remain with Ernest. He drives it through his enemy's throat, who dies. Then he struggles up to see the closing scene of the drama, but not in time to help in it. Mazooku has wounded his man badly, and is following to kill him. And Jeremy? He has struck at one of the Kafirs with his sword. The blow is received on the edge of the cow-hide shield, and sinks half-way through it, so that the hide holds the steel fast. With a sharp twist of the shield the weapon is jerked out of his hand, and he is left defenceless, with nothing to trust to except his native strength. Surely he is lost! But no—with a sudden rush he seizes both Zulus by the throat, one in each hand, and, strong men as they are, swings them wide apart. Then with a tremendous effort he jerks their heads together with such awful force that they fall senseless, and Mazooku comes up and spears them.

Thus was the fight ended.

Ernest and Jeremy sank upon the bloody grass, gasping for breath. The firing from the direction of the camp had now died away, and after the tumult, the shouts, and the shrieks of the dying, the silence seemed deep.

There they lay, white man and Zulu, side by side in the peaceable sunlight; and in a vague bewildered way Ernest noticed that the faces, which a few minutes before looked so grim, were mostly smiling now. They had passed through the ivory gates and reached the land of smiles. How still they all were! A little black-and-white bird, such as flies from ant-hill to ant-hill, came and settled upon the forehead of a young fellow, scarcely more than a boy, and the only son of his mother, who lay quiet across two Zulus. The bird knew why he was so still. Ernest had liked the boy, and knew his mother, and began to wonder as he lay panting on the grass what she would feel when she heard of her son's fate. But just then Mazooku's voice broke the silence. He had been standing staring at the body of one of the men he had killed, and was now apostrophising it in Zulu.

"Ah, my brother," he said, "son of my own father, with whom I used to play when I was little; I always told you that you were a perfect fool with an assegai; but I little thought that I should ever have such an opportunity of proving it to you. Well, it can't be helped; duty is duty, and family ties must give way to it. Sleep well, my brother; it was painful to kill you—very!"

Ernest lifted himself from the ground, and laughed the hysterical laugh of shattered nerves, at this naive and thoroughly Zulu moralising. Just then Jeremy rose, and came to him. He was a fearful sight to see—his hands, his face, his clothes, were all red; and he was bleeding from a cut on the face, and another on the hand.

"Come, Ernest," he said, in a hollow voice, "we must clear out of this."

"I suppose so," said Ernest.

On the plain at the foot of the hill several of the horses were quietly cropping the grass, till such time as the superior animal, man, had settled his differences. Among them was Ernest's black stallion, "The Devil," which had been wounded, though slightly, on the flank. They walked towards the horses, stopping on their way to arm themselves from the weapons which lay about. As they passed the body of the man Ernest had killed in his last struggle for life, he stopped and drew the broken assegai from his throat. "A memento!" said he. The horses were caught without difficulty, and "The Devil" and the two next best animals selected. Then they mounted, and rode towards the top of the ridge over which Ernest had seen the body of Zulus lying in reserve. When they were near it Mazooku got down and crept to the crest on his stomach. Presently, to their great relief, he signalled to them to advance: the Zulus had moved on, and the valley was deserted. So the three passed over the neck, that an hour and a half before they had crossed with sixty-one companions, who were now all dead. "I think we have charmed lives," said Jeremy, presently. "All gone except us two. It can't be chance."

"It is fate," said Ernest, briefly.

From the top of the neck they got a view of the camp, which now looked quiet and peaceful, with its white tents and its Union Jack fluttering as usual in the breeze.

"They must be all dead too," said Ernest; "which way shall we go?"

Then it was that Mazooku's knowledge of the country proved of the utmost service to them. He had been brought up in a kraal in the immediate neighbourhood, and knew every inch of the land. Avoiding the camp altogether, he led them to the left of the battle-field, and after two hours' ride over rough country, brought them to a ford of the Buffalo which he was acquainted with, some miles below where the few survivors of the massacre struggled across the river, or were drowned in attempting to do so. Following this route they never saw a single Zulu, for these had all departed in the other direction, and were spared the horrors of the stampede and of "Fugitive's Drift."

At last they gained the farther side of the river, and were, comparatively speaking, safe on Natal ground.

They determined, after much consultation, to make for the little fort at Helpmakaar, and had ridden about a mile or so towards it, when suddenly the Zulu's quick ear caught the sound of firing distant to their right. It was their enemy, the Undi Corps, attacking Rorke's Drift. Leaving Mazooku to hold the horses, Ernest and Jeremy dismounted, and climbed a solitary koppie or hill which just there cropped out from the surface of the plain. It was of an iron-stone formation, and on the summit lay a huge flat slab of almost pure ore. On to this they clambered, and looked along the course of the river, but could see nothing. Rorke's Drift was hidden by a rise in the ground.

All this time a dense thunder-cloud had been gathering in the direction of Helpmakaar, and was now, as is common before sunset in the South African summer season, travelling rapidly up against the wind, set in a faint rainbow as in a frame. The sun, on the other hand, was sinking towards the horizon, so that his golden beams, flying across a space of blue sky, impinged upon the black bosom of the cloud, and were reflected thence in sharp lights and broad shadows, flung like celestial spears and shields across the plains of Zululand. Isandhlwana's Mountain was touched by one great ray which broke in glory upon his savage crest, and crowned him that day's king of death, but the battle-field over which he towered was draped in gloom. It was a glorious scene. Above, the wild expanse of sky broken up by flaming clouds, and tinted with hues such as might be reflected from the jewelled walls of heaven. Behind, the angry storm set in its rainbow-frame like ebony in a ring of gold. In front, the rolling plain, where the tall grasses waved, the broad Buffalo flashing through it like a silver snake, the sun-kissed mountains, and the shadowed slopes.

It was a glorious scene. Nature in her most splendid mood flung all her colour streamers loose across the earth and sky, and waved them wildly ere they vanished into night's abyss. Life, in his most radiant ecstasy, blazed up in varied glory before he sank, like a lover, to sleep awhile in the arms of his eternal mistress—Death.

Ernest gazed upon it, and it sank into his heart, which, set to Nature's tune, responded ever when her hands swept the chords of earth or heaven. It lifted him above the world, and thrilled him with indescribable emotion. His eyes wandered over the infinite space above, searching for the presence of a God; then they fell upon Isandhlwana, and marked the spot just where the shadows were deepest; where his comrades lay, and gazed upon the splendid sky with eyes that could not see; and at last his spirit gave way, and, weakened with emotion and long toil and abstinence, he burst into a paroxysm of grief.

"O Jeremy," he sobbed, "they are all dead, all except you and I, and I feel a coward that I should still live to weep over them. When it was over, I should have let that Zulu kill me but I was a coward, and I fought for my life. Had I but held my hand for a second, I should have gone with Alston and the others, Jeremy."

"Come, come, old fellow, you did your best, and fought the corps like a brick. No man could have done more."

"Yes, Jeremy, but I should have died with them; it was my duty to die. And I do not care about living, and they did. I have been an unfortunate dog all my life. I shot my cousin, I lost Eva, and now I have seen all my comrades killed, and I, who was their leader, alone escaped. And perhaps I have not done with my misfortunes yet. What next, I wonder; what next?"

Ernest's distress was so acute, that Jeremy, looking at him and seeing that all he had gone through had been too much for him, tried to soothe him, lest he should go into hysterics, by putting his arm round his waist and giving him a good hug.

"Look here, old chap," he said, "it is no use bothering one's head about these things. We are just so many feathers blown by the wind, and must float where the wind blows us. Sometimes it is a good wind, and sometimes a bad one; but on the whole it is bad, and we must just make the best of it, and wait till it doesn't think it worth while to blow our particular feathers about any more, and then we shall come to the ground, and not till then. Now we have been up here for more than five minutes, and given the horses a bit of a rest. We must be pushing on if we want to get to Helpmakaar before dark, and I only hope we shall get there before the Zulus, that's all. By Jove, here comes the storm—come on!" And Jeremy jumped off the lump of iron ore, and began to descend the koppie.

Ernest, who had been listening with his face in his hands, rose and followed him in silence. As he did so, a breath of ice-cold air from the storm-cloud, which was now right overhead, fanned his hot brow, and when he had gone a few yards he turned to meet it, and to cast one more look at the scene.

It was the last earthly landscape he ever saw. For at that instant there leaped from the cloud overhead a fierce stream of jagged light, which struck the mass of iron-ore on which they had been seated, shivered and fused it, and then ran down the side of the hill to the plain. Together with the lightning there came an ear-splitting crack of thunder.

Jeremy, who was now nearly at the bottom of the little hill, staggered at the shock. When he recovered, he looked up where Ernest had been standing, and could not see him. He rushed up the hill again, calling him in accents of frantic grief. There was no answer. Presently he found him lying on the ground, white and still.

BOOK III

CHAPTER I

THE CLIFFS OF OLD ENGLAND

It was an April evening; off the south coast of England. The sun had just made up his mind to struggle out from behind a particularly black shower-cloud, and give that part of the world a look before he bade it good-night.

"That is lucky," said a little man, who was with difficulty hanging on to the bulwark netting of the R.M.S. Conway Castle; "now, Mr. Jones, look if you can't see them in the sunlight."

Mr. Jones accordingly looked through his glasses again.

"Yes," he said, "I can see them distinctly."

"See what?" asked another passenger, coming up.

"The cliffs of old England," answered the little man, joyously.

"Oh, is that all?" said the other; "curse the cliffs of Old England!"

"Nice remark for a man who is going home to be married, eh?" said the little man, turning to where his companion had stood.

But Mr. Jones had shut up his glasses, and vanished aft.

Presently he reached a deck-cabin, and entered without knocking.

"England is in sight, old fellow," he said, addressing somebody who lay back smoking in a cane-chair.

The person addressed made a movement as though to rise, then put up his hand to a shade that covered his eyes.

"I forgot," he answered, with a smile; "it will have to be very much in sight before I can see it. By the way, Jeremy," he went on, nervously, "I want to ask you something. These doctors tell such lies." And he removed the shade. "Now, look at my eyes, and tell me honestly, am I disfigured? Are they shrunk, I mean, or have they got a squint, or anything of that sort?" and Ernest turned up his dark orbs, which except that they had acquired that painful, expectant look peculiar to the blind, were just as they always had been.

Jeremy looked at them, first in one light, then in another.

"Well!" said Ernest impatiently. "I can feel that you are staring me out of countenance."

"Hamba gachlé," replied the imperturbable one. "I am di—di—diagnosing the case. There, that will do. To all appearance, your optics are as sound as mine. You get a girl to look at them, and see what she says."

"Ah, well; that is something to be thankful for."

Just then some one knocked at the cabin-door. It was the steward.

"You sent for me, Sir Ernest?"

"O yes, I remember. Will you be so good as to find my servant? I want him."

"Yes, Sir Ernest."

Ernest moved impatiently.

"Confound that fellow, with his everlasting 'Sir Ernest'!"

"What, haven't you got used to your handle yet?"

"No, I haven't, and I wish it were at Jericho, and that is a fact. It is all your fault, Jeremy. If you had not told that confoundedly garrulous little doctor, who went and had the information printed in the Natal Mercury, it would never have come out at all. I could have dropped the title in England; but now all these people know that I am Sir Ernest, and Sir Ernest I shall remain for the rest of my days."

"Well, most people would not think that such a dreadful misfortune."

"Yes, they would, if they had happened to shoot the real heir. By the way, what did the lawyer say in his letter? As we are so near home, I suppose I had better post myself up. You will find it in the despatch-box. Read it, there's a good fellow."

Jeremy opened the box, battered with many years of travel, and searched about for the letter. It contained a curious collection of articles, prominent among which was a handkerchief, which once belonged to Eva Ceswick; a long tress of chestnut hair tied up with a blue ribbon; ditto of golden, which had come—well, not from Eva's locks; a whole botanical collection of dead flowers, tender souvenirs of goodness knows who, for, after a while, these accumulated dried specimens are difficult to identify; and many letters and other curiosities.

At last Jeremy came to the desired document, written in a fair clerk's hand; and having shovelled back the locks of hair, &c., began to read it aloud:

"St. Ethelred's Court, Poultry,
"22nd January, 1879.

"Sir,—"

"You see," broke in Ernest, "while we were fighting over there at Isandhlwana, those beggars were writing to tell me that I was a baronet. Case of the 'bloody hand' with a vengeance, eh?"

"Sir" (began Jeremy again), "it is out duty to inform you of the death, on the 16th of the present month, of our esteemed client, Sir Hugh Kershaw, Bart., of Archdale Hall, Devonshire, and of the consequent devolution of the baronetcy to yourself, as only son of the late Sir Hugh's only brother, Ernest Kershaw, Esq.

"Into the question of the unhappy manner in which you came to be placed in the immediate succession it does not become us to enter. We have before us at this moment a certified copy of Her Majesty's pardon, granted to you under the Transvaal Amnesty Act of 1877, and forwarded to us by Reginald Cardus, Esq., of Dum's Ness, Suffolk, which we have neither the wish nor the will to dispute. It is clear to us that, under this pardon, you are totally free from any responsibility for the breach of the law which you perpetrated some years since; and of this it is our duty to advise you. Your title to succeed is also clear under the original patent.

"As was only to be expected under the circumstances, the late Sir Hugh did not bear any feeling of good-will towards you. Indeed, we do not think that we shall be exaggerating if we say that the news of your free pardon materially hastened his end. On the attainment of full age by the late Hugh Kershaw, Esq., who fell by your hand, the entail of the family estates was cut, and only the mansion-house of Archdale Hall, the heirlooms, which are numerous and valuable, therein contained, and the deer-park, consisting of one hundred and eighty-five acres of land, were resettled. These consequently pass to you, and we shall be glad to receive your instructions concerning them, should you elect to honour us with your confidence. The estates pass, under the will of the late Baronet, to a distant cousin of his late wife's, James Smith, Esq., 52 Camperdown Road, Upper Clapham. We now think that we have put you in possession of all the facts connected with your accession to the baronetcy, and, awaiting your instructions, have the honour to remain,

"Your obedient servants,
"Paisley & Paisley." (Signed)

"Ah, so much for that!" was Ernest's comment. "What am I to do with Archdale Hall, its heirlooms, and its deer-park of one hundred and eighty-five acres, I wonder? I shall sell them if I can. Mine is a pretty position: a baronet with about sixpence halfpenny per annum to support my rank on; a very pretty position!"

"Hamba gachlé," replied Jeremy; "time enough to consider all that. But now, as we are on the reading lay, I may as well give you the benefit of my correspondence with the officer commanding Her Majesty's forces in Natal and Zululand."

"Fire away!" remarked Ernest, wearily.

"First letter, dated Newcastle, Natal, 27th January, from your humble servant to officer commanding, &c.:

"'Sir,—I have the honour to report, by order of Lieutenant and Adjutant Kershaw, of Alston's Horse, at present incapacitated by lightning from doing so himself—'

"Very nearly put that, I think," interpolated Jeremy.

"Very. Go on."

—"'that on the 22nd inst., Alston's Horse, having received orders to check the flanking movement of the Undi Corps, proceeded to try and do so. Coming to a ridge commanding the advance of the Undi, the corps, by order of their late commander, Captain Alston, dismounted, and opened fire on them at a distance of about three hundred yards, with considerable effect. This did not, however, check the Undi, who appeared to number between three and four thousand men, so Captain Alston issued an order to charge the enemy. This was done with some success. The Zulus lost a number of men; the corps, which passed right through the enemy, about twenty troopers, Captain Alston, and his son Roger Alston, who acted as his aide-de-camp. Several horses and one or two men were also severely wounded, which crippled the further movements of the corps.

"'Lieutenant and Adjutant Kershaw, on taking command of the corps, determined to attempt to retreat. In this attempt, however, he failed, owing to the presence of dismounted and wounded men; to the detachment of a body of about three hundred Zulus to intercept any such retreat; and to the presence of a large body of Zulus on the farther side of the pass leading to the valley through which such retreat might be conducted.

"'Under these circumstances he determined to fight the remains of the corps to the last, and dismounting them, took possession of a fairly advantageous position. A desperate hand-to-hand encounter ensued. It ended in the almost total extermination of Alston's Horse, and in that of the greater part of the attacking Zulus. The names of the surviving members of Alston's Horse are—Lieutenant and Adjutant Kershaw, Sergeant-Major Jeremy Jones, Trooper Mazooku (the only native in the corps).

"'These ultimately effected their escape, the enemy having either been all destroyed or having followed the track of the Undi. Lieutenant and Adjutant Kershaw regrets to have to state that in process of effecting his escape he was struck by lightning and blinded.

"'He estimates the total loss inflicted on the enemy by Alston's Horse at from four hundred to four hundred and fifty men. In face of such determined bravery as was evinced by every one of his late gallant comrades, Lieutenant Kershaw feels that it would be invidious for him to mention any particular names. Every man fought desperately, and died with his face to the enemy. He begs to enclose a return of the names of those lost, the accuracy of which he cannot, however, guarantee, as it is compiled from memory, the papers of the corps having all been lost. Trusting that the manoeuvres attempted by Lieutenant Kershaw under somewhat difficult circumstances will meet with your approval, I have, &c.—By order of Lieutenant Kershaw,

(Signed)
"'Jeremy Jones,
"'Sergeant-Major.'

"Then follows the reply, dated Maritzburg, 2nd February:

"'Sir,—1. I have to direct you to convey to Lieutenant and Adjutant Kershaw, and the surviving members of the corps known as Alston's Horse, the high sense entertained by the Officer, &c., of the gallant conduct of that corps in the face of overwhelming odds at Isandhlwana on the 22nd of January.

"'2. It is with deep regret that the Officer, &c., learns of the heavy misfortune which has befallen Lieutenant Kershaw. He wishes to express his appreciation of the way in which that officer handled the remnants of his corps, and to inform him that his name will be forwarded to the proper quarter for the expression of Her Majesty's pleasure with regard to his services.[*]

"'3. I am directed to offer you a commission in any of the volunteer corps now on service in this campaign.—I have, &c.,

(Signed)
"'Chief of the Staff.'"

[*] It may be stated here that, if this was ever done, the War Office did not consider Ernest's services worthy of notice, for he never heard anything more about them.

Then comes a letter from Sergeant-Major Jones, gratefully acknowledging the expression of the high opinion of the Officer, &c., and declining the offer of a commission in another volunteer corps.

Next is a private letter from the Officer, &c., offering to recommend Sergeant-Major Jeremy Jones for a commission in the army.

And, finally, a letter from Sergeant-Major Jones to the Officer, &c., gratefully declining the same.

Ernest looked up sharply. The raison d'etre of the movement was gone, for he could no longer see, but the habit remained.

"Why did you decline the commission, Jeremy?"

Jeremy moved uneasily, and looked through the little cabin-window.

"On general principles," he answered presently.

"Nonsense! I know you would have liked to go into the army. Don't you remember, as we were riding up to the camp at Isandhlwana, you said that you proposed that if the corps did anything, we should try and work it?"

"Yes."

"Well?"

"Well, I said we!"

"I don't quite follow you, Jeremy."

"My dear Ernest, you can't go in for a commission now, can you?"

Ernest laughed a little bitterly.

"What has that to do with it?"

"Everything. I am not going to leave you in your misfortune to go and enjoy myself in the army. I could not do it; I should be wretched if I did. No, old fellow, we have gone through a good many things side by side, and, please God we will stick to each other to the end of the chapter."

Ernest was always easily touched by kindness, especially now that his nerves were shaken, and his heart softened by misfortune, and his blind eyes filled with tears at Jeremy's words. Putting out his hand, he felt about for Jeremy's, and, when he had found it, grasped it warmly.

"If I have troubles, Jeremy, at least I have a blessing that few can boast—a true friend. If you had gone with the rest at Isandhlwana yonder, I think that my heart would have broken. I think we do bear one another a love 'passing the love of women.' It would not be worth much if it didn't, that is one thing. I wonder if Absalom was a finer fellow than you are, Jeremy? 'from the sole of his foot even to the crown of his head there was no blemish in him.' Your hair would not weigh 'two hundred shekels after the king's weight' though" (Jeremy wore his hair cropped like a convict's); "but I would back you to throw Absolom over your shoulder, hair and all."

It was his fashion to talk nonsense when affected by anything, and Jeremy, knowing it, said nothing.

Just then there came a knock at the door, and who should enter but Mazooku, and Mazooku transformed. His massive frame, instead of being clothed in the loose white garments he generally wore, was arrayed in a flannel shirt with an enormous stick-up collar, a suit of pepper-and-salt reach-me-downs several sizes too small for him, and a pair of boots considerably too large for his small and shapely feet; for, like those of most Zulus of good blood, his hands and feet were extremely delicately made.

To add to the incongruity of his appearance, on the top of his hair, which was still done in ridges, Zulu fashion, and decorated with long bone snuff-spoons, was perched an extremely small and rakish-looking billycock hat, and in his hand he carried his favourite and most gigantic knobstick.

On opening the cabin-door he saluted in the ordinary fashion, and coming in, squatted down on his haunches to await orders, forgetting that he was not in all the freedom of his native dress. The results were most disastrous. With a crack and a bang the reach-me-down trousers, already strained to their utmost capacity, split right up the back. The astonished Zulu flew up into the air, but presently discovering what had happened, sat down again, remarking that there was "much more room now."

Jeremy burst out laughing, and having sketched his retainer's appearance for the benefit of Ernest, told him what had happened.

"Where did you get those things from, Mazooku?" asked Ernest.

Mazooku explained that he had bought the rig-out for three pound ten from a second-class passenger, as the weather was growing cold.

"Do not wear them again. I will buy you clothes as soon as we get to England. If you are cold, wear your great-coat."

"Koos!"

"How is 'The Devil'?" Ernest had brought the black stallion on which he had escaped from Isandhlwana home with him.

Mazooku replied that the horse was well, but playful. A man forward had been teasing him with a bit of bread. He had waited till that man passed under his box, and had seized him in his teeth, lifted him off the ground by his coat, and shaken him severely.

"Good! Give him a bran-mash to-night."

"Koos!"

"And so you find the air cold. Are you not regretting that you came? I warned you that you would regret."

"Ou ka Inkoos" ("O no, chief"), the Zulu answered, in his liquid native tongue. "When first we came upon the smoking ship, and went out on to the black water out of which the white men rise, and my bowels twisted up and melted within me, and I went through the agonies of a hundred deaths, then I regretted. 'O, why,' I said in my heart, 'did not Mazimba my father kill me rather than bring me on to this great moving river? Surely if I live I shall grow like a white man from the whiteness of my heart, for I am exceedingly afraid, and have cast all my inside forth.' All this I said, and many more things which I cannot remember, but they were dark and heavy things. But behold! my father, when my bowels had ceased to melt, and when new ones had grown to replace those which I had thrown forth, I was glad, and did eat much beef, and then I questioned my heart about this journey over the black water. And my heart answered and said, 'Mazooku, son of Ingoluvu, of the tribe of the Maquilisini, of the people of the Amazulu, you have done well. Great is the chief whom you serve; great is Mazimba on the hunting-path; great was he in the battle; all the Undi could not kill him, and his brother the lion (Jeremy), and his servant the jackal (Mazooku), who hid in a hole and then bit those who digged. O yes, Mazimba is great, and his breast is full of valour; you have seen him strike the Undi down; and his mind is full of the white man's knowledge and discretion; you have seen him form the ring that spat out fire so fast that his servants the horsemen were buried under the corpses of the Undi. So great is he, that the 'heaven above' smelled him out as 'tagati,' as a wizard, and struck him with their lightning, but could not kill him then. And so now my father wanders and wanders, and shall wander in the darkness, seeing not the sun or the stars, or the flashing of spears, or the light that gathers in the eyes of brave men as they close in the battle, or the love which gleams in the eyes of women. And how is this? Shall my father want a dog to lead him in the darkness? Shall his dog Mazooku, son of Ingoluvu, prove a faithless dog, and desert the hand that fed him, and the man who is braver than himself? No, it shall not be so, my chief and my father. By the head of Chaka, whither thou goest thither will I go also, and where thou shalt build thy kraal there shall I make my hut. Koos! Baba!"

And having saluted after the dignified Zulu fashion, Mazooku departed to tie up his split trousers with a bit of string. There was something utterly incongruous between his present appearance and his melodious and poetical words, instinct as they were with qualities which in some respects make the savage Zulu a gentleman, and put him above the white Christian, who for the most part regards the "nigger" as a creature beneath contempt. For there are lessons to be learned even from Zulu "niggers," and among them we may reckon those taught by a courage which laughs at death; an absolute fidelity to those who have a right to command it, or the qualities necessary to win it; and, in their raw and unconverted state, perfect honesty and truthfulness.

"He is a good fellow, Mazooku," said Ernest, when the Zulu had gone; "but I fear that one of two things will happen to him. Either he will get homesick and become a nuisance, or he will get civilised and become drunken and degraded. I should have done better to leave him in Natal."

CHAPTER II

About nine o'clock in the morning following Mazooku's oration, a young lady came running up the stairs of the principal Plymouth hotel, and burst into a private sitting-room, like a human bomb-shell of attractive appearance, somewhat to the astonishment of a bald old gentleman who was sitting at breakfast.

"Good gracious, Dorothy, have you gone suddenly mad?"

"O Reginald, the Conway Castle is nearly in, and I have been to the office, and got leave for us to go off in the launch; so come along, quick!"

"What time does the launch leave?"

"A quarter to ten exactly."

"Then we have three-quarters of an hour."

"O please, Reginald, be quick; it might go before, you know."

Mr. Cardus smiled, and, rising, put on his hat and coat, "to oblige Dorothy," he said; but, as a matter of fact, he was as excited as she was. There was a patch of red on each of his pale cheeks, and his hand shook.

In a quarter of an hour they were walking up and down the quay by the Custom House, waiting for the launch to start.

"After all these years," said Mr. Cardus, "and blind!"

"Do you think that he will be much disfigured, Reginald?"

"I don't know, dear; your brother said nothing about it."

"I can hardly believe it; it seems so strange to think that he and Jeremy should have been spared out of all those people. How good God is!"

"A cynic," replied Mr. Cardus with a smile, "or the relations of the sixty other people who died might draw a different conclusion."

But Dorothy was thinking how good God was to her. She was dressed in pink that morning, and

"Oh, she looked sweet,
As the little pink flower that grows in the wheat."

Dorothy neither was, nor ever would be, a pretty woman, but she was essentially a charming one. Her kindly puzzled face (and, to judge from the little wrinkles on it, she had never got to the bottom of the questions which contracted her forehead as a child), her steady blue eyes, her diminutive rounded form, and, above all, the indescribable light of goodness which shone round her like a halo, all made her charming. What did it matter if the mouth was a little too wide, or the nose somewhat "tip-tilted"? Those who can look so sweet are able to dispense with such fleshly attributes as a Grecian nose or chiselled lips. At the least, they will have the best of it after youth is past; and let me remind you, my young and lovely reader, that the longer and dustier portion of life's road winds away towards the pale horizon of our path on the farther side of the grim mile-post marked "30."

But what made her chiefly attractive was her piquante taking manner and the chic of her presence. She was such a perfect lady.

"All aboard, if you please," broke in the agent. "Run in the gangway!" and they were off towards the great grey vessel with a blue pennant at the top.

It was a short run, but it seemed long to Dorothy and the old gentleman with her. Bigger and bigger grew the great vessel, till at last it seemed to swallow up their tiny steamer.

"Ease her! Look out for the line there! Now haul away! Make fast?"

It was all done in an instant, and next moment they stood upon the broad white deck, amid the crowd of passengers, and were looking round for Ernest and Jeremy.

But they were not to be seen.

"I hope they are here," faltered Dorothy.

Mr. Cardus took his hat off, and wiped his bald head. He too hoped that they were there.

At that moment Dorothy became aware of a black man, clad in a white smock pulled on over a great-coat, and carrying a big spear and a kerrie in his hand, who was pushing his way towards them. Next moment he stood before them saluting vigorously.

"Koos!" he said, thrusting his spear into the air before Mr. Cardus's astonished nose.

"Inkosikaas!" (chieftainess) he repeated, going through the same process before Dorothy. "This way, master; this way, missie. The chief without eyes send me to you. This way; the lion bring him now."

They followed him through the press towards the after part of the ship, while, giving up the unfamiliar language, he vociferated in Zulu (it might have been Sanskrit, for all they knew):

"Make way, you low people, make way for the old man with the shining head, on whose brow sits wisdom, and the fair young maiden, the sweet rosebud, who comes," &c.

At that moment Dorothy's quick eye saw a great man issuing from a cabin, leading another man by the hand. And then she forgot everything, and ran forward.

"O Ernest, Ernest!" she cried.

The blind man's cheek flushed at the music of her voice. He drew his hand from Jeremy's, and stretched out his arms towards the voice. It would have been easy to avoid them—one never need be kissed by a blind man—but she did not avoid them. On the contrary, she placed herself so that the groping arms closed round her, while a voice said: "Dorothy, where are you?"

"Here, Ernest, here!" and in another moment he had drawn her to him, and kissed her on the face, and she had returned the kiss.

Next she kissed Jeremy too, or rather Jeremy lifted her up two or three feet and kissed her—it came to the same thing. Then, Mr. Cardus wrung them both by the hand, wringing Ernest's the hardest; and Mazooku stood by, and, Zulu fashion, chanted a little song of his own improvising, about how the chiefs came back to their kraal after a long expedition, in which they had, &c.; and how Wisdom, in the shape of a shining headed and ancient one, the husband without any doubt of many wives, and the father of at least a hundred children, &c.; and Beauty, in the shape of a sweet and small one, &c.; and finally they all went very near to crying, and dancing a fling on the quarter-deck together.

After these things they all talked at once, and set about collecting their goods in a muddle-headed fashion. When these had been put in a pile, and Mazooku was seated, assegai and all, upon the top of them, as a solemn warning to thieves (and ill would it have gone with the thief who dared to meddle with that pile), they started off to inspect Ernest's great black horse, "The Devil."

Behold! Dorothy stroked "The Devil's" nose, and he recognising how sweet and good she was, abandoned his usual habits, and did not bite her, but only whinnied and asked for sugar. Then Ernest, going into the box with the horse, which nobody but he and Mazooku were fond of taking liberties with, felt down his flank till he came to a scar inflicted by an assegai in that mad charge through the Undi, and showed it to them. And Dorothy's eyes filled with tears of thankfulness, as she thought of what that horse and its rider had gone through, and of the bleaching bones of those who had galloped by their side; and she would have liked to kiss Ernest again, only there was no excuse. So she only pressed his hand, feeling that the sorrow of the empty years which were gone was almost atoned for by this hour of joy.

Then they went ashore to the hotel, and sat together in the pleasant sitting-room, which Dorothy had chosen, and made sweet with great bunches of violets (for she remembered that Ernest loved violets), and talked. At length Mr. Cardus and Jeremy went off to see about getting the things through the Custom House, where they arrived to find Mazooku keeping half a dozen gorgeous officials, who wanted to open a box, at bay with his knobsticks, and plastering them with offensive epithets, which fortunately they did not understand.

"Doll," said Ernest, presently, "it is a beautiful day, is it not? Will you take me for a walk, dear? I should like to go for a walk."

"Yes, Ernest, of course I will."

"You are sure you do not mind being seen with a blind man? You must give me your hand to hold, you know."

"Ernest, how can you?"

Mind giving him her hand to hold, indeed! thought Dorothy to herself, as she ran to put her bonnet on. O, that she could give it to him for always! And in her heart she blessed the accident of his blindness, because it brought him so much nearer to her. He would be helpless without her, this tall strong man, and she would be ever at his side to help him. He would not be able to read a book, or write a letter, or to move from room to room without her. Surely she would soon be able so to weave herself into his life that she would become indispensable to it.

And then, perhaps—perhaps—and her heart pulsed with a joy so intense at the mere thought of what might follow that it became a pain, and she caught her breath and leaned against a wall. For every fibre of her frame was thrilled with a passionate love for this blind man whom she had lost for so many years, and now had found again; and in her breast she vowed that if she could help it she would lose him no more. Why should she? When he had been engaged to Eva, she had done her best for him and her, and bitterly had she felt the way in which he had been treated. But Eva had taken her own course, and was now no longer in the outward and visible running, whatever place she might still hold in the inward and spiritual side of Ernest's nature. Dorothy did not underrate that place; she knew well that the image of her rival had sunk too deep into his heart to be altogether dislodged by her. But she was prepared to put up with that.

"One can't have everything, you know," she said, shaking her wise little head at her own reflection in the glass, as she tied her bonnet-strings.

Dorothy was an eminently practical little person, and having recognised the "eternal verity" of the saying that half a loaf is better than no bread, especially if one happens to be dying of hunger, she made up her mind to make the best of the position. Since she could not help it, Eva would be welcome to the inward and spiritual side of Ernest, and only she could secure the outward and visible side; "for after all, that is real and tangible, and there isn't much human comfort in spiritual affection, you know," she said, with another shake of the head.

In short, the arguments which proved so convincing to her were not unlike those that carried conviction home to the gentle breast of Mr. Plowden, when he made up his mind to marry Eva in the teeth of her engagement to, and love for, Ernest; but, putting aside the diversity of the circumstances, there was this difference between them. Mr. Plowden recognised no higher spiritual part at all; he did not believe in that sort of thing; he contracted for Eva as he would have contracted to buy a lovely animal, and when he had got the given quantity of flesh and blood he was satisfied. Of the soul—the inner self—which the human casket held and which loathed and hated him, he took no account. He had got the woman, what did he care about the woman's soul? Souls, and spiritual parts, and affinities with what is good and high, and the divinity of love, &c., &c., were capital things to preach about, but they did not apply to the affairs of every-day life. Besides, if he had been asked, he would have given it as his candid opinion that women did not possess any of these things.

There are hundreds of educated men who think like Mr. Plowden, and there are thousands of educated ladies who give colour to such opinions by their idle, aimless course of life, their utter inappreciation of anything beyond their own little daily round, and the gossip of the dozen or so of families who for them make up what they call society and the interests of existence, and by their conduct in the matter of marriage. Truly the great factor in the lowering of women is woman herself. But what does it matter? In due course they have their families, and the world goes on!

Now, Dorothy did believe in all these things, and she knew what an important part they play in human affairs, and how they dominate over, and direct, finer minds. So did she believe in the existence of the planets, and in the blooming of roses in walled gardens; but as she could not get near to know the beauties of the stars, or to see the opening rosebuds, she had to satisfy herself with the light that poured from the one, and the scent that came from the other. When one is star-stricken, or mad in the matter of roses, that is better than nothing.

So, taking Ernest by the hand, she led him through the crowded streets with tender care, and on to the quiet Hoe. And as they passed, the people turned to look at the handsome young fellow who was blind, and some thought that they would not mind a little blindness if it led to being personally conducted by so sweet a maid.

Soon they reached the gardens.

"Now, tell me about yourself, Ernest. What have you been doing all these long years, besides growing bigger and handsomer, and getting that hard look about the mouth?"

"A great many things, Doll. Shooting, fighting, playing the fool."

"Pshaw! I know all that, or at least I can guess it. What have you been doing in your mind, you know?"

"Why, thinking of you, of course, Doll."

"Ernest, if you talk to me like that, I will go away, and leave you to find your own way home. I know well of whom you have been thinking every day and every night. It was not of me. Now, confess it."

"Don't let's talk of her, Doll. If you talk of the devil, you know, you sometimes raise him; not that he requires much raising in this instance," he laughed bitterly.

"I was so sorry for you, Ernest dear, and I did my best; indeed I did. But I could do nothing with her. She must have been off her head, or that man" (Dorothy always spoke of Plowden as "that man") "and Florence had some power over her; or perhaps she never really cared for you; there are some women, you know, who seem very sweet, but cannot truly care for anybody except themselves. At any rate, she married, and has a family of children, for I have seen their births in the paper. Oh, Ernest, when I think of all you must have suffered out there about that woman, I cease to be sorry for her, and begin to hate her. I am afraid you have been very unhappy, Ernest, all these years."

"Ah, yes, I have been unhappy sometimes—sometimes I have consoled myself. There, what is the use of telling lies?—I have always been unhappy, and never more so than when I have been in process of consolation. But you should not hate her, poor girl! Perhaps she has her bad times too; only, unfortunately, you women cannot feel, at least not much—not like us, I mean."

"I don't know about that," put in Dorothy.

"Well, I will qualify my remark—most women. And, besides, it is not quite her fault; people cannot help themselves much in this world. She was appointed to be my evil destiny, that is all, and she must fulfil her mission. All my life she will probably bring me trouble, till at last the fate works itself out. But, Dolly, my dear, there must be an end to these things, and Nature, always fertile in analogies, teaches us that the end of sorrow will be happiness. It is from the darkness of night that day is born, and ice and snow are followed by the flowers. Nothing is lost in the world, as old Alston used to say, and it is impossible to suppose that all the grief and suffering are alone wasted; that they are the only dull seeds which will not, when their day comes, bloom into a beautiful life. They may seem to be intangible things now; but, after all, the difference between tangible and intangible is only a difference of matter. We know that intangible things are real enough, and perhaps in a future state we shall find that they are the true immortal parts. I think so myself."

"I think so too."

"Well, then, Doll, you see, if once one gets the mastery of that idea, it makes the navigation easier. Once admit that everything works to an end, and that end a good and enduring one, and you will cease to call out under your present sorrows. But it is hard for the little boy to learn to like being whipped, and we are all children, Doll, to the end of our days."

"Yes."

"And you see, Doll, for some reason I have been picked out for the rods. It does seem rather hard that a woman like that should be allowed to turn all the wine of a man's life into vinegar; but so it often is. Now, if she had died, that would have been bad enough; but I could have borne it, and bided my time in the hope of joining her. Or if she had ceased to love me, and learned to love the other man, I think I could have borne that, because my pride would have come to my rescue, and because I know that the law of her affections is the only law which the heart of woman readily acknowledges, to however many others she may be forced to conform; and that a woman of refined nature who has ceased to love you, and is yet forced to live with you, is in consequence a thing worthless to you, and dishonoured in her own eyes. Besides, I ask no favours in such matters. I have no sympathy, as a general rule, with people who raise a din because they have lost the affection of their wives or sweethearts, for they should have been able to keep them. If any man could have cut me out, he was welcome to do so, for he would have proved himself the better man, and as for the lady, I would not have her without her heart. But I gather that was not quite the case with Eva."

"O, no, indeed; at least she said that she was wretched."

"Exactly as I thought. Well, now, you will understand that it is rather hard. You see I did love her dearly, and it is painful to think of this woman, whose love I won, and who by that divine right and by the law of nature should have been my wife, as forced into being the wife of another man, however charming he may be; and I hope for her sake that he is charming. In fact, it fills me with a sensation I cannot describe."

"Poor Ernest!"

"Oh no, don't pity me. Everybody has his troubles—this is mine."

"Oh, Ernest, but you have been unfortunate, and now your sight has gone; but perhaps Critchett or Couper would be able to do something with that."

"All the Critchetts and Coupers in the world will never do anything for it, my dear. But you must remember that where I only lost my sight, many others lost their lives, and it is supposed to better to lose your sight than your life. Besides, blindness has its advantages; it gives you more time to think, and it humbles you so much. You can have no idea what it is like, Doll. Intense, everlasting blackness hedging you in like a wall: one long, long night, even when the sunlight is beating on your face; and out of the night, voices and the touching of hands, like the voices and the touchings of departed spirits. Your physical body is as helpless and as much at the mercy of the world as your spiritual body is in the hands of the Almighty. Things grow dim to you too: you begin to wonder what familiar faces and sights are like, as you wonder about the exact appearance of those who died many years ago, or of places you have not seen for years. All of which, my dear Doll, is very favourable to thought. When next you lie awake for five or six hours in the night, try to reckon all the things which occupy your brain; then imagine such wakefulness and its accompanying thoughts extended over the period of your natural life, and you will get some idea of the depth and breadth and height of total blindness."

His words struck her, and she did not know what to answer, so she only pressed his hand in token of her mute sympathy.

He understood her meaning; the faculties of the blind are very quick.

"Do you know, Doll," he said, "coming back to you and your gentle kindness is like coming into the peace and quiet of a sheltered harbour after bearing the full brunt of the storm." Just then a cloud which had obscured the sun passed away, and its full light struck up on his face. "There," he went on, "it is like that. It is like emerging into the sweet sunshine after riding for miles through the rain and mist. You bring peace with you, my dear. I have not felt such peace for years as I feel holding your hand to-day."

"I am very glad, dear Ernest," she answered; and they walked on in silence. At that moment, a little girl, who was trundling a hoop down the gravel-path, stopped her hoop to look at the pair. She was very pretty, with large dark eyes, but Dorothy noticed that she had a curious mark upon her forehead. Presently Dorothy saw her run back towards an extremely tall and graceful woman, who was sauntering along, followed at some distance by a nurse with a baby in her arms, and turning occasionally to look at the beds of spring flowers, hyacinths and tulips, which bordered the path.

"O mother," she heard the little girl call out, in the clear voice of childhood, "there is such a nice blind man! He isn't old and ugly, and he hasn't a dog, and he doesn't ask for pennies. Why is he blind if he hasn't a dog, and doesn't ask for pennies?"

Blindness, according to this little lady's ideas, evidently sprang from the presence of a cur and an unsatisfied hunger for copper coin. Sometimes it does.

The tall graceful lady looked up carelessly, saying, "Hush dear!" She was quite close to them now, for they were walking towards each other, and Dorothy gave a great gasp, for before her stood Eva Plowden: there was no doubt about it. She was paler and haughtier-looking than of yore; but it was she. No one who had once seen her could mistake that queenly beauty. Certainly Dorothy could not mistake it.

"What is the matter, Doll?" said Ernest, carelessly. He was thinking of other things.

"Nothing; I hurt myself."

They were quite close now.

Eva, too, looked at them. She, too, saw a face she had never thought to see again. With all her eyes and with her lips parted as though to cry out, she gazed at the sight before her—slowly, slowly taking in all it meant.

They were nearly level now.

Then there leaped up into her eyes which a second before had been so calm—a wild light of love, an intensity of passionate and jealous desire, such as is not often to be seen on the faces of women.

"Ernest there, and Ernest blind, being led by the hand of Dorothy, and looking happy with her! How dared Dorothy touch her love! How dared he look happy with her!" Those were the thoughts which flashed through her troubled mind.

She made a step towards them, as though to address him, and the blind eyes fell upon her lovely face, and wandered over it. It made her mad. His eyes were on her, and yet he could not see her. O God!

Dorothy saw the motion, and, moved by an overmastering instinct, threw herself between them in an attitude of protection not unmixed with defiance. So, for a second, their eyes flashing and their bosoms heaving with emotion, the two women stood face to face, and the blind pathetic eyes wandered uneasily over both, feeling a presence they were unable to define.

It was a tragic, almost a dreadful scene. The passions it revealed were almost too intense for words, as no brush can justly paint a landscape made vivid by the unnatural fierceness of the lightning.

"Well, Doll, why do you stop?" Ernest said, impatiently.

His voice broke the spell. Eva withdrew her arm, which was half outstretched, and touched her lips with her fingers as though to enjoin silence. Then a deep misery spread itself over her flushed face, her head sank low, and she passed thence with rapid steps. Presently the nurse with the baby followed her, and Dorothy noticed vaguely that this child had also a mark upon its forehead. The whole incident had not lasted forty seconds.

"Doll," said Ernest, in a wild voice, and commencing to tremble, "who was it that passed us."

"A lady," was the answer.

"A lady; yes, I know that—what lady?"

"I don't know—a lady with children."

It was a fib; but she could not tell him then; an instinct warned her not to do so.

"Oh, it is strange, Doll, strange; but, do you know, I felt just now as though Eva were very near me. Come, let us go home!"

Just then the cloud got over the sun again, and they walked home in the shadow. Apparently, too, all their talkativeness had gone the way of the sun. They had nothing to say.

CHAPTER III

INTROSPECTIVE

Eva Plowden could scarcely be said to be a happy woman. A refined person who has deliberately married one man when she loves another is not as a rule happy afterwards, unless indeed, she is blessed or cursed, with a singularly callous nature. But there are degrees and degrees of unhappiness. Such a fate as Eva's would have killed Dorothy, and would have driven Florence, bad as she might otherwise be, to suicide or madness. But with Eva herself it was not so; she was not sufficiently finely strung to suffer thus. Hers was not a very happy life, but that was all. She had been most miserable; but when the first burst of her misery had passed, like the raving storm that sometimes ushers in a wet December day, like a sensible woman, she had more or less reconciled herself to her position. The day was always rather wet, it is true; but still the sun peeped out now and again, and if life was not exactly a joyous thing, it was at least endurable.

Yet with it all she loved Ernest in her heart as much as ever; his memory was inexpressibly dear to her, and her regrets were sometimes very bitter. On the whole, however, she had got over it wonderfully—better than anybody would have thought possible who could have witnessed her agony some years before, when Florence told her the whole truth immediately after the wedding. The Sabine women, we are told, offered a very reasonable resistance to their rape by the Romans, but before long they gave the strongest proofs of reconciliation to their lot. There was something of the Sabine woman about Eva. Indeed, the contrast between her state of mind as regarded Ernest, and Ernest's state of mind as regarded her, would make a curious study. They each loved the other, and yet how different had the results of that love been on the two natures! To Eva it had been and was a shamed sorrow, sometimes very real; to Ernest, the destruction of all that made life worth living. The contrast, indeed, was so striking as to be almost pitiable; so wide a gulf was fixed between the two. The passion of the one was a wretched thing compared to the other. But both were real; it remained merely a difference of degree. If Eva's affection was weak when measured by Ernest's, this was because the soil in which it grew was poorer. She gave all she had to give.

As for Mr. Plowden, he could not but feel that on the whole his matrimonial speculation had answered very well. He was honestly fond of his wife, and, as he had a right to be, very proud of her. At times she was cold and capricious, and at times she was sarcastic; but, take it altogether, she made him a good and serviceable wife, and lifted him up many pegs in the social scale. People saw that though Plowden was not a gentleman, he had managed to marry a lady, and a very lovely lady too; and he was tolerated, indeed to a certain extent courted, for the sake of his wife. It was principally to attain this end that he had married her, so he had every reason to be satisfied with his bargain, and he was, besides, proud to be the legal owner of so handsome a creature.

Eva often thought of her old lover, though, except in the vaguest way, she had heard nothing of him for years. Indeed, she was, as it happened, thinking of him tenderly enough that very morning when her little girl had called her attention to the "nice blind man." And when at last, in a way which seemed to her little short of miraculous, she set eyes again upon his face, her smothered, smouldering passion broke into flame, and she felt that she still loved him with all her strength, such as it was. At that moment indeed she realised how great, how bitter, how complete was the mistake she had made, and what a beautiful thing life might have been for her if things had gone differently. But, remembering how things were, she bowed her head and passed on, for the time completely crushed.

Presently, however, two points became clear in the confusion of her mind, taking shape and form as distinct and indisputable mental facts, and these were—first, that she was wildly jealous of Dorothy; second, that it was her fixed determination to see Ernest. She regretted now that she had been too overcome to go up and speak to him, for see him she must and would; indeed, her sick longing to look upon his face and hear his voice, filled her with alarm.

Eva reached her home, after the meeting on the Hoe, just before luncheon-time. Her husband was now acting as locum tenens for the rector of one of the Plymouth parishes. They had moved thus from place to place for years, waiting for the Kesterwick living to fall vacant, and Eva liked the roving life well enough—it diverted her thoughts.

Presently she heard her husband enter, bringing somebody else with him, and summoned up the sweet smile for which she was remarkable to greet him.

In another instant he was in the room, followed by a fresh-faced subaltern, whose appearance reminded her of the pictures of cherubs. Mr. Plowden had changed but little since we saw him last, with the exception that his hair was now streaked with white, and the whole face rather stouter. Otherwise the cold grey eyes were as cold as ever, and the countenance of Plowden was what the countenance of Plowden had always been—powerful, intelligent, and coarse-looking.

"Let me introduce my friend Lieutenant Jasper to you, my dear," he said, in his full strong voice, which was yet unpleasant to the ear. "We met at Captain Johnstone's, and, as it is a long way to go to the barracks for lunch, I asked him to come and take pot-luck with us."

The cherubic Jasper had screwed an eyeglass into his round eye, and through it was contemplating Eva with astonished ecstasy. Like most very beautiful women, she was used to that sort of thing, and it only amused her faintly. Mr. Plowden, too, was used to it, and took it as a personal compliment.

"I am delighted," she murmured, and held out her hand.

The cherub, suddenly waking to the fact, dropped his eyeglass, and, plunging at the hand, seized it as a pike does a little fish, and shook it with enthusiasm.

Eva smiled again.

"Shall we go to lunch?" she said, sweetly: and they went to lunch, she sailing down in front of them with the grace of a swan.

At lunch itself the conversation lagged rather—that is, Mr. Plowden talked with all the facility of an extemporary preacher; the cherub gazed at this pale, dark-eyed angel; and Eva, fully occupied with her own thoughts, contributed a great many appreciative smiles and a few random remarks. Just as they were, to her intense relief, nearing the conclusion of the meal, a messenger arrived to summon Mr. Plowden to christen a dying baby. He got up at once, for he was punctilious in the performance of his duties, and, making excuses to his guest, departed on his errand, thus forcing Eva to carry on the conversation.

"Have you been in Plymouth long, Mr. Jasper?" she asked.

The eyeglass dropped spasmodically.

"Plymouth? O dear, no; I only landed this morning."

"Landed? Indeed! where from? I did not know that any boat was in except the Conway Castle."

"Well, I came by her, from the Zulu war, you know. I was invalided home for fever."

The cherub suddenly became intensely interesting to Eva, for it struck her that Ernest must have come from Africa.

"Indeed! I hope you had a pleasant voyage. It depends so much on your fellow-passengers, does it not?"

"O yes, we had a very nice lot of men on board, wounded officers mostly. There were a couple of very decent civilians, too—a giant of a fellow called Jones, and a blind baronet, Sir Ernest Kershaw."

Eva's bosom heaved.

"I once knew a Mr. Ernest Kershaw; I wonder if it is the same? He was tall, and had dark eyes."

"That's the man; he only got his title a month or two ago. A melancholy sort of chap, I thought; but then he can't see now. That Jones is a wonderful fellow, though—could pull two heavy men up at once, as easily as you would lift a puppy-dog. Saw him do it myself. I knew them both out there."

"Oh? Where did you meet them!"

"Well, it was rather curious. I suppose you heard of the great disaster at that place with that awful name. Well, I was at a beastly hole called Helpmakaar, when a fellow came riding like anything from Rorke's Drift, telling us what had happened, and that the Zulus were coming. So we all set to and worked like mad, and just as we had got the place a little fit for them, somebody shouted that he saw them coming. That was just as it was getting dark. I ran to the wall to look, and saw, not the Zulus, but a great big fellow carrying a dead man in his arms, followed by a Kafir leading three horses. At least, I thought the fellow was dead, but he wasn't—he had been struck by lightning. We let him in; and such a sight as they were you never saw, all soaked with blood from top to toe!"

"Ah! And how did they come like that?"

"They were the only survivors of a volunteer corps called Alston's Horse. They killed all the Zulus that were attacking them, when the Zulus had killed everybody except them. Then they came away, and the blind fellow—that is, Sir Ernest—got struck in a storm; fellows often do out there."

Eva put further questions, and listened with breathless interest to the story of Ernest's and Jeremy's wonderful escape, so far as the details were known to Mr. Jasper, quite regardless of the pitiless fire that young gentleman was keeping on herself through his eyeglass. At last, reluctantly enough, he rose to go.

"I must be off now, Mrs. Plowden; I want to go and call on Sir Ernest at the hotel. He lent me a Derringer pistol to practise at a bottle with, and I forgot to give it back."

Eva turned the full battery of her beautiful eyes upon him. She saw that the young gentleman was struck, and determined to make use of him. Women are unscrupulous when they have an end in view.

"I am sorry you must go; but I hope you will come and see me again, and tell me some more about the war and the battles."

"You are very kind," he stammered. "I shall be delighted."

He did not think it necessary to add that he had not had the luck to see a shot fired himself. Why should he?

"By the way, if you are going to see Sir Ernest, do you think you could give him a private message from me? I have a reason for not wishing it to be overheard."

"O yes, I daresay I can. Nothing would give me greater pleasure."

"You are very good." Another glance. "Will you tell him that I wish he would take a fly and come to see me? I shall be in all this afternoon."

A pang of jealousy shot through the cherubic bosom, but he comforted himself with the reflection that a fine woman like that could not care for a "blind fellow."

"O, certainly, I will try."

"Thank you"; and she extended her hand.

He took it, and intoxicated by those superb eyes, ventured to press it tenderly. A mild wonder took possession of Eva's mind that anybody so very young could have developed such an astonishing amount of impudence, but she did not resent the pressure. What did she care about having her hand squeezed when it was a question of seeing Ernest?

Poor deluded cherub!

CHAPTER IV

AFTER MANY DAYS

Within an hour of the departure of Lieutenant Jasper, Eva heard a fly draw up at the door. Then came an interval and the sound of two people walking up the steps, one of whom stumbled a good deal; then a ring.

"Is Mrs. Plowden at home?" said a clear voice, the well-remembered tones of which sent the blood to her head and then back to her heart with a rush.

"Yes, sir."

"Oh! Wait here, flyman. Now, my good girl, I must ask you to give me your hand, for I am not in a condition to find my way about strange places."

Another pause, and the drawing-room opened, and the maid came in, leading Ernest, who wore a curious, drawn look upon his face.

"How do you do?" she said, in a low voice, coming and taking him by the hand. "That will do, Jane."

He did not speak till the door closed; he only looked at her with those searching blind eyes.

Thus they met again after many years.

She led him to a sofa, and he sat down.

"Do not leave go of my hand," he said quickly; "I have not yet got used to talking to people in the dark."

She sat down on the sofa beside him, feeling frightened and yet happy. For awhile they remained silent; apparently they could find nothing to say, and, after all, silence seemed most fitting. She had never thought to sit hand in hand with him again. She looked at him; there was no need to keep a guard over her loving glances, for he was blind. At length she broke the silence.

"Were you surprised to get my message?" she asked, gently.

"Yes; it was like getting a message from the dead. I never expected to see you again. I thought that you had quite passed out of my life."

"So you had forgotten me?"

"Why do you say such a thing to me? You must know Eva, that it is impossible for me to forget you; I almost wish that it were possible. I meant that you had passed out of my outward life, for out of my mind you can never pass."

Eva hung her head and was silent though his words sent a thrill of happiness through her. So she had not quite lost him after all.

"Listen, Eva," Ernest went on, gathering himself together, and speaking sternly enough now, with a strange suppressed energy that frightened her. "How you came to do what you have done you best know."

"It is done; do not let us speak of it. I was not altogether to blame," she broke in.

"I was not going to speak of it. But I was going to say this, now while I have the chance, because time is short, and I think it right that you should know the truth. I was going to tell you first that for what you have done I freely forgive you."

"O Ernest!"

"It is," he went on, not heeding her, "a question that you can settle with your conscience and your God. But I wish to tell you what it is that you have done. You have wrecked my life, and made it an unhappy thing; you have taken that from me which I can never have to give again; you have embittered my mind, and driven me to sins of which I should not otherwise have dreamed. I loved you, and you gave me proofs that I could not doubt that I had won your love. You let me love you. Then when the hour of trial came you deserted and morally destroyed me, and the great and holy affection that should have been the blessing of my life has become its curse."

Eva covered her face with her hands and sat silent.

"You do not answer me, Eva," he said presently, with a little laugh. "Perhaps you find what I have to say difficult to answer, or perhaps you think I am taking a liberty."

"You are very hard," she murmured.

"Had you not better wait till I have done before you call me hard? If I wished to be hard, I should tell you that I no longer cared for you, that my prevailing feeling towards you was one of contempt. It would, perhaps, mortify you to think that I had shaken off such heavy chains. But it is not the truth, Eva. I love you now, as I always have loved you, as I always shall love you. I hope for nothing, I ask for nothing; in this business it has always been my part to give, not to receive. I despise myself for it, but so it is."

She laid her hand upon his shoulder. "Spare me, Ernest," she whispered.

"I have very little more to say, only this: I believe all that I have given you has not been given uselessly. I believe that the love of the flesh will die with the flesh. But my love for you has been something more and higher than that, or how has it loved without hope, and in spite of its dishonour, through so many years? It is of the spirit, and I believe that its life will be like that of the spirit, unending, and that when this hateful existence is done with I shall in some way reap its fruits with you."

"Why do you believe that, Ernest? It seems too happy to be true."

"Why do I believe it? I cannot tell you. Perhaps it is nothing but the fantasy of a mind broken down with brooding on its grief. In trouble we grow towards the light—like a plant in the dark, you know. As a crushed flower smells sweet, so all that is most aspiring in human nature is called into life when God lays His heavy hand upon us. Heaven is sorrow's sole ambition. No, Eva, I do not know why I believe it—certainly you have given me no grounds for faith—but I do believe it, and it comforts me. By the way, how did you know that I was here?"

"I passed you on the Hoe this morning, walking with Dorothy."

Ernest started. "I felt you pass," he said, "and asked Dorothy who it was. She said she did not know."

"She knew, but I made a sign to her not to say."

"Oh!"

"Ernest, will you promise me something?" asked Eva, wildly.

"What is it?"

"Nothing. I have changed my mind—nothing at all!"

The promise that she was about to ask was that he would not marry Dorothy, but her better nature rose in rebellion against it. Then they talked awhile of Ernest's life abroad.

"Well," said Ernest, rising after a pause, "good-bye, Eva."

"It is a very cruel world," she murmured.

"Yes, it is cruel, but not more cruel than the rest."

"It has been a happiness to see you, Ernest."

He shrugged his shoulders as he answered. "Has it? For myself I am not sure if it has been a happiness or a misery. I must have a year or two of quiet and darkness to think it over before I make up my mind. Will you kindly ring the bell for the servant to take me away?"

Half unconsciously, she obeyed him. Then she came and took his hand, looking with all her eyes and all her soul into his face. It was fortunate that he could not see her.

"O Ernest, you are blind!" she said, scarcely knowing what she said.

He laughed—a hard little laugh. "Yes, Eva, I am blind now as you have been always."

"Ernest! Ernest! how can I live without seeing you? I love you!" and she fell into his arms.

He kissed her once—twice, thrice, nor did he kiss alone. Then, he never knew how, he found the strength to put her from him. Perhaps it was because he heard the servant coming.

Next moment she came and led him away.

As soon as he was gone Eva flung herself down on the sofa and sobbed as though her heart would break.

When Dorothy saw a fresh-faced young officer, who had come up to see Ernest, mysteriously lead him aside, and whisper something in his ear which caused him to turn first red and then white, being a shrewd observer, she thought it curious. But when Ernest asked her to ring the bell and ordered a fly to be brought round at once, the idea of Eva at once flashed into her mind. She and no other must be at the bottom of this mystery. Presently the fly was announced, and Ernest went off without a word, leaving her to the tender mercies of the cherub, who was contemplating her with his round eye as he had contemplated Eva, and finding her also charming. It must be remembered that he had but just returned from South Africa, and was prepared, faute de mieux, to fall in love with an apple-woman. How much more, then, would he succumb to the charms of the stately Eva and the extremely fascinating Dorothy! It was some time before the latter could get rid of him and his eyeglass. On an ordinary occasion she would have been glad enough to entertain him, for Dorothy liked a little male society. Also the cherub, though he did look so painfully young, was not a bad fellow, and after all his whole soul was in his eyeglass, and his staring was meant to be complimentary. But just now she had a purpose in her mind, and was heartily glad when he departed to reflect over the rival attractions of the two charmers.

It was very evident to Dorothy, who was always strictly practical, that to keep Eva and Ernest in the same town was to hold dry tow to a lighted match over a barrel of gunpowder. She only hoped that he might come back now without having bred more trouble.

"Oh, what fools men are!" she said to herself, with a stamp; "a pretty face and a pair of bright eyes, and they count the world well lost for them. Bah! if it had been a plain woman who played Ernest that trick, would he be found dangling about after her now? Not he. But with her, she has only to say a soft word or two, and he will be at her feet, I'll be bound. I am ashamed of them both."

Meanwhile she was putting on her bonnet, which was a very favourite time with her for meditation, having already made up her mind as to her course of action. Ernest had authorised her to make arrangements for an interview with an oculist. She proceeded to make those arrangements by telegram, wiring to a celebrated surgeon to know if he could make an appointment for the following afternoon. Then she took a walk by herself to think things over. In an hour she returned, to find Ernest in the sitting-room looking extremely shaken and depressed.

"You have been to see Eva?" she asked.

"Yes," he answered.

Just then there was a knock at the door, and the servant brought in a telegram. It was from the occulist. He would be glad to see Sir Ernest Kershaw at four o'clock on the following afternoon.

"I have made an appointment for you with an eye-doctor, Ernest, at four o'clock to-morrow."

"To-morrow!" he said.

"Yes. The sooner you get your eyes looked to the better."

He sighed. "What is the good? However, I will go."

So next morning they all took the express, and at the appointed time Ernest found himself in the skilful hands of the oculist. But though an oculist can mend the sight, he cannot make it.

"I can do nothing for you, Sir Ernest," he said, after an exhaustive examination. "Your eyes will remain as they are, but you must always be blind."

Ernest took the news with composure.

"I thought as much," he said; but Dorothy put her handkerchief to her face and wept secretly.

Next morning he went with Jeremy to call on Messrs. Paisley and Paisley, and told them to try and let Archdale Hall, and to lock up the numerous and valuable heirlooms, as unfortunately he was unable to see them. Then they went on home to Dum's Ness, and that night Ernest lay awake in the room where he had slept for so many years in the boyhood which now seemed so dim and remote, and listened to the stormy wind raving round the house, and thought with an aching heart of Eva, but was thankful that he had bid her farewell, and wondered if he could find the strength to keep away from her.

And Eva, his lost love, she too lay by the sea and listened to the wind, and thought of him. There she lay in her beauty, seeking the sleep that would not settle on her. She could not sleep; forgetful sleep does not come readily to such as she. For her and those like her are vain regrets and an empty love and longing, and the wreath of thorns that crowns the brow where sorrow is enthroned.

Yet, Eva, lift that fevered head, and turn those seeking eyes to heaven. See, through the casement, above the tumult of the storm, there gleams a star. For you too, there shines a star called Hope, but it is set in no earthly sky. Have patience, wayward heart, there is but a space of trouble. As you suffer, so have millions suffered, and are they not at peace? So shall millions suffer:

"While thou, that once didst make the place thou stoodst in lovely, shalt lie still,
Thy form departed, and thy face remembered not in good or ill."

For of this we may be sure—if suffering is not the widest gate of heaven, then heaven has no gates. Unhappy woman, stretch out those longing arms in supplication to the God of sorrows for strength to bear your load, since here it shall not be lightened. The burdens which Providence binds on our backs, Providence will sometimes lessen, but those which our own folly fastens remain till death deliver us.

So, Eva, dry your tears, for they can avail you naught, and go get you to your daily task—go tend your children, and smile that sweet sad smile on all alike, and wait. As you have sowed so shall you reap, but seed-time is not done; not yet is the crop white to the harvest.

CHAPTER V

HOME AGAIN

It was very peaceful, that life at Kesterwick, after all the fierce racket and excitement of the past years. Indeed, as day succeeded day, and brought nothing to disturb his darkness but the sound of Dorothy's gentle voice, and the scent of flowers on the marshes when the wind blew towards the ocean, and the sharp strong odour of the sea when it set upon the land, Ernest could almost fancy that the past was nothing but a dream more or less ugly, and that this was a dream more or less pleasant, from which he should presently awake and find himself a boy again.

English villages change but little. Now and again a person dies, and pretty frequently some one is born; but, on the whole, the tide of time creeps on very imperceptibly, and though in the course of nature the entire population is changed every sixty years or so, nobody seems to realise that it is changing. There is so little in such places by which to mark the change. The same church-tower makes a landmark to the eye as it did centuries ago in the eyes of our ancestors, and the same clouds sweep across the same blue space above it. There are the same old houses, the same streams, and, above all, the same roads and lanes. If you could put one of our Saxon forefathers down in the neighbourhood of most of our country towns, he would have little difficulty in finding his way about. It is the men who change, not the places.

Still there were some few changes at Kesterwick. Here and there the sea had taken another bite of the cliff, notably on the north side of Dum's Ness, out of which a large slice had gone, thus bringing the water considerably nearer to the house. Here and there a tree, too, had been cut down, or a cottage built, or a family changed its residence. For instance, Miss Florence Ceswick had suddenly shut up the Cottage, where she had remained ever since Eva's marriage, seeing nothing of her sister or her sister's husband, and had gone abroad—people said to Rome, to study art. For Florence had suddenly electrified the Kesterwick neighbourhood by appearing as an artist of tragic force and gruesome imagination. A large picture by her hand had been exhibited in the Royal Academy of the previous year, and, though the colouring was somewhat crude, and the drawing not faultless, it made a deserved sensation, and finally sold for a considerable sum.

This picture represented a promontory of land running out far into a stormy ocean. The sky above the sea was of an inky blackness, except where a fierce ray of light from the setting sun pierced it, and impinged upon the boiling waters which surged round the low cliff of the promontory. On the extreme edge of the cliff stood a tall and lovely woman. The wind caught the white robe she wore and pressed it against her, revealing the extraordinary beauty of her form, and, lifting her long fair locks, tossed them in wild confusion. She was bending forward, pointing with her right hand at the water, with such a look of ghastly agony upon her beautiful face and in the great grey eyes, that people of impressionable temperament were wont to declare it haunted their sleep for weeks. Down below her, just where the fierce ray lit up the heaving waters, gleamed a naked corpse. It was that of a young man, and was slowly sinking into the unfathomable darkness of the depths, turning round and round as it sank. The eyes and mouth were wide open, and the stare of the former appeared to be fixed upon those of the woman on the cliff. Lastly, over the corpse, in the storm-wreaths above, there hovered on steady wings a dim female figure, with its arm thrown across the face as though to hide it. In the catalogue this picture was called "The Lost Lover," but speculation was rife as to what it meant.

Dorothy heard of it, and went to London to see it. The first thing that struck her about the work was the extraordinary contrast it presented to the commonplace canvases by which it was surrounded, of reapers, of little girls frisking with baa-lambs and nude young women musing profoundly on the edge of pools, as though they were trying to solve the great question—to wash or not to wash. But soon the horror of the picture laid hold upon her, and seemed to fascinate her, as it had so many others. Then she became aware that the faces were familiar to her, and suddenly it broke upon her mind that the sinking corpse was Ernest and the agonised woman, Eva. She examined the faces more attentively. There was no doubt about it. Florence, with consummate art, had changed the colouring of the hair and features, and even to a great extent altered the features themselves; but she had preserved the likeness perfectly, both upon the dead face of the murdered man, and in the horror-inspired eyes of his lover. The picture made her sick with fear—she could not tell why—and she hurried from Burlington House full of dread of the terrible mind that had conceived it.

There had been no intercourse between the two women since Eva's marriage. Florence lived quite alone at the Cottage, and never went out anywhere; and if they met by any chance, they passed with a bow. But for all that, it was a relief to Dorothy to hear that she was not for some long time to see that stern face with its piercing brown eyes.

In Dum's Ness itself there appeared to be no change at all. Except that Mr. Cardus had built a new orchid-house at the back—for as he grew older his mania for these flowers increased rather than diminished—the place was exactly the same. Even the arrangement of the sitting-room was unchanged, and on its familiar bracket rested the case which Jeremy had made to contain the witch's head.

The people in the house to all appearance had changed as little as the house itself. Jeremy confided to Ernest that Doll had grown rather "tubby," which was his elegant way of indicating that she had developed a very pretty figure, and that Grice (the old housekeeper) was as skinny as a flayed weasel, and had eyes like the point of a knife. Ernest maliciously repeated these sayings to the two ladies concerned, with the result that they were both furious. Then he retreated, and left them to settle it with Jeremy.

Old Atterleigh, too, was almost exactly the same, except that of late years his intellect seemed to have brightened a little. It was, however, difficult to make him understand that Ernest was blind, because the latter's eyes looked all right. He retained some recollection of him, and brought him his notched stick to show him that, according to his ("Hard-riding Atterleigh's") calculation, his time of service with the devil, otherwise Mr. Cardus, would expire in a few months. Dorothy read what the old man wrote upon his slate, and repeated it to Ernest for, he being practically dumb and Ernest being blind, that was the only way in which they could communicate.

"And what will you do then?" asked Ernest. "You will be wretched without any writs to fill up. Who will look after the lost souls, I should like to know?"

The old man at once wrote vigorously on his slate:

"I shall go out hunting on the big black horse you brought with you; he will carry my weight."

"I should advise you not to try," said Ernest, laughing; "he does not like strange riders." But the old man, at the mere thought of hunting, was striding up and down the room, clanking his spurs and waving his hunting-crop with his uninjured arm.

"Is your grandfather as much afraid of your uncle as ever, Doll?"

"Oh yes, I think so; and do you know, Ernest, I don't quite like the way he looks at him sometimes."

Ernest laughed. "I should think that the old boy is harmless enough," he said.

"I hope so," said Dorothy.

When first they came back to Dum's Ness, Jeremy was at a great loss to know what to do with himself, and was haunted by the idea that Mr. Cardus would want him to resume that stool in his office which years before he had quitted to go in search of Ernest. A week or so after his arrival, however, his fears were set at rest very pleasantly. After breakfast, Mr. Cardus sent for him to come into his office.

"Well, Jeremy," he said, letting his soft black eyes wander round that young gentleman's gigantic form—for it was by now painfully large—not so much in height, for he was not six feet three—as in its great width, which made big men look like children beside him, and even dwarfed his old grandfather's enormous frame—"well, Jeremy, and what do you think of doing? You're too big for a lawyer; all your clients would be afraid of you."

"I don't know about being too big," said Jeremy, solemnly, "but I know that I am too great an ass. Besides, I can't afford several years to spend in being articled at my time of life."

"Quite so. Then what do you propose doing?"

"I don't know from Adam."

"Well, how would you like to turn your sword to a plough-share, and become a farmer?"

"I think that would suit me first-rate. I have some capital laid by. Ernest and I made a little money out there."

"No, I would not advise you to take a farm in that way; these are bad times. But I want a practical man to look after my land round here—salary £150. What do you say?"

"You are very kind; but I doubt if I can boss that coach; I don't know anything of the work."

"Oh, you will very soon learn; there is a capital bailiff; Stamp—you remember him—he will soon put you up to the ropes. So we will consider that settled."

Thus it was that our friend Jeremy entered on a new walk in life, and one which suited him very well. In less than a year's time he grew aggressively agricultural, and one never met him but what he had a handful of oats, or a carrot in his coat-tail pocket, which he was ready to swear were samples of the finest oats, carrot, or whatever the particular agricultural product might be, that ever had been, or were ever likely to be, grown.

CHAPTER VI

HOW IT ALL CAME ABOUT

How did it all come about?

Let us try and discover. Dorothy and Ernest were together all day long. They only separated when Mazooku came to lead the latter off to bed. At breakfast-time he led him back again, and handed him over to Dorothy for the day. Not that our Zulu friend liked this; he did not like it at all. It was, he considered, his business to lead his master about, and not that of the "Rosebud," who was, as he discovered, after all nothing but a girl connected with his master neither by birth nor marriage. On this point there finally arose a difference of opinion between the Rosebud and Mazooku.

The latter was leading Ernest for his morning walk, when Dorothy, perceiving it, and being very jealous of what she considered her rights, sallied out and took his hand from the great Zulu's. Then did Mazooku's long-pent indignation break forth.

"O Rosebud, sweet and small Rosebud!" he commenced, addressing her in Zulu, of which, needless to say, she understood not one word, "why do you come and take my father's hand out of my hand? Is not Mazimba my father blind, and am I not his dog, his old dog, to lead him in his blindness? Why do you take his bone from a dog?"

"What is the man saying?" asked Dorothy.

"He is offended because you come to lead me; he says that he is my dog, and that you snatch his bone from him. A pretty sort of bone, indeed!" he added.

"Tell him," said Dorothy, "that here in this country I hold your hand. What does he want? Is he not always with you? Does he not sleep across your door? What more does he want?"

Ernest translated her reply.

"Ow!" said the Zulu, with a grunt of dissatisfaction.

"He is a faithful fellow, Doll, and has stood by me for many years; you must not vex him."

But Dorothy, after the manner of loving women, was tenacious of what she considered her rights.

"Tell him that he can walk in front," she said, putting on an obstinate little look—and she could look obstinate when she liked. "Besides," she added, "he cannot be trusted to lead you. I am sure he was tipsy last night."

Ernest translated the first remark only—into the latter he did not care to inquire, for the Zulu vowed that he could never understand Dorothy's English, and Mazooku accepted the compromise. Thus for awhile the difference was patched up.

Sometimes Dorothy and Ernest would go out riding together; for, blind as he was, Ernest could not be persuaded to give up his riding. It was a pretty sight to see them; Ernest mounted on his towering black stallion, "The Devil," which in his hands was as gentle as a lamb, but with everybody else fully justified his appellation, and Dorothy on a cream-coloured cob Mr. Cardus had given her, holding in her right hand a steel guiding-rein linked to "The Devil's" bit. In this way they would wander all over the country-side, and sometimes, when a good piece of turf presented itself, even venture on a sharp canter. Behind them Mazooku rode as groom, mounted on a stout pony, with his feet stuck, Zulu fashion, well out at right angles to his animal's side.

They were a strange trio.

So from week's end to week's end Dorothy was ever by Ernest's side, reading to him, writing for him, walking and riding with him, weaving herself into the substance of his life.

At last there came one sunny August day, when they were sitting together in the shade of the chancel of Titheburgh Abbey. It was a favourite spot of theirs, for the grey old walls sheltered them from the glare of the sun and the breath of the winds. It was a spot, too, rich in memories of the dead past, and a pleasant place to sit.

Through the gaping window-places came the murmur of the ocean and the warmth of the harvest sunshine; and gazing out by the chancel doorway, Dorothy could see the long lights of the afternoon dance and sparkle on the emerald waves.

She had been reading to him, and the book lay idle on her knees as she gazed dreamily at those lights and shadows, a sweet picture of pensive womanhood. He, too, had relapsed into silence, and was evidently thinking deeply.

Presently she roused herself.

"Well, Ernest," she said, "what are you thinking about? You are as dull as—as the dullest thing in the world, whatever that may be. What is the dullest thing in the world?"

"I don't know," he answered, awakening. "Yes, I think I do; an American novel."

"Yes, that is a good definition. You are as dull as an American novel."

"It is unkind of you to say so, Doll, my dear. I was thinking of something, Doll."

She made a little face, which of course he could not see, and answered quickly:

"You generally are thinking of something. You generally are thinking of—Eva, except when you are asleep, and then you are dreaming of her."

Ernest coloured up.

"Yes," he said, "it is true; she is often more or less in my mind. It is my misfortune, Doll, not my fault. You see, I do not do things by halves."

Dorothy bit her lip.

"She should be vastly flattered, I am sure. Few women can boast of having inspired such affection in a man. I suppose it is because she treated you so badly. Dogs love the hand that whips them. You are a curious character, Ernest. Not many men would give so much to one who has returned so little."

"So much the better for them. If I had a son, I think that I should teach him to make love to all women, and to use their affection as a means of amusement and self-advancement, but to fall in love with none."

"That is one of your bitter remarks, for which I suppose we must thank Eva. You are always making them now. Let me tell you that there are good women in the world; yes, and honest, faithful women, who, when they have given their heart, are true to their choice, and would not do it violence to be made Queen of England. But you men do not go the right way to find them. You think of nothing but beauty, and never take the trouble to learn the hearts of the sweet girls who grow like daisies in the grass all round you, but who do not happen to have great melting eyes or a splendid figure. You tread them underfoot, and if they were not so humble they would be crushed, as you rush off and try to pick the rose; and then you prick your fingers and cry out, and tell all the daisies how shamefully the rose has treated you."

Ernest laughed, and Dorothy went on:

"Yes, it is an unjust world. Let a woman but be beautiful, and everything is at her feet, for you men are despicable creatures, and care for little except what is pleasant to the senses. On the other hand, let her be plain, or only ordinary-looking—for the fate of most of us is just to escape being ugly—and you pay as much regard to her as you do to the chairs you sit on. And yet, strange as it may seem to you, probably she has her feelings, and her capacities for high affections, and her imaginative power, all working vigorously behind her plain little face. Probably, too, she is better than your beauty. Nature does not give everything. When she endows a woman with perfect loveliness, she robes her either of her heart or her brains, or perhaps of both. But you men don't see that, because you won't look; so in course of time all the fine possibilities in Miss Plain-face wither up, and she becomes a disappointed old maid, while my Lady Beauty pursues her career of selfishness and mischief-making, till at last she withers up too, that's one comfort. We all end in bones, you know, and there isn't much difference between us then."

Ernest had been listening with great amusement to Dorothy's views. He had no idea that she took such matters into her shrewd consideration.

"I heard a girl say the other day that, on the whole, most women preferred to become old maids," he said.

"Then she told fibs; they don't. It isn't natural that they should—that is, if they care for anybody. Just think, there are more than ten hundred thousand of our charming sisterhood in these islands, and more women being born every day! Ten hundred thousand restless, unoccupied, disgusted, loveless women! It is simply awful to think of. I wonder they don't breed a revolution. If they were all beautiful, they would."

He laughed again.

"Do you know what remedy Mazooku would apply to this state of affairs?"

"No."

"The instant adoption of polygamy. There are no unmarried women among the Natal Zulus, and as a class they are extremely happy."

Dorothy shook her head.

"It wouldn't do here; it would be too expensive."

"I say, Doll, you spoke just now of our 'charming sisterhood'; you are rather young to consider yourself an old maid. Do you want to become one?"

"Yes," she said sharply.

"Then you don't care for anybody, eh?"

She blushed up furiously.

"What business is it of yours, I should like to know?" she answered.

"Well, Doll, not much. But will you be angry with me if I say something?"

"I suppose you can say what you like."

"Yes; but will you listen?"

"If you speak I cannot help hearing."

"Well, then, Doll—now don't be angry, dear."

"O Ernest, how you aggravate me! Can't you get it out and have done with it?"

"All right, Doll, I'll steam straight ahead this time. It is this. I have sometimes lately been vain enough to think that you cared a little about me, Doll, although I am as blind as a bat. I want to ask you if it is true. You must tell me plain, Doll, because I cannot see your eyes to learn the truth from them."

She turned quite pale at his words, and her eyes rested upon his blind orbs with a look of unutterable tenderness. So it had come at last.

"Why do you ask me that question, Ernest? Whether or no I care for you, I am very sure that you do not care for me."

"You are not quite right there, Doll, but I will tell you why I ask it; it is not out of mere curiosity.

"You know all the history of my life, Doll, or at least most of it. You know how I loved Eva, and gave her all that a foolish youngster can give to a weak woman—gave it in such a way that I can never have it back again. Well, she deserted me; I have lost her—certainly for this world and perhaps for all others if there are any others, since I cannot see why people in a new existence should differ greatly from what they were in the old. The leopard does not change its spots, you know! The best happiness of my life has been wrecked beyond redemption; that is a fact which must be accepted as much as the fact of my blindness. I am physically and morally crippled, and certainly in no fit state to ask a woman to marry me on the ground of my personal advantages. But if, dear Doll, you should, as I have sometimes thought, happen to care about anything so worthless, then, you see, the affair assumes a different aspect."

"I don't quite understand you. What do you mean?" she said, in a low voice.

"I mean that in that case I will ask you if you will take me for a husband."

"You do not love me, Ernest; I should weary you."

He felt for her hand, found it, and took it in his own. She made no resistance.

"Dear," he said, "it is this way: I can never give you that passion I gave to Eva, because, thank God, the human heart can know it but once in a life; but I can and will give you a husband's tenderest love. You are very dear to me, Doll, though it is not in the same way that Eva is dear. I have always loved you as a sister, and I think that I should make you a good husband. But, before you answer me, I want you to thoroughly understand about Eva. Whether I marry or not, I fear that I shall never be able to shake her out of my mind. At one time I thought that perhaps if I made love to other women I might be able to do so, on the principle that one nail drives out another. But it was a failure; for a month or two I got the better of my thoughts, then they would get the better of me again. Besides, to tell you the truth, I am not quite sure that I wish to do so. My trouble about this woman has become a part of myself. It is, as I told you, my 'evil destiny'; and goes where I go. And now, dear Doll, you will see why I asked you if you really cared for me, before I asked you to marry me. If you do not care for me, then it will clearly not be worth your while to marry me, for I am about as poor a catch as a man can well be; if you do—well, then it is a matter for your consideration."

She paused awhile and answered:

"Suppose that the positions were reversed, Ernest; at least, suppose this: suppose that you had loved your Eva all your life, but she had not loved you except as a brother, having given her heart to some other man, who was, say, married to somebody else, or in some way separated from her. Well, supposing that this man died, and that one day Eva came to you and said, 'Ernest, my dear, I cannot love you as I loved him who has gone, and whom I one day hope to rejoin in heaven; but if you wish it, and it will make you the happier, I will be your true and tender wife.' What should you answer her, Ernest?"

"Answer? why, I suppose that I should take her at her word and be thankful. Yes, I think that I should take her at her word."

"And so, dear Ernest, do I take you at your word; for as it is with you about Eva, so it is with me about you. As a child I loved you; ever since I have been a woman I have loved you more and more, even through all those cold years of absence. And when you came back, ah, then it was to me as it would be to you if you suddenly once more saw the light of day. Ernest, my beloved, you are all my life to me, and I take you at your word, my dear. I will be your wife."

He stretched out his arms, found her, drew her to him, and kissed her on the lips.

"Doll, I don't deserve that you should love me so; it makes me feel ashamed that I have not everything to give you in return."

"Ernest, you will give me all you can; I mean to make you grow very fond of me. Perhaps too one day you will give me 'everything.'"

He hesitated a little while before he spoke again.

"Doll," he said, "you are sure quite that you do not mind about Eva?"

"My dear Ernest, I accept Eva as a fact, and make the best of her, just as I should if I wanted to marry a man with a monomania that he was Henry VIII."

"Doll, you know I call her my evil destiny. The fact is, I am afraid of her; she overpowers my reason. Well, now, Doll, what I am driving at is this: supposing—not that I think she will—that she were to crop up again, and take it into her head to try and make a fool of me! She might succeed, Doll."

"Ernest, will you promise me something on your honour?"

"Yes, dear."

"Promise me that you will hide from me nothing that passes between Eva and yourself, if anything ever should pass, and that in this matter you will always consider me not in the light of a wife, but of a trusted friend."

"Why do you ask me to promise that?"

"Because then I shall, I hope, be able to keep you both out of trouble. You are not fit to look after yourselves, either of you."

"I promise. And now, Doll, there is one more thing. Notwithstanding what I said just now it is somehow fixed in my mind that my fate and that woman's are intertwined. I believe, perhaps foolishly enough, that what we are now passing through is but a single phase of interwoven existence; that we have already passed through possibly many stages and that many higher stages and developments await us. The question is, do you care to link your life with that of a man who holds such a belief?"

"Ernest, I daresay your belief is a true one, at any rate to you who believe it, for it seems probable that as we sow so shall we reap, as we spiritually imagine so shall we spiritually inherit, since causes must in time produce effects. These beliefs are not implanted in our hearts for nothing, and surely in the wide heavens there is room for the realisation of them all. But I too have my beliefs, and one of them is, that in God's great hereafter every loving and desiring soul will be with the soul thus loved and desired. For him or her, at any rate, the other will be there, forming a part of his or her life, though, perhaps, it may elsewhere and with others also be pursuing its own desires and satisfying its own aspirations. So you see, Ernest, your beliefs will not interfere with mine, nor shall I be afraid of losing you in another place.

"And now, Ernest, my heart's love, take my hand, and let me lead you home; take my hand as you have taken my heart, and never leave go of it again till at last I die."

So hand in hand they went home together, through the lights and shadows of the twilight.

CHAPTER VII

MAZOOKU'S FAREWELL

Dorothy and Ernest returned to Dum's Ness just in time to dress for dinner, for since Ernest and Jeremy had come back, Dorothy, whose will in that house was law, had instituted late dinner. The dinner passed over as usual, Dorothy sitting between Ernest and her grandfather, and attending to the wants of those two unfortunates, both of whom would have found it rather difficult to get through their meal without her gentle, unobtrusive help. But when dinner was over and the cloth removed, and Grice had placed the wine upon the table and withdrawn, an unusual thing happened.

Ernest asked Dorothy to fill his glass with port, and when she had done so he said:

"Uncle and Jeremy, I am going to ask you to drink a health."

The old man looked up sharply. "What is it, Ernest, my boy?"

As for Dorothy, she blushed a rosy red, guessing what was coming, and not knowing whether to be pleased or angry.

"It is this, uncle—it is the health of my future wife, Dorothy."

Then came a silence of astonishment. Mr. Cardus broke it:

"Years ago, Ernest, my dear nephew, I told you that I wished this to come to pass; but other things happened to thwart my plans, and I never expected to see it. Now in God's good time it has come, and I drink the health with all my heart. My children, I know that I am a strange man, and my life has been devoted to a single end, which is now drawing near its final development; but I have found time in it to learn to love you both. Dorothy, my daughter, I drink your health. May the happiness that was denied to your mother fall upon your head, her share and your share too! Ernest, you have passed through many troubles, and have been preserved almost miraculously to see this day. In Dorothy you will find a reward for everything, for she is a good woman. Perhaps I shall never live to see your happiness and the children of your happiness—I do not think I shall; but may the solemn blessing I give you now rest upon your dear heads! God bless you both, my children. All peace go with you, Dorothy and Ernest!"

"Amen!" said Jeremy, in a loud voice, and with a vague idea that he was in church. Next he got up and shook Ernest's hand so hard in his fearful grip that the latter was constrained to cry out, and lifted Dolly out of her chair like a plaything, and kissed her boisterously, knocking the orchid-bloom she wore out of her hair in the process. Then they all sat down again and beamed at one another and drank port-wine—at least the men did—and were inanely happy.

Indeed, the only person to whom the news was not satisfactory was Mazooku.

"Ou!" he said, with a grunt, when Jeremy communicated it to him. "So the Rosebud is going to become the Rose, and I shan't even be able to lead my father to bed now. Ou!" And from that day forward Mazooku's abstracted appearance showed that he was meditating deeply on something.

Next morning his uncle sent for Ernest into the office. Dorothy led him in.

"O, here you are!" said his uncle.

"Yes, here we are, Reginald," answered Dorothy; "what is it? Shall I go away?"

"No, don't go away. What I have to say concerns you both. Come and look at the orchids, Ernest; they are beautiful. Ah!" he went on, stammering, "I forgot you can't see them. Forgive me."

"Never mind, uncle, I can smell them;" and they went into the blooming-house appropriated to the temperate kinds.

At the end of this house was a little table and some iron chairs, where Mr. Cardus would sometimes come to smoke a cigarette. Here they sat down.

"Now, young people," said Mr. Cardus, wiping his bald head, "you are going to get married. May I ask what you are going to get married on?"

"By Jove," said Ernest, "I never thought of that! I haven't got much, except a title, a mansion with 'numerous and valuable heirlooms, and one hundred and eighty acres of deer park,'" he added laughing.

"No, I don't suppose you have; but, luckily for you both, I am not so badly off, and I mean to do something for you. What do you think would be the proper thing? Come, Dorothy, my little housewife, what do you reckon you can live on—living here, I mean, for I suppose that you do not mean to run away and leave me alone in my old age, do you?"

Dorothy wrinkled up her forehead as she used to as a child, and began to calculate upon her fingers. Presently she answered:

"Three hundred a year comfortably, quietly on two."

"What!" said Mr. Cardus, "when the babies begin to come?"

Dorothy blushed, old gentlemen are so unpleasantly outspoken, and Ernest jumped, for the prospect of unlimited babies is alarming till one gets used to it.

"Better make it five hundred," he said.

"Oh," said Mr. Cardus, "that's what you think, is it? Well, I tell you what I think. I am going to allow you young people two thousand a year and to pay the housekeeping bills."

"My dear uncle, that is far more than we want."

"Nonsense, Ernest! it is there and to spare; and why should you not have it, instead of its piling up in the bank or in investments? There are enough of them now, I can tell you. Everything that I have touched has turned to gold; I believe it has often been the case with unfortunate men. Money! I have more than I know what to do with, and there are idiots who think that to have lots of money is to be happy."

He paused awhile and then went on:

"I would give you more, but you are both comparatively young, and I do not wish to encourage habits of extravagance in you. The world is full of vicissitudes, and it is impossible for anybody to know how he may be pecuniarily situated in ten years' time. But I wish you, Ernest, to keep up your rank—moderately, if you like, but still to keep it up. Life is all before you now, and whatever you choose to go in for, you shall not want money to back you. Look here, my children, I may as well tell you that when I die you will inherit nearly all I have got; I have left it to be divided equally between you, with reversion to the survivor. I drew up that will some years back, and I do not think that it is worth while altering it now."

"Forgive me," said Ernest, "but how about Jeremy?"

Mr. Cardus's face changed a little. He had never got over his dislike of Jeremy, though his sense of justice caused him to stifle it.

"I have not forgotten Jeremy," he said, in a tone that indicated that he did not wish to pursue the conversation.

Ernest and Dorothy thanked the old man for his goodness, but he would not listen, so they went off and left him to return to his letter-writing. In the passage Dorothy peeped through the glass half of the door which opened into her grandfather's room.

There sat the old man writing, writing, his long iron-grey hair hanging all about his face. Presently he seemed to think of something, and a smile, which the contorted mouth made ghastly, spread itself over the pallid countenance. Rising, he went to the corner and extracted a long tally-stick on which notches were cut. Sitting down again, he counted the remaining notches over and over, then took a penknife and cut one out. This done, he put the stick back, and looking at the wall, began to mutter—for he was not quite dumb—and to clasp and unclasp his powerful hand. Dorothy entered the room quickly.

"Grandfather, what are you doing?" she said sharply.

The old man started, and his jaw dropped. Then the eyes grew dull, and his usual apathetic look stole over his face. Taking up his slate, he wrote, "Cutting out my notches."

Dorothy asked him some further questions, but could get nothing more out of him.

"I don't at all like the way grandfather has been going on lately," she said to Ernest. "He is always muttering and clinching his hand as though he had some one by the throat. You know he thinks that he has been serving the fiend all these years, and that his time will be up shortly, whereas, though Reginald had no cause to love him, he has been very kind to him. If it had not been for Reginald, my grandfather would have been sent to the madhouse; but because he was connected with his loss of fortune, he thinks he is the devil. He forgets how he served Reginald; you see even in madness the mind only remembers the injuries inflicted on itself, and forgets those it inflicted on others. I don't at all like his way."

"I should think that he had better be shut up."

"Oh, Reginald would never do it. Come, dear, let us go out."

It was a month or so after Mr. Cardus's announcement of his pecuniary intentions that a little wedding-party stood before the altar in Kesterwick Church. It was a very small party, consisting, indeed, only of Ernest, Dorothy, Mr. Cardus, Jeremy, and a few idlers, who, seeing the church door open, had strolled in to see what was going on. Indeed, the marriage had been kept a profound secret; for since he had been blind, Ernest had developed a great dislike to being stared at. Nor, indeed, had he any liking for the system under which a woman proclaims with loud and unseemly rejoicings that she has found a man to marry her, and the clan of her relations celebrate her departure with a few outward and visible tears and much inward and spiritual joy.

But among that small crowd, unobserved by any of them, quite close up in the shadow of one of the massive pillars, sat a veiled woman. She sat quite quiet and still; she might have been carved in stone;

but as the service went on she raised her thick veil, and fixed her keen eyes upon the two who stood before the altar. As she did so, the lips of this shadowy lady trembled a little, and a mist of trouble rose from the unhealthy marshes of her mind and clouded her fine-cut features. Long and steadily she gazed, then dropped the veil again, and said beneath her breath:

"Was it worth while for this? Well, I have seen him."

Then this shadowy noble-looking lady rose, and glided from the church, bearing away with her the haunting burden of her sin.

And Ernest? He stood there and said the responses in his clear manly voice; but even as he did so there rose before him the semblance of the little room in far-away Pretoria, and the vision which he had seen of this very church, and of a man standing where he himself stood now, and a lovely woman standing where stood Dorothy his wife. Well, it was gone, as all visions go—as we, who are but visions of a longer life, go too. It was gone—gone into that limbo of the past which is ever opening its insatiable maw and swallowing us and our joys and our sorrows—our virtues and our sins—making a meal of the atoms of to-day that it may support itself till the atoms of to-morrow are ready for its appetite.

It was gone, and he was married, and Dorothy his wife stood there wreathed in smiles and blushes which he could not see, and Mr. Halford's voice, now grown weak and quavering, was formulating heartfelt congratulations, which were being repeated in the gigantic echo of Jeremy's deep tones, and in his uncles quick jerky utterances. So he took Dorothy his wife into his arms and kissed her, and she led him down the church to the old vestry, into which so many thousand newly-married couples had passed during the course of the last six centuries, and he signed his name where they placed his pen upon the parchment, wondering the while if he was signing it straight, and then went out, and was helped into the carriage, and driven home.

Ernest and his wife went upon no honeymoon; they stopped quietly there at the old house, and began to accustom themselves to their new relationship. Indeed, to the outsider at any rate, there seemed to be little difference between it and the former one; for they could not be much more together now than they had been before. Yet in Dorothy's face there was a difference. A great peace, an utter satisfaction which had been wanting before, came down and brooded upon it, and made it beautiful. She both looked and was a happy woman.

But to the Zulu Mazooku this state of affairs did not appear to be satisfactory.

One day—it was three days after the marriage—Ernest and Dorothy were walking together outside the house, when Jeremy, coming in from a visit to a distant farm, advanced, and, joining them, began to converse on agricultural matters; for he was already becoming intensely and annoyingly technical. Presently, as they talked, they became aware of the sound of naked feet running swiftly over the grass.

"That sounds like a Zulu dancing," said Ernest, quickly.

It was a Zulu: it was Mazooku, but Mazooku transformed. It had been his fancy to bring a suit of war finery, such as he had worn when he was one of Cetywayo's soldiers, with him from Natal; and now he had donned it all, and stood before them, a striking yet an alarming figure. From his head a single beautiful grey feather, taken from the Bell crane, rose a good two feet into the air; around his waist hung a kilt of white ox-tails, and beneath his right knee and shoulder were small circles of white goat's hair. For the rest, he was naked. In his left hand he held a milk-white fighting-shield made of ox-hide, and in his right his great "bangwan," or stabbing assegai. Still as a statue he stood before them, his plume bending in the breeze; and Dorothy, looking with wondering eyes, marvelled at the broad chest scarred all over with assegai wounds, and the huge sinewy limbs. Suddenly he raised the spear, and saluted in sonorous tones:

"Koos! Baba!"

"Speak," said Ernest.

"I speak, Mazimba, my father. I come to meet my father as a man meets a man. I come with spear and shield, but not in war. With my father I came from the land of the sun into this cold land, where the sun is as pale as the white faces it shines on. Is it not so, my father?"

"I hear you."

"With my father I came. Did you my father and I stand together for many a day? Did I not slay the two Basutos down in the land of Secocoeni, chief of the Bapedi, at my father's bidding? Did I not once save my father from the jaws of the wild beast that walks by night—from the fangs of the lion? Did I not stand by the side of my father at the place of the Little Hand, when all the plain of Isandhlwana was red with blood? Do I dream in the night, or was it so, my father?"

"I hear you. It was so."

"Then when the heavens above smelt out my father, and smote him with their fire, did I not say, 'Ah, my father, now art thou blind, and canst fight no more, and no more play the part of a man. Better that thou hadst died a man's death, O my father! But as thou art blind, lo! whither thou goest, thither I will go also and be my father's dog.' Did I not say this, O Mazimba, my father?"

"Thou didst say it."

"And so we sailed across the black water, thou, Mazimba, and I and the great Lion, like unto whom no man was ever born of woman, and came hither, and have lived for many moons the lives of women, have eaten and drunken, and have not fought or hunted, or known the pleasure of men. Is it not so, Mazimba, my father?"

"Thou speakest truly, Mazooku; it is even so."

"Yes, we sailed the black water in the smoking ship, sailed to the land of wonders, which is full of houses and trees, so that a man cannot breathe in it, or throw out his arms lest they should strike a wall; and, behold! there came an ancient one with a shining head wonderful to look on, and a girl Rosebud, small but very sweet, and greeted my father and the Lion, and led them away in the carriages which put the horses inside them, and set them in this place, where they may look for ever at the sadness of the sea.

"And then, behold, the Rosebud said, 'What doth this black dog here? Shall a dog lead Mazimba by the hand? Begone, thou black dog, and walk in front or ride behind; it is I who will hold Mazimba's hand.'

"Then my father, sinking deep in ease, and becoming a fat man, rich in oxen and waggons and corn, said to himself, 'I will take this Rosebud to wife.' So the Rosebud opened her petals, and closed them round my father, and became a rose; and now she sheds her fragrance round him day by day and night by night, and the black dog stands and howls outside the door.

"Thus, my father, it came to pass that Mazooku, thy ox and thy dog, communed with his heart, and said: 'Here is no more any place for thee. Mazimba thy chief has no longer any need of thee, and behold! O Soldier in this land of women thou, too, shalt grow like a woman. So arise and go to thy father, and say to him, "O my father, years ago I put my hand between thy hands, and became a loyal man to thee; now I would withdraw it, and return to the land whence we came; for here I am not wanted, and here I cannot breathe."' I have spoken, O my father and my chief."

"Mazooku, umdanda ga Ingoluvu, umfana ga Amazulu" (son of Ingoluvu, child of the Zulu race), answered Ernest, adopting the Zulu metaphor, his voice sounding wonderfully soft as the liquid tongue he spoke so well came rolling out, "thou hast been a good man to me and I have loved thee. But thou shalt go. Thou art right: now is my life the life of a woman; never again shall I hear the sound of rifles or the ringing of steel in war. And so thou goest, Mazooku. It is well. But at times thou wilt think of thy blind master Mazimba, and of Alston, the wise captain who sleeps, and of the Lion who threw the ox over his shoulder. Go, and be happy. Many be thy wives, many thy children, and countless thy cattle! The Lion shall take thee by the hand and lead thee to the sea, and shall give thee of my bounty wherewith to buy a little food when thou comest to thine own land, and a few oxen, and a piece of ground, or a waggon or two, so that thou shalt not be hungry, nor want for cattle to give for wives. Mazooku, fare thee well!"

"One word, Mazimba, my father, and I will trouble thine ears no more, since for thee my voice shall be silent for ever. When the time has come for thee to die, and thou dost pass, as the white men say, up 'into the heavens above,' and thy sight dawns again, and thou art once more a man eager for battle, then turn thee and cry with a loud voice: 'Mazooku, son of Ingoluvu, of the tribe of the Maquilisini, where art thou, O my dog? Come thou and serve me!' And surely, if I still live, then I shall hear thy voice, and groan and die, that I may pass to thee; and if I be already dead, then shall I be at thy side, even as thou callest. This thou wilt do for me, O Mazimba, my father and my chief, because, lo! I have loved thee as the child loves her who suckled it, and I would look upon thy face again, O my father from the olden time, my chief from generation to generation!"

"If it be in my power, this I will do, Mazooku."

The great Zulu drew himself up, raised his spear, and for the first and last time in his life gave Ernest the royal salute—to which, by the way, he had no right at all—"Bayète, Bayète!" Then he turned and ran swiftly thence, nor would he see Ernest again before he went. "The pain of death was over," he said.

As the sound of his footsteps grew faint, Ernest turned his head aside and sighed.

"There goes our last link with South Africa, Jeremy, my boy. It is a good thing, for he was growing too fond of the bottle and the women; they all do here. But it makes me very sad, and sometimes I think that, as Mazooku says, it is a pity we did not go under with Alston and the others. It would all have been over now."

"Thank you," said Jeremy, after reflecting; "on the whole, I am pretty comfortable as I am."

CHAPTER VIII

MR. CARDUS ACCOMPLISHES HIS REVENGE

Mr. de Talor owed his great wealth not to his own talents, but to a lucky secret in the manufacture of the grease used on railways discovered by his father. Talor pere had been a railway-guard till his discovery brought him wealth. He was a shrewd man, however, and on his sudden accession of fortune did his best to make a gentleman of his only son, at that date a lad of fifteen. But it was too late; the associations and habits of childhood are not easily overcome, and no earthly power or education could accomplish the desired object. When his son was twenty years of age, old Jack Talor died, and his son succeeded to his large fortune and a railway-grease business which supplied the principal markets of the world.

His son had inherited a good deal of his father's shrewdness, and set himself to make the best of his advantages. First he placed a "de" before his name, and assumed a canting crest. Next he bought the Ceswick Ness estates, and bloomed into a country gentleman. It was shortly after this latter event that he made a mistake, and fell in love with the beauty of the neighbourhood, Mary Atterleigh. But Mary Atterleigh would have none of him, being at the time secretly engaged to Mr. Cardus. In vain did he resort to every possible means to shake her resolution, even going so far as to try to bribe her father to put pressure upon her; but at this time Atterleigh, "Hard-riding Atterleigh," as he was called, was well off, and resisted his advances. Thereupon De Talor, in a fit of pique, married another woman, who was only too glad to put up with his vulgarity in consideration of his wealth and position as a county magnate.

Shortly afterwards three events occurred almost simultaneously. "Hard-riding Atterleigh" got into money difficulties through over-gratification of his passion for hounds and horses; Mr. Cardus was taken abroad for the best part of a year in connection with a business matter; and a man named Jones, a friend of Mr. de Talor's staying in his house at the time, fell in love with Mary Atterleigh. Herein De Talor saw an opportunity of revenge upon his rival, Mr. Cardus. He urged upon Jones that his real road to the possession of the lady lay through the pocket of her father, and even went so far as to advance him the necessary funds to bribe Atterleigh; for though Jones was well off, he could not at such short notice lay hands upon a sufficient sum in cash to serve his ends.

The plot succeeded. Atterleigh's scruples were overcome as easily as the scruples of men in his position without principle to back them generally are, and pressure of a most outrageous sort was brought to bear upon the gentle-minded Mary, with the result that when Mr. Cardus returned from abroad he found his affianced bride the wife of another man, who became in due course the father of Jeremy and Dolly.

This cruel and most unexpected bereavement drove Mr. Cardus partially mad, and when he came to himself there arose in his mind a monomania for revenge on all concerned in bringing it about. It became the passion and object of his life. Directing all his remarkable intelligence and energy to the matter, he early discovered the heinous part that De Talor had played in the plot, and swore to devote his life to the unholy purpose of vengeance. For years he pursued his enemy, trying plan after plan to achieve his ruin, and as one failed fell back upon another. But to ruin a man of De Talor's wealth was no easy matter, especially when, as in the present instance, the avenger was obliged to work like a mole in the dark, never allowing his enemy to suspect that he was other than a friend. How he ultimately achieved his purpose the reader shall now learn.

Ernest and Dorothy had been married about three weeks, and the latter was just beginning to get accustomed to hearing herself called Lady Kershaw, when one morning a dog-cart drove up to the door and out of it emerged Mr. de Talor.

"Dear me, how Mr. de Talor has changed of late!" said Dorothy, who was looking out of the window.

"How? Has he grown less like a butcher?" asked Ernest.

"No," she answered; "but he looks like a used-up butcher about to go through the Bankruptcy Court.'

"Butchers never go bankrupt," said Ernest; and at that moment Mr. de Talor came in.

Dorothy was right; the man was much changed. The fat cheeks were flabby and fallen, the insolent air was gone, and he was so shrunken that he looked not more than half his former size.

"How do you do, Lady Kershaw? I saw Cardus 'ad got some one with him, so I drove round to pay my respects and congratulate the bride. Why, bless me, Sir Ernest, you 'ave grown since I saw you last. Ah, we used to be great friends then. You remember how you used to come and shoot up at the Ness" (he had once or twice given the two lads a day's rabbit-shooting). "But, bless me, I hear that you have become quite a fire-eater since then, and been knocking the niggers right and left—eh?"

He paused for breath, and Ernest said a few words, not many, for he disliked the man's flattery as much as in past years he used to dislike his insolence.

"Ah," went on De Talor, looking up and pointing to the case containing the witch's head, "I see you've still got that beastly thing your brother once showed me; I thought it was a clock, and he pretty well frightened me out of my wits. Now I think of it, I've never 'ad any luck since I saw that thing."

At this moment the housekeeper Grice came to say that Mr. Cardus was ready to see Mr. de Talor if he would step into the office. Dorothy thought that their visitor turned paler at this news, and it evidently occupied his mind sufficiently to cause him to hurry from the room without bidding them good-bye.

When Mr. de Talor entered the office he found the lawyer pacing up and down.

"How do you do, Cardus?" he said jauntily.

"How do you do, Mr. de Talor?" was the cold reply.

De Talor walked to the glass door and looked at the glowing mass of blooming orchids.

"Pretty flowers, Cardus, those, very. Orchids, ain't they? Must have cost you a pot of money."

"They have not cost me much, Mr. de Talor; I have reared most of them."

"Then you are lucky; the bill my man gives me for his orchids is something awful."

"You did not come to speak to me about orchids, Mr. de Talor."

"No, Cardus, I didn't; business first, pleasure afterwards—eh?"

"Yes," said Mr. Cardus, in his soft jerky way. "Business first, pleasure afterwards."

Mr. de Talor fidgeted his legs about.

"Well, Cardus, about that mortgage. You are going to give me a little more time, I hope?"

"On the contrary, Mr. de Talor, the interest being now eight months overdue, I have given my London agents orders to foreclose, for I don't conduct such business myself."

De Talor turned pale. "Foreclose! Good God, Cardus! It is not possible—on such an old friend too!"

"Excuse me, it is not only possible, but a fact. Business is business, even where old friends are concerned."

"But if you foreclose, what is to become of me, Cardus?"

"That, I imagine, is a matter for your exclusive consideration."

His visitor gasped, and looked like an unfortunate fish suddenly pulled out of the water.

"Let us recapitulate the facts. I have at different periods within the last several years lent you sums of money secured on your landed estates at Ceswick's Ness and the neighbourhood, amounting in all"—referring to a paper—"to one hundred and seventy-six thousand five hundred and thirty-eight pounds ten shillings and fourpence; or, reckoning in the overdue interest, to one hundred and seventy-nine thousand and fifty-two pounds eight shillings. That is so, I think."

"Yes, I suppose so, Cardus."

"There is no supposition about it. The documents prove it."

"Well, Cardus?"

"Well, Mr. de Talor; and now, as you cannot pay, I have instructed my London agents to commence an action in Chancery for the sale of the lands, and to buy in the property. It is a most desirable property."

"O Cardus, don't be rough on me! I am an old man now, and you led me into this speculation."

"Mr. de Talor, I also am an old man; if not very old in years, at least as old as Methuselah in heart."

"I don't understand it all, Cardus."

"It will give me the greatest pleasure to explain. But to do so I must go back a little. Some ten or twelve years ago, you may remember," he began, sitting down with his back to the light, which struck full on the wretched De Talor's face, "that a firm named Rastrick and Codley took out a patent for a new railway-grease, and set up an establishment in Manchester not far from the famous De Talor house, which was established by your father."

"Yes, curse them!" groaned De Talor.

Mr. Cardus smiled.

"By all means curse them. But what did this enterprising firm do, Mr. de Talor? They set to work and sold a grease superior to the article manufactured by your house, at about eighteen per cent. cheaper. But the De Talor house had the ear of the markets, and the contracts with all the leading lines and Continental firms, and for awhile it seemed as though the new house must go to the wall; and if they had not had considerable capital at command, they must have gone to the wall."

"Ah, and where did they get it from? That's the mystery," said De Talor.

"Precisely; that was the mystery. I shall clear it up a little presently. To return. After awhile the buyers began to find that Rastrick and Codley's grease was a better grease and a cheaper grease, and as the contracts lapsed, the companies renewed them, not with the De Talor house, but with the house of Rastrick and Codley. Doubtless you remember."

Mr. de Talor groaned in acquiescence, and the lawyer continued: "In time this state of affairs produced its natural results—De Talor's house was ruined, and the bulk of the trade fell into the hands of the new firm."

"Ah, I should just like to know who they really were—the low sneaks!"

"Would you? I will tell you. The firm of Rastrick and Codley were—Reginald Cardus, solicitor, of Dum's Ness."

Mr. de Talor struggled out of his chair, looked wildly at the lawyer, and sank down again.

"You look ill; may I offer you a glass of wine?"

The wretched man shook his head.

"Very good. Doubtless you are curious to know how I, a lawyer, and not otherwise connected with Manchester, obtained the monopoly of the grease trade, which is, by the way, at this moment paying very well. I will satisfy your curiosity. I have always had a mania for taking up inventions, quite quietly, and in the names of others. Sometimes I have made money over them, sometimes I have lost; on the whole, I have made largely. But whether I have made or lost, the inventors, as a rule, have never known who was backing them. One day, one lucky day, this railway grease patent was brought to my notice. I took it up and invested fifty thousand in it straight off the reel. Then I invested another fifty thousand. Still your firm cut my throat. I made an effort and invested another fifty thousand. Had I failed, I should then have been a ruined man; I had strained my credit to the utmost. But fortune favours the brave, Mr. de Talor, and I succeeded. It was your firm that failed. I have paid all my debts, and I reckon that the railway-grease concern is worth, after paying liabilities, some two hundred thousand pounds. If you should care to go in for it, Messrs. Rastrick and Codley will, I have no doubt, be most happy to treat with you. It has served its purpose, and is now in the market."

De Talor looked at him with amazement. He was too upset to speak.

"So much, Mr. de Talor, for my share in the grease episode. The failure of your firm, or rather its stoppage from loss of trade, left you still a rich man, but only half as rich as you had been. And this, you may remember, made you furious. You could not bear the idea of losing money; you would rather have lost blood from your veins than sovereigns from your purse. When you thought of the grease which had melted in the fire of competition, you could have wept tears of rage. In this plight you came to me to ask advice."

"Yes; and you told me to speculate."

"Not quite accurate, Mr. de Talor. I said—I remember the words well—'You are an able man, and understand the money market; why don't you take advantage of these fluctuating times, and recoup yourself for all you have lost?' The prospect of gain tempted you, Mr. de Talor, and you jumped at the idea. You asked me to introduce you to a reliable firm, and I introduced you to Messrs. Campsey and Ash, one of the best in the City."

"Confound them for a set of rogues!" answered De Talor.

"Rogues! I am sorry you think so, for I have an interest in their business."

"Good heavens! what next?" groaned De Talor.

"Well, notwithstanding the best efforts of Messrs. Campsey and Ash on your behalf, in pursuance of written instructions as you from time to time communicated to them, and to which you can no doubt refer if you please, things went wrong with you, Mr. de Talor, and year by year, when your balance sheet was sent in, you found that you had lost more than you had gained. At last, one unlucky day, about three years ago, you made a plunge against the advice, you may remember, of Messrs. Campsey and Ash, and lost. It was after that, that I began to lend you money. The first loan was for fifty thousand; then came more losses, and more loans, till at length we had reached the present state of affairs."

"O Cardus, you don't mean to sell me up, do you? What shall I do without money? And think of my daughters: 'ow will they manage without their comforts? Give me time. What makes you so rough on me?"

Mr. Cardus had been walking up and down the room rapidly. At De Talor's words he stopped, and going to a despatch-box, unlocked it, and drew from a bundle of documents a yellow piece of stamped paper. It was a cancelled bill for ten thousand pounds in the favour of Jonas de Talor, Esquire. This bill he came and held before his visitor's eyes.

"That, I believe, is your signature," he said quietly, pointing to the receipt written across the bill.

De Talor turned almost livid with fear, and his lips and hands began to tremble.

"Where did you get that?" he asked.

Mr. Cardus regarded him, or rather all round him, with the melancholy black eyes that never looked straight at anything, and yet saw everything, and then answered:

"Among your friend Jones's papers. You scoundrel!" he went on, with a sudden change of manner, "now perhaps you begin to understand why I have hunted you down step by step: why for thirty years I have waited, and watched, and failed, and at last succeeded. It is for the sake of Mary Atterleigh. It was you who, infuriated because she would have none of such a coarse brute, set the man Jones on to her. It was you who lent him the money with which to buy her from old Atterleigh. There lies the proof before you. By the way, Jones need never have repaid you that ten thousand pounds, for it was marriage-brokerage, and therefore not recoverable at law. It was you, I say, who were the first cause of my life being laid waste, and who nearly drove me to the madhouse, ay, who did drive Mary, my betrothed wife, into the arms of that fellow, whence, God be praised! she soon passed to her rest."

Mr. Cardus paused, breathing quick with suppressed rage and excitement; the large white eyebrows contracted till they nearly met, and, abandoning his usual habit, he looked straight into the eyes of the abject creature in the chair before him.

"It's a long while ago, Cardus; can't you forgive, and let bygones be bygones?"

"Forgive! Yes, for my own sake, I could forgive; but for her sake, whom you first dishonoured and then killed, I will never forgive. Where are your companions in guilt? Jones is dead; I ruined him. Atterleigh is there; I did not ruin him, because, after all, he was the author of Mary's life; but his ill-gotten gains did him no good; a higher power than mine took vengeance on his crime, and I saved him from the madhouse. And Jones's children, they are here, too, for once they lay beneath her breast. But do you think that I will spare you, you coarse, arrogant knave—you, who spawned the plot? No, not if it were to cost me my own life, would I forego one jot or tittle of my revenge!"

At that moment Mr. Cardus happened to look up, and saw through the glass part of the door of his office, of which the curtain was partially drawn, the wild-looking head of "Hard-riding Atterleigh." He appeared to be looking through the door, for his eyes, in which there was a very peculiar look, were fixed intently upon Mr. Cardus's face. When he saw that he was observed, he vanished.

"Now go," said the lawyer sternly to the prostrate De Talor; "and never let me see your face again!"

"But I haven't any money; where am I to go?" groaned De Talor.

"Wherever you like, Mr. de Talor—this is a free country; but, if I had control of your destination, it should be—to the devil!"

The wretched man staggered to his feet.

"All right, Cardus; I'll go, I'll go. You've got it all your own way now. You are damned hard, you are; but perhaps you'll get it taken out of you some day. I'm glad you never got hold of Mary; it must have been pleasant to you to see her marry Jones."

In another second he was gone, and Mr. Cardus was left thinking, among other things, of that look in old Atterleigh's eyes, which he could not get out of his mind. Thus did he finally accomplish the revenge to which he had devoted his life.

CHAPTER IX

MAD ATTERLEIGH'S LAST RIDE

A month had passed since Mr. de Talor had crept, utterly crushed, from the presence of the man whom he had wronged. During this time Mr. Cardus had been busy from morning till night. He was always a busy man, writing daily with his own hand an almost incredible number of letters; for he carried on all, or nearly all, his great affairs by correspondence, but of late his work seemed to have doubled.

In the course of that month the society in the neighbourhood of Kesterwick experienced a pleasurable sensation of excitement, for suddenly the De Talor family vanished off the face of the Kesterwick world, and the Ceswick Ness estates, after being advertised, were put up for sale, and bought, so said report, by a London firm of lawyers on behalf of an unknown client. The De Talors were gone, where to nobody knew, nor did they much care to inquire—that is with the exception of the servants whose wages were left unpaid, and the tradespeople to whom large sums were owing. They inquired vigorously enough, but without the smallest result; the De Talors had gone and left no trace, except the trace of bankruptcy, and Kesterwick knew them no more, but was glad over the sensation made by their disappearance.

But on one Saturday Mr. Cardus's business seemed to come to a sudden stop. He wrote some letters and put them in the post bag. Then he went to admire his orchids.

"Life," he said aloud to himself, "shall be all orchids now; my work is done. I will build a new house for tropical sorts, and spend two hundred pounds on stocking it. Well, I can afford it."

This was about five o'clock. Half an hour later, when he had well examined his flowers, he strolled out Titheburgh Abbey way, and here he met Ernest and his wife, who had been sitting in their favourite spot.

"Well, my dears," he said, "and how are you?"

"Pretty well, uncle, thank you; and how are you?"

"I? O, I am very jolly indeed for an old man; as jolly as an individual who has just bid good-bye to work for ever should be," he said.

"Why, Reginald, what do you mean?"

"Mean, Dorothy, my dear? I mean that I have wound up my affairs and retired on a modest competence. Ah, you young people should be grateful to me, for let me tell you that everything is now in apple-pie order, and when I slip off you will have no trouble at all, except to pay the probate duty, and that will be considerable. I never quite knew till a week ago how rich I was; but, as I said the other day, everything I have touched has turned to gold. It will be a large fortune for you to manage, my dears; you will find it a great responsibility."

"I hope you will live many years to manage it yourself," said Ernest.

"Ah, I don't know. I am pretty tough; but who can see the future? Dolly, my dear girl," he went on, in a dreamy way, "you are growing like your mother. Do you know, I sometimes think that I am not far off her now; you see I speak plainly to you two. Years ago I used to think—that is, sometimes—that your mother was dust and nothing more; that she had left me for ever; but of late I have changed my ideas. I have seen," he went on, speaking in an absent way, as though he were meditating to himself, "how wonderfully Providence works even in the affairs of this imperfect world, and I begin to believe that there must be a place where it allows itself a larger development. Yes, I think I shall find your mother somewhere, Dorothy, my dear. I seem to feel her very near me sometimes. Well, I have avenged her."

"I think that you will find her, Reginald," she answered; "but your vengeance is wicked and wrong. I have often made bold to tell you so, though sometimes you have been angry with me, and I tell you so again. It can only bring evil with it. What have we poor creatures to do with vengeance, who do not understand the reason of things, and can scarcely see an inch before our noses? What right have we to judge others, who, if we knew everything, would probably be the first to pardon them?"

"Perhaps you are right, my love—you generally are right in the main; but my desire for vengeance upon that man De Talor has been the breath of my nostrils, and I have achieved it. Man, if he only lives long enough, and has strength of will enough, can achieve everything except happiness. But man fritters away his powers over a variety of objects; he is led astray in pursuit of the butterfly Pleasure, or the bubble Ambition, or the Destroying Angel Woman; and his purposes fall to the ground between a dozen stools. Most men, too, are not capable of a purpose. Men are weak creatures; and yet what a mighty seed lies hid in every human breast. Think, my children, what man might, nay, may become, when his weakness and follies have fallen from him, when his rudimentary virtues have been developed, and his capacities for physical and mental beauties brought to an undreamed of perfection! Look at the wild flower and the flower of the hothouse—it is nothing compared to the possibilities inherent in man, even as we know him. It is a splendid dream! Will it ever be fulfilled, I wonder? Well, well—

"'Whatever there is to know
That we shall know one day.'

"Come, let us turn; it will soon be time to dress for dinner. By the way, Dorothy, that reminds me. I don't quite like the way that your respected grandfather is going on. I told him that I had no more deeds for him to copy, that I had done with deeds, and he went and got that confounded stick of his, and showed me that according to his own little calculations his time was up; and then he got his slate and wrote about my being the devil on it, but that I had no more power over him, and that he was bound for heaven. The other day, too, I caught him staring at me through the glass of the door with a very queer look in his eyes."

"Ah, Reginald, so you have noticed it! I quite agree with you; I don't at all like his goings-on. Do you know, I think that he had better be shut up."

"I don't like to shut him up, Dorothy. However, here we are; we will talk about it to-morrow."

Having led Ernest to his room, Dorothy, before beginning to dress herself, went to the office to see if her grandfather was still there. And there, sure enough, she found him, pacing up and down, muttering and waving his long stick, out of which all the notches had now been cut.

"What are you doing, grandfather?" she asked; "why haven't you gone to dress?"

He snatched up his slate and wrote rapidly upon it:

"Time's up! Time's up! Time's up! I've done with the devil and all his works. I'm off to heaven on the big black horse to find Mary. Who are you? You look like Mary."

"Grandfather," said Dolly, quietly taking the slate out of his hand, "what do you mean by writing such nonsense? Let me hear no more of it. You ought to be ashamed of yourself. Now, mind, I will have no more of it. Put away that stick, and go and wash your hands for dinner."

The old man did as he was bid somewhat sulkily, Dorothy thought; but when he arrived at the dinner-table there was nothing noticeable about his manner.

They dined at a quarter to seven, and dinner did not take them very long. When it was over, old Atterleigh drank some wine, and then, according to his habit, went and sat in the ancient inglenook which had presumably been built by the forgotten Dum for his comfort on winter evenings. And on winter evenings, when there was a jolly wood-fire burning on the hearth, it was a pleasant spot enough; but to sit there in the dark on a lovely summer night was an act, well—worthy of old Atterleigh.

After dinner the conversation turned upon that fatal day when Alston's Horse was wiped out at Isandhlwana. It was a painful subject both to Ernest and Jeremy, but the former was gratifying his uncle's curiosity by explaining to him how that last dread struggle with the six Zulus came to determine itself in their favour.

"And how was it?" asked Mr. Cardus, "that you managed to get the better of the fellow with whom you rolled down the hill?"

"Because the assegai broke, and, fortunately enough, the blade was left in my hand. Where is it, Doll?" (for Jeremy had brought it home with him).

Dorothy got up and reached the broken assegai, which had about eight inches of the shaft, from its place over the mantelpiece.

"Now then, Jeremy, if you would be so good as to sprawl upon your back upon the floor, I will just show my uncle what happened."

Jeremy complied, not without grumbling about dirtying his dress-coat.

"Jeremy, my boy, where are you? O, there! Well, excuse my taking the liberty of kneeling on your chest, and holloa out of the assegai goes into you. If we are going to have a performance at all, it may as well be a realistic one. Now, uncle, you see when we finished rolling, which was just as this assegai snapped in two, as luck would have it I was uppermost, and managed to get my knee on my friend's left arm and to hold his right with my left. Then, before he could get loose, I drove this bit of spear through the side of his throat, just there, so that it cut the jugular vein, and he died shortly afterwards; and now you know all about it."

Here Ernest rose and laid the spear upon the table, and Jeremy, entering into the spirit of the thing, began to die as artistically as a regard for his dress-coat would allow. Just then Dorothy, looking up, saw her grandfather Atterleigh's distorted face peering round the wall of the inglenook, where he was sitting in the dark, and looking at the scene of mimic slaughter with that same curious gaze which he had worn on several occasions lately. He withdrew his head at once.

"Get up, Jeremy!" said his sister, sharply, "and stop writhing about there like a great snake. You look as though you had been murdered; it is horrible!"

Jeremy arose laughing, and, having obtained Dorothy's permission, they all lit their pipes, and, sitting there in the fading light, fell to talking about that sad scene of slaughter which indeed appeared that night to have a strange fascination for Mr. Cardus. He asked Ernest and Jeremy about it again and again—how this man was killed, and that?—did they die at once? and so on.

The subject was always distressing to Ernest, and one to which he rarely alluded, full as it was for him of the most painful recollections, especially those connected with his dear friend Alston and his son.

Dorothy knew this, and knew too that Ernest would be low spirited for at least a day after the conversation, which she did her best to stop. At last she succeeded; but the melancholy associations connected with the talk had apparently already done their work, for everybody lapsed into the most complete silence, and sat grouped together at the top-end of the old oak table as quietly as though they were cut in stone. Meanwhile, the twilight deepened, little gusts of wind arose, and gently shook the old-fashioned window-lattices, making a sound as though feeble hands were trying to throw them open. The dull evening light crept from place to place, and threw great shadows about the room, glanced upon the armour on its panelled walls, and at last began to die away into darkness. The whole scene was eerie, and for some unknown reason it oppressed Dorothy. She wondered why everybody was so silent, and yet she herself did not feel equal to breaking the silence; there was a load upon her heart.

Just then a curious thing happened. As may be remembered, the case containing the wonderful mummied head, found by Eva Ceswick, had years before been placed by Jeremy upon a bracket at the end of the room. Round about this case hung various pieces of armour, and among others, above it, suspended by a piece of string from a projecting hook, was a heavy iron gauntlet. For many years—twenty or more—it had hung from the hook, but now at last the string was worn through, and even as Dorothy was wondering at the silence, it gave. Down came the heavy iron hand with a crash, and, as it passed, it caught the latch of the long air-tight case, and jarred the door wide open.

Everybody in the room sprang to their feet, and, as they did so, a last ray from the setting sun struggled through one of the windows, and rested upon the open case, staining it, and all about it, the hue of blood, and filling the fearful crystal eyes within with a lurid light. How they glowed and shone, to be sure, after their long sleep!—for the case had scarcely been opened for years—while their tremulous glance, now dull, now intense, according as the light played upon them, appeared to wander round and round the room, as though in search of somebody or something.

It was an awful sight which that ray of sunlight showed, as it played upon the trembling crystal orbs, the scornful, deathly features, and the matchless hair that streamed on either side. Together with the sudden break in the silence, caused by the crashing fall of the gauntlet, as it had done many years before, it proved altogether too much for the beholders' nerves.

"What is that?" asked Ernest, with a start, as the gauntlet fell.

Dorothy glanced up and gave a little cry of horror. "Oh, that dreadful head! it is looking at us."

They all rose to their feet, and Dorothy, seizing Ernest by one hand, and covering her eyes with the other, retreated slowly, followed by the others, towards the swing-door. Soon they had reached the door, were through it, down the passage, and out into the peaceful stillness of the evening. Then Jeremy spoke, and his language was more forcible than polite.

"Well, I am blowed!" he said, wiping the cold perspiration from his forehead.

"Oh, Reginald, I do wish you would get that horrible thing out of the house; there has been nothing but misfortune ever since it has been here. I cannot bear it, I cannot bear it!" said Dolly, hysterically.

"Nonsense, you superstitious child!" answered Mr. Cardus, who was now recovering from his start. "The gauntlet knocked the door open, that was all. It is nothing but a mummied head; but, if you don't like it, I will send it to the British Museum to-morrow."

"Oh, please do, Reginald," answered Dorothy, who appeared quite unhinged.

So hurried had been their retreat from the room that everybody had forgotten "Hard-riding Atterleigh" sitting in the dark in the inglenook. But the bustle in the room had attracted him, and already, before they were gone, he had projected his large head covered with the tangled grey locks, and begun to stare about. Presently his eyes fell upon the crystal orbs, and then, to him, the orbs appeared to cease their wanderings and rest upon his eyes. For awhile the two heads stared at each other thus—the golden head without a body in the box, and the grey head that, thrust out as it were from the ingle-wall, seemed to have no body either. They stared and stared, till at last the golden head got the mastery of the grey head, and the old man crept from his corner, crept down the room till he was almost beneath the baleful eyes, and nodded, nodded, nodded at them.

And they, too, seemed to nod, nod, nod at him. Then he retreated backwards as slowly as he had come, nodding all the while, till he came to where the broken assegai lay upon the table, and, taking it, thrust it up his sleeve. As he did so, the ray of light faded and the fiery eyes went out. It was as though the thick white lids and long eyelashes had dropped over them.

None of the other four returned to the sitting-room that night.

When he had recovered from his fright, Jeremy went into his little room, the same in which he used to stuff birds as a boy, and busied himself with his farm accounts. Mr. Cardus, Dorothy, and Ernest walked about together in the balmy moonlight, for, very shortly after the twilight had departed, the great harvest-moon came up and flooded the world with light. Mr. Cardus was in a talkative, excited mood that night. He talked about his affairs, which he had now finally wound up, and about Mary Atterleigh, mentioning little tricks of manner and voice which were reproduced in Dorothy. He talked too about Ernest's and Dorothy's marriage, and said what a comfort it was to him. Finally, about ten o'clock, he said that he was tired and going to bed.

"God bless you, my dears; sleep well! Good-night," he said. "We will settle about that new orchid-house to-morrow. Good-night, good-night."

Shortly afterwards Dorothy and Ernest also went to bed, reaching their room by a back entrance, for they neither of them felt inclined to come under the fire of the crystal eyes again, and soon they were asleep in each other's arms.

The minutes stole on one by one through the dead silence of the night, bearing their records with them to the archives of the past. Eleven o'clock came and fled away; midnight came too, and swept across the world. Everywhere—on land, sky, and sea—there was silence, nothing but silence sleeping in the moonlight.

Hark! Oh, heavens, what was that!

One fearful, heartrending yell of agony, ringing all through the ancient house, rattling the casements, shaking the armour against the panelled walls, pulsing and throbbing in horrible notes out into the night, echoing and dying far away over the sea! Then silence again, silence sleeping in the moonlight.

They sprang from their beds, did every living soul beneath that roof, and rushed in their night-gear, men and women together, into the sitting-room. The crystal eyes seemed to be awake again, for the moon was up and played upon them, causing them now and then to flash out in gleams of opalescent light.

Somebody lit a candle, somebody missed Mr. Cardus; surely he could never have slept through that! Yes, he had slept through it. They ran and tumbled, a confused mass of white, into the room where he lay. He was there sure enough, and he slept very sound, with a red gash in his throat, from which the blood fell in heavy drops, down, down to the ground.

They stood aghast, and as they stood, from the courtyard outside there came a sound of galloping hoofs. They knew the sound of the galloping; it was that of Ernest's great black stallion!

A mile or more away out on the marshes, just before you come to the well-known quicksands, which have, tradition says, swallowed so many unfortunates, and which shudder palpably at times and are unpleasant to look on, stands a lock-house, inhabited by one solitary man, who has charge of the sluice. On this very night it is necessary for him to open his sluice-gates at a particular moment, and now he stands awaiting that propitious time. He is an ancient mariner; his hands are in his pockets, his pipe is in his mouth, his eyes are fixed upon the sea. We have met him before. Suddenly he hears the sound of a powerful horse galloping furiously. He turns, and his hair begins to rise upon his head, for this is what he sees in the bright moonlight:

Fast, fast towards him thunders a great coal-black horse, snorting with mingled rage and terror, and on its bare back there sits a man with a grip of iron—an old man, for his grey locks stream out behind him—who waves above his head the fragment of a spear.

On they come. Before them is the wide sluice; if they are mortal, they will turn or plunge into it. No; the great black horse gathers himself, and springs into the air.

By heaven, he has cleared it! No horse ever took that leap before, or will again. On at whirlwind speed towards the shuddering quicksand two hundred yards away!

Splash! Horse and man are in it, making the moist mass shake and tremble for twenty yards round. The bright moonlight shows it all. The horse shrieks in fear and agony, as only a horse can; the man on his back waves the spear.

The horse vanishes, the man vanishes; the spear glitters an instant longer in the moonlight, and then vanishes too. They have all vanished for ever.

They have all vanished, and again the perfect silence sleeps in the moonlight.

"Bust me!" says the ancient one, aloud, and shaking with a mortal dread; "bust me, I have stood still and seed many a queer thing, but I never seed a thing like that!" Then he turned and fled fast as his old legs would carry him, forgetful of Dutch cheeses and of sluice-gates, forgetful of everything except that demon horse and man.

Thus ended "Hard-riding Atterleigh's" maddest gallop, and thus, too, ended the story of Mr. Cardus and his revenge.

CHAPTER X

DOROTHY'S TRIUMPH

Some years passed before Eva Plowden returned to Kesterwick, and then she was carried thither. Alive she did not return, nor during all these years did she and Ernest ever meet.

They buried her, in obedience to her last wishes, in the churchyard, where lay generation upon generation of her ancient race, and the daisies grew above her head. Twice had they bloomed above her before Sir Ernest Kershaw stood by the spot hallowed with the presence of what once enshrined the spirit of the woman he had loved.

Ernest was now getting well into middle life, and Dorothy's bright hair was slightly lined with grey, when they stood that summer evening by Eva's grave. Many things had happened to the pair since Mr. Cardus's tragic death. They had children born to them—some they had lost, some remained—honest English lads and lasses, with their father's eyes. They had enjoyed great wealth, and spent it royally, giving to all who needed. They had drunk deep of the cup of this world's joys and sorrows. Ernest had gone into Parliament for a couple of years, and made something of a name there. Then, impatient for the active life of other days, he had accepted a high Colonial appointment, for which, notwithstanding his blindness, his wealth and parliamentary reputation eminently fitted him. Now he was just about to leave to fill the governorship of one of the Australian colonies.

Long years had passed, many things had happened; and yet as he stood by that heap of turf, which he could not see, it seemed but yesterday when—and he sighed.

"Not quite cured yet, Ernest?" said Dorothy, interrogatively.

"Yes, Dorothy," he answered, with a little sigh, "I think I am cured. At any rate," he went on, as she took his hand to lead him away from the grave, "I have learned to accept the decrees of Providence without murmuring. I have done with dreams and outlived pessimism. Life would, it is true, have been different thing for me if poor Eva had not deserted me, for she poisoned its waters at the fount, and so they have always tasted bitter. But happiness is not the end and object of man's existence; and if I could I would not undo the past. Take me to the old flat tombstone, Dolly, near the door."

She led him to it, and he sat down.

"Ah," he went on, "how beautiful she was! Was there ever woman like her, I wonder? And now her bones lie there; her beauty is all gone; and there lives of her only the unending issues of what she did. I have only to think, Dolly, and I can see her as I saw her a score of times passing in and out of this church-door. Yes, I can see her, and the people round her, and the clothes she wore, and the smile in her beautiful dark eyes—for her eyes seemed to smile, you remember, Dolly. How I worshipped her, too, with all my heart and soul and strength, as though she were an angel! And that was my mistake, Dolly. She was only a woman—a very weak woman."

"You said just now that you were cured, Ernest; one would hardly think it to hear you talk," put in Dorothy, smiling.

"Yes, Doll, I am cured; you have cured me, my dear wife, for you have crept into my life, and taken possession of it, so that there is little room for anybody else; and now, Dorothy, I love you with all my heart."

She pressed his hand and smiled again, for she knew that she had triumphed, and that he did love her, truly love her, and that this passion for Eva was a poor thing compared to what it had been years before—more indeed of a tender regret, not unmingled with a starry hope, than a passion at all. Dorothy was a clever little person, and understood something of Ernest and the human heart in general. She had thought long ago that she would win Ernest altogether to her in the end. By what tenderness, by what devotion and nobility of character she had accomplished this, those who know her can well imagine, but in the end she did accomplish it, as she deserved to do. The contrast between the conduct of the two women who had mainly influenced his life was too marked for Ernest, a man of a just and reasonable mind, to altogether ignore; and when once he came to comparisons the natural results followed. Yet, though he learned to love Dorothy so dearly, it cannot be said that he forgot Eva; because there are things that some men can never forget, since they are a part of their inner life, and of these, unfortunately, first love is one.

"Ernest," went on Dorothy, "you remember what you told me when you asked me to marry you in Titheburgh Abbey, about your belief that your affection for Eva would outlast this world. Do you still believe that?"

"Yes, Doll, to some extent."

His wife sat and thought for a minute.

"Ernest," she said presently.

"Yes, dear."

"I have managed to hold my own against Eva in this world, when she had all the chances and all the beauty on her side, and what I have to say about your theories now is, that when we get to the next, and are all beautiful, it will be very strange if I don't manage to hold my own there. She had her chance, and she threw it away: now I have got mine, and I don't mean to throw it away, either in this world or the next."

Ernest laughed a little. "I must say, my dear, it would be a very poor heaven if you were not there."

"I should think so, indeed. 'Those whom God hath joined let not man put asunder'—nor woman either. But what is the good of our stopping here to talk such stuff about things of which we really understand nothing? Come, Ernest, Jeremy and the boys will be waiting for us."

So hand in hand they went on homeward through the quiet twilight.

H. Rider Haggard – A Short Biography

Sir Henry Rider Haggard, KBE was born on June 22nd 1856 at Bradenham in Norfolk, England.

More familiarly known as H. Rider Haggard, he was the eighth of ten children born to Sir William Meybohm Rider Haggard, a barrister (born, incidentally, in St Petersburg, Russia), and Ella Doveton, an author, poet and daughter of a merchant in the East India Trading Company.

Haggard was initially schooled at Garsington Rectory in Oxfordshire where he studied under the tutelage of Reverend H. J. Graham. His elder brothers, who seemed to find more favour with their father, graduated from various private schools whilst Haggard was sent to Ipswich Grammar School, saving his father a considerable sum in fees.

He failed his army entrance exam, and was therefore sent to a private crammer in London in preparation for the entrance exam to the British Foreign Office, which he appears never to have sat. However, it was during his two years in London that Haggard came into contact with a circle of people interested in the study of psychical phenomena and for which he too now developed a life-long interest together with a series of enduring friendships.

In 1875, Haggard's father used his family's connections to send him to Southern Africa to take up an unpaid position as assistant to the secretary to Sir Henry Bulwer, Lieutenant-Governor of the Colony of Natal. In 1876 he was transferred to the staff of Sir Theophilus Shepstone, Special Commissioner for the Transvaal. It was in this role that Haggard was present in Pretoria in April 1877 for the official announcement of the British annexation of the Boer Republic of the Transvaal. The official who had been nominated to read out the Proclamation lost his voice and Haggard was his replacement. It was a moment in history.

Haggard was to remain in the country for six years, during which time he served as Master of the High Court of the Transvaal and an adjutant of the Pretoria Horse.

It was here that he fell in love with Mary Elizabeth "Lilly" Jackson. He hoped to marry her once he obtained more certainty in his career path.

In 1878 he became Registrar of the High Court in the Transvaal and now the time seemed opportune to write to his father to tell him of his hope to marry. The reply from his father was uncompromising. He forbade it until his son had made a proper career for himself.

The following year, 1879, Lily married Frank Archer, a well-to-do banker.

Haggard returned briefly to England to marry a friend of his sister's, Marianna Louisa Margitson, a 21 year old, in 1880, and the couple travelled to Africa together. Haggard's years in Africa had proved, at least on a writing level, rich and inspirational for him, and while still in Natal he wrote two articles for The Gentleman's Magazine describing his experiences.

Moving back to England in (and accounts here differ as to whether it was 1881 or 1882) the couple settled in Ditchingham, Norfolk, Louisa's ancestral home. Later they moved to Kessingland and established connections with the church in Bungay, Suffolk. The marriage produced four children. A son named Jack (who tragically died at age 10 of measles) and three daughters, Angela, Dorothy and Lilias. (Lilias grew to become an author and her father's biographer.)

In England Law was to be the fulcrum of his career. However, although he studied, writing was growing in its appeal to him. His first book, Cetywayo and His White Neighbours, was an account and study of Britain's policies in South Africa.

From this point his career as a writer began to take substantial hold and with it a dramatic shift to fiction. Two years later he published his first fiction, Dawn followed in 1885 by arguably his most popular novel, King Solomon's Mines—detailing the life of the adventurer Allan Quatermain. This was followed the following year, 1886, by She: A History of Adventure, which introduced the female character Ayesha. Both characters, Quatermain and Ayesha, developed a series of books about their adventures.

The study of Law now fell away entirely. He appeared also to have a keen sense of his commercial appreciation. Rather than sell the copyright of his first best-seller, King Solomon's Mines, for a £100 fee he, instead, accepted a 10% royalty. This book is also generally accepted as the first of the Lost World writing genre.

Haggard obviously thought there were many further adventures to tell and it would be hard to find a publisher who would disagree given the start he had made. Sequels soon followed. Allan Quatermain continued his epic and swash-buckling adventures in Africa whilst the sequel to She entitled Ayesha played out her adventures in Tibet. Interestingly Haggard would later extend his characters adventures around the world with Eric Brighteyes, being the basis for an epic Viking romance.

The Haggard family lived at 69 Gunterstone Road in Hammersmith, London, from mid-1885 to mid-1888. It was here that he wrote his most famous works. His time in Africa had given him the experience and atmosphere as well as several observations and friendships of the people who would so influence his fictional characters. Chief among them were the larger-than-life adventurers Frederick Selous and Frederick Russell Burnham. Both were men of Empire and huge ambition as they helped uncover the great mineral wealth of Africa, as well as the ruins of ancient lost civilisations of the continent, such as Great Zimbabwe.

Three of Haggard's books, The Wizard (1896), Black Heart and White Heart; a Zulu Idyll (1896), and Elissa; the Doom of Zimbabwe (1898), are dedicated to Burnham's daughter Nada, the first white child born in Bulawayo; she had been named after Haggard's 1892 book Nada the Lily.

As is typical of the writing of the time his novels contain many of the stereotypes associated with colonialism, yet they also sympathise, to a degree, with the native populations. Africans often play heroic roles in the novels, although the protagonists are more often than not European. The time around the turn of the century was, after all, the great sprint to Empire by many European countries intent on gaining possessions of land, people and resources.

Three of Haggard's novels were written in collaboration with his friend Andrew Lang who shared his interest in the spiritual realm and paranormal phenomena and who was also a greatly admired editor.

Haggard's stories are still widely read today. Ayesha, the female protagonist of She, has been cited as a prototype by psychoanalysts such as Sigmund Freud (in The Interpretation of Dreams) and Carl Jung. Her epithet is, of course, "She Who Must Be Obeyed" and has for decades been used tongue-in-cheek to describe the presumed balance of influence between the sexes.

As a legacy it is easy to establish Haggard, and his pioneering work, as the author of the Lost World branch of writing and its influence of such other writers as Edgar Rice Burroughs, Robert E. Howard and Talbot Mundy. The Allan Quatermain character influenced many 'serials' in Hollywood during the 30s & 40s and can readily be seen as a template for Indiana Jones, the American archaeologist and explorer and huge box office film character.

Years later, when Haggard was a successful novelist, he was contacted by his former love, Lilly Archer, née Jackson. Lily had been deserted by her husband, who had embezzled funds and fled bankrupt to Africa. Haggard installed her and her sons in a house and saw to the children's education. Lilly eventually followed her husband to Africa, where he infected her with syphilis before dying of it himself. Lilly returned to England in late 1907, where Haggard again supported her until her death on April 22nd, 1909.

Haggard also wrote about agricultural and social reform, in part inspired by his experiences in Africa, but also based on what he saw in Europe. By the end of his life, he was adamantly opposed to Bolshevism, a position that he shared with his life-long friend Rudyard Kipling. The two had found friendship upon Kipling's arrival at London in 1889 largely on the strength of their shared opinions.

Haggard was extremely interested in the social affairs of the Country and eager to play a more active part in attempting reform. In 1895 he stood unsuccessfully for Parliament as a Conservative candidate for the Eastern division of Norfolk losing by 198 votes.

Also in 1895 he served on a government commission to examine Salvation Army labour colonies. This, and his heavy involvement in agriculture reform, led to him being a member of several further commissions on land use and related affairs, work that involved several trips to the Colonies and Dominions. This work, in part, helped lead to the passage of the 1909 Development Bill.

In 1911 he served on the Royal Commission examining coastal erosion.

He was an absorbed and dedicated writer of letters to The Times, nearly one hundred were published by them and the bibliography attached below reveals much in the range of subjects he wished to bring attention to.

He was made a Knight Bachelor in 1912 and a Knight Commander of the Order of the British Empire in 1919. Haggard was a member of several clubs including the Athenaeum, Savile, and Authors' clubs.

The district of Rider in British Columbia, Canada, was named in his honour.

Henry Rider Haggard died on May 14th, 1925 at the age of 68. His ashes were buried at Ditchingham Church. His papers are held at the Norfolk Record Office.

The first chapter of his book People of the Mist (1894) is credited with inspiring the 1912 motto of the Royal Air Force (formerly the Royal Flying Corps), Per ardua ad astra. "Through adversity to the stars" (or alternately "Through struggle to the stars") it is also used by other Commonwealth air forces such as the RAAF, RCAF, RNZAF, and the SAAF.

H. Rider Haggard – A Concise Bibliography

Novels
Dawn (1884) Published in three volumes
The Witch's Head (1884) Published in three volumes
King Solomon's Mines (1885) Allan Quatermain series
She: A History of Adventure (1886) Ayesha series
Allan Quatermain (1887) Allan Quatermain series
Jess (1887)
A Tale of Three Lions (1887) Allan Quatermain series
Maiwa's Revenge, or the War of the Little Hand (1888) Allan Quatermain series
Colonel Quaritch, VC (1889) Published in three volumes
Cleopatra (1889)
Beatrice (1890)
The World's Desire (1890) Co-written with Andrew Lang
Eric Brighteyes (1891)
Nada the Lily (1892)
An Heroic Effort (1893)
Montezuma's Daughter (1893)
The People of the Mist (1894)
Heart of the World (1895)
Joan Haste (1895)
The Wizard (1896)
Doctor Therne (1898)
Swallow: A Tale of the Great Trek (1899)
Lysbeth (1901)
Pearl Maiden (1903)

Stella Fregelius: A Tale of Three Destinies (1903)
The Brethren (1904)
Ayesha: The Return of She (1905) Ayesha series
The Way of the Spirit (1906)
Benita (1906)
Fair Margaret (1907)
The Ghost Kings(1908)
The Yellow God (1908)
The Lady of Blossholme (1909)
Morning Star (1910)
Queen Sheba's Ring (1910)
Red Eve (1911)
The Mahatma and the Hare (1911)
Marie (1912) Allan Quatermain series
Child of Storm (1913) Allan Quatermain series
The Wanderer's Necklace (1914)
The Holy Flower (1915) Allan Quatermain series
The Ivory Child (1916) Allan Quatermain series
Finished (1917) Allan Quatermain series]
Love Eternal (1918)
Moon of Israel (1918)
When the World Shook (1919)
The Ancient Allan (1920) Allan Quatermain series
She and Allan (1921) Allan Quatermain series / Ayesha series
The Virgin of the Sun (1922)
Wisdom's Daughter (1923) Ayesha series
Heu-Heu (1924) Allan Quatermain series]
Queen of the Dawn (1925)
The Treasure of the Lake (1926) Allan Quatermain series
Allan and the Ice-Gods (1927) Allan Quatermain series
Mary of Marion Isle (1929)
Belshazzar (1930)

Short Story Collections
Allan's Wife and Other Tales (1889)
Black Heart and White Heart: A Zulu Idyll (1900)
Smith and the Pharaohs (1920)

Publications in Periodicals and Newspapers
A Zulu War-Dance (July 1877) The Gentleman's Magazine
A Visit to the Chief (September 1877) The Gentleman's Magazine
Hydrophobia (letter) (3 November 1885) The Times
The Land Question (letter) (28 April 1886) The Times
About Fiction (February 1887) The Contemporary Review
Mr Rider Haggard and His Critics (letter) (27 April 1887) The Times
Our Position in Cyprus (July 1887) The Contemporary Review

American Copyright (letter) (11 October 1887) The Times
On Going Back (November 1887) Longman's Magazine
Delagoa Bay (letter) (17 December 1887) The Times
South African Policy (letter) (27 December 1887) The Times
Suggested Prologue to a Dramatised Version of She (March 1888) Longman's Magazine
Mr. Meeson's Will (18 June 1888) The Illustrated London News
The Wreck of the Copeland (18 August 1888) The Illustrated London News
Cleopatra (3 December 1888) The Illustrated London News
Hydrophobia and Muzzling (letter) (25 October 1889) The Times
The Annals of Natal (23 November 1889) The Saturday Review
Mummy at St Mary/Woolnoth's (letter) (25 December 1889) The Times
Mummies (letter) (27 December 1889) The Times
The Fate of Swaziland (January 1890) The New Review
In Memoriam (17 May 1890) Thompson's Seasons
American Copyright (letter) (5 June 1890) The Times
Mr Herbert Ward and Mr Stanley (10 November 1890) The Times
Nada the Lily (2 January 1892) The Illustrated London News
A New Argument Against Creation (19 December 1892) The Times
My First Book. Dawn. By H. Rider Haggard (April 1893) The Idler
The Tale of Isandlwana and Rorke's Drift (4 October 1893) The True Story Book
Lobengula (letter) (19 October 1893) The Times
The New Sentiment (letter) (6 November 1893) The Times
Wanted—Imagination   (25 December 1893) The Times
The Fate of Captain Patterson's Party (28 December 1893) The Times
The Three Volume Novel (letter) (27 July 1894) The Times
The Adventures of John Gladwyn Jebb (letter) (30 October 1894) The Times
Agriculture in Norfolk (letter) (30 October 1894) The Times
The Nelson Bazaar (letter) (16 February 1895) The Times
Everything is Peaceful (letter) (20 March 1895) The Times
Lord Kimberley in Norfolk (letter) (17 April 1895) The Times
The East Norfolk Election (letter) (23 July 1895) The Times
The East Norfolk Election (letter) (29 July 1895) The Times
Wilson's Last Fight (7 October 1895) The True Story Book
The Crisis in the Transvaal (letter) (2 January 1896) The Times
The Transvaal Crisis (letter) (13 January 1896) The Times
Jameson's Surrender (letter) (14 March 1896) The Times
The Rinderpest in South Africa (letter) (5 November 1896) The Times
Mr Rider Haggard and Dr Neufeld (letter) (9 January 1899) The Times
Shrinkage of Population in Agricultural Districts (letter) (9 May 1899) The Times
The South African Crisis—An Appeal (letter) (1 July 1899) The Times
Commandant-General Joubert and Mr H Rider Haggard (letter) (8 September 1899) The Times
Anglo-African Writers' Club (17 October 1899) The Times
The War (letter) (25 October 1899) The Times
Farming in 1899 (letter) (22 December 1899) The Times
Farming in 1899 (letter) (1 January 1900) The Times
Settlement of Soldiers in South Africa (letter) (5 May 1900) The Times
1881 and 1900 (letter) (2 October 1900) The Times
Farming in 1900 (letter) (1 January 1901) The Times

Central and Associated Chambers of Agriculture (letter) (6 November 1901) The Times
Small Holdings (letter) (8 November 1901) The Times
Rural England (letter) (4 February 1903) The Times
Mr Rider Haggard on Rural Depopulation (3 May 1903) The Times
Agricultural Distress (letter) (11 June 1903) The Times
The Motor Problem (letter) (24 June 1903) The Times
Fiscal Policy and Agriculture (letter) (16 December 1903) The Times
Telepathy Between a Human Being and a Dog (letter) (21 July 1904) The Times
Telepathy Between a Human Being and a Dog (letter) (9 August 1904) The Times
Mr Rider Haggard on Small Holdings (12 September 1904) The Times
Case L.1139 Dream (October 1904) Journal of the Society for Psychical Research
Mr Rider Haggard on Agriculture (22 October 1904) The Times
Mr Rider Haggard on Rural Housing (27 October 1904) The Times
The Deserted Village (letter) (25 August 1905) The Times
Decrease of Population and the Land (letter) (6 January 1906) The Times
Prevention of Cruelty to Children (3 February 1906) The Times
The New Land and Tenure Bill (letter) (12 March 1906) The Times
Garden City Association (17 March 1906) The Times
Mr H. Rider Haggard on the Zulus (19 May 1906) The Illustrated London News
To Be Proof against British Bullets: A Zulu Incantation (19 May 1906) The Illustrated London News
Housing of the Working Classes (26 June 1906) The Times
Mr Rider Haggard on Small Holdings (4 July 1906) The Times
The Unemployed and Waste City Lands (letter) (19 July 1906) The Times
Mr Rider Haggard on the Transvaal Constitution (7 August 1906) The Times
Vanishing East Anglia (1 September 1906) The Saturday Review
The Land Grabbing at Plaistow (5 September 1906) The Times
The Land Tenure Bill (22 November 1906) The Times
Publishers and the Public (letter) (19 February 1907) The Times
The Careless Children (2 March 1907) The Saturday Review
The Government and the Land (letter) (29 April 1907) The Times
Chambers of Agriculture (2 May 1907) The Times
The Government and the Land (letter) (8 May 1907) The Times
Miss Jebb on Small Holdings (15 June 1907) Country Life
Rural Housing and Sanitation Association (27 June 1907) The Times
St Thomas Hospital Medical School (28 June 1907) The Times
The Land Question (4 July 1907) The Times
A Plea for the Sitting Tennant (letter) (12 August 1907) The Times
A Literary Coincidence (letter) (19 October 1907) The Spectator
Town Planning Conference (26 October 1907) The Times
Dr Barnardo's Homes (16 November 1907) The Times
The Proposed Agricultural Party (5 December 1907) The Times
Mr Rider Haggard and Small Holdings (10 January 1908) The Times
Mr Haggard and Children's Legislation (13 March 1908) The Times
The Drink Trade and Common Sense (letter) (2 April 1908) The Times
The Zulus: The Finest Savage Race in the World (June 1908) The Pall Mall Magazine
Sparrows (letter) (18 August 1908) The Times
Sparrows, Rats and Humanity (letter) (5 September 1908) The Times
The Letters of Queen Victoria (letter) (26 November 1908) The Times

The Romance of the World's Greatest Rivers (December 1908) Travel Magazine
Afforestation. Mr Rider Haggard's View (1 March 1909) The Times
The Late Sir Marshal Clarke (letter) (13 April 1909) The Times
Mr Rider Haggard on Agriculture (27 November 1909) The Times
Mr Rider Haggard on South Africa (11 March 1910) The Times
Why? (letter) (25 April 1910) The Times
Mr Rider Haggard on Irish Agriculture (23 May 1910) The Times
Why Not? (letter) (12 July 1910) The Times
Mr Rider Haggard on Agriculture (16 September 1910) The Times
Mr Rider Haggard on Vermin (8 November 1910) The Times
Danish High Schools (21 December 1910) The Times
Sugar Beet Growing in Norfolk (6 March 1911) The Times
Rural Denmark (letter) (22 March 1911) The Times
Rural Denmark (letter) (3 April 1911) The Times
The Copyright Bill (letter) (6 June 1911) The Times
Mr Rider Haggard on Poverty. The Burden of Civilization (15 July 1911) The Times
Mr Rider Haggard and the Public Records (28 July 1911) The Times
The Farmers' Burden (1 December 1911) The Times
Egyptian Date Farm. The Financial Aspect (11 October 1912) The Times
Umslopogaas and Makokel. Sir H. Rider Haggard on Zulu Types (letter) (16 August 1913) The Times
The Death of Mark Haggard (letter) (10 October 1914) The Times
On the Land. Old Problems and New Ways. The War—and After. (15 March 1915) The Times
Soldiers as Settlers. After-War Problem for the Empire (20 August 1915) The Times
Raids by Air. Zeppelins and Zeppelins (letter) (22 October 1915) The Times
Women's Work on the Land. A Palliative in Hard Times (letter) (29 November 1915) The Times
Women on the Land. Town Girls' Unfitness for Farm Work (letter) (9 December 1915) The Times
Soldiers as Settlers. Sir Rider Haggard's Oversea Mission (2 February 1916) The Times
Soldiers as Settlers (letter) (7 February 1916) The Times
Soldier Settlers. The Future of Rural England (letter) (10 February 1916) The Times
Farewell Luncheon to Sir Rider Haggard (March 1916) United Empire
Soldier Settlers for the Empire. Offer from Victoria (18 April 1916) The Times
Sir R Haggard's Tour. Land for Ex-Service Men (22 July 1916) The Times
Sir H. Rider Haggard's Mission. Land for Ex-Soldiers (1 August 1916) The Times
Land for Ex-Soldiers. Outline of Sir R. Haggard's Report   (12 August 1916) The Times
Empire Land Settlement Deputation to the Secretary of State for the Colonies and the President of the Board of Agriculture (September 1916) United Empire
Empire Land Settlement by Sir Rider Haggard (December 1916) United Empire
A Journey through Zululand by Sir H Rider Haggard (December 1916) The Windsor Magazine
Mr Wilson's Note. British Publicity (28 December 1916) The Times
Home Produce (letter) (22 February 1917) The Times
The Milk Supply (letter) (11 April 1917) The Times
Corn Production Bill. A National Measure (letter) (13 June 1917) The Times
A Protest and a Plea. Farmers and Meat (letter) (9 October 1917) The Times
Pig-Breeding. A Subject for Municipal Enterprise (letter) (22 February 1918) The Times
The German Colonies. Interests of the Dominions (letter) (5 November 1918) The Times
Light—More Light! (letter) (19 November 1918) The Times
A Great American. Tributes to the Late Mr Roosevelt (letter) (8 January 1919) The Times
Shut the Door (letter) (10 March 1919) The Times

Population and Housing. Emigration v Birth Control (25 March 1919) The Times
The Ex-Kaiser (letter) (11 April 1919) The Times
Empire Birth-Rate. Sir Rider Haggard on Emigration (17 April 1919) The Times
Ex-Service Men Abroad. Warnings from California (letter) (10 May 1919) The Times
Edith Cavell (letter) (16 May 1919) The Times
The Ex-Kaiser. Uncertainties of Trial (letter) (8 July 1919) The Times
Race Suicide Peril. Western Civilization Threatened (11 October 1919) The Times
The British Cinema. Production of Reputable Films (letter) (5 November 1919) The Times
Horrors on the Film. Limits of Publicity (letter) (19 November 1919) The Times
The British Museum (letter) (24 January 1920) The Times
Air Exploration and Empire (letter) (7 February 1920) The Times
The Liberty League. A Campaign Against Bolshevism (letter) (3 March 1920) The Times
Bolshevist Peril. Counter-Propaganda (4 March 1920) The Times
The Empire's Vacant Lands. Settlers and the Food Supply (14 April 1920) The Times
Films and Happy Endings. The Tyranny of a Convention (letter)   (21 April 1921) The Times
Land and its Burdens. Evil of Grinding Taxation (letter) (8 August 1921) The Times
Boy Emigrants (letter) (31 March 1922) The Times
Migration and Morals. Declining Birther Rate (7 April 1922) The Times
Labour Party's Programme. Confiscation and Class Hatred (letter) (28 October 1922) The Times
Efficient Denmark. Keeping the People on the Land (7 December 1922) The Times
The Egyptian Find. Tombs of Eighteenth Dynasty Queens (letter) (19 December 1922) The Times
King Tutankhamen. Reburial in Great Pyramid (letter) (13 February 1923) The Times
The Norfolk Dispute. A Truce while There is Time (letter) (3 April 1923) The Times
Rural Post and Telephone. Minister's Reply to Deputation (19 April 1923) The Times
Liberalism and Land Reform (letter) (1 May 1923) The Times
Small Holdings. Influence of Heredity (letter) (4 July 1923) The Times
Agricultural Parcel Post (26 July 1923) The Times
Country Houses for Sale. Empty East Anglian Mansions (letter) (14 June 1924) The Times
Plight of Agriculture (24 July 1924) The Times
Loans From the British Museum (letter) (30 July 1924) The Times
Zinovieff Letter. Mr MacDonald and a Political Plot (letter) (29 October 1924) The Times
Two Centuries of Publishing. Tributes to Messrs. Longmans (6 November 1924) The Times
Imagination and War (26 November 1924) The Times

Non-Fiction
Cetywayo and His White Neighbours (1882)
A Farmer's Year (1899)
The Last Boer War (1899)
A Winter Pilgrimage (1901)
Rural England (1902)
A Gardener's Year (1905)
The Poor and the Land (1905)
Regeneration (1910)
Rural Denmark (1911)
The Days of My Life (1926)

King Solomon's Mines

This novel has been adapted at least six times. The first version, King Solomon's Mines, directed by Robert Stevenson, premiered in 1937. The best known version premiered in 1950: King Solomon's Mines, directed by Compton Bennett and Andrew Marton, was followed in 1959 by a sequel, Watusi. In 1979 a low-budget version directed by Alvin Rakoff, King Solomon's Treasure, combined both King Solomon's Mines and Allan Quatermain in one story. The 1985 film King Solomon's Mines was a tongue-in-cheek parody of the story, with a 1987 sequel in the same vein, Allan Quatermain and the Lost City of Gold. Around the same time an Australian animated TV film came out, King Solomon's Mines. In 2008 a direct-to-video adaptation, Allan Quatermain and the Temple of Skulls, was released.

She

She has been adapted for the cinema at least ten times, and was one of the earliest films to be made, in 1899 as La Colonne de feu (The Pillar of Fire), by Georges Méliès. A 1911 version starred Marguerite Snow, a British-produced version appeared in 1916, and in 1917 Valeska Suratt appeared in a production for Fox which is lost. In 1925 a silent film of She, starring Betty Blythe, was produced with the active participation of Rider Haggard, who wrote the intertitles. This film combines elements from all the books in the series.

A decade later another cinematic version of the novels was released, featuring Helen Gahagan, Randolph Scott and Nigel Bruce. Unlike the book and the other films, this 1935 version was set in the Arctic, rather than Africa, and depicts the ancient civilisation of the story in an Art Deco style, with music by Max Steiner.

The 1965 film She was produced by Hammer Film Productions; it starred Ursula Andress as Ayesha and John Richardson as her reincarnated love, with Peter Cushing and Bernard Cribbins as other members of the expedition.

In 2001 another adaption was released direct-to-video with Ian Duncan as Leo Vincey, Ophélie Winter as Ayesha and Marie Bäumer as Roxane.

Dawn

The film Dawn was released in 1917, starring Hubert Carter and Annie Esmond.

Jess

This book was filmed in 1912, featuring Marguerite Snow, Florence La Badie and James Cruze, in 1914 with Constance Crawley and Arthur Maude, and in 1917 as Heart and Soul, starring Theda Bara in the title role.

Beatrice

The book was adapted into a 1921 Italian silent drama film called The Stronger Passion, directed by Herbert Brenon and starring Marie Doro and Sandro Salvini.

Swallow

The novel was adapted into a 1922 South African film.

Stella Fregelius

The book was adapted into a 1921 British film, Stella.

Moon of Israel
This novel was the basis of a script by Ladislaus Vajda, for film-director Michael Curtiz in his 1924 Austrian epic known as Die Sklavenkönigin (Queen of the Slaves).

www.ingramcontent.com/pod-product-compliance
Lightning Source LLC
Chambersburg PA
CBHW071138170626
46809CB00002B/679